STAR SPLINTER

BOOK 1 OF THE FRACTURED SPACE SERIES

J G CRESSEY

Star Splinter
Book one of the Fractured Space Series

Copyright © 2014 by J G Cressey
www.jgcressey.com

This is a work of fiction. Any resemblance to actual persons, places or events
is purely Coincidental.

First Printing, 2014

Edited by Amanda Shore
Cover art and design by J Cressey and Alisha at www.damonza.com
Formatting by Polgarus Studio

If you would like to learn more about the book and the author please
visit www.jgcressey.com where you can also sign up to a release date
newsletter

For my wife, Liz. Thanks for the encouragement and unyielding support.

Part One:

Chapter One
GUILT AND REGRET

Lieutenant Callum Harper felt no satisfaction from the punch. He watched grimly as the big man stumbled back across the office, his arms flailing like some sort of faulty windup toy before a collision with a hefty metal desk bounced him face first to the floor. The man lay still, seemingly out cold. Cal cursed. Violence had never been his intention, but now that the time had come, he'd found it impossible to hold back. In truth, he was surprised it hadn't happened sooner. Patiently, he waited for the man to come to. It started with a confused shifting, which before long turned into a clumsy panic. The man was bordering on obesity, and getting to his hands and knees was proving a struggle. Then there was something close to a whimper as he caught sight of his tooth set neatly in a little pool of blood beneath him.

Oh bloody hell. Cal felt his jaw tighten as well has his fist. He could take raging expletives, violence, or even arrogance and spite, but not self-pity and blubbing. There was no way he could put up with the man crying, not *this* man. He'd just have to knock him out again. Fortunately, the tears didn't materialize, and Cal relaxed his fist.

The floored man was Captain Laurence Decker, someone whom,

3

to Cal's utter bewilderment, had been deemed worthy of commanding a Class One Military Starship. Even more confusing was the fact that he was the son of the highly revered Admiral James Decker, a man who'd worked his way up the ranks with unrivalled determination, wit, and charm. How the hell could such a great military leader have produced a son who fell so short of the mark? The only logical explanation was that the Admiral's greatness simply didn't stretch to his parenting skills. There were, after all, plenty of rumours to back that up, talk of inflated grades at the Admiral's hand and echoes of disgust relating to his son's absurd leapfrog from academy to starship command. Cal had started military training shortly after Laurence Decker had graduated, but the rumours had lingered on. He had even heard talk of a discreet bodyguard being hired in the early years to deal with bullies.

Laurence Decker had more than a few bodyguards now, and they were far from discreet. The sound of multiple cutting lasers on the other side of the sealed office door pulled Cal away from his thoughts, and he briefly turned to the sound. "It seems your guards are finally coming to your rescue, Decker. But they won't be getting through that door seal anytime soon."

Decker didn't react to the words; he was still staring at his front tooth, seemingly struggling to come to terms with the fact that it was no longer in his mouth.

"Stand up and face me, Decker."

As if trying to prevent any more teeth from spilling out, Decker placed a hand over his mouth and finally looked up at his attacker. There was unmistakable fear in that look, fear that this man who'd punched his tooth out might not be finished with him. Cal had never considered himself a particularly imposing man, and the level of the Decker's dread took him by surprise.

Good, let the bastard be scared.

Clumsily, Decker shifted back against the same desk that he'd recently bounced off, his eyes darting wildly about the office no doubt in search of an escape from his nightmare. But there was no escape. Not unless you counted the exterior viewing panel, which, even if he could break through it, would make for a rather messy, unceremonious exit out into the cold vacuum of deep space. There was only one exit, and Cal had activated the door's heavy duty punch locks and placed himself between that exit and the captain.

"Are you going to stand up and face me, or am I going to have to come over there and haul you up?" Cal hoped for the former. He didn't relish the idea of lifting that much weight.

Leaning back against the desk to steady himself, Decker managed to struggle to his feet. "Anything you want. I'll give you anything, just name it."

Here we go. "Let's dispense with the begging and bribing," Cal replied evenly. "You know why I'm here." *Why the hell am I here?* Would pounding his fist into this man really do any good?

"Open that door, Lieutenant. Open it now, and your career will remain intact." The shaking in Decker's voice drowned out any inkling of authority it might once have contained. "My career ended when I failed to stop you sending good soldiers on yet another suicide mission." *I'm here to try and knock some sense into you, you useless bastard.*

"But I had no choice," Decker reasoned weakly. "I had to send at least one squad in. The pirates—"

"They weren't the threat. You're a weak, dim-witted fool, Decker, but even you should have seen that."

"You're wrong... There were orders... I—"

"Shut your damn mouth," Cal shouted more in frustration than anger. All he wanted was to get through to the man. He wanted him to realize what a fool he was. He wanted him to realize the weight that his command carried and the cost of his foolishness. He also wanted to punch him again. "The order came from you. You know it, and I know it." The lazy bastard probably hadn't even read the mission brief. "I can't let you do it again, Decker."

Decker didn't reply. He gripped the desk behind him and shot nervous glances between Cal, the exit, and the exit's locking mechanism. Cal could still hear the guards battling furiously with the sealed door, but he wasn't concerned. There was still time. He stared at Decker, reading the man like a book. The pathetic excuse for a captain had tried begging, making excuses for his actions, and of course pulling rank. They'd all failed, and now, Cal saw a level of desperation that suggested a last ditch effort at physical action. It seemed that apologizing and admitting his guilt would never occur to such a man.

"Don't bother—" Cal began, but the captain was already launching his ample weight forward.

Swiftly, Cal twisted aside, easily tripping the man and once again setting the arms flailing. Decker's journey was a short one that ended abruptly as his head connected with the rear wall.

Cal rubbed his face and eyes. What the hell was he doing? He'd never get through to a man like this, not with fists and certainly not with words. Stepping towards the crumpled captain, he was amazed to see that he'd somehow remained conscious. Reaching down, he clamped a fist around his collar and dragged him up onto his knees.

Decker pawed at the fist with weakened fingers. "I'm sorry... I'm sorry they died." The words were quiet but clear.

Cal paused, not quite trusting his ears. He stared into the man's terrified eyes, searching for some sincerity, some truth. Releasing his grip, he allowed the captain to slump to the floor. "Is there none of your father in you?" he asked, his brow creased in frustration.

After a few moments of silence, Cal shook his head and turned away. Maybe it hadn't been a complete waste. Maybe something had made it through. "You can take this as my resignation," he said as he walked slowly over to the office door and activated its release mechanism. The military would have to do without him from now on. He'd had enough of foolish orders and bullshit missions. He'd had enough of men like Captain Laurence Decker. And he'd had enough of being responsible for people. From now on, he'd be responsible for himself and leave it at that. *No more taking orders, no more giving orders, and no more responsibility.* With that in mind, Cal almost smiled as Captain Decker's guards burst in and surrounded him with pulse rifles raised.

"What d'you want done with him, sir?" asked the guard who had taken up position directly in front of Cal. His voice was aggressive, and the muzzle of his weapon was practically touching his nose.

Suddenly feeling much calmer, Cal looked down at the crumpled man.

Remaining on the floor, Decker took a few moments before answering. "Earth," he said simply, his voice sounding as broken as his face. "Send him back to Earth."

As the guards escorted him from the office, Cal caught a glimpse of an unfamiliar expression on Captain Laurence Decker's face. It was the unmistakable look of guilt and regret.

Chapter Two
JUMPER

Jumper Decoux was lost in thought as he stared at the huge, skeletal form of the Bullseye walker that lay crippled in the lush jungle ravine below. It was still morning in Mars' Big Game Zone, but already, the sun was beating down mercilessly, rapidly evaporating the last of the morning mist that hung limply over the jungle's canopy. Sweat rolled down Jumper's dark skin. He wiped it from his brow without moving his gaze from the distant wreck. He'd seen the crippled walker countless times over the last forty years but had never lost interest in the contrast of machine and nature. This was the only one of the SD181 Bullseye walkers remaining, all the others having been recovered by Federation scrappers long ago. Jumper could only guess why this one was left to corrode.

He would have liked to have seen one of the machines in action, but they'd been before his time, used in place of human hunters during the Food Planet's early days. They would stomp through the vast areas of the Big Game Zone, picking off just enough animals for the transport ships to ferry back to the hungry mouths on Earth. Of course, truthfully, no one on Earth was anywhere close to hungry. As Jumper understood it, the Bullseye walkers had worked well, but they were expensive, and the Federation hated nothing more than wasting money. Humans were cheap. He sighed and wiped again at his brow. Dirt bloody cheap.

Jumper remembered his first encounter with this walker wreck as a boy, how out of place it had seemed settled amongst the lush foliage. Its slick metal shielding would have been shiny enough to shave in back then had a fourteen year old trainee hunter really needed to shave. Every year since, when passing through this sector of the Big Game Zone, he'd always taken the time to locate the lone wreck and witness its ever-losing battle with the elements. Tall trees loomed over its weakening frame now, casting shadows like a giant, open maw. Stains from fallen fruits created a blood-like illusion as thick creeper vines mercilessly clung and tugged at the twisted metal as if pulling it slowly into a muddy grave.

The metallic skeleton reminded Jumper of his own aging body. Maybe this planet was doing the same to him, eating away his strength bit by bit, turning him into a lonely, forgotten old man. In truth, Jumper suspected he was fitter and sharper than most men half his age, but the lonely part was a different matter. Food Planet Hunters had an isolated career. The only people he ever saw were those on his once yearly shrink assessment at Big Game Headquarters, but ironically, the sanity of those manning the headquarters was iffy at best, most notably the shrink, so he never stayed for long.

As a younger man, Jumper had reveled in the seclusion. He'd always done well on his own and felt at home in the wild. Mars had been the right place to be, particularly the Big Game Zone. But one year ago to this very day, during his last visit to the Bullseye wreck, the thought had occurred that maybe he should be elsewhere. *Scrap metal belongs with scrap metal; people belong with people.* He had made a conscious decision that day to leave Mars for good and seek out a new, altogether more social life. After all, he'd be a rich man by now.

Big Game Hunters weren't well paid by any means, but with not a credit spent after forty years of service, his accounts had built up. If he was honest, though, the money meant little. A convenience, nothing more. It was human company he longed for. That and avoiding the same sorry fate as this derelict walker.

Unfortunately, abandoning the only lifestyle he'd known for forty years was no mean feat, and here he was, one year later, with nothing changed but a few extra gray hairs peppering his afro. Jumper was ashamed to admit that it was fear that stopped him from leaving, fear of rejoining a civilization that would no doubt be worlds apart from the one he'd left as a boy. No, this planet wasn't going to let him go without a fight.

A faint, rhythmic thump abruptly yanked Jumper from his thoughts. Without hesitation, he snatched his Long Eye bliss rifle from his back, closed his eyes, and listened. The thumping became louder. Spinning on his heel, he made a rapid descent down the ravine and, reaching a large cluster of rocks, dove behind them just as the culprit of the ominous thumping revealed itself. Jumper didn't need to risk a look; of all the creatures on the planet, it was the footfall of this particular beast that he was most familiar with.

The thumping stopped.

Damn it's hot, he thought, checking his rifle was loaded and clean. The sun had fully cleared the horizon now, and sweat was practically flowing off the end of his nose. What the hell was going on with the damned atmos-tweekers?

A deafening roar echoed down the ravine, reverberating through the boulders and in turn through Jumper's spine. Very slowly, he straightened up to assess the situation. As he'd guessed, the Tyrannosaurus rex stood in its menacing haunch at the very crest of the ravine, its cold, soulless eyes surveying the multitude of creatures inhabiting the wrecked walker below.

Jumper remained calm. The giant beast was a mere sixty feet from him, but he was well used to such events. During his forty years on the planet, he'd faced hundreds of dinosaur species, and every year, the Federation would *rebirth* more. Some believed they'd begun the experiments for archaeological research, others for the profits of theme park attractions and Jurassic zoos, but Jumper suspected they did it simply because they *could*, showing off on a grand scale. Using them as a food source had come later once it had been discovered that most dinosaur meat was surprisingly agreeable. From high quality stegosaurus steak to fast food T-rex burgers, never underestimate the potential profits of a good gimmick. With money in mind, the Federation had decided that free range was the way to go; feeding and breeding naturally proved far more cost effective. And thus, the Big Game Zone of Mars was born, allowing the Federation to well and truly begin cashing in.

The Tyrannosaurus indulged in one last ground-shuddering roar before lurching in to a thunderous charge down the ravine. Feeling the reassuring grip of his rifle in his hands, Jumper also made his move. Diving clear of the rocks, he tucked into a well-practiced roll and landed smoothly in a small clearing of dusty, red mud. Coming up on one knee, he leveled his rifle and, calm as a kid shooting cans, watched the creature grow large in his sights. With only a few precious meters left before the beast was upon him, Jumper pulled the trigger of his impressive-looking weapon, and a decidedly unimpressive dart hissed from its long barrel.

The great brute's charge ended there, its huge body abruptly losing all power as the dart did its job and sent it into a state of pure bliss—or as close to that state as such a creature could reach. Seconds later, it died, its body thundering into the dirt like a toppling tree, its giant head coming to rest just inches from the tip of Jumper's rifle.

Jumper took a few deep breaths. Despite having witnessed the effects of the bliss darts thousands of times, he still marvelled at their effectiveness. Slinging his rifle over his shoulder, he climbed onto the dinosaur's back, pulled the spent dart from its neck, and placed it carefully into his ammo belt. He was glad for the darts; not only did they avoid the rather messy business of pulse rifles, but they were infinitely more humane.

"Rest in peace, old girl," he whispered whilst gently running a hand along the dinosaur's rough hide. Then, reaching into his backpack, he plucked out a small locator device, flicked it on, and clamped it onto the creature's back.

"Okay, she's all yours," he said looking up to the sky.

Sliding to the floor, Jumper strolled over to a nearby tree; plucked a plump, red fruit from a low-hanging branch; and settled himself into a comfortable nook between two large, twisted roots. He hadn't waited for a Scooper ship in thirty years. There had never been any point. The ships had always worked like clockwork, flying in and quite literally scooping up the dead beasts within minutes. Until a few days ago, however, the atmos-tweekers had also worked like clockwork. So this time, Jumper decided to wait. More than anything, he hated to think that such an impressive beast had died for nothing.

After an hour of waiting, Jumper climbed to his feet and stared upwards, confusion creasing his brow. Not only had the scooper ship not arrived, but he had caught sight of a small, black dot moving across the pale blue sky. The dot was undoubtedly a small craft, but Jumper knew from decades of experience that a craft of that size had no place in the Mars sky. Snatching up his longeye rifle, he flicked the sights to the highest level and used them to peer at the new arrival. It was an ugly craft, that much was clear, little more than an oblong hunk of metal.

After a few moments of tracking its path, Jumper swore out loud. He was no expert on ships or indeed flying, but even to his untrained eye, it was plain to see that the little craft was on a collision course.

Slinging his longeye rifle over his back, he glanced up one last time then snatched up his pack and set off at a run.

Chapter Three
REJECT RAFT

Cal's eyes flickered open and struggled to focus through the ice-covered glass of the coffin-like cryo-capsule. A flow of warm air had begun to fill the capsule whilst an impossibly smooth female voice issued instructions. *Remain calm. An early awakening from your cryo-sleep has been deemed necessary. Please lay still, breathe deeply, and—*

Shit.

Cal slammed his elbow into the cryo-capsule's manual override and stiffly kicked it open to let a rush of cold air shock his body into action. Something was wrong, *seriously* wrong. Waking a crew early from a cryo-sleep was a last resort, especially a crew of rejects. The sudden recollection of his situation made him wince. *A fucking reject raft.* Still, he had to be thankful he was at least being ferried back to Earth. Decker could have just as easily sent him to one of the thousands of subpar colonies or even a fringe space prison planet.

Stumbling onto his bare feet, which partially stuck to the near frozen metal grating, Cal looked around the ship's interior and attempted to assess the situation as fast as his foggy brain would allow. The rest of the crew were still in their capsules, probably caught in the grip of panic and oblivious to the ship's soothing instructions. Everything else appeared normal. Quickly, he moved to the flight controls, his cold limbs protesting all the way.

"Where the hell are we?" he muttered whilst hitting the shield release for the exterior viewing panel. The thick barrier lazily slid upwards to reveal the dazzling glare of an outside world. Cal's eyes took a moment to adjust then grew wide. Two things were immediately apparent: The first was that he and his fellow rejects had not arrived at Earth, and the second was that they were in deep shit.

The hover beacon, which was rapidly filling the viewing panel, had a ludicrous number of lights, none of which were illuminated that suggested that it was offline, something that Cal had never encountered in all his years of piloting. The beacon wasn't even being detected by the ship's systems.

Ignoring the supplied hammer, Cal punched his fist through the protective glass covering the manual controls. Shoving his hand into the flight glove, he braced himself against the console and twisted the glove hard right, causing the ship to bank sharply. A second later, the ship's left landing wing tore into the beacon, and a stabilizer was wrenched clean out of its housing. Cal's grip within the flight glove instantly failed him as his body was launched sideways. Pain exploded in his side as he collided with a cold, unforgiving wall. The impact turned his vision into a color-filled haze, which, once dissipated, allowed him a blurred view of shuddering metal and glass. A screeching warning alarm filled the ship's cramped interior, an excessive sound that seemed entirely redundant in a ship that was quiet obviously crashing.

The ship was listing severely and Cal had to dig his fingers into the deck's metal grating in order to drag himself back towards the flight console. It was an effort that wasn't helped by the hale of dislodged ice fragments that were now freely raining down on him. Hauling himself into the flight chair and jamming his hand back into the flight glove, he did his best to level the ship. Blood trickled down his forehead. He wiped it away and fixed his eyes on the vast canopy of lush jungle vegetation that was rushing by below.

Too much ground, not enough sky, he thought grimly as he heaved back on the flight glove.

Heat created by the ship's entry into the planet's atmosphere had finally reached the interior walls and was causing any remaining ice to melt and drip freely. Cal wiped a mixture of this melted ice and his own blood from his eyes and risked a glance back at the cryo-capsules. Only one of them had opened, out of which a young man with tanned skin and a tangle of long, blond hair was sitting up and staring at him with wide eyes. He was fiercely gripping the side of his shuddering capsule.

"*What the hell?*" the young man yelled over the piercing alarm.

Ignoring him, Cal turned back to the flight console and hit a control, which promptly closed the capsule's lid on the man's head, forcing him to lie back down as the vacuum seal muted any further cries of distress. Before turning his attentions back to the outside world, Cal quickly locked the other three capsules.

The hull of the ship was skimming the tops of the trees now. With his free hand, Cal fumbled at the manual crash restraints on the top of the flight chair. He was used to smart-straps that closed around the body at the touch of a button. Unfortunately, it seemed rejects weren't worth the expense. Unable to fasten the restraints, he tried loosening his grip on the flight glove, but the ship immediately started to tip.

A huge branch thudded into the front of the ship, and the resulting lurch threw Cal painfully against the controls. Well aware that he could soon be sharing a similar fate to the bugs smeared on the viewing panel, he unlocked the flight seat with his free hand, spun it around so it faced the rear of the ship, and locked it in place.

Sitting reversed in the chair, he braced his legs beneath the arm rests.

As the ship bored its way through the canopy, Cal caught a brief glimpse of huge, pillar-like tree trunks bestrewn with twists of thick, knotted vines. *Exactly how I remember it*, he thought as he buried his chest and face into the back of the chair and waited for the inevitable impact.

Chapter Four
AN UNLIKELY TRIO

Cal clung to the flight chair like driftwood in a stormy sea. With his eyes shut tight and his face pressed hard against the worn padding, every bang and bump seemed painfully amplified as the ship barrelled its way through a seemingly endless array of branches and tangled vines. Eventually, the ship slowed, then Cal felt it flip and begin to drop upside-down. He gritted his teeth and clung tighter still, horribly aware that if his grip failed him, his head would pay the price. Thankfully, the landing turned out to be surprisingly and mercifully soft.

The inverted ship had turned dark. Doing his best to drop gracefully to its ceiling, Cal peered through the gloom and tried to assess the state of the craft. It seemed relatively stable, but the viewing panel was mostly blocked, and only a few dim, blinking lights offered any illumination. Every inch of his body throbbed painfully as he made his way to the ship's external door. Fortunately, his head had stopped bleeding, and nothing felt broken. He activated the opening mechanism, and the thick, metallic door hissed and groaned eerily as it attempted to slide open. After a moment of mechanical strain, a tall gap about two feet wide opened up to the bright outside world. Satisfied, Cal stiffly made his way to first cryo-capsule—the one from which the young blond man had made a brief appearance—and reached up to its control panel. A shower of dried crash foam rained down on Cal as the blond man spilled out. Shielding his eyes from the foam, Cal did his best to break the man's fall.

"What the hell's going on?"

"Relax, you've been in a crash," Cal explained as he pulled the man to his feet and directed him towards the partially opened door. Some of the dried foam had turned to floating dust and was making the already dim cabin darker still.

"I can't bloody see."

"It's just the dust. Head towards the light."

Turning back around, the young man felt for Cal with panicked hands. "Am I dead, bro?"

Cal almost laughed. "No, you're very much alive," he said and firmly turned the man back towards the door. "Just head towards the bright gap. It's a door, not the afterlife."

By the time Cal had opened the other two capsules and helped the surprisingly small occupants down and out of the gap, the interior of the ship was literally filled with thick dust. Coughing loudly and avoiding the temptation to wipe his eyes, Cal exited the ship into the brightness of day and took a moment to suck in a couple of deep breaths. His bewildered companions were already a dozen paces from the ship, sprawled out on a bank of soft, rusty colored mud. He looked around at the surrounding jungle then glanced up at the sky. *Christ.* Why the hell had they been redirected here?

Brushing himself down, Cal made his way over to his new companions. They were certainly not what he had expected. He'd been a last minute addition to the reject raft and hadn't seen the three who had entered the cryo-capsules a good hour before him.

They were the most unlikely trio to have come from a Class One Military Starship that he could possibly imagine even if they were rejects.

The young, blond man looked half asleep, possibly a little dazed from a knock to the head. Cal guessed that he was probably in his late teens or maybe early twenties. He certainly appeared strong and healthy enough to be a soldier, but Cal thought him more suited to riding a surfboard than firing a pulse rifle. Next to him was a girl of a similar age. She was pretty; petite; and, if it weren't for her military style buzz cut and combat fatigues, would have appeared straight from the cover of a teen fashion shoot. The girl seemed unhurt and was already climbing to her feet. The last member of the crew was definitely just a boy, Cal guessed maybe fourteen or fifteen.

This trio wasn't going to get far without him, not on a planet like this. Cal shook his head and smiled at the irony. *No more giving orders, no more responsibility.* Fate could be a bitch. He rubbed the back of his head. "Well, I got us on the ground," he said, glancing back at the inverted ship.

"Crappy landing," the boy mumbled.

Cal noticed he was clasping his left shoulder. "Are you hurt?"

Before he could get an answer, the girl with the buzz cut straightened up and gave a ridged salute. "Sorry, sir, didn't recognize you. Private Cole, division one ten."

Cal waved her hand down, finding himself a little taken aback by the volume of her voice. "No need for that. What's your first name, Private Cole?"

"Edwina, sir, friends call me Eddy."

Cal nodded. "Okay, Eddy, you mind doing something for me?"

"Name it, sir."

"First, call me Cal, and second, have a rummage around the ship for a med kit?" *More of a request than an order.*

"Right away, sir," The girl replied before eagerly darting back towards the wrecked ship.

Cal turned back to the boy. "She's a live one, eh?"

The boy shot him a small, unconvincing smile.

"Mind if I take a look at that shoulder?"

"S'no big deal. I reckon it'll be okay in a minute," the boy replied, a wobble in his voice.

"Good, but it won't hurt to check it just in case." Before the boy could protest, Cal bent down and began to examine the injury. "What's your name?"

"Viktor."

"Well, Viktor I'm afraid your shoulder's dislocated."

The boy shook his head, allowing a couple of tears to escape. "It'll be okay, don't worry about it."

"You're right. It will be okay once I deal with it."

Looking fearful, the boy awkwardly shuffled back a little way.

"It'll be quick," Cal assured him.

The boy screwed up his face. "Will it hurt?"

"A little." *A bloody lot.*

Cal turned to see that the girl named Eddy was already exiting the ship. She ran towards them, holding up a small, white box as she did so. The boy had also turned to look. Taking advantage of his distraction, Cal reached down, grabbed his skinny arm, and gave it a quick, hard yank, expertly popping it back into its socket.

The boy yelped. "*What the hell, you bloody psycho!*" He scrambled out of Cal's reach, teeth gritted.

"Sorry, but a dislocated shoulder's better sorted out sooner rather than later," Cal said as Eddy bounded up, holding out the med kit. Cal took it and, after a quick dig around, pulled out a small white disc. He looked down at the boy, who was now watching him with an understandably wary eye. "You're a brave chap, Viktor. Most soldiers cry like babies after having their shoulders popped." He tossed the little white disc to him. "This pain patch will get rid of the burning; just slap it on the front of your shoulder."

Viktor snatched the pain patch up without a second thought and managed a small nod of thanks.

Passing the med kit back to Eddy, Cal saw that the young, blond man was on his feet and was peering over the girl's shoulder. "Got any of the good stuff in that kit?'

"You hurt?" Cal asked.

"No, not really. But I've a keen interest pharmaceuticals," he replied, reaching over towards the kit.

"Get your damn junky fingers outa there, blondie, or I'll break 'um off," the girl warned.

The blond man chuckled at that.

"What ya laughin' at, idiot?" she snapped.

"Chill out, little chick, I just—"

Cal never thought it possible that such a delicate-looking girl could pack such a powerful punch. The blond man hit the mud with a dull thud. Understandably, it seemed to take him a few moments to register what had just happened, but eventually, he propped himself up on one elbow and glared at the girl. "What the hell?" he protested, cupping his bloody nose.

"Don't call me chick," Eddy replied simply as she casually returned her attentions to the med kit.

The blond man wiped some blood off his chin roughly with his sleeve. "Okay, point taken." He looked up at Cal, bemused.

Definitely not getting far without me. Cal offered the young man a hand up which was promptly accepted.

"Thanks. At least someone around here's got some manners," he said, his voice slightly muffled as he pressed his sleeve up under his nose. "I'm loving the old school English accent by the way."

22

Cal replied with a smile. "Sorry for shutting the cryo-capsule on your head earlier, but you'd have been far worse off otherwise."

"Reckon you'd be right on that score, um, Cal right?"

"That's *sir* to you, blondie," Eddy interjected.

The young man removed his arm from under his nose to reveal a broad, white-toothed grin. "Despite being proud of my fine blond locks, I prefer the name Toker," he said. "How'd a pretty little thing like you get so damn hostile?"

The girl scowled.

"Actually, Eddy, I never did like being called sir," Cal said as he turned on the spot to have another good look at their surroundings. "But let's finish our introductions later. Our crash may have attracted attention."

At this statement, the odd trio fell silent and joined him in looking about. At first, the surrounding jungle seemed quiet and still. After a few moments of peering into the huge trees, however, life became obvious shuffling, creeping and fluttering in just about every direction. High above them, small birds streaked through the jungle canopy in colorful, aerobatic displays, the odd one swooping down to the jungle floor where a myriad of insects busied themselves amongst the red mud and fallen fruits. In contrast, large, slow creatures, full of fur and long, curved claws, lazily crawled among the mammoth tree trunks and vines with seemingly little enthusiasm.

The boy Viktor was the first to break the silence. "Does anyone even know where we are?"

Cal noted a dreamy tone in his voice from the fast-acting pain patch.

"Well, it certainly ain't Earth," Toker replied as he ran a hand through his long hair. "Too many trees and too damn hot."

"He's right; it's not Earth," Cal said, continuing to scope the surrounding trees. "Don't ask me how, but we've ended up crashing deep in the Big Game Zone."

"Mars…? The Big Game Zone…?" Toker asked, his tanned skin rapidly losing its colour. "You're screwing with us, right?" Suddenly, a great deal of the cool edge had left the young man's voice.

"Afraid not," Cal replied. "We'll be okay, but we should get moving." He glanced at each of them. "Best collect anything useful from the ship. But bear in mind we've a long trek ahead and might have to run at times."

Toker and a wobbly looking Viktor wasted no time hurrying back over to the ship, leaving Cal and Eddy standing alone.

"Nothing you want from the ship, Eddy?" Cal asked, keeping his attention on the trees.

"No, sir. Bastards wouldn't let me take me guns on board."

Cal nodded. "Bastards indeed. Would've been handy having a few guns."

"You reckon there's hostiles nearby, Cal, sir?"

"If you mean animals big enough to tip us off the peak of the food chain, then yep."

"There's a scalpel here in the med kit. D'you wannit?" she asked, eagerly pulling out the tiny, silver blade.

"Er, you hold onto it for now," Cal suggested. He was beginning to suspect that size was of little importance to this girl. "So how did you end up on a reject raft, Eddy?"

"Permission to speak freely, Cal, sir?" she asked after a slight hesitation.

"Sure. And just call me Cal."

"Right, yeah… Cal… sorry," the girl said, looking a little conflicted. "Thing was…my commanding officer was a bit of an arsehole, thought I was out of control, endangering missions cos I was too eager to kick arse. Said I was nuts."

24

"And he put you on the reject raft for being over eager?' Cal asked, puzzled. Even for the military, the punishment seemed a little harsh.

"Well, he had a real go at me one day, talked at me all high and mighty like…so I kinda ended up kicking *his* arse."

Cal grinned.

"Well I never let any of my brothers get away with talkin' at me like that," she continued, "not even big Frank or Joe, so I don't see why I should let some poncy officer get away with it."

"Sounds like he had it coming."

The girl beamed. It was a radiant smile that took Cal by surprise.

"And you, sir. On some sort of secret mission, are you?"

"No," Cal shook his head. "No, I was given the boot too."

The girl eyed him, seemingly unsure if he was jesting. "But you're Lieutenant Harper. You won that Federation bravery award like three times."

Cal winced. He loathed those bloody awards. "It's true, Eddy."

"But how come?"

Cal thought for a moment then said, "My commanding officer was a bit of an arsehole… Did a bit of arse kicking myself."

Eddy snorted in a particularly unladylike laugh and was still snorting when a jittery Toker bounded up behind them carrying a small backpack. "Sure we should be moving?" he said. "Couldn't we just sit tight in the ship 'till help arrives?"

"There's no help coming, Toker. I'm not going to lie to you, the fact we've ended up on Mars means something on Earth's gone seriously wrong, and if that's the case, there's no chance anyone's going to waste time looking for a lost reject raft or its occupants."

"Buggers," Toker muttered, sitting himself on a nearby log and burying his hands into his tangle of blond hair.

Cal wished it was an exaggeration, but in truth, he couldn't think of a single reason why the reject raft would have been redirected to Mars. Even in the searing heat, the thought left him feeling cold.

"Permission to climb on top of the ship, Cal, sir?" Eddy asked. "Just whilst we wait for the kid. I could keep a lookout for hostiles an' all that."

"Sure, Eddy. Might be a good idea to tell the boy to hurry up though whilst you're over there."

"Right you are, sir... I mean, Cal," she called over her shoulder as she scampered off towards the ship.

"She's a bloody lunatic," Toker blurted as soon as the girl was out of earshot. "Can you believe it? Punched me square in the face."

Cal shrugged. He had to disagree; the girl wasn't nuts, just highly strung. He'd had plenty like her under his command. "It was an impressive punch though, you have to admit."

"Just caught me off balance is all."

Cal nodded. "So what's your story, Toker? You don't strike me as the soldier type."

"You got that right. I'm more lover than fighter."

"So how'd you end up on a Class One Military Starship?"

"To be honest, it's kind of a long story," Toker said then quickly grinned. "Actually, that's not an exact truth. It's not long, it's just, shall we say, kind of embarrassing."

Cal raised an eyebrow. "Well now you've got me intrigued."

Toker paused a few moments as if weighing Cal up. "Okay, I'll tell you, bro, but you gotta promise not to tell little knuckles over there."

"She won't hear it from me."

"Okay, I'm trusting you, but only because of that posh English accent. You sound like a bloke that honors a promise."

Cal nodded and smiled in reply.

"You ever watch the holo-show, Nine Lives Nutters?"

"No, not familiar."

"Really. Oh, man, you're missing out, and I'm not just saying that because I'm in it. It's truly a…"

Toker's voice trailed off, his eyes suddenly widening as they fixed on something over Cal's shoulder. Whatever had attracted the young man's attention seemed to be preventing his mouth from closing. Cal twisted around and instantly understood. A strikingly beautiful, six-foot-tall blonde woman had emerged from the wrecked ship and was making a surprisingly successful attempt at walking through the mud in high heel shoes and a skirt that was little more than a belt.

What the…

Before Cal could make sense of what he was seeing, Eddy had leapt from the top of the ship, scalpel clamped dangerously between her teeth, and landed on the blonde woman's back. It was an assault that should have smashed the unfortunate woman face first into the mud. But instead, the girl bounced off the woman like a deflected pin ball and hit the ground hard. Undeterred, Eddy quickly scrabbled to her feet and leaped once again onto the tall woman's back, this time wrapping her left arm around her neck and holding the scalpel to her jugular. The woman didn't scream. In fact, she barely reacted at all.

"Who the hell are you?" Eddy growled into the woman's ear.

Cal began moving towards the pair cautiously. "Take it easy, Eddy, everything's fine." *Shit, maybe she is a little nuts.* "Carefully slide off her, put the scalpel down, and slowly back away."

"Yeah, what the hell are you doing?" Toker added. "She's obviously off the ship, just like us."

Eddy showed no sign of obeying. "Yeah, where the hell was she then? There's only four cryo-capsules. She's a big, blonde, unanswered question, an', until it's answered, she's bloody well a hostile.'

"You ever heard of innocent 'til proven guilty? Or how's about anger management? That's one you should look up," Toker said, taking a brief moment to shoot Cal a grin.

Cal shook his head, hoping it would shut him up, then continued moving slowly towards the two women. "Trust me, Eddy, it's in your best interest to get off her, and do it carefully. She's not a hostile, she's a—"

"Melinda, a hand please?" Viktor's voice echoed from inside the ship, cutting Cal off mid-sentence.

The blonde woman reacted immediately. Swinging back towards the wrecked craft, she snatched Eddy's scalpel-wielding arm and, as if simply ridding herself of a bothersome cobweb, flung the girl away.

Leaping forward, Cal managed to break the worst of Eddy's fall while narrowly avoiding a scalpel in his ear. Having already grasped a fairly good understanding of how the girl's brain handled information—or didn't, as the case may be—Cal restrained her as she made an attempt to jump up and pursue her unanswered question.

"But, Cal, sir, she could be a danger," Eddy said, struggling against his unyielding grip. "Let me go an'…I'll handle this.'

"I'll let you go, Eddy, but how's about I answer your unanswered question first."

The girl's struggling eased but didn't stop.

"Now, I don't know where the hell she was hiding or why, but she didn't require a cryo-capsule because she doesn't breathe or feel the cold. She's a synthetic, a military synthetic combat soldier."

Eddy shook her head. "No disrespect, sir, but I've seen pictures of synthetic combat soldiers. I even seen one for real once, and they sure don't look nuffin' like the bimbo over there."

"Granted, there seem to have been a few less than standard

adjustments," Cal reasoned, "but think about it, Eddy. The synthetics are always female, she's the right height and build, and call me crazy, but the biggest giveaway was the way you bounced off her back like a rubber ball off concrete."

Eddy stopped struggling. "She did seem weirdly strong."

"She sure kicked your ass, soldier girl," Toker said, obviously amused by the turn of events. "A synthetic, eh? Who'd've thought a friggin' android could be so...well, attractive. They always make them that hot, Cal?"

Cal looked over to the ship where Viktor was passing a large, apparently broken, hovercase down to the blonde synthetic, who it seemed was named Melinda. Cal knew he could keep a cool head longer than most, but he was seriously starting to doubt his grip on reality. Eddy was right about one thing; unanswered questions could be dangerous. He got to his feet and pulled Eddy up with him. "No, Toker, they never make them that hot. But the questions are going to have to wait. It's time we started moving. Viktor, we're moving out. Best tell your girlfriend to lose the high heels and follow us."

"Okay, we're right behind you. But she's not my girlfriend, she's my wife."

Cal led the way into the jungle and, for the sake of his sanity, pretended that he hadn't heard the boy's last comment.

Chapter Five
BOY GENIUS

The jungle remained as lively as ever as Cal and his new companions made their way through tangled vines and over massive, twisting tree roots. A huge variety of God's creations—and some that were more likely the result of human genetic tinkering—were flying, crawling, hopping, slivering, and occasionally squelching all around them. Fortunately, none of the local wildlife encountered so far was particularly large or vicious or indeed taking the slightest interest in them.

It had been many years since Cal had spent time on Mars, and he was finding the diversity of plant and animal life astounding, far more than he'd seen as a boy. Another startling difference to the Mars of his memories was the heat. The jungles of the Big Game Zone were always intended to be hot, but the sizzling rays penetrating the gaps in the jungle's canopy seemed excessive. The atmos-tweekers were undoubtedly malfunctioning just as the landing beacon had been. Cal didn't like to think what could have caused such malfunctions. The running systems for both were fortified with a large number of backups and a similarly large number of skilled staff. Something or someone had majorly screwed up, that much was clear, and he and his companions were paying the price. He looked up and wiped his brow with a damp sleeve. If it weren't for the mass of foliage above their heads, that price would be a severe roasting.

Cal made a point of regularly looking back at the oddball convoy he was leading. The girl, Eddy, was close behind him, hacking away with her tiny medical scalpel at branches that weren't even in her way. The young blond man, Toker, trailed a few paces behind her, snapping his head around nervously at every sound. Then, bringing up the rear, was the buxom blonde—who Cal had to keep reminding himself was one of the most sophisticated weapons the military had ever developed—and the pale, skinny kid stumbling along beside her. Cal noticed that the boy still looked a little unsteady from the effects of the pain patch. Despite the ominous situation, he couldn't help but grin at the sight of the pair.

As he battled on through the tricky terrain, Cal tried to think of the possible reasons why the reject raft hadn't made it to Earth. Scenarios came and went, but each one seemed more ludicrous than the last. Frustrated, he eventually decided to concentrate on a mystery closer to home. Taking a quick pause, he instructed Eddy on their direction and nominated the young girl to lead the way. She may be bordering on psychotic, but she was at least alert. He then waited for Viktor to catch up.

"How's the shoulder, Viktor?"

"I've had worse," the boy replied.

Cal smiled, impressed with the duration of the pain patch's effects. "Good chap." He looked over at Melinda. It was incredible how human she looked. He'd always thought the real giveaway with the synthetics was their lifeless eyes and lack of personality. Melinda, however, was different—strikingly so. Her gender was the norm; all of the synthetics were designed in the female form, the military's reasoning being that the enemy would find a female less threatening and therefore underestimate her in combat. Despite meeting some pretty lethal women in his time, Cal in general could see the logic in this. Where the logic evaporated for him, however, was in the decision to make these passive, wouldn't-hurt-a-fly females six feet tall and, due to hair being considered an encumbrance during battle, completely bald. In contrast, Melinda had beautiful long locks, and more importantly, Cal could see life in her eyes.

"Mind if we talk whilst we walk?" He asked the boy.

"Fine by me."

Cal glanced again at the synthetic. "Do you think Melinda would mind if we talked in private?" He asked the question with an air of caution. He knew all synthetics were fitted with behaviour inhibitors to prevent them harming a human without a direct order from a suitably ranked officer, but he couldn't be sure if Melinda's remained intact. He definitely didn't want her to take offence.

"Would you mind dropping back for a bit, M?"

"Of course," Melinda replied in a soft tone. She then stood perfectly still as Cal and Viktor continued on.

"She'll decrease her hearing capability and follow us once we're out of earshot," Viktor said confidently.

Cal nodded. "So, I hope you don't mind me asking, but I'm a little confused as to how you ended up on a reject raft with a synthetic soldier."

"She's not a synthetic soldier anymore," he replied defensively. "She's nothing like those mindless drones."

"Yes, she's quite a beauty," Cal agreed.

"Isn't she just."

Cal thought for a moment how to broach the subject then decided to come right out with it. "So, um...*wife?*"

The boy reddened. "It's not impossible, you know. I heard about a woman who married her AI companion once."

Cal shot him a wry smile.

"Yeah, I know. Stupid, eh? I had to say something though. They're gonna try and take her away from me and after all the improvements I'd made."

"*You* made?"

"Yeah, I worked quite a bit on her facial features, see, especially the smile—the smile's the most important thing—and the eyes. And she's got the most perfect nose you've ever seen, right?' the boy continued, hardly stopping for a breath. "Those damn Military designers have no clue what makes a good bone structure. They put no love into their work, Cal. Plus, they set the facial muscles all wrong, and they wonder why the hell they don't have realistic expressions. And the lack of hair, bloody hell, and don't even get me started on the personality programming. I've seen toy dolls with better personalities. I don't own toy dolls, you understand—'

"Viktor, sorry to disrupt your flow, but I think you might need to start your story a bit further back so I can get the full picture."

"Uh…sorry, yeah, I go off on one sometimes. They're just so stupid though, you know, these military guys. Not you, but some of the others, you know what I mean?'

"Yep."

"So I guess you wanna know how I got on a military starship?"

"Sounds like the perfect place to start."

"I was invited. I'm what they call gifted in the world of science. I mean, I don't like to brag, but they call me a genius."

Cal suspected that the boy did like to brag, but a little bragging where bragging was due was fine in his book.

"When I was twelve, I designed and built a synthetic dog and entered into Earth's most prestigious science fair, the…er…fifth Quantum Star Science event. Pretty sure it was the fifth. Can you believe that some idiot woman in the entries office tried to put me and my dog into the junior competition?"

After a brief pause, Cal realized that the boy was actually waiting for a response. "What an idiot," he replied, trying his best for genuine sincerity.

"Too right. Wasn't a problem though. Quick little hack into their entries system, and me and Rex, that was the dog, were in with the big boys. Just as well too cos I only went and bloody well won it."

Cal smiled. "Congratulations. So the military took a keen interest in your talents?"

"Yep, they're always hanging out at the big science fairs. Kinda like scouts at the college spike ball games I guess. So anyway, they sent me to the best science college to develop my skills, which was a load of crap by the way. Those professors really don't have a clue. Still, I s'pose I got all the best equipment to mess around with. Then I turn fourteen, see, an' they offer me a crap ton of credits to work on one of their starships, fixing up their battle robots 'n synthetics 'n stuff."

"Huh. You ever work on a battle robot called Max? He was part of my team."

"Sure, Max. I worked on him quite a bit. Made a few alterations. He was a good bot." The boy looked up and shot Cal a smile. "The job they gave me was a bunch of crap though, see. I wasn't destined to fix things. I'm an inventor, see, Cal. I like to create things, not play around with stuff or fix up some dipshit's shoddy designs. I mean how's science meant to advance if they don't let guys like me open their minds and think outside of the box, eh, Cal, eh?"

Cal rubbed his face. He felt his own mind was being opened a little too wide for comfort. But at least a few of the pieces of the puzzle were starting to come together. "So I guess they didn't take kindly to you thinking outside of the box?"

"I'm not too good with rules, see, Cal. They were pissed when I introduced them to Melinda. What they were too dim to realize, though, was that I was doing them a favor. They kept going on about the bigger boobs and the blonde hair as if all I'd done was alter her looks. If they'd let me put her in the ring with one of their stupid drones, like I suggested, they'd have seen that my Melinda could destroy those pathetic synthetics with one arm tied behind her back."

Cal looked back at Melinda whilst Viktor struggled over a cluster of particularly large, slippery tree roots. The cybernetic woman was standing stock still about twenty meters behind them, waiting dutifully for Viktor to continue forwards. The boy undoubtedly had talent; unlike her counterparts, Melinda could easily pass as human. Cal wondered about the extent of her combat alterations. Considering their location, he doubted he'd be wondering for long. Although the synthetics were still relatively new within the military, Cal had already seen them in combat many times, and he had to admit, he was glad she was with them.

"Can't keep your eyes off her, eh?" Viktor said, sounding triumphant at having finally made it over the cluster of roots.

Cal smiled. "Just curious."

"They were sending her back on the reject raft cos none of them on the starship could work out what I'd done to her. Bloody dipshits were confused to hell."

Cal could sympathise. "Probably best to call her back over now, Viktor. And do me a favor, will you?"

The boy looked at him questioningly.

"Keep her close."

Chapter Six
JUNGLE BRAWL

It was beginning to get dark. Cal and his new companions had been trekking through the dense jungle for two long days with little rest. The previous night had been spent in the relative safety of a large tree, precariously perched among the high branches. None of them had achieved much sleep that night, and with the fierce heat during the day, they were near the point of exhaustion.

Wiping the sweat from his eyes, Cal turned and ordered a pit stop. After pointing out some edible fruits and picking a few for himself, he took a much-needed seat on a tree root and regarded his companions. Eddy was looking wobbly on her feet but showed no sign of quitting. She had a seemingly inexhaustible grin on her face, and Cal had to wonder whether her body's exhaustion had even registered in her somewhat unhinged brain. Toker, despite clearly still suffering anxiety as he peered around at the surrounding jungle, was obviously a fit guy and was managing to keep pace. Of all of them, Cal expected that Viktor would be the one suffering the most from the hard slog, but fortunately, this wasn't the case. Since the middle of the first day, the boy had opted to walk arm in arm with the synthetic, and Cal suspected that his feet had barely touched the ground since.

Although used to jungle trekking, it pained Cal to admit that it was he who was most likely to slow them down. The battering he'd taken during the crash combined with the long trek had aggravated an old injury in his lower back that had occurred four years previously when the snapping jaws of a Panthelon ice lizard had forced him off a high cliff. Fortunately, a deep snow drift had broken the worst of his fall, but his back had paid the price. A constant string of follow up missions had left him no opportunity to have the injury dealt with.

As he called the others over, he couldn't ignore a pang of envy at their youth. He was only thirty-five, but the current state of his body made him feel twice that. Kneading his knuckles into his back, he made a resolution to get the injury seen to as soon as he made it back to Earth. He just hoped to God they could fix it. "I think it's time we found somewhere to rest up. It'll be dark again soon," he said, looking at each of them in turn. He'd briefly considered taking advantage of the cooler temperatures and continuing on through the night but had quickly dismissed the idea. So far, they'd been extremely fortunate not to have encountered any large predators. The darkness of night, however, was hunting time for many of the Big Game residents. If they remained on the move, their luck would likely run out.

"Maybe we should light a big fire, eh, keep any beasties at bay?"

"Usually, you'd be right, Toker. But certain beasties around here aren't put off by fire. It would just illuminate their dinner. We're best off doing the same as last night and scaling a tree. This one will do nicely." Cal pointed to an enormous tree that was covered with rugged green bark. "It's a couching tree. Plenty of hand and foot holds in the bark, so it should be an easy enough climb. Any objections?"

"Course not, Cal, you know best," Eddy said as she stared up at the tree. "You're the leader."

Cal winced. *Just get them to the headquarters.*

"Want me to get up there and scope it out, Cal?"

Cal looked up into the ominous tangle of branches that seemed to stretch endlessly into the rapidly darkening sky. "Okay, Eddy. Shout once you've found a good place to rest."

She gave a quick salute, which almost landed her beloved scalpel in her right temple.

"Oh, and Eddy, try to take it slow, eh?"

The girl nodded and, gripping the little blade in her teeth, completely ignored the suggestion and practically ran up the tree's thick trunk to the first branch.

"She's like a little squirrel," Toker said, sounding genuinely impressed.

"She's certainly agile," Cal agreed as they watched her ascend out of sight.

"So, Toker, you didn't finish telling me how you ended up on a military starship."

Toker frowned. "Kinda hoped you'd forgotten about that," he said, looking around to check that the boy and the synthetic weren't listening in. Viktor was sat on his broken hovercase on the other side of the clearing with Melinda standing tall over him.

"How could I forget?" Cal replied. "You've got me intrigued."

Toker sighed but cracked a little grin nonetheless. "Okay, bro, where did I get to?"

"The holo-show. Nine Live Nutters."

"Oh right, yeah, can't believe you never seen it." Toker paused as if expecting Cal to suddenly recollect the show. "So anyway, there's nine of us, right, four girls and five guys, an' it's like a competition show. Basically, we all have to come up with a stunt, then every Thursday night, each of us attempts to pull off that stunt, and it's shown on live holo-screens everywhere, even the fringe space colonies apparently. It's a popular show. I'm actually quite famous, bro," he said, flashing another of his big, white-toothed grins. "So anyway, the winner gets a prize, right, a new speed board or Flint Fusion hover boots, something like that. Thing is, none of us do it for the prize. We do it for the love of the rush. I'm talkin' adrenalin pumpin' through your veins 'till they feel like they're gonna pop. You ever experienced that, Cal?"

"Sure, once or twice."

"Right, then you'll know how addictive it is. Thing is, lately, it's been getting harder and harder to come up with a winning stunt, you know, one good enough to top the last."

"So who decides on the winner?"

"Not who, bro, but what." Toker snatched up his backpack and started digging around inside.

"Used to be that the public voted on the winner, but that didn't last because you know what, all the chicks watching voted for one of the girls because of all that girl power stuff, an' the guys voted for one of the girls too because they bloody fancied them. Just wasn't fair. Not until they came up with this..." Toker pulled a small device with an electronic dial and a short smart-strap from his bag and held it out with a grin. "It's an Ando Adrenalin Cuff, the best damn invention since the surfboard."

Cal took it and gave it a quick study. "Measures your adrenalin levels?"

"You got it in one, bro. It measures both the level and length of the high. Best reading goes home a winner."

"Sounds fair," Cal said, handing back the cuff. "So..."

"Oh, so yeah, still doesn't explain being on the starship, right? This is where the story gets kinda embarrassing," Toker continued, once again having a quick look around. "Like I said, it gets harder and harder to come up with a stunt to top the last, right, and it was the season finale, so the pressure was really on. I tell ya, I was seriously struggling. My head was empty like a cracked coconut. So I decide to go visit a mate of mine. He lives in the desert, the one in the old zone of California. The desert helps me think, you see. So there I am, sitting in this bloody desert on the top of this huge bloody dune, no one around as far as the eye can see, which is pretty damn rare on Earth, right? So anyway, that's when it came to me: *the orbit death jump!*"

"Huh."

"Uh huh," Toker agreed with an enthusiastic nod. "See, when I was sitting on that dune, searching for my inspiration, it only went and flew right over my bloody head." Toker took another pause, seemingly lost in thought. "You ever seen one of those big ass military supply vessels, Cal? Those humongous bloody great things that take all sorts of crap out to the starships and colonies?"

"I have."

"Yeah, course you have—"

Toker's words were cut short as a long, hissing shadow suddenly dropped between them from above. Both men jumped back, Toker with a small cry of terror. The python hit the ground hard then slithered hurriedly over the couching tree's protruding roots to disappear into the thick undergrowth.

"Heads up," came Eddy's faint voice from somewhere high in the darkness.

"Damn that bloody chick," Toker blurted. "Teeth. Everywhere I turn, man, frickin' teeth, goddamn pointy bloody teeth."

Cal checked to make sure the snake had gone. He wasn't overly fond of them himself. "So?" he said, turning back to Toker.

"Right, yeah," Toker replied, straightening himself up and attempting to regain some sort of composure. "So the supply ships…well, it's one hell of a display when they take off, right? So I figured if I could hitch a ride on one, then I could jump out of the thing just before it left Earth's atmosphere. I could retire from the show a bona fide legend."

Cal rubbed his injured back and briefly mused how surreal his life had suddenly become. "Sounds like a winning stunt to me."

"Too right. I was prepared too, right down to the last detail: state-of-the-art jump pack, heat proof body armor, oxygen…hell, I even had four hover cameras programmed to follow me down."

"So what happened?"

"Well, turned out the military were less than keen for me to hitch a ride on one of their precious supply ships, so I had to do it on the sly. Didn't even tell the producers of the show. To tell you the truth, it was a lot easier than I thought, sneaking onto that ship. I hid amongst the livestock. Not a great idea though, bro, cow crap everywhere, plus I had wads of time before the launch, so I decided to take a little nap, you know, calm the nerves."

"Uh oh," Cal said with a grin.

"You catch on fast. Damn right, uh oh. There's only one thing that I'm better at than stunts, and that's sleeping. Next thing I know, I'm waking up in zero G with nothing but a bunch of floating cows for company."

Cal laughed out loud. His life was in turmoil, but at least he was entertained. "Lucky you hid in the livestock section. Oxygen's always handy."

"Reckon I'd have been better off without it. That ship took five damn weeks to get to your starship. You any idea what it's like eating chicken and cow feed for five weeks in zero G? An' you know the worst thing? My adrenalin cuff didn't go higher than three bars the whole friggin' trip."

Cal's laughter suddenly caught in his throat as a distant shout from Eddy echoed from above. "Somethin's comin' our way, an' it's movin' fast."

The whites of Toker's eyes grew a little larger in the darkness. "If you're messing with us, little chick, I swear—"

"Quiet," Cal said, laying a hand on Toker's shoulder and peering into the surrounding trees. There was a rustling of leaves and snapping of dry twigs. The sounds seemed to be coming from more than one direction and were fast becoming louder.

"Viktor, stay close to Melinda. We might have trouble," Cal shouted, looking towards the boy who was already caught up in the synthetic woman's protective embrace.

A fast-moving shadow suddenly shot across Cal's peripheral vision. Grabbing Toker's arm, he threw himself to the ground, taking the young man with him as the shadow tore through the space where their heads had been. The dark attacker let out a blood-curdling roar and landed with a thud the on the other side of the clearing just a few paces from Viktor and Melinda.

Ignoring an explosion of pain in his lower back, Cal got to his feet. "Viktor, stay completely still."

"What the hell is it, Cal?" Toker whispered as he backed up towards the base of the huge couching tree.

"Not a bloody clue," he whispered back. The creature was similar to one of Earth's silverback gorillas but for two alarming differences: Firstly, the beast had no fur. Instead, it was covered with jet black scales that glimmered hauntingly with each aggressive movement. And secondly, in place of forearms and fists, it had dark, crab-like claws that it was using to scuff the ground with frightening force. The creature looked at each of them in turn, noisily snorting air in and out of its flattened nose. Cal couldn't judge whether it considered them a threat encroaching on its territory or prey doing a poor job of running away. The silvery drool dripping from its long fangs suggested the latter.

Toker was shaking his head and mumbling. "Teeth, more bloody teeth. Can my life get any deeper in the shitter?"

As if in answer to his question, two smaller, but just as vicious looking, creatures of the same breed slowly emerged from the surrounding darkness to join their companion.

The largest of the trio fixed its menacing eyes on Viktor.

"Viktor, I think it's time to give Melinda instructions."

"No need, Cal," the boy replied, sounding confident despite the tremble in his voice.

With a ferocity that outdid even that of their earthly counterparts, the lead creature bolted towards Viktor. Without hesitation, Melinda grabbed the boy by the back of his shirt, swung him once around, and threw him with incredible precision into an overhead branch. Despite executing the move with lighting speed, the synthetic woman barely had time to turn and meet the attacking creature head on. There was a titanic clash, and the two became a strange blur of black and blonde as they rolled, punches flying, into the surrounding trees.

"Toker, get up the tree," Cal shouted then turned to see that the young man was already above him, scrabbling desperately up the trunk. Cal had an overwhelming urge to bolt up after him, but his rational brain overruled it. These beasts were sure to be efficient climbers, so instead, he pressed his back against the tree's mammoth trunk and braced himself. As predicted, one of the two remaining creatures launched itself towards him in a kinetic bust of fury that sent dark chunks of mud flying. Cal stayed put until he was sure he could feel the creature's hot, snorting breath on his face. Then he threw himself clear. There came a satisfying crunch as the creature's head connected with the unforgiving tree trunk. Hitting the ground in a roll, Cal sprang to his feet as fast as his protesting back would allow and span around. To his great relief, his attacker was slumped unconscious among the tangle of roots.

The third creature, perhaps having learned from its companion's mistake, came at Cal with more caution but no less aggression. Seizing a nearby log, Cal attempted to raise it threateningly above his head, but another explosion of pain in his back forced him to abort the effort. Clutching his back and retreating slowly, he cursed his own stupidity while his eyes and mind searched franticly for options, an escape, a weapon, any bloody thing…

Then Eddy dropped from the sky directly in front of him.

Oh fucking hell.

"I got him," the girl growled, wielding her little scalpel in front of her as if it were a four-foot-long broadsword. The creature paused for just a second, possibly bewildered by the lack of fear in its prey. It was all the time Cal needed. Reaching forward, he pulled Eddy towards him just as the creature took a swipe at her head with one massive, razor sharp claw. Stumbling backwards, Cal caught his retreating heel on a root and fell to the ground. Her arms flailing, Eddy followed him down, winding him with her skinny shoulder as she did so. Seeing its chance, the creature leapt, bloodthirsty rage emanating from its eyes as it swung its great claw downwards in a killing blow.

Fortunately, the blow didn't come.

There was a loud thud and a splintering of roots as Melinda hit the ground, the creature's thick neck clasped tightly between her powerful, cybernetic hands. After a brief and confusing tussle, the synthetic managed to slip behind her opponent and wrap all four of her long limbs around it, instantly putting a stop to the lashing of its deadly claws. Witnessing what he thought to be a stalemate, Cal surged to his feet. Then he stopped short; the synthetic woman's long, blonde hair had begun to lengthen. Not only that but it started to snake its way around the creature's neck and tighten.

Seconds later, the beast was unconsciousness.

"Holy shit, she did it. She used her hair," Viktor shouted triumphantly as he clumsily tumbled from his high perch and bounded towards Cal. 'What did I tell you, Cal, my girl kicks arse."

Cal watched with fascination as Melinda's long hair unravelled from the unconscious creature's limp neck and retracted back to its normal length. He nodded at the boy, feeling a little dumbfounded. "She really does," he mumbled in reply. Rubbing the throbbing ache in his back, he turned to see Eddy climbing to her feet while Toker reluctantly crawled back down the tree.

"That's the first chance she's had to use it," Viktor said as he sidled up to the synthetic woman. "Other than making her look gorgeous of course."

Melinda, despite being covered in mud, did indeed still look gorgeous as she smiled down serenely at the boy.

"I used some of the latest Claxo smart-sync nano threads, modified slightly of course. What d'ya reckon, Cal?"

Cal continued rubbing his back. It felt like a red hot poker had been pushed into his lower spine. "I reckon, Viktor, that it's the most impressive hair I've ever seen."

The boy gave an impossibly wide smile and looked about to reply when a loud voice rang out from the darkness of the surrounding trees. "You used to say that about mine."

The sound made all of them, bar Melinda, jump in fright. Cal turned to see a tall black man with undeniably impressive hair emerge from the shadows to step into the moonlight. "Jumper Decoux," Cal said with a sudden grin. "Well I'll be damned."

Chapter Seven
FRIENDS REUNITED

With warmth from the early morning sun against his face and a sweet jungle chorus filling his ears, Cal slowly roused from a deep, dreamless sleep. His eyes fluttered open to a radiant sunrise pouring over a blanket of mist that spread to the horizon and beyond. As he stretched and breathed in the fresh, fruity air, some of his boyhood memories flooded into his mind and brought with them a wide smile. With so much of his time spent in the cold, silent expanse of space, he'd sorely missed the jungles of Mars. And now he was back, albeit unexpectedly, and was adamant he'd enjoy it while it lasted. Closing his eyes, he took a moment to let the medley of birdsong swim through his ears and cleanse his mind. God knows it needed a damn good cleanse.

Cal had only been thirteen for one week when he'd first arrived on Mars and been introduced to his hunting mentor. The tall man, who'd introduced himself as Jumper Decoux, had seemed intimidating at first, but then Cal had seen the kindness in his eyes. The year that he'd gone on to spend in Jumper's company before being carted off to military academy held some of his fondest memories.

Opening his eyes, Cal marvelled at the spectacle before him. The view from the massive, twisted branch on which he was perched was nothing short of spectacular. The previous night, Jumper had led them through the darkness to a tree so large it seemed a trick of the eye. Its mammoth trunk soared, skyscraper-like, through the jungle canopy while its multitude of branches spread far and wide like the outstretched arms of giants. Cal had never seen its like. It made the surrounding jungle look like a garden of mere bonsai trees in comparison.

He looked over to an adjacent branch where his companions lay, still deep in sleep. He was relieved to see that none of them had sleepwalked during the night. Viktor was enclosed in Melinda's gentle but immovable embrace. The two of them appeared asleep, but Cal knew the synthetic woman would be fully aware. Much to his amusement, Viktor and Melinda weren't the only ones embracing. He suspected, however, that Toker's embrace of Eddy was probably a case of dream-induced mistaken identity. For Toker's sake, he hoped that the young man woke before she did.

Cal climbed to his feet and was relieved to find that the pain in his back had subsided a little after the long night's sleep. It still bloody hurt, but it was easily bearable compared to the searing, almost crippling pain of the previous evening. Having one last careful stretch, he began to climb downwards. He knew that his old friend Jumper would be perched a few levels below, making sure that no unwanted visitors were venturing up to meet them. Cal could think of no one better for the job. Despite his relaxed manner, Jumper was more alert and capable than any person he knew.

Sure enough, he found him a few branches below, sitting with his back against the tree's wall-like trunk, busily dissecting a large, bright red fruit with an equally large survival knife.

"Beautiful morning, eh?" Jumper said without looking up.

"Yep," Cal replied, settling himself down beside him. "This is quite a campsite you've found us."

Jumper cut a large wedge from the fruit and passed it to Cal. "Biggest tree you've ever seen, right? It's an Alvorian Oak."

"Alvor. I should have guessed. All the biggest and best things seem to come from that planet." Cal took a large bite from the fruit, and his eyes grew wide. "Alvorian fruit?"

Jumper gave a knowing nod. "Pretty good, huh?"

"Unbelievably good," Cal replied, taking another generous bite.

"Only the richest cats get to sample this back on Earth. Alvor's pretty far away, so it gets costly importing any type of food. That's why this tree is here. It's an experiment to see how Alvorian vegetation takes to Mars soil."

"Seems to be taking well."

Jumper shrugged and passed him another wedge of fruit.

"You don't agree?" Cal asked puzzled.

"Don't get me wrong. When I saw how this tree grew and first sampled its fruit, I thought I'd died and gone to heaven."

"But?"

"But it's been my responsibility to monitor the tree's growth and compare it to charts of the growth rates on Alvor."

"You're saying they get bigger than this on Alvor?"

"Twice as big. And as good as this fruit is, I'm willing to bet every curly hair on my head that the fruit growing on Alvor is twice as tasty."

Cal wiped his chin and tried to picture the jungles of Alvor. "Maybe you'll find out one day... Maybe we both will."

"Maybe," Jumper agreed with a smile.

Cal thought he detected sadness in the smile and decided not to push the subject.

The two men sat in comfortable silence for a little while, enjoying the view and continuing to devour the fruit.

Eventually, Jumper broke the silence, "So how's the back feeling?"

Cal turned to him with a raised eyebrow. "I don't remember telling you about that."

Jumper shrugged. "You couldn't keep your hands off it last night, and you didn't exactly spring up this tree."

Cal shook his head and grinned. "Observant bugger, aren't you? It's just an old injury. It got stirred up from the crash and the trek. To be honest, it's making me feel a hundred years old, especially around these kids."

"Don't worry, you've got a *real* old man with you now."

Cal shook his head again and laughed quietly. "You're not the only observant one, Jumper. Unlike me, you *did* spring up this tree last night. Put every one of us to shame. And I'd wager you weren't even trying." Cal studied him for a moment. "And I have to say, you haven't aged a day."

Jumper shrugged.

"So, what's your secret?"

Jumper cut another piece of fruit and held it out to Cal. "Good diet," he said with a grin.

Cal laughed and took the wedge of fruit. "You're probably right."

The two men enjoyed another moment of silence as they finished their breakfast. Cal stared out at the far-reaching view. The mist was burning away now, and the daytime heat was already increasing rapidly. It was good to be in the company of his old friend again. It had been twenty years since Jumper had trained him in the ways of a food planet hunter. Every year since on Jumper's check in at headquarters, Cal had sent a message filling him in on the route his life was taking, and every year, Jumper would reply.

"So, I couldn't help but notice quite a few things have changed around here in the last twenty years," Cal said, sucking the last of the fruit juice from his fingers.

Jumper shrugged. "I suppose my afro's a little smaller.'

Cal grinned. "It's still pretty large."

"I'll get it cut one of these days. You're right though; the planet's changed quite a bit since you were a boy. They've introduced a lot of weird and wonderful things, especially over the last couple of years. Mostly weird. Here in the Big Game Zone, there's twice as many predators. Certainly makes my job a hell of a lot more difficult. Those gorilla creatures you met last night are a new addition. I only met them myself a couple of months ago. Federation guys say they're alien, but personally, I think they've been messing around with genetics again."

"Not much demand for black-scaled gorillas in the restaurant business I'd guess. Are they for the zoos, theme parks?"

"Maybe. But there's plenty of new motives."

"Oh?"

"Security for one. Once some of the nastier beasts are fully grown, Federation salesmen cart them off to valuable factory planets or to those super rich colonies, places like that. Apparently, men and dogs don't cut it these days. And then there's always the military. You know how they like to train up a beast or two. Also the pet business."

"*Pets.*"

"There's some pretty weird people out there, Cal." Jumper grinned. "Still, all these new creatures aren't the strangest things around here lately. Atmosphere's been going haywire. I'm getting no replies from headquarters, and the scooper and pickup ships have been non-existent. Then of course, there's the icing on the cake; my good friend, Callum Harper, goes and drops out of the sky in the ugliest hunk of metal I've ever seen."

Cal grinned. "You saw our ship come in?"

"Couldn't miss it. That was a beautiful landing by the way."

"Cheeky bastard. I got us on the ground, didn't I?"

"I suppose so. Sorry it took me a while to get to you. I had to scale down the western cliffs. Thought I'd arrived too late 'till that tall blonde saved your skins. I almost put a bliss dart in her by accident."

"I doubt it would've caused her much of a problem. She's a synthetic."

"Ah, I'd guessed some sort of superhero, but I suppose a synthetic makes more sense. I never knew they were so attractive. No wonder you joined up."

Cal laughed; he always enjoyed the way Jumper played down his intelligence. In truth, his old friend was far smarter, and certainly wiser, than most. In fact, it never ceased to amaze Cal how clued up he was considering his solitary lifestyle.

"The Big Game Zone's pretty huge. A lucky coincidence, you being in the area when we came down?" Cal asked.

"Maybe not. I've been making my way to headquarters since the atmos-tweekers screwed up. And I'm guessing your less than perfect landing was due to a crapped out beacon. I think we've both ended up in the same part of shit creek because our paddles malfunctioned."

"Well at least we're in shit creek together." *You can bloody help me keep these kids on a leash.* "So I guess you're wondering what I'm doing back in this star cluster?"

"A fresh start?" Jumper suggested with a knowing look.

"Possibly. Hopefully. I've been given the military boot. They were sending me back to Earth. That ugly hunk of metal we came in on was supposed to be taking us on a direct route. It's what military types like to call a reject raft."

"Reject raft, huh? Well, I've not known your companions long, but they all seem a decent, capable lot. I'm sure a more suitable crew could be found for a reject raft."

"They were tired when you met them," Cal replied with a crooked grin. "To be honest though, Jumper, I'm glad I got the boot."

"So am I...purely for selfish reasons of course. What are yours?"

No more taking orders, no more giving orders, and no more responsibility. "Let's just say it's not for me anymore. Felt a bit like a pawn of greed, property of the Federation."

"Yeah, I know the feeling."

"Maybe I should have stayed here with you, become a lifelong jungle man."

Jumper had a good long look at him before shaking his head. "There's too much fire in your blood, Cal. You just weren't meant to stay in one place too long. Trust me, you wouldn't want that fire to go out."

Again, Cal sensed a hint of melancholy in his friend's expression even though his voice gave nothing away.

"So why didn't your reject raft make it to Earth?"

"Honestly, Jumper, I have no clue. I've been trying my best not to think of it because nothing I come up with makes any bloody sense. But I'm no expert; there might be something I'm missing."

"Some kind of computer error back on Earth?"

Cal shook his head. "A computer error that stretches to the problems you've been experiencing here... I don't know, Jumper, it doesn't seem possible."

Jumper nodded in agreement.

"Whatever's going on, it's tied a bastard knot of anxiety in my gut. I can't shake the feeling that something bad has happened. I mean proper shit creek bad."

Jumper spent some time staring at the horizon. Then he climbed to his feet. "Okay, best we focus on what's in front of us then. Concentrate on getting our backsides to the Big Game Headquarters." He offered Cal a hand up.

"Agreed," Cal said, letting his old friend pull him to his feet. "Let's just hope they don't get bitten on the way."

Chapter Eight
TEETH

Cal perched on the top of a tall boulder which, due to an ever-growing layer of cloud cover, was not quite hot enough to scorch his flesh. The group of boulders were nestled amongst the last of the jungle vegetation before the terrain became a vast expanse of desert known as the Big Game flat lands. As he peered through Jumper's digi-scope binoculars, a deep crease developed across his forehead. On any normal day, the flat lands were fairly empty with only occasional herds of relatively harmless beasts roaming. Today, however, the binoculars revealed something quite different, a riot of some of God's most vicious creatures plus a few with a hint of man's influence.

Cal had found it strange, and rather unsettling, that their trek through the jungle had been devoid of the usual variety of large predators. Even Jumper had been at a loss to explain it. All they'd encountered were groups of herbivores lacking their usual fight or flight jitters. It was as if they didn't have a care in the world. Now, after peering deep into the flat lands, Cal realized that they didn't. Every predator he'd ever encountered on Mars, and a whole bunch of new ones, were gathered far out in the center of the vast plain. Every pixel of the digi-scope binoculars seemed overwhelmed with squirming, leathery hides, glimmering scales, and bristling fur all combined with a multitude of gnashing teeth, horns, and bloody claws.

"Problem?" Jumper asked as he heaved himself up onto the boulder and perched himself next to Cal.

"You might say that."

Raising an eyebrow, Jumper brought up his bliss rifle and scanned the plains through his sights. "The storm brewing?"

"No. Look lower, the middle of the plains."

"Fuck me," Jumper said after a moment.

"Uh huh," Cal agreed, his eyes still glued to the binoculars. "And I think I've found the reason for it."

Jumper adjusted the angle of his rifle to follow his line of sight.

"See those mountains of dead flesh?"

It only took a couple of seconds for Jumper to find what Cal was referring to. "*Christ.*"

"Yep, I think we're encountering the largest dinner banquet in the history of this universe."

"*Any* universe."

"Where the hell did those carcasses come from?" Cal asked. "I've never seen anything like them. They must be the size of ten blue whales."

"Hunkar lizards," Jumper replied. "The Federation brought them over from one of the planets in the Arean system a couple of years ago. Big success, tasty, feed a lot of people."

"I can't imagine even a team of T-rexes tackling something that big. What do you think brought them down?"

"My guess? The heat killed them," Jumper said. "Being stuck out on those open plains during the day with the atmosphere going haywire, you'd be like a bug under some evil kid's magnifying glass."

"I see your point."

"The smell of the rotting carcasses has probably been drifting across the plains and into the jungle for days now. I reckon just about every predator and his brother has caught a whiff."

Cal lowered the binoculars. "Not many turn down a free meal I suppose," he said, turning to look over his shoulder. "I guess they take cover back here in the jungle during the heat of the day…wait in the shade of the trees until the coolness of night allows them to head back out for another feast."

"Right, and now with that storm taking shape, the cloud cover's made the daytime heat bearable for an early dinner," Jumper added. "Lucky thing too, else we'd be rubbing shoulders with them right now."

Cal grimaced at the thought and took another look through the binoculars. He raised the sights to the horizon, where thick clouds were eagerly taking shape, then focused back on the monstrous feast. "They're right between us and the headquarters."

Jumper slowly scanned his rifle from side to side. "Yep, an' they're spread too wide to skirt around before that storm hits even in the buggies. Looks like it's gonna be a big bastard of a storm too, probably worsened by the messed up heat."

Cal continued to peer at the distant creatures, unable to deny the hint of excitement stirring in him. If only it were just him and Jumper, he might just be revelling in it. "Are the buggies close?"

Before Jumper could answer, a scuffling sound from below caught their attentions. Toker's head emerged over the lip of the boulder, revealing his usual white-toothed grin. "Room for one more up there, chaps?"

Cal reached down and pulled him up.

"Had to get some distance from Eddy. She's driving me nuts. I can't say a word without getting a smack."

Cal gave him a half-hearted grin.

"So, we must be pretty near the headquarters now, right?"

"Not far," Jumper replied. "It's in the centre of this desert."

Toker glanced over the huge expanse of flat ground, blissfully unaware of the distant activity that his naked eyes couldn't register. "Hey, looks like there's a storm building up. Excellent, I like a good storm."

"There's one every week," Jumper informed him. "They program them into the atmosphere. Usually works like clockwork."

"Huh, clever buggers, aren't they?"

Jumper shrugged.

"*Usually* works like clockwork?" Cal asked.

"It's not due for another two days. One more bit of screwed up tech."

Toker continued to stare out at the ever-darkening plains. "A storm like that would bring some killer waves back home. Can't wait to get back for a decent surf." He turned to them and grinned again. "Not that I haven't had a blast here. Always up for a bit of adventure, trekking in the jungle and all that. You know, Mars isn't half as bad as I thought. Apart from those gorilla things the other night, this Big Game Zone doesn't seem anything like the man-eating mecca people say it is. I used to have nightmares about this place, you know. The thought of getting eaten and all that…scares the hell outa' me."

Cal glanced at Jumper, but his old friend shook his head to opt out of the news breaking role.

"Had a bit of a nasty experience as a kid," Toker continued. "Was out surfing back on Earth and almost got myself chomped by a great white. The shark repeller on my board was bust up. Luckily, the toothy bugger found my board tastier than me. I didn't get a scratch. Had a whopping great mental scar though. Couldn't go back in the water for a couple of years after that." He looked at them both in turn, his grin slowly faltering. "Zoos were out too. Any place with pointy teeth, you know. Hell, even my girlfriend's pet bloody cat used to freak me out a little."

Shooting Toker a sympathetic smile, Cal handed the young man the binoculars. "I'm afraid we've run into a spot of trouble, Toker. It's probably best you know what we're up against." He nodded in the direction of the plains.

Toker looked at him questioningly, his fading grin vanishing completely as he registered the expression on Cal's face. Taking the digi-scope binoculars, he directed them out towards the plains.

With the power of foresight, Cal grasped the young man's arm before he wobbled off the boulder.

By the time Toker had been aided back to ground level, Cal and Jumper had worked out a plan or had at least selected the best option from a very small bunch of very bad options.

"Our biggest problem," Cal explained to the others, "is the heat from the malfunctioning atmosphere. So far, the jungle canopy's prevented us from being burned to a crisp. But that heat's only going to get worse, and soon, no amount of foliage is going to protect us. Our only chance is to get to the Big Game Headquarters, and to do that, we're going to have to cross those plains."

Toker looked petrified. He opened his mouth as if to say something but failed to create any sound. Eddy, in contrast, had eyes almost as wide as her grin as she grabbed the binoculars from Cal and, for the hundredth time, peered out at the distant feast.

"I don't get it, Cal," Viktor said. The boy was looking anxious as Melinda stood behind him, stroking his hair. "Wouldn't it be best to wait for all those creatures to finish eating? Then they'll leave the plains, right? We could go across tomorrow night, when we won't get eaten or burned."

"It's a good plan, Viktor, but there're a couple of problems: First, it looks like there's still enough meat on those Hunkar lizards to last a good few nights. Second, that storm is going to hit within the next half hour, and when it does, even the most ferocious beast is going to get freaked and run from it. And unfortunately, it's going to push them in this direction."

"So we could hide in the trees, right? Wait for them to run past," Viktor said hopefully.

"That's good thinking, kid," Jumper said. "But there's a problem with that too. My experience tells me that once they reach the cover of the trees, they'll feel safe and stop running. That would leave us camped out among them. Even the best hiding place wouldn't last long."

"So we just go for it then, yeah?" Eddy piped up. "Hit 'um head on, push on through."

Still open mouthed, Toker turned to look at her as if she were the conductor of his nightmares. He was still unable to make any sound leave his lips.

"Believe it or not, yes, that's sort of the plan," Cal replied, still not quite believing that was the best he could come up with.

"You're joking, right, Cal?" Viktor blurted out. "They're too quick; we won't be able to just run through them."

"We won't be going on foot," Jumper said, reaching into his pack and pulling out a small device. "If you all back up a few paces, I'll show you why."

Once they'd done as he'd asked, Jumper directed the device at the area of ground on which they'd been standing and pressed a button. There was a loud, pneumatic hiss followed by a deafening whirring noise, which caused Toker to practically jump out of his skin. Suddenly, a large, square section of the dusty floor began to shift directly in front of them. The square shuddered slightly and then began to flip on a central axis. Loose rocks and gritty sand slid off the tilting section to drop down into a dark, hollow space that was slowly being revealed beneath. As the square platform continued to turn, it soon became apparent that something was attached to its underside. Within seconds, the platform had completed its rotation and had once again sealed the desert floor. Sitting on the platform were a pair of rugged, powerful looking dune buggies. Thick smart-straps, which had secured the vehicles during their inverted positioning, popped free and retracted back into the platform.

"Holy shit, you chaps have been holding out on me," Toker said, his legs suddenly finding strength and springing him up and over to the vehicles. Cal was pleased to see that his young friend's look of eternal horror had failed in its eternity.

Each buggy was identical with huge, knobbly tires and a thick set of roll bars. Toker ran his hand over the nearest vehicle, staring at it as if it were a holy relic. "Man, these are beautiful."

"Are you kidding?" Viktor asked, looking and sounding disgusted. "They're ancient…with frickin' *wheels*. They should be in a museum."

Toker ignored him and was studying the huge exhausts jutting out from behind each door. Eddy scampered over for a closer inspection too though her interest was focused on the large guns mounted on the rear of each vehicle.

"Bliss blasters," Jumper informed her. "They can fire twenty bliss darts a second."

"Dunno what a bliss dart is, but I reckon these things could bring down anythin'."

"You reckon right," Jumper replied. "We use them to bring down the huge Hunkar lizards that roam the plains. They're the biggest land creatures ever discovered. Takes a fair amount of bliss formula to bring them down, I can tell you. We use the buggies and the blasters because the Hunkars are too big and fast to get on foot with just a rifle."

"Why not use hover vehicles or ships?" Viktor asked.

"The Federation don't like shelling out for ships or all terrain hover vehicles," Jumper informed the flabbergasted boy. "And the flat lands aren't exactly suited for hover tracks."

"Can I be on one of the blasters, Cal?' Eddy pleaded, causing Cal to swallow a curse.

"Actually, Eddy, I really need you for a more difficult task," he replied with as much conviction as he could muster. He wasn't convinced that Eddy could man the blaster and remain calm enough not to shoot the other vehicle or indeed herself. Fortunately, the girl seemed convinced.

"Course, Cal, name it."

"I need someone next to me proficient in close quarters combat. If anything gets past the bliss darts, they'll need dealing with."

The girl sniffed loudly, looking a little disappointed. "Sure, Cal. No worries."

Cal looked at Jumper. His old friend was grinning and watching the young girl with fascination as she pulled her little scalpel out from her boot. Seeming to decide that it couldn't hurt to boost her natural confidence little further, Jumper pulled out his gleaming survival knife, expertly flipped it in his hand, and offered it to her. "A gift," he said, shooting Cal a swift look of apology as the girl grabbed the knife. "Just promise me to go slow, take your time."

The girl nodded silently, but Cal suspected her expression was more than enough thanks for Jumper.

Whilst Jumper and Melinda checked that the bliss blasters were fully loaded, Cal took a moment to stretch. His lower back was still playing up, but the throbbing had now turned to a deep, constant burn that he was able to mostly ignore. He hoped the stretching would prevent him from seizing up during the mad dash.

He noticed Toker leaning against the bonnet of one of the buggies and staring out across the plains. The burst of excitement resulting from the reveal of the buggies had once again abandoned the young man's face to be replaced by a look of distressed exhaustion. Finishing up his routine, Cal walked over and joined him in staring out over the plains. The distant storm was building fast, bringing the darkness of night early.

"Sorry we have to do this, Toker," he said after a moment of silence.

Toker looked down at his boots with a furrowed brow and started scuffing the hard, dusty floor. "No worries, Cal... Got no choice, right?"

"Afraid not."

"It's a funny thing, fear...don't you think?" the young man said quietly, still staring at his feet. "How is it that I don't think twice about jumping from a huge spaceship that's about to burst from Earth's atmosphere, but throw a few pointy teeth into the equation, and my guts turn to jelly?"

"We all have different fears, I guess."

Toker turned to him with an unconvincing hint of a smile. "I hope this isn't where you give me the spiel about facing my fears and it'll make 'um go away?"

"No, that only works occasionally—when you face them enough times and get a real close look."

"Trust me, bro, if I get through this, I don't plan on facing this particular fear ever again, so I guess I'll never get over it."

Cal rubbed at his chin. "Well, never say never... Luckily for you,

I might just have a short cut for getting rid of this particular fear."

Toker looked up again, this time with a glimmer of hope in his eyes. "Yeah, what's the deal? Clue me up."

Cal pointed up to the mounted bliss blaster on the back of the buggy. "You shoot the shit out of them." He left Toker with a hard slap on the shoulder.

Chapter Nine
THE FLATLAND RUN

The two dune buggies tore across the desert floor, clouds of dust billowing in their wake. The combined roar of the G-shock engines was so great that it even drowned out the rumbling thunder of the fast-approaching storm. Night had fallen now, but lightning periodically illuminated the landscape with the power of a thousand flares. Cal manned the driving seat of one of the buggies with Eddy sitting restlessly by his side, the blade Jumper had given her glinting as she peered into the distance.

Cal could feel his heart thudding against his ribs. Driving through the desert plains in broad daylight was challenging enough, let alone on a dark, stormy night. The buggy's smart-glass windscreen was constructed from a pretty old version of the tech, but it still offered a half decent view of the desert before him. The problem with the flat lands was that they were far from flat. A multitude of rocks and potholes were constantly presenting themselves, some large enough to dislodge a wheel or tear through the buggy's chassis. It was seriously dangerous driving. So much so that Cal had to keep reminding himself that he shouldn't be grinning.

The storm was getting close now. Cal risked a quick glance to the rear of the vehicle where Toker was wedged into the mounted bliss blaster's swivel seat. The young man's fingers were poised over each trigger, and a holographic targeting sight glowed red before his eyes. To Cal's relief, the eyes were full of determination, not just fear. *We might just get through this,* he thought confidently. Then he turned back just in time to swerve sharply around a large boulder, almost flipping the vehicle over as he did so. *Shit.* "Sorry," he called out, feeling a little of his cockiness seep out of him.

Cal very much doubted that Melinda, who was driving the other buggy a short distance to his left, was under quite the same pressure. Her reactions and eyesight were far better than that of any human. If it weren't for the huge torrent of dust and stones being left in her wake, Cal would have been happy to follow her driving path. Viktor was at the synthetic's side, which was undoubtedly the safest place for the boy not least because Jumper was manning the bliss blaster at the vehicle's rear. Cal had total faith in his old friend's marksmanship and knew from personal experience that he would risk his own life to protect the boy.

The wind was howling now. The rain, however, was yet to hit them, so the visibility was still good. A blip on the buggy's scanner bumped Cal's heart rate up a notch. He flicked on the comm unit. "Here they come," he said, making sure his voice was loud enough to be heard over the roar of engines. It wasn't long before the lone blip was accompanied by a multitude of others, and soon, a staggered line of red dots was moving fast down the scanner.

The first of the fleeing beasts became visible—a seemingly endless row of very large, ghostly white shapes lumbering towards them out of the darkness. Cal knew immediately that these particular creatures had not been in residence during his time on Mars as a boy. He knew this because such incredibly unique beasts could hardly have been missed or forgotten. Everything about them was long: six long legs, a long body and tail, all covered in long, flowing white fur. Even their heads seemed ridiculously elongated. Instinctively, Cal felt that these beasts posed no great threat other than an accidental collision. They were very large, but it was a lanky sort of large, completely lacking any of that imposing, muscular bulk. They were obviously the fastest of the bunch, but with a storm of this magnitude, the rest wouldn't be far behind.

Gripping the steering controls hard, Cal searched for the safest route between the beasts. Picking a gap, he pumped the accelerator and, unable to resist a quick glimpse up, saw rows of sharp, cone-shaped teeth lining massive, slack maws. The pale fur about the beasts' heads and shoulders were streaked crimson, the remnants of the great feast.

As Cal had suspected, fear of the storm overruled any aggressive tendencies, and the creatures paid them little attention. "Hold your fire with these ones, Toker." He hoped the lack of reply was due to concentration rather than an untimely loss of consciousness. Risking a glance to his left, he saw Eddy hanging out of the side of the buggy, possibly attempting to get a better look at the fleeing beasts or possibly trying to attack them. Leaning over, he grabbed her by the belt of her combat trousers and pulled her back in. "I recommend staying in the vehicle, Eddy," he shouted, trying to keep his cool as he swerved the vehicle away from a long, whipping tail. "Don't worry about these ones. They're too scared of the storm to cause us any trouble."

"Right you are, Cal."

Finally, the last of the lanky, white-haired aliens thundered past, and Cal relaxed his grip on the vehicle controls. For a few blessed moments, the dark plains appeared to still.

Then they came.

Beasts of all shapes and sizes erupted out of the darkness. It was as if the storm itself had collided with the desert floor and manifested into an army of kinetic flesh and bone. Some of the beasts appeared to be all teeth, flashing them viciously with each lightning strike. Others sported long, ivory horns protruding from thick-boned foreheads. Still more were armed with multitudes of spikes, huge shards of bone jutting erratically from the ends of wildly lashing tales. Many of the beasts were as different as night and day, but all had a frighteningly lethal quality. Aided by his night vision glasses, Cal could see that the fleeing hordes were spread far and wide. With no other option available, he and Melinda charged the two vehicles directly into the fray.

Seconds later, a large Utahraptor, one of the biggest Cal had ever seen, mastered its fear of the storm and set its cold eyes on the buggies.

"Toker, we've got an incoming—" Cal's warning was drowned out by his young companion's battle cry and the sound of the bliss blaster hammering out twenty darts per second. The raptor thundered into the ground before it even got close. Unfortunately, the sight of the toppled beast did little to deter others whose fleeing lines also began to gravitate towards the buggies. Cal risked a quick turn of the head to see Jumper sat atop his mounted blaster, entirely more composed than Toker as he shot his weapon. Both men were doing an impressive job at dropping any beasts that came too close, but for every one that hit the ground, another leapt instantly into its place.

Rain began to lash down mercilessly, drenching clothes and stinging exposed skin. Cal continued forward as fast as he dared, Melinda keeping pace all the way. With the core of the storm directly overhead, the beasts had begun running in all directions in a mass instinctual panic. To Cal, the next ten minutes felt more like ten hours. The world had become a nightmarish blur of teeth and claws, all glimpsed through sheets of sweeping rain, bright white under the relentless lightning. He swerved the buggy with sometimes little more to go on than a nearby roar to his left or a blast of foul carnivorous breath to his right. Glancing at Eddy, he couldn't quite believe they both still possessed all their limbs. The continuous pumping of the bliss blaster suggested that Toker was also still in one piece. Even more unbelievable was the fact that the two buggies had remained in relatively close proximity. Somehow, he and Melinda had managed to blindly snake the vehicles through the deadly barrage without a single collision. Even Melinda, with her synthetic skills, must have been relying heavily on luck.

Finally, the number of oncoming beasts thinned, and the plains became more desert-like. Rocks and grit gave way to smooth sand. The rain had also eased. Realizing this, Cal risked a little extra pressure on the accelerator. At the rate Toker was expelling bliss darts, he feared they'd be left defenseless on the home stretch.

Even with their increased speed, it seemed an age before the buggies arrived at the huge, dark forms of the dead Hunkar lizards, the blameless cause of all the chaos. Only a small handful of carnivorous feasters had found it within themselves to brave the storm and continue feeding. The rain had stopped completely now, and the wind had diminished to a gentle breeze. Cal and Melinda slowed the vehicles in order to navigate the massive torn lumps of flesh and shards of chewed bones that protruded like splintered remains of bleached trees.

Apart from the low growl of the buggy engines and the distant rumbling of thunder, the night had become eerily quiet. Even Eddy and Toker remained silent due in no small part to the covering of their mouths to shield from the sickening stench. Indeed, the only sound of note was the occasional crunch of bone as the few remaining carnivores continued their feast.

There were sighs of relief all around as the two buggies finally exited the labyrinth of foul-smelling gore. Cal peered ahead across the dark plains. The visibility was now good enough to make out the tall, distant form of the Big Game Headquarters. There was a glow emanating from the central tower that he took as an encouraging sign.

As he fixed his eyes on their target, he found himself grinning again. They'd just swept through the jaws of death with little more than a scratch on any of them. Such a miracle deserved a grin.

Chapter Ten
PALE MENACE

Cal stared at the dead comm unit feeling that knot of anxiety once again tighten in his gut. What the fuck was up with all this tech? Taking a step back, he craned his neck and looked to the top edge of the huge barriers, which stretched vertically before them like a flawlessly smooth cliff. In the darkness of the night, he could just about make out the glow emanating from the headquarters nestled within. It seemed there was power, and at the very least, some lights were working within the compound. He looked back down at the firmly closed gates. They wouldn't be prying those open any time soon. They were built to defend against animals of immense power and size. Even the small, man-size entrance at which they stood was crafted from ten inches of the most frustratingly durable metal.

Shit.

"Not much of a welcome party," Toker pointed out.

Cal agreed with a shake of the head and shared a concerned look with Jumper. Malfunctioning tech was bad enough, but this ominous lack of humans turned the situation from a worrying puzzle to a potential panic. What the hell could explain it? If it had been a pirate attack, then the place would be swarming with troops by now. Maybe there was an outbreak? Some sort of disease? But where were the assessment and med teams?

Approaching the door, Eddy flipped the big survival knife in her hand and slammed the handle against the hard metal. "Open up, ya buggers."

The alarming volume of the girl's voice rang out into the silent night.

"Jesus, Eddy," Toker exclaimed, "you wanna shout any louder? Maybe call a few beasties to come join us?"

They all turned around at that statement and peered past the low-level lights of the buggies into the surrounding blackness. Now that the storm had passed, the night had become eerily quiet, and the darkness seemed to be pressing in on them. Jumper raised his rifle and peered through the sights. "We're good at the moment," he said as he scanned back and forth.

"I can get us in."

Cal turned to see that Viktor was crouched down with his hands buried in his faulty hovercase. Inside, Cal could see a mass of tools and complex gizmos, some state-of-the-art and expensive, others clunky and undoubtedly homemade.

"Off with the control panel if you please, M," the boy said, holding up a slim-line punch tool. Melinda didn't hesitate and got to work on the metal panel whilst Viktor plunged his rummaging hands back into the case. Cal was impressed to see how well the boy was holding up. Most his age, or any age for that matter, would have been bawling at the first sight of giant, gnashing teeth.

Not bothering to loosen the bottom section of the panel, Melinda grasped the metal and forced it open, bending it down to reveal the workings of the security system.

"Thanks, M." Viktor stood, a small gizmo in his hands. He had a confident smile on his face and seemed to be revelling in his chance to contribute some skills. Fixing the gizmo to the exposed panel, he began manipulating the controls. "Should have this open in just—"

Suddenly, the boy lurched forward, his head hitting the metal door so hard that blood was left running down the metal as his limp body crumpled to the ground. There was a pale blur. Cal stumbled back, struggling to register what was happening. Melinda was moving fast. She had seized a white, lizard-like creature by its thick neck and was forcing it to the floor. Planting a knee in its back, she grasped its jaw and yanked its head back hard. There was a loud crack of vertebra. Then there was a cry from Toker and two shots from Jumper's rifle. Another pale blur, and Viktor's limp body was dragged away through the sand at frightening speed to disappear into the darkness. All this in a few seconds. Another few seconds, and Melinda had bolted into the darkness after the assaulted boy.

"*What the fuck…*" Toker gasped, sounding as shocked as Cal felt.

Eddy had her knife in hand, and Jumper once again had his rifle up and was peering through his sights.

"Jumper?"

"Can't see him, Cal…or Melinda." Jumper replied as he slowly moved in the direction they had disappeared.

Cal watched with gritted teeth as his old friend walked into the darkness. He could hear sounds in the distance. A lot of scuffling, even a strange, eerie whistling, but the sounds seemed to echo and were hard to pinpoint.

"Eddy, Toker, see if you can get this fucking door open," he said as he made for the nearest buggy.

"Bugger that," Eddy said as she ran past him towards the far vehicle.

"Eddy, hold—" *Damn it.* Cal let her go. She couldn't cause much more trouble than they were already in. Climbing up into the nearest buggy, he quickly planted himself in the mounted bliss blaster and flicked on the night targeting screen. Setting the zoom to its maximum setting, he swivelled left and right searching for any sign of his friends.

Something moved, a pale shape, maybe five feet long, just like the one Melinda had dealt with. It was incredibly fast. Then there was another and another. Eddy fired a couple of short blasts from the other bliss blaster. Cal was impressed and surprised by her controlled shooting.

He carried on scanning, staring at the targeting screen and refraining from firing any of his own shots in favor of his search.

Then she appeared.

Melinda was running flat out, Viktor's limp form in her arms. Cal would have thought it impossible in a machine—even in one as sophisticated as Melinda—but he could see real anger on her face, anger to the point of fury. He was beginning to suspect that Viktor's modifications ran far deeper than he'd first imagined. Cal locked the targeting onto her and tracked her progress. One of the pale creatures darted at her with near impossible speed and snapped its jaws around her thigh. Melinda ignored the attacker, but it slowed her down considerably. Careful not to hit Viktor, Cal fired a couple of darts. One found its mark, and the creature instantly tumbled into the darkness. Cal barely had time to take a breath, however, before two more attackers bolted at her and attached themselves to the synthetic woman's legs. Cal fired again and again. One fell just as another clamped on.

Cal dealt with the newest attacker before leaping up. Melinda was close now. "Eddy, we're leaving," he shouted as he slid down the rear of the buggy

Too consumed in her torrent of bliss blaster fire, the girl didn't respond. He ran over to her. "Eddy, move it… Eddy." Just as he was about to climb onto the buggy and drag her off, the girl ceased her fire and looked down at him. Her eyes were wild, almost feral.

"We're—"

Cal didn't get a chance to finish before the girl leapt at him, the big blade suddenly in her fist, which was pulled back, ready for a killing blow.

With barely time to swear, Cal ducked away, narrowly missing the blade as it arced downwards. There was a sickening thud. Turning, he saw Eddy on her knees. She was struggling to twist the big knife, which was embedded deep within the skull of one of the pale creatures. Failing in her attempts, she simply yanked it out and looked up at him.

"Thanks, Eddy. I owe you one," he said, pulling her to her feet. Some of the wildness dissipated from her grubby face and was replaced by a grin.

The two of them ran back to Toker, who was hunched at the still unopened door. "*Help me,*" His voice was panicked as he fumbled desperately with Viktor's device. "This tech is confusing to hell."

Cal stared at it hopelessly and had to agree.

The sound of Jumper's rifle stole his attention. His old friend stood twenty paces away, his longeye rifle planted firmly against his shoulder as he fired it into the night. Seconds later, Melinda burst out of the darkness. Thankfully, Jumper seemed to have dealt with all but one of her assailants, and she was once again moving fast. Not only that but Viktor looked to be stirring in her arms.

Cal moved to meet the synthetic woman and relieved her of the boy so she could deal with the last creature trying so relentlessly to drag her down. She ended its attempts with fast and lethal efficiency.

Cal ran back to the door and set Viktor down. He was relieved to see that the boy was at least partially conscious. "Viktor, we need you to get this door open quickly." The words felt harsh seeing as the dazed boy had blood pouring from a gash on his forehead, but they needed to be said. To his credit, Viktor reacted relatively quickly considering his condition. As Cal helped support him, he began to manipulate the controls on his gizmo with noticeably clumsier fingers than his earlier efforts. At least he seemed to know what the hell he was doing. Cal looked back to see that the others had formed a tight, protective arc around them. Eddy had her knife in hand. Jumper was firing off round after round while Melinda was practically twisting the head off one of the white beasts. Even Toker was standing with his fists raised defiantly. Cal didn't have time to assess the numbers of the pale attackers, but the increase of the strange whistling sounds didn't bode well.

Suddenly, Cal felt Viktor sag in his arms.

Fearing the worst, he looked back to the door, but there was no door, just a blessed gap within the barrier. The boy had managed to hold onto consciousness just long enough. *Brave lad.*

"We're in." Cal had barely finished shouting the words before Viktor was snatched from his arms, and Melinda was bearing him through the gap.

"Toker, get—"

"Shit, Cal. Shit, it's got me." Toker fell to the ground, one of the creatures gnawing at his arm. Cal dropped to his knees and began slamming his fist into its head. The beast was resilient, and only after a few blows to its eyes did it let go. Cal kicked the attacker away, and both men scrambled back towards the entrance. Eddy was also heading for the door, stumbling backwards whilst slashing her knife wildly at four new aggressors.

Cal sucked in a sharp breath as he took in the sight of countless pale shapes swarming around the buggies. "You first, Toker," he shouted. The young man didn't argue and scrambled though the entrance with desperate enthusiasm. Cal was no sooner on his feet when Eddy piled into him, white jaws clamped to her knife-wielding arm. Together, they tumbled back, hitting the ground halfway through the gap. Eddy was letting out a sort of animalistic snarl as she tried to shake off her biting foe. Having no success, she returned the favor by sinking her teeth into its neck. Cal tried to aid her by jabbing at its eye, but there was no need. Jumper was leaping over them, planting a dart in the creature's back as he did so.

Eddy shoved the lifeless beast aside. Before Cal could push her to her feet, however, a hand grasped his shirt and dragged them both backwards. It was so effortless that there was no doubt Melinda was the one responsible. The view through the door was a mass of white movement. One of the creatures pilled though the gap only to be met with Eddy's boot. Ironically she probably saved its life as the kick sent the beast toppling back just out of range of the door, which slid shut with lethal force.

All of them spent a few wordless moments breathing hard. Cal looked up to check on Viktor's condition; the boy was conscious again, but Melinda was bearing most of his weight. "Well done, Viktor. You okay?"

"Think so, Cal. Not really sure what happened."

Reaching into his pack, Jumper pulled out a med pack and began seeing to the gash on Viktor's head.

Still breathing hard, Cal climbed to his feet and turned on the spot to take in the surroundings. There was little to see, just a few dim lights illuminating the empty space between numerous lifeless buildings. A damn ghost town. "Everyone else okay? Eddy, Toker, you hurt?"

"Ain't nothing," Eddy answered quickly.

Toker moved his arm about. "Bit bruised. The buggers were more gums than teeth."

Call looked down at the dead creature and gave its white, scaly body a nudge with his boot. "Damn lucky for us. More new additions, Jumper?"

Without turning his attentions from Viktor's head, Jumper nodded. "Fairly. They only come out at night. I'm usually safe up a tree."

Cal shook his head, still not quite believing they'd all made it to the headquarters more or less intact. He looked over at Melinda. The synthetic had one or two gashes covering her legs. They were already filled with a blue, gel-like substance that Cal recognized as a smart healing glue common to all synthetics of value. It would replace or repair artificial flesh in a matter of hours, leaving no visible scar. Melinda was once again wearing her usual serene smile that Cal found far less human than the anger he'd witnessed on the other side of the barricade.

"I reckon we should shift ourselves up to the main control center," Jumper suggested, having finished patching up Viktor's head. "Find out what been causing all this chaos."

No one disagreed.

The Big Game Headquarters were every bit as ominous as the barricades that surrounded them. It was comprised of a number of dark, dome-shaped buildings and one huge cylindrical tower that reached at least as high as the Alvorian oak that they'd slept in a couple of nights previously. Cal and the others followed Jumper through the tower's entrance then down a long, featureless corridor that eventually led to a brightly lit, silver-walled elevator.

"This place is bigger than I was expecting," Toker said as he stepped into the lift. "Do a lot of people work here?"

"Actually, not so many," Jumper answered as he tapped a code into the elevator's control panel. "The first four hundred feet of this tower is a solid block, supposedly extra security in case the gates fail."

"Makes sense, I guess," Toker replied as the elevator began a smooth but rapid ascent.

"Maybe," Jumper said, a hint of a smile on his lips. "Personally, I think it's got more to do with the human obsession of all things large and phallic."

Eddy sniggered, "Yeah, whoever designed it was obviously a man."

"Yeah," Toker agreed, grinning. "A small man at that."

Viktor blurted out a laugh, but Cal could see that the meaning of the joke was lost on the boy.

Looking at them each in turn, Cal observed the wide, twitchy eyes that accompanied their nervous chuckling. He'd seen this many times before: a post-battle reaction. They shared the look of those who had gone into battle and literally slipped through the jaws of death. They were an odd bunch, but Cal had to admit, they worked well together, a group of misfits who, when thrown together, just seemed to fit. He was glad of that not least because he had a nasty feeling that their trials were just beginning.

Chapter Eleven
BIG BLUE

As far as high-tech rooms were concerned, the control center of the Big Game Headquarters was right up there with the best of them. It was a huge, cylindrical room filled with smooth consoles neatly concealing a host of scanning, communication, and monitoring systems. There were no walls as such, just a crystal-clear exterior viewing panel that reached from floor to ceiling and wrapped itself around the entire circumference of the large, circular space. Other than the obstruction of the elevator shaft situated in the very center of the room, a person could see three hundred and sixty degrees of far-reaching views, a vast sea of desert leading to jungles and distant mountains. One simple flick of a control wand, and those mountains would appear not so distant thanks to the multi-league zoom technology that was integrated into every inch of the impenetrable smart-glass. Multiple holo-maps could also be beamed from numerous ports located in the brightly lit ceiling to detail the locations of the hunters and scooper ships dotted around the vastness of the Big Game Zone.

That immaculate, technologically advanced room was exactly what Cal expected to see as he stepped though the elevator doors. What he actually saw was a chaotic array of destruction. Every single console had been shattered, mass tangles of circuitry spewing out of them to lay strewn across the glossy floor like the guts of some giant cyborg. None of the holo-maps were active, and Cal could see that each of the beaming ports in the ceiling had also been smashed.

"What the hell happened?" Eddy asked, rushing past Cal to examine one of the mangled consoles.

"Seems we're not the only ones who've been through a battle," he replied, moving forward and putting a protective hand on the girl's shoulder. "Careful what you touch, Eddy. Whoever dropped in for a visit could have left a few surprises."

"Right you are. Look at these though, eh," Eddy replied, doing her best keep her hands at her sides. "These ain't like no plasma hits I ever saw. I mean, there's no scorching. It don't look there was any heat at all."

Cal took a closer look, impressed with the girl's observation.

"So they just fell apart then, eh?" Toker said.

"Watch it, mush nut," Eddy warned, "Else I might just make your face fall apart."

"Eddy's right," Cal said. "Whatever weapon shattered these consoles wasn't your usual military fare… In fact, I don't know of any weapons that would cause damage like this. You, Jumper?"

Jumper gave a puzzled frown and shook his head.

"But if there's been weapons and a battle and whatnot, where's all the bodies or like…blood an' stuff?" Toker reasoned. "I mean, where the hell is everyone?"

Limping and still a little unsteady on his feet, Viktor joined Eddy in getting a closer look at the damaged consoles. "Who could do such a thing to all this beautiful tech?" he asked no one in particular. The boy wore a look that suggested he was indeed looking at blood and dead bodies.

"The headquarters is pretty big," Jumper said after a moment.

"Maybe we should do a search, see if anyone's still around?"

Cal nodded in agreement.

"I could maybe save us some time," Viktor said, seeming to snap out of his horrified state. "Melinda."

The synthetic strode over to him, carrying the broken hovercase as if it were filled with feathers, and placed it on a nearby work station. Viktor flicked it open. "Somewhere in here, I've got a scanner," he said, pulling out numerous devices and setting them neatly on the desk. "It'll scan this place and all the surrounding buildings in seconds."

"How accurate is it?" Cal asked.

"Here," the boy said, pulling out a small device with a screen crudely taped to its side. "It may not look like much, but it's *very* accurate, Cal. My own design."

Cal didn't doubt it for a second; his faith in the boy's tech abilities was growing exponentially. Nobody moved or uttered a word as they awaited the results of the little machine.

Viktor looked up, his bruised and battered face solemn as he shook his head. "There's no one here. This place is completely lifeless."

"I don't know about you guys, but this is starting to creep me out a little," Toker whispered after a moment.

"You're a bloody pansy," Eddy scoffed without even bothering to look his way. "So what now, Cal?"

Cal looked up to see them all staring at him, uncertainty in their eyes. Even Jumper looked more unsure than Cal had ever seen him. He sighed inwardly. It seemed the answers were going to be a harder find than he first thought. Not only that but his young companions and his old friend were putting their faith in him to find them. But where the hell to start? His mind felt full yet strangely empty. And he had to agree with Toker: The situation was starting to creep him out. Even if the crew of the headquarters had been attacked and the bodies taken, this whole place would be filled with Federation officials and engineers by now. They might not give a damn about a lost reject raft, but Mars was big business, a food supply that Earth couldn't do without. A reaction should have been instant.

Turning on his heel, he walked over to a collection of smashed up storage pods, and with a supporting hand on his aching back, he stooped down to pick up some of the drink canisters strewn on the floor. "Now we do something that my old combat instructor taught me," he said, throwing each of them a canister. All of them deftly snatched the canisters out of the air bar Viktor, who was happy for Melinda to do the catching for him.

"We're all a little wired to say the least," Cal continued. "It's time to take a quick time out. Time to sit, drink, and think."

None of them argued. Instead, they all sank to the floor, cracked open the canisters, and began to guzzle on the cool liquid they contained. As Cal knew it would, the break gave them all a chance to calm their buzzing minds, quiet their ringing ears, and rehydrate their aching bodies. Cal took a moment to look at each of them in turn. Eddy and Toker were slouched on the floor opposite him. The safety of the headquarters seemed to have already restored some of Toker's relaxed manner. In contrast, Eddy looked like a coiled spring, and Cal suspected that it was taking a great deal of effort for the girl to stay put. Not for the first time, he wondered what invisible force was supplying her with such seemingly inexhaustible energy. To his left, Viktor was leaning against Melinda. Understandably, the boy looked exhausted from the ordeals he'd just endured, but he was doing a good job at putting a brave face on it. Despite their oddness, Cal was finding himself warming to them all.

Finally he looked at Jumper. His old friend was frowning and staring at one of the shattered consoles. Cal didn't blame him; he felt like frowning at that particular puzzle himself. He was sure he'd seen every type of weapon blast known to man. This damage, however, was like nothing he'd ever witnessed. What the hell could have caused it? He rubbed his head. No answers, just more questions. Deciding to finally break the silence, he said, "Viktor, do you think you could get any of these consoles up and running?"

With Melinda's help, the boy climbed to his feet as if he'd simply been waiting for his cue. "Course, Cal… At least, I'll give it a go." Pulling a few of his gizmos from his case, the boy shuffled over to a nearby console. "This station here looks not too bad. All the holo-ports and screens look totally bust up, but I've got a little portable screen I can rig up."

"Good lad." Cal climbed to his feet and turned to the rest of them, who were following suit. "I'm going to take a trip down to the hangar and check out the transport situation. I'd like to know that we can get off this planet under our own steam if need be. Unless, of course, you all fancy becoming permanent Mars residents?"

"Hey man, don't even joke," Toker blurted.

"Thought as much," Cal said with a quick grin. "Want to join me, Jumper?"

Jumper slung his bliss rifle over his back. "Absolutely."

"Can I come too, Cal?" Eddy asked.

Cal nodded, and the girl wasted no time heading for the elevator. Toker took a moment to look about the room then shook his head and followed her with a sigh.

"We'll be back shortly, Viktor." The boy already had his head immersed inside the shattered console and simply waved a distracted hand in reply.

"So where are the ships?" Eddy asked as the lift began its speedy descent. "I didn't see none outside."

"They're in the hangar underneath the base," Jumper explained. "Sections of the desert open up to allow for launch."

"Yeah?"

The lift came to a stop, and the doors smoothly slid open. Cal led the way into a dimly lit room that had a large, glass panel on the far wall. Eddy immediately ran ahead of them and pressed her forehead against the panel.

Toker joined her and peered disappointed though the glass. "Well, that truly sucks."

Cal was inclined to agree. The large hangar contained two spacecraft, both of which would have been impressive if it weren't for the gaping holes riddling their hulls.

Eddy stepped back and shook her head. "Think we can fix 'um, Cal?"

"Maybe, if we had the equipment and materials, which we don't."

"So we're stuck here," Toker said somberly. "We're gonna have to bloody well wait for someone to come pick us up."

Cal didn't answer; if help were coming, it would have arrived days ago. Silently, he continued to run over their options in his head, a distinct gnawing feeling that he was missing something. Then it hit him. He turned to Jumper and saw on his old friend's face that the idea had dawned on him too.

"*Big Blue,*" they said aloud in unison.

"Big what now?" Toker asked.

With renewed vigor, Cal strode over to a large, steel trap door, which was barely visible in the corner of the room. With Jumper's help, he heaved it open to reveal a metal ladder that stretched vertically down a dark, narrow shaft.

Toker whistled. "That'll be one dark hole."

Two hundred rungs later, Cal planted his feet on flat concrete. Rubbing his throbbing back, he resolved that he'd take the freight lift back up. He looked about a featureless room that contained nothing more than a single bolted door. The sleek, shiny appearance of the headquarters above had gone, and instead, the walls were damp and stained. Approaching the door, he slid the bolts aside and swung it open. "We're in."

"In where?" Eddy asked, as she stepped off the last rung of the ladder and barged past Toker for a better look.

"The bone yard," Jumper answered as he hopped nimbly off the ladder.

Eddy screwed up her face and followed Cal through the door, Toker close behind. Cal grinned as the pair of them gasped. Row upon row of ridiculously powerful lights illuminated an enormous space. The small platform on which they stood was a few hundred feet from the floor and the same distance again from the huge beams that supported the vast ceiling.

"Man, would you look at the size of this place?" Toker breathed.

"I don't think I can even see the other side," Eddy added, squinting as she leaned recklessly over the platform railings.

The space was filled as far as the eye could see with piles of twisted scrap metal as well as numerous crafts that appeared little more than scrap themselves.

"Excellent." Toker clapped his hands and rubbed them briskly. "So one of these hunk o' junk ships is gonna get us the hell outa here, right?"

"With any luck," Cal replied.

"What about one of those?" Eddy suggested. "The one's with the big ass guns on the side."

"Those are Bullseye walkers, Eddy. Even if we managed to get inside one, we wouldn't get very far off the ground. *Big Blue* is the only ship here that has a chance of getting us out of orbit."

Toker and Eddy followed the line of Cal's pointing finger to a hunk of metal far in the distance, which, as its name suggested, was big and indeed blue. In fact, it was immense.

"That huge lump of scrap's gonna get us back to Earth?" Toker asked, sounding unconvinced. "You certain we'll all fit?"

"I guess if we're lacking room, you could always bunk in with the cattle," Cal retorted. "*Big Blue*'s actually a fine ship. One of the best cargo ships ever built."

Jumper nodded in agreement. "I always thought it was a crime leaving it down here to rot. I think perhaps it's time we pulled her out of retirement."

Cal turned and saw a familiar twinkle returning to his old friend's dark eyes. He suspected that Jumper was rather looking forward to getting off this planet.

Arriving back at the control center, they found Viktor with his head and arms immersed deep inside a console that was stripped of its casing.

"Viktor…everything okay?" Cal asked. "How you getting on?"

"Good timing. Think I've got it," the boy replied without so much as glance in their direction. "Just finished rigging up my screen." He pulled up a seat and positioned himself in front of a portable key pad. His fingers were a blur as they skimmed over the keys, his nose practically touching the little holographic screen as he worked.

"Got it, we're in."

"Good lad.'

"I'll see if I can get us a communication link with Earth's prime hub. Shouldn't be a problem, just got to…" The boy's voice faded, but his fingers didn't slow for a second. "Uh...that's odd."

"Bugger," Toker mumbled.

"Something wrong?" Cal asked.

Viktor didn't answer. His fingers just moved faster still. "That's not right... That *can't* be right," he said, sounding increasingly distressed. "A mistake...there must be a mistake."

"What, Viktor? What's a mistake?"

The boy's fingers finally stopped moving, and his nose slowly retracted from the screen. As he turned to face them, Cal saw that his eyes were spilling tears.

"Viktor?"

"It's gone... Earth, it's not there... The system says it's been destroyed."

Part Two:

Chapter Twelve
BOREDOM, BOAR BACON, AND BLISS

Cal woke with a start, and immediately, the left side of his face began to throb. Lifting his head, he attempted to rub the pain away and discovered a surprisingly detailed map of the flight console imprinted on his cheek. He took a brief moment to gaze out of the cockpit's huge window only to see the same view he'd witnessed for the past three months: the cold, blackness of space splattered with an array of frustratingly distant stars.

Despite weeks of trying, Cal and the rest of the gang had been unsuccessful in locating any other humans on Mars. Viktor had rigged up a makeshift communications console from which they'd sent a looped message to the Big Game Hunters as well as to the other food sectors. No replies came, and it had soon become apparent that Jumper had been extremely lucky being stationed in relatively close proximity to the headquarters. Without the pickup ships operational, the other hunters must have perished in the rising heat. Viktor had eventually managed to stabilize the planet's atmosphere but only after the planet had reached oven-like temperatures. Only the toughest of the planets' inhabitants would have survived such heat. Unfortunately, humans weren't among them.

Cal was comforted by Viktor's assurance that the G28 solar systems powering the atmos-tweekers would, in theory, last thousands of years. Even with the possibility of no human intervention, whatever life remained on Mars would still have the opportunity to thrive for many centuries to come. As for the future of the human race, Cal had no idea.

It had taken them three weeks to get the immense cargo ship, Big Blue, fit for zero G and then a further two weeks to prep the engines for the big push out of Mars' atmosphere. During that time, Viktor had attempted to extract further clues from the headquarter computers that might shed some light on the undeniably bleak situation. His attempts had proved futile. Whoever or whatever had destroyed Earth and attacked Mars remained shrouded in mystery. Long-range communications had also failed, the interplanetary airwaves remaining eerily silent. This was a mystery made worse by the fact that Mars' long-range satellites were all intact. Not even Viktor could offer any theories as to the cause. It was a situation frightening and frustrating in equal measures. Without long-range communications, Cal suspected that the tens of thousands of colonies within fringe space could fall into chaos very quickly.

There had been few words shared between the gang during those five weeks other than those necessary for the structural overhaul of *Big Blue*. The shock of Earth's destruction had understandably hit them all hard. Cal had no living relatives that he knew of and, with all of his close friends being stationed on roaming starships or residing on distant colonies, he had spent very little time on the home planet. Still, he mourned the billions of strangers who had lost their lives in the ominous disaster. An aching emptiness had formed deep in his gut as if a vital organ had been removed, leaving a gaping hole in its wake. None of the others had spoken to him about loved ones lost. Like him, it seemed they preferred to mourn in silence.

Occasionally, he would hear crying behind closed doors, which was something he felt like doing himself from time to time, but the tears would never come. Perhaps his experiences as a child followed by those in the military had hardened him to such losses. Or maybe he just couldn't bear to give in to the grief.

But time had proved an ever reliable healer, and as the weeks passed, the crying eased, and eventually, laughter began—though slow and quiet at first, as if it were inappropriate and should never be appropriate again after such sadness. But then time dispersed the guilt too, and the laughter came easier. That had helped Cal more than anything, the sight of his friends, old and new, allowing the joy back in. He felt the hole in his gut begin to fill and, by the time they'd successfully launched *Big Blue*, a renewed sense of hope and vigor had become apparent in them all.

Big Blue had proved to be a sturdy, reliable ship. Having successfully burst out of Mars' atmosphere, enough power still remained in the cargo ship's energy cells to allow for a good ten years of roaming in zero G. As far as Cal was concerned, the ship's only problem resided in its dated engines. Sluggish didn't even come close. A distance that had already taken them months could have been crossed in mere days in a modern ship, even a cheap one. During those months, they had crossed paths with no less than twelve human colonies. Arriving at the first two, they had all agreed to use *Big Blue*'s dropship to see with their own eyes what the scans and lack of communication from the planet surfaces suggested: The colonies were deserted.

Turning away from the cockpit's huge window, Cal took some time to stretch, a routine that he performed at least three times daily. It had done wonders for his back injury, so much so that he almost felt like his old self again. Once he felt sufficiently supple, he began his usual morning jog, timing it just as the ship's sun-cycle lights began simulating dawn. If it weren't for the noise of his feet clanging against metal grating, he could have closed his eyes and almost fooled his brain into believing he was running in a sunlit park.

The daily run was not only for fitness, but also to cut away a small slice of the incredible boredom that was an inevitable part of long haul space travel. Such boredom would have been less of an issue had *Big Blue* still been in its original state. But as it was, anything of value had been removed long ago, including the entertainment systems. There was literally nothing to watch but the stars and nothing to read but star charts. Even the ship's cryo-lockers had been removed although dreaming away their journey deep in cryo-sleep wasn't the best idea considering recent events.

Cal had not been the only one to suffer from boredom over the months. Nearly all of the gang had become increasingly irritable with only Viktor, and presumably Melinda, being the exceptions. Other than at meal times, the pair were rarely seen. Cal had little doubt that this was due to the double cabins' worth of damaged technical equipment the boy had lugged on board from Mars then twice that amount from the other two colonies. What he was doing with all the mangled equipment, Cal couldn't even hazard a guess. "Just tinkering," was the only reply he ever got out of the boy

Eventually, all of them conceived of new and inventive ways to amuse themselves and fill the long days. Cal had revived his long lost love for rock climbing by fashioning countless hand and foot holds out of smoothed bits of scrap metal and attaching them all over the docking bay walls and walkways to create a mammoth climbing wall. He'd spent hours every day hanging, swinging, and traversing and had been pleased at the rate at which his skill and strength had progressed. On occasion, Jumper would join him, and as always, Cal would be astounded at his older friend's unparalleled agility.

As well as showing off his skills on the climbing wall, Jumper had also proven himself to be quite the chef. Rummaging every day through their abundance of salvaged food stores, the older man had concocted meal after mouth-watering meal for the whole gang. Thanks to Jumper, mealtimes had fast become the highlight of their days.

As for Eddy, the girl had created a hobby born from her admiration of Jumper's other talent: stealth. In an attempt to hone her skills, the girl had inexhaustibly stalked the ship, launching constant sneak attacks on the other members of the gang. Much to her annoyance, the only success she had was with Toker—no great achievement considering he spent most of his time asleep. In fact, if such a thing were possible, Cal could have sworn his young blond friend had some sort of implanted cryo-sleep mechanism. He had personally witnessed Eddy pounce on the sleeping man and administer a minute-long headlock while he snored peacefully throughout.

Cal had been unsuccessful dissuading Eddy from choosing Melinda as an intended victim. Subsequently, he'd needed Jumper's help to pry the girl from the crumpled clothes locker in which the synthetic had cocooned her. It had taken the two of them a good hour. Undeterred by being gift wrapped in steel, Eddy had gone on to choose an even more dangerous target: Viktor. Melinda had dealt with that attempt without the boy even being aware it had occurred. The synthetic woman had wrapped the girl in the docking bay loading chains, leaving her suspended forty feet in the air—a restraint that had taken Cal and Jumper a full two and a half hours to remedy.

They had passed two more colony planets during this time but had still received no replies to their signal. Quick to remind them that they'd still barely brushed the surface of the massive number of human colonies, Cal also pointed out that with the destruction of

Earth, the natural human response would be to flee as far from that destruction as possible. The further afield they travelled, the greater the chance they had of finding occupied colonies. He just hoped to God he was right.

Cal ended his jog in his quarters. His room was small and charmless with no viewing window and a big hole in the wall where the entertainment system had once been. What the room lacked in charm, however, it made up for in comfort with a large bunk and a fully functioning cleanse cube. Pulling off his clothes, he threw them down the wash chute—which he still wasn't entirely sure was operational—then entered the cube, which automatically sealed shut behind him. After a long steam and an even longer vapor shower, he waited for the warm air jets to dry him then left the cube feeling pleasantly refreshed. Hitting a button next to his bunk, a shelf ejected, revealing new underwear, a crisp pair of dark gray combat trousers, and an immaculate white t-shirt. The stock counter next to the shelf showed two hundred and twelve identical sets of clothing still available, plenty of time yet to check the wash chute was operational.

Having had nothing but the filthy clothes on their backs, they had all raided the stores back at the Big Game Headquarters and had found more than enough in the way of suitable clothing. Cal had been particularly lucky in his search after prying open a jammed locker down in one of *Big Blue*'s cargo holds and discovering an old Corrian Explorer combat jacket. The jacket was considered a classic, and its dark brown leather bore enough scuff marks to suggest a history of action. Cal loved the jacket; it was rugged, fitted him perfectly, and possessed none of the gimmicks of its modern counterparts like body temperature control or locator devices.

Pulling on his boots, Cal followed his nose and headed for breakfast. The smell of something truly astonishing was wafting through the corridors, and by the time he reached its source, his stomach was rumbling. *Big Blue*'s kitchen was huge, but Jumper had set up a table near to the stove, enabling him to chat with the rest of the gang while he cooked. As he approached, Cal could see that Viktor and Melinda were already sitting at the table, staring at the flames as they danced around Jumper's wok. Melinda, who didn't require food as sustenance, was doing an excellent job at impersonating a ravenous human.

"Morning," Cal said as he moved towards the stove. "As always, my friend, breakfast looks and smells divine."

Jumper smiled. "That compliment might just earn you an extra portion of Seke mushrooms."

"Very nice. And what's in there?" he asked, laying a hand on Jumper's back as he leaned over the stove to peek at the sizzling contents of the other pans.

"Silverside boar bacon. We have the planet Slion to thank for that particular delight. Supposedly, it's the very stuff that gave the vegetarian movement a wobble a few generations back. I read it somewhere, George Tennekay's book I think, *Food Trends Through the Centuries* or something, wasn't it?'

Viktor looked up, twiddling his fork. "Sure, Jumper…sounds right," he said, looking and sounding a little confused.

Tearing himself from the stove, Cal took a seat next to the boy. "No sign of Eddy and Toker? It's not like them to miss out on one of your meals, Jumper."

"I was wondering about those two myself," Jumper replied, wiping his hands on his spotlessly clean apron and strolling over to the kitchen's comm unit. "I'm usually having to fend off their greedy fingers with the carving knife by now," he continued while peering at the comm's locator screen. "That's weird…"

Cal shot him a questioning look.

"The locater's showing them both in my quarters," Jumper said as he activated the comm. "You kids'll miss out on the boar bacon if you don't get your arses in gear. You better not be messing up my room."

No reply.

"Maybe the comm's broken," Viktor suggested. "Couldn't we just start without them?"

Jumper stared at the silent comm then at Viktor. "You know the rules, kid. No one starts until we're all sat at the table."

Cal sighed. The only time he ever saw Jumper get annoyed was when someone interrupted his meal preparations. It was also one of the rare times that he saw his old friend apply any rules.

Jumper turned his ear to the silent comm for another few seconds then shook his head. "Guess I'll have to go down and drag them here myself. Melinda," he said, turning to the synthetic woman, "Would you be so kind as to stir my mushrooms while I'm gone?"

Giving no vocal answer, Melinda stood and elegantly glided over to the wok to begin stirring its contents in a slow, precise motion.

"Good…thanks," Jumper muttered, eyeing Cal and Viktor suspiciously. He pointed an accusing finger at them. "She's the only one of you that I trust with my food."

As he left the room, Cal and Viktor shrugged at each other before leaning back in their seats and allowing their eyes to drift back towards the stove.

"Really does smell good," Cal said after a few moments.

"Yeah…it's a good smell, Cal."

They both nodded and sat for a little while longer, Cal drumming his fingers on the table, Viktor twiddling his fork.

"You know, Cal," the boy said eventually, "Melinda will do anything I ask her to."

By the time Cal swallowed his sixth ration of bore bacon, Jumper's voice rang out through the kitchen's comm unit.

"Cal, I'm down in my quarters with Toker and Eddy... You better turn off the stove and get down here."

Jumper's voice was calm as always, but Cal detected a hint of uncharacteristic seriousness. Filling their cheeks with one last mouthful each, Cal and Viktor hastily made their way out of the kitchen and over to the lift pods. A minute later, they arrived at the open door of Jumper's quarters just in time to see a drooling Eddy stumble, arms wide, straight past a giggling Toker and headfirst into a clothes locker. Toker was sitting on Jumper's bunk, busily attempting to put his right foot behind his head. The left one was already there.

"Huh," Cal said for lack of a better expression. "Guess they're not hungry."

Jumper held up an empty glass vial. "Found this in the sink. They must've swiped it from my stash."

Cal raised an eyebrow. "And yet they still seem to be living."

"They must have only used a drop. Then I guess they combined their two brain cells to work out how to dilute it suitably," Jumper replied as he watched the laughing Toker crouch on the ground and begin rolling head over heels until the wall brought his progress to an abrupt halt. "Luckily, they seem to have got it about right, otherwise we'd definitely have two less crew members by now."

"We still might if they keep that up," Cal said. "We better restrain them until it wears off."

Jumper nodded and walked over to his locker to pull out some smart-cord.

"What's going on, guys?" Viktor asked. "They drunk or what?"

"Oh, they're drunk alright," Cal said as he moved to restrain

Eddy. She was spinning in circles in the center of the room. "But it's got nothing to do with alcohol. Right now, they're probably experiencing levels of bliss and love that even the likes of Casanova could never dream of." Eddy started to giggle uncontrollably whilst pointing up at a blank section of ceiling. "Probably a few hallucinations too."

"Cassa who?"

"Never mind… Our idiot crew members have gone and sampled some of Jumper's Alvorian bliss formula."

"The stuff in bliss darts?"

"The very same."

"Will they be okay?"

Holding her at arm's length, Cal looked into Eddy's eyes. She was desperately attempting to lick his face with the expression of a toddler who'd just spied a toffee apple. "That depends on your definition of fine. If you mean will they go back to how they were before, then yes, Viktor, I think they'll be fine."

"Why don't we all do some then? Looks like fun."

"You're right, kid, it is fun," Jumper answered, doing his best to ignore Toker, who was poking at his afro with wonderment in his eyes. "Cal and I both experienced the bliss formula as part of our training on Mars. The after effects, however, really aren't fun."

"Thought you said they'd be fine," Viktor said, sounding more disappointed than worried.

"Eventually, yes… Try and imagine pure, unadulterated bliss, then imagine the complete opposite of that."

Viktor screwed up his face.

"You got it? Now double that, an' you'll get an idea of the hangover they'll be experiencing in a few hours. Trust me, kid, it ain't pretty," Jumper explained as he and Cal began tying the writhing, giggling pair to the bunk. "And then, of course, they'll be having to endure an ear full from me for letting the silverside boar bacon go to waste."

Cal looked at Viktor and did his best to stifle a grin.

Chapter Thirteen
MAGNET CITY

Randal Meeks strode briskly along a wide, pristine corridor. To his right, a long window offered a far-reaching view of the Golden Hall, a lavish, mile-long casino filled exclusively with the richest and most attractive of people. Meeks didn't so much as glance. He'd seen the view countless times, and it only served to remind him what he didn't have. He wasn't poor by any means, but he wasn't filthy rich either. Not that wealth would matter for much longer. The twittering fools could bury their heads as deep into their piles of gold and diamonds as they liked, but sooner or later, they'd have to face up to the facts. Earth was gone, long-range communications were down, and if it wasn't already, the Federation would soon be in tatters.

Meeks came to a neat stop in front of an ornate, gold-trimmed door that marked the end of the corridor, pressed a shiny silver button and looked expectantly up towards the spot he knew the camera to be.

"Damn it, Meeks. As always, your timing stinks."

Meeks smoothed his slick, black hair—a habit of his whenever he was annoyed—then looked down at the comm with a sigh. "This is precisely the time you asked me to arrive," he replied in a bored tone to match his expression. The door slid open, and he entered a lavish office. Surveying the room, he saw his boss, Aaron Hogmeyer, standing at its rear, pouring himself a drink.

"You brought the figures?" Hogmeyer asked gruffly.

"Have I ever not brought the figures?"

The reply earned Meeks a look that suggested the man might stride around his huge, empty desk and throw a gold-ringed fist at his nose. Meeks wasn't worried. His boss was a big man with a small fuse, but talented accountants with such disregard for the rules were hard to come by. Meeks knew it was this fact, and this fact only, that prevented him from being marched to the nearest airlock. Hogmeyer held the look for a moment longer then gulped noisily at his drink. Meeks didn't bother hiding his disgust at the sight. He could barely look at the man. That unsightly belly protruding in a round, pregnant bulge was replicated on a smaller scale at chin level. A weird bulk considering his arms and legs were so long and shapeless. Then there were those greasy threads of hair stretched desperately over his glistening baldness.

As Hogmeyer poured another drink, Meeks turned to stare out of the pulse, blast, and fire-proof smart-glass that made up the front end of the office. Even the sight of the multitudes of gambling fools was better than looking at his boss. If it weren't for the people, Meeks had to admit the casino made quite a sight: a mile of marble and gold filled with gambling stations and elegant cocktail bars. Even more impressive was the seemingly endless array of translucent, single-person tube lifts that snaked their way up to the silver and gold pleasure pods, which filled the vast ceiling like big, floating eggs. Meeks sniffed, feeling something close to appreciation as he took in the sight. *Yes, a real shame about the people.* From this height, they looked and sounded like nothing more than a swarm of mindless birds.

Hearing Hogmeyer pour yet another drink, Meeks smoothed his hair and continued to stare at the view. Despite his loathing of the big man, he had to admit that he'd done well. It was hard to imagine that the lavish space had once been the interior of a huge mining ship. *Someone else's huge mining ship.* As Hogmeyer told it, he'd scammed the ship and the enormous stack of gold it was transporting from a hapless crew of traders. His boss recounted an impressive story of his genius, but Meeks was inclined to believe the other story, the one that Hogmeyer had so violently attempted to quash. It told of how the big man had in fact crashed his little cruiser into the mining ship's flight window while on the run from debt collectors. Apparently, he'd had gambling debts up to his fat neck and, after five days on the run, had fallen asleep at the controls of his little ship, allowing it to drift into a shipping lane. The little cruiser had wedged itself in the massive mining ship's cockpit and killed the crew instantly.

Whatever the truth may be, his boss had acquired the ship and claimed it as his own. Then, remaining a gambler at heart, had taken a big risk and used every piece of the gold that it contained to transform its vast cargo hold into a casino capable of travelling to all the richest colonies. He'd named the casino "The Golden Hall" and had refurbished it accordingly, decorating everything from the floors to the dice with real gold. He'd also remained loyal to his little ship by revamping it and suspending it high above the crowds to serve as his office. Granting access to only the very richest, most attractive of people, Hogmeyer had become a tycoon practically overnight. But he hadn't stopped there, not by a long shot. He'd bought more ships, then more still, refurbishing each and every one and attaching them to the original cargo ship. This expansion process had continued until he'd created what could only be described as a vast, metal city drifting through space.

Not wanting to deprive his deep pockets of the credits of poorer or indeed less attractive people, Hogmeyer had constructed suitable gambling establishments for each and every class. In fact, he'd even gone as far as to section off the entire city according to class from the gold and silver sectors for the rich and famous right down to the tin and copper taverns for the ugly, sickly scum. Everyone had been catered to. Meeks had always thought it ironic that it had been those lower classes who'd ultimately coined the city's name: *Magnet City.* Despite its origin, however, Hogmeyer had embraced the name, finding the word *magnet* entirely fitting for a city as attractive as his. In actuality, the name had been born from the difficulty of escaping the place once you were stuck there, something of which Hogmeyer seemed oblivious, or perhaps he simply didn't give a shit. Meeks had never been brave enough to broach the subject.

Bored of waiting for his boss to finish drinking, Meeks pulled a small, white cube from his pocket and placed it carefully in the center of the desk. As he stepped back, a stream of bright light burst forth from the cube, forming a large hologram.

"Bloody hell, Meeks, how many times do I have tell you? Keep those damned graphs out of my view." Approaching the desk, Hogmeyer pulled a control wand from his back pocket and struck the cube, sending it and its holographic projection spinning away.

"My apologies, sir, I was under the illusion that you had some interest in how your little empire was performing."

"I pay you for summaries, you dull little man—quick facts and conclusions—not to bore me with your bloody graphs."

"Very well," Meeks said, resisting the urge to touch his hair. "Obviously, it's impossible for me to know exact rates while long-range communications are down, but with the instructions you've given the city banks and your pawn brokers, profits are the highest they've ever been."

Hogmeyer nodded and walked back to his mini bar with a hint of a smile. "Of course they are. That's what happens when you get the opportunity to set your own rates, your own rules. Might as well take advantage while the system is down, eh?"

And what if the system never comes back up? What will your numbers on the screen mean then? Meeks feigned his agreement with a nod.

"Of course, it also helps when your competition gets blown to smithereens," Hogmeyer continued. Throwing a couple of ice cubes into a glass, he filled it almost to the brim with a thick, red liquid. "Alvorian port, Meeks?"

"Don't mind if I do."

The big man tossed a fist full of ice cubes into a second glass and accompanied them with a dribble of the red liquid.

"Your generosity knows no bounds," Meeks said, walking forward to take the glass and holding it up to the light to view the short measure.

Ignoring the comment, Hogmeyer moved back to his desk and settled himself into a large, leather, spring-backed chair. Lifting his long legs, he slammed his gold-capped, stegosaurus skin boots down on the desk and stared out at his beloved casino. "I tell you, Meeks, whoever or whatever destroyed Earth and its damned pleasure moon did me a serious favor."

Idiotic fool. Meeks had never known a man who could be so bright and so dim simultaneously. Surely, he could see the long term ramifications of the situation. Surely, he could see that chaos was looming. Wealth, customers, power...soon, it will all be turned on its head. How the hell could he not see it? "Yes, a big favor indeed, sir. We've even had to turn punters away for lack of room."

Hogmeyer's head snapped up. "*What?*" he barked, port-infused spittle taking flight. "Why wasn't I informed?"

"What would be the point? We simply don't have the capacity for more customers."

"So we bloody increase capacity, buy more ships, *expand, damn it.* There's no excuse for turning away profit bringers, you understand me, Meeks?"

Blind fool. Unperturbed by his boss' sudden rage, Meeks drained his measly measure of port and calmly set the glass down. "Loud and clear, sir." Silently, he cursed. Who was he kidding? He was burying his head in the sand just as much as his fat boss, just as much as the hoard of gambling fools below. After all, he was still working for this idiot, he was still residing in this ridiculous drifting city. But where the hell else would he go? What would he do? There was no running or hiding from this disaster. Its ripples would have spread far and wide by now.

"How the pods doing?"

Meeks turned and gazed toward the large, egg-like structures that filled the casino's vast ceiling. "Excellent. By all accounts, they're an excellent investment." The pleasure pods were a relatively new addition to the casinos. Utilizing a mixture of virtual reality, drugs, and sensory links enabled their occupants to fulfil their greatest fantasies—or at least to make them think they were, and that was good enough for most. *What better way to escape present circumstances?* Meeks mused. Those who desired—and could afford it—often spent weeks at a time cocooned within the high-tech little eggs. All necessary bodily functions were taken care of, allowing an uninterrupted experience for the user as they busily became the greatest lover, the toughest fighter, or simply more popular than God.

"At this rate, they'll soon be bringing in as much as the gambling."

"I told you, Meeks." Hogmeyer's mouth made an approximation

of a grin. "I told you they'd be a success."

Meeks did his best to smile back. "Of course...there have been a few complaints."

Hogmeyer scoffed. "Aren't there always bloody complaints? Ignore them."

"I would sir, but the complaints have been connected to a few casualties."

"Casualties?"

"Deaths, actually. It seems the drug input is a little on the high side."

"Of course it is, makes for a better experience. And the drugs are cheap. What's to lose? There are other establishments with these pods, you know, Meeks. I won't have mine being thought of as inferior just because of a few weaklings." Using the tip of his control wand, Hogmeyer scratched at his shoulder. Then he pointed the wand at Meeks. "You realize this city has a reputation to uphold."

Oh, that it has, Meeks thought, wondering if his boss actually believed his own bullshit. "And what if a few of those *weaklings* have been from the higher class sector of the city?"

Hogmeyer looked ready to bark out a reply then stopped short. Twiddling his wand, he gazed out at his beloved Golden Hall and seemed to consider for a moment. "Reputations are tricky beasts, Meeks... Okay, reduce the drugs in the higher class pods." Again, he thrust the control wand in Meeks' direction. "But the higher class only."

Only after Meeks had nodded his understanding did Hogmeyer redirect the wand. Pointing it at the huge smart-glass window, he gave it a lazy flick. Instantly, the view of the Golden Hall disappeared, and a grid of no less than two hundred large squares took its place. Within each square were viewpoints from bug cameras stationed throughout the city. About half of those squares showed crowds of people roaming the various gambling halls, hotel lobbies, and shopping centers. The other half consisted of a mix, ranging from busy spaceship hangars to health spa saunas—similarly busy with nude women. Meeks couldn't help but notice that one of those flesh-filled scenes was marked as last viewed. It was also on that scene that the green targeting beam of the control wand now fell.

"I'm done with you now, Meeks," Hogmeyer said without bothering to tear his eyes from the screen. "Get out of my sight. I've work to do."

"Of course," Meeks replied as he scooped up his little white holo-cube and strode smoothly towards the door.

As the little accountant left the office, he couldn't help but smooth back his hair and mumble a single word. "Pervert."

Before Hogmeyer could bark a retort, the door had slid shut behind him.

Chapter Fourteen
KUNG FU PUPPETS

The soft, fine sand felt good under Cal's bare feet. Strolling out from under the shade of the palm trees, he looked up and took a moment to enjoy the warmth of the sun. The beach was completely deserted. The only sounds he could hear came from the gentle, lapping of waves as they met the shore and the twittering and occasional squawking of tropical birdlife. He shielded his eyes and looked out over the calm, glittering sea.

"Pretty cool, eh, Cal?" The voice was Viktor's.

Cal looked over to the boy, who had seemingly appeared out of nowhere a little further up the beach. "It's incredible, Viktor. Excellent choice of venue."

"I'm glad you like it," the boy replied, walking toward him. He came to a stop about five metres away. "Of course, we're not here to admire the view."

Cal smiled, amused at the seriousness of his young friend.

Planting his feet shoulder width apart, Viktor brought his clenched fists up in front of him. "You ready?" There was an attempt at menace in the boy's tone, but his high voice made it unconvincing.

"As ready as I'll ever be I guess."

Cal had barely finished his reply before Viktor launched himself into the air, an impossibly high jump, and targeted his outstretched foot at Cal's head. Managing to twist away from the attack in the nick of time, Cal found himself stumbling backwards in an attempt to steady himself. But Viktor allowed him little time to gather his wits or balance. The boy had barely hit the sand before launching a second airborne attack, this time making full use of his bony fists to unleash a barrage of lethal punches. Cal was forced back further still, blocking punch after punch, each one testing his speed and skill to the limit. After two narrowly missed elbow strikes and a roundhouse kick that practically took his nose off, Cal found himself thigh deep in the sea. Rather than following him in any deeper, Viktor once again ignored the laws of gravity and leapt backwards in a high, arching backflip to land effortlessly on the dry sand.

"Up for any more punishment, Cal?" the boy inquired, beckoning him forward.

"On my way," Cal muttered as he waded back towards the shore. Before reaching it, however, he noticed what appeared to be a green fireball, about half a meter in diameter, hovering before his young opponent. He had two seconds to ponder the fireball's existence before an indecipherable shout from Viktor sent the fiery mass careening toward him with the speed of a professionally thrown spikeball. Hitting him square in the chest, it sent him spinning through the air to plunge straight back into the sea.

Cal didn't surface. Instead, he found himself in one of *Big Blue*'s recreation rooms, his clothes as dry as a bone. He was standing on a large platform facing a disappointed-looking Viktor, who was perched on a similar platform a few meters opposite. The boy looked ridiculous; he was wearing a stim-suit that had more wires protruding from it than a porcupine had spines. Of course, he too was wearing a similar suit and didn't imagine for a second that he looked any less ridiculous.

"You gotta at least try and fight me back, Cal. I thought you were good at all this kung fu stuff."

"Well, this virtual fighting is a little different to real life, Viktor. To be honest, I've never had to try and block a green fireball before," Cal replied. He could hear hysterical laughter behind him, and he turned to see Toker and Eddy falling about one another on the floor. Jumper was standing behind them, his perfect white teeth displayed in a wide grin that suggested he was teetering on the edge of a giggle fit himself.

"What's so funny?" Viktor asked, sounding genuinely puzzled.

"Viktor...that was priceless," Toker said though his laughter. "I dunno what it looked like in your virtual kung fu land, but your...arms and legs...everywhere...brilliant..."

"You...you were like..." Eddy was clutching her gut and was having similar trouble getting her words out, "A little drunk...kung fu puppet."

"Perfect, yes. Good one," Toker wholeheartedly agreed. "Drunk kung fu puppet...spot on."

"You have to move your arms and legs, idiots. The stim-suits read your moves then puts 'em in the game."

"Oh...those were moves, were they?" Toker said, sitting up and wiping away his tears.

"Yes, they were, and I can assure you, the moves I was pulling off were kicking Cal's arse, and they'll kick yours when it's your turn."

"You think, little squirt?" Toker replied, his laughter rapidly subsiding to his competitive edge. "I'll have you know I completed Dragon Warrior eight, Zin's Revenge in three days."

"Ha, Zin's Revenge. That's a kiddie's game. I bet you played it on one of those crappy Centor virtual world machines too."

Toker spluttered as he climbed to his feet. "What you talking about? Centors are the best credits can buy. You're saying your heap of wires and spare parts is better than a Centor? Man, you're nuts."

Viktor shook his head. "Another dimwit sucker falling for Centor marketing. If you had even half a proper brain, you'd realize they're using old school technology. My machine is leagues ahead. And the wires are only there cos the sensor platforms aren't finished, idiot."

"Now now, kids, let's leave the fighting for the beach, shall we?" Cal interjected. "Toker can take my next go, and then you can work out who's got the biggest, greenest fireballs."

"Sounds good to me," Toker said, striding forward.

"Wait up, Cal," Viktor said with a raised hand. "I'll gladly kick this Centor sucker's arse, but you've gotta finish three rounds first. That's the rules."

Before Cal could even make an attempt at getting out of it, Viktor had activated the game's second round. Once again, he had the strange sensation of his senses and surroundings changing in an instant. This time, he found himself standing on a grassy plateau amid lush, alpine mountains. A truly breathtaking view and stunning in its detail. "I've got to give it to you, Viktor, your venues are great."

"Might as well have a good view while I'm woppin' your butt." Cal laughed. "We'll see."

"Ready?"

"Yep."

Not wanting to be caught off guard again, Cal leapt towards the boy. Before reaching him, however, his young opponent had miraculously disappeared in a cloud of mystical smoke only to reappear five meters further back. Viktor's face was as smug as his stance was cocky.

"You're sure that's not against the rules?"

"Winners make the rules, Cal. Losers just have to suck 'em up."

"Programmer makes the rules," Cal mumbled as he crept forward, fully aware that Viktor could appear directly in front of him at any moment.

As it turned out, it wasn't Viktor who he suddenly found himself nose to nose with. Instead, three glistening, bikini-clad girls who were donning boots and hats of the old cowboy variety had materialized directly in his path. Oddly, the girls seemed to be appearing in 2D. Unsure how to react to such a strange occurrence, Cal simply stood in dumb confusion and stared at the odd trio. He couldn't have imagined a weirder sight amid the beautiful mountain vista. Then what he recognized as old style country and western music began to sound and rapidly increased in volume. Seeming to take the music as their cue, the trio of plastic-looking beauties looked directly at him and broke into a provocative dance.

"Hi there, cowboy," the three of them said in unison, followed by an exaggerated wink. "The great Aaron Hogmeyer invites you and your crew to Magnet City's *Lucky Deuce,* the real man's gambling hall. All the girls and gamble you can handle. Just make sure you follow our signal now though, big boy. Don't wanna end up in the wrong part of the city." Blowing him a kiss and performing one last wink, the girls vanished as abruptly as they'd appeared.

The next thing Cal saw was Viktor excitedly hopping towards him across the lush grass, a wide grin plastered on his face.

"Er, I'm a little confused, Viktor."

"This could be it, Cal," the boy said, barely managing to contain his excitement.

"It?"

"People, Cal, fellow humans. I wired up the ship's communications to the virtual reality, see, just in case an incoming signal came through while we were deep in a game. It's another colony, Cal, an' I reckon this one sounds promising."

Chapter Fifteen
FELLOW HUMANS

Standing at *Big Blue*'s flight controls, Cal and the rest of the gang peered eagerly out of the cockpit's window. Cal had heard plenty of rumors regarding Magnet City but had never actually visited it. From what he'd been told, he would never want to. His present situation was of course an exception. At last, they were going to reconnect with fellow humans. He tried to remain calm, but he couldn't deny the excitement building within him, and it was clear the rest of the gang were feeling the same. The months of creeping through the cold emptiness of space had been hard, the questions surrounding their plight often evoking grim emotions. Would they ever learn the truth behind Earth's destruction? What was lying in wait at the other colonies? Were they the only ones left? Cal was good at pushing such questions out of his mind, but on occasion, they had inevitably snuck through.

Barring Aldular, the floating city on the ocean planet of Aqualorian Prime, Magnet City was the only mobile city Cal had ever heard of. It was akin to a space station, which over time had developed and expanded to become the size of a small moon. Lacking a planet surface to bury its roots in, the city drifted through space, only occasionally utilizing its massive oscillator engines to propel it to a specific destination. The reason for the city's acquired name was glaringly obvious: a hulking mass of adjoined ships appearing as though a huge magnetic force had pulled them from far and wide to a single collision point. Some of the adjoined ships were small, some large, and others as immense as *Big Blue*. All were melded together haphazardly with seemingly little thought given to design. Cal felt the erratic shape and jagged edges gave the city an ominous appearance, a sort of monstrous, metallic sea urchin squashed and adrift in the black sea of deep space. As the city grew larger in the cockpit window, however, floating neon billboards and great bundles of flashing lights came into view, turning it from ominous to plain tacky.

"I can see ships," Toker blurted excitedly.

"Of course you can, idiot, the whole thing's made of ships," Viktor said sharply. The boy was still a little bitter at having his virtual combat mocked.

"I mean flying ships, smart ass."

"So we ain't alone then," Eddy said, more as a statement than a question.

"Well that's a relief, eh?" Toker said, giving the girl a nudge. "Thought for a moment it was gonna be up to you an' me to get down and dirty with the repopulating."

Cal was surprised to see Eddy react with a little smirk. "Who said I'd have chosen you?" she replied coolly.

"Yeah, the human race would be doomed if it had to rely on your genes, thickie," Viktor added.

"Too right," Eddy agreed. "Maybe I'd choose you, eh, Vik?" she said, taking hold of the boy and pulling him close. "Least our kids'd be smart then, eh?"

Toker looked put out for a moment before the expression on Viktor's flushed face brought laughter instead.

Cal grinned. All jokes aside, he could see the relief in his young friends' eyes. He didn't blame them. The sight of activity around the city made him feel like he'd just burst from the surface of the sea and sucked in a much-needed lungful of air.

As *Big Blue* moved ever closer, Cal wondered whether the city would hold the answers they'd all been hoping for. It was possible that the city's residents were no wiser than themselves. But at least they weren't alone.

"Why d'you suppose this colony isn't abandoned like the others?" Viktor asked.

"Who knows?" Cal replied. "Maybe because it's much further from Earth's destruction. Also, it's always on the move."

"Could be that people feel safer in numbers too," Jumper added. "The other colonies we've seen were much smaller."

Cal nodded in agreement. When there's a potential killer on the loose, people always feel safer in a crowd. It was human nature. As was seeking out distraction from trouble and traumatic events even to the point of ignoring their existence. And what better place to do such a thing than in a city designed to lose yourself in gambling, drugs, and who knew what else.

Before long, the city was dominating *Big Blue*'s entire flight window. One of the hovering billboards maneuvered directly into their path, displaying the very same scantily dressed girls that Cal had faced during Viktor's game.

"Glad you made it, boys...and girls," said the buxom blonde in the middle of the three. "Are you all ready for some fun? Thought so," she said with a giggle. "Just lock onto our signature, and we'll guide you directly to the *Lucky Deuce*. More girls and gamble than you can handle."

"Lots of horny men for you too, little lady," the equally buxom brunette on the left added as she winked in Eddy's direction.

Eddy scoffed.

"How'd they know who's on board?" Toker asked.

"Probably an illegal scan of the ship," Cal suggested. "I've heard that the running of this place falls a way short of law abiding."

"Can't be much of a scanner if it thinks Melinda is a real chick," Toker pointed out.

"She *is* a real chick," Viktor said defensively.

Toker turned to him with a raised eyebrow, and after a moment, the boy sighed and gave a shrug. "She can fool any scanner that comes her way...doesn't take much; it's pretty basic tech."

Cal glanced at Melinda. "Good. It's probably best we don't attract any attention, at least until we know what's what."

"Do we have to follow those dirty chicks, Cal?" Eddy asked. "The other end of the city looks much nicer."

Cal turned back to the flight console. "It seems the city's been divided into different sections, split according to wealth and class. From what I can tell from the readouts, the scan's ranked us second from the bottom."

Eddy sniffed loudly. "So can't we just ignore the stupid bimbo billboard and head for the good stuff?"

Toker shook his head. "No way. I vote we follow the dirty chicks."

"You would, perv," Eddy spat.

"Probably shouldn't break the rules on our first day," Jumper pointed out. "Best play it safe and follow the billboard at least until we get some information about what's been going on."

Toker grinned. "Dirty chicks it is."

The Lucky Deuce gambling hall was a colossal space filled to the brim with booze, fighting, naked flesh, and of course gambling.

Numerous pole dancing stages on which countless shiny girls slivered under a neon glow seedily graced the center of the hall. Cal could see a struggling man who'd been tied, gagged, and suspended above the nearest strip stage. A large sign was strapped to his chest, stating, *"Touch flesh without paying, an' you'll be joining me."* Enforcing the threat, hulking bouncers garbed in black, stab-proof clothing roamed the bars, occasionally dishing out blows to the back of troublemaking heads with shock-sticks.

Looking up, Cal saw countless egg-shaped pleasure pods hanging from the high ceiling. Each of them had a translucent tube lift coiling up to it, most of which seemed less than secure. In one of the lifts, he spotted a man who'd become jammed halfway up. No one seemed bothered that the poor soul looked close to death.

"Maybe we should have ignored the dirty chicks," Toker mumbled as the six of them stood on the rickety entrance platform that overlooked the hall.

"Looking at a place like this kind of makes me wish we *were* alone," Jumper added.

"Not much of a reintroduction to the human race for you, Jumper," Cal said. He'd almost forgotten that, for the last few decades, his old friend was only used to looking at a handful of people at most. "But now we're here, I guess we should make the most of it," he said, rubbing his hands together in a lackluster attempt to rustle up some enthusiasm. "I'm going to see if I can weed out some useful info."

"I'll come with you," Jumper said, sounding less than optimistic but giving Cal a slap on the back nonetheless.

Despite probably being way out of his comfort zone, Cal was pleased to see that his old friend seemed as cool and collected as ever. "Good. The rest of you have fun exploring," he said, sounding a little more like a parent than he'd have liked. "Viktor, it's probably best you stick close to Melinda."

The boy nodded. "I wouldn't let her wander around a place like this without an escort."

"Well, quite. Everyone, try and stay out of trouble, eh?" Cal said, shooting one last deliberate glance at Eddy and Toker before strolling off.

Cal and Jumper searched for a good hour among the rowdy crowds for someone willing to discuss Earth's destruction. After some spilt drinks, a few near miss fights, and a myriad of expletives, they finally discovered their man. Nick Rail had once been the captain of *The Swan Queen,* a class one pleasure cruiser that had left Earth space only a few minutes before the planet met its end. After a brief introduction, Nick led them through the noisy hordes to a relatively quiet section of the gambling hall. Here, they found an area of enclosed booths where the people were at least eating more than they were drinking. Selecting the least overlooked booth, they sat and began to talk.

"What d'you want to know?" Nick asked as he buried his fingers into a bowl of nuts.

"Everything…from the beginning," Cal said, refusing an offer of the damp-looking nuts with a forced smile and a raised hand.

"The beginning of the end," Nick mumbled.

Cal liked the look of the former captain. He had intelligent eyes, but it was plain to see that he was physically and mentally exhausted. Whatever stresses he'd endured over the past months had obviously taken their toll.

"We know that Earth was destroyed," Jumper informed him, "but not by who…or what."

"My God, where've you guys been living, a jungle?"

"Yes," Jumper replied.

Nick made a lackluster attempt at a smile before continuing. "It was an alien race called Carcarrions, or so I'm told." Nick shifted uncomfortably. "Came straight towards Earth in three of the biggest ships I've ever seen…monstrous cubes, each bigger than this city if you can believe it. They obliterated Earth without the slightest warning."

"Impossible," Cal said with a sudden sinking feeling. Maybe they didn't have their man after all. "You've been misinformed. I know of the Carcarrions; they're a primitive race, practically still living in caves."

"So I've heard," Nick replied, shooting them a look that suggested he'd heard those particular words a thousand times before. "But my ship somehow escaped the attack as did thirty or forty others. Every one of those ships managed to run scans of the attacking crafts before they struck. They only picked up one life form: Carcarrions."

Cal's brow creased. "Maybe the scanners were fooled."

Nick shrugged.

"How did you escape?"

"They ignored us as if we were insignificant. There were a few military ships that tried to counterattack, but they were ignored too. Their weapons deflected like pinballs. Once Earth was destroyed, the military ships fled like the rest of us. I'm not sure where." Nick flicked a nut into his mouth. "I don't know where these Carcarrions found their technology, but it was certainly a damned sight more advanced than ours."

"So you witnessed the actual destruction?"

Nick nodded and stared down at his hands. "My ship had just left Earth's airspace. We were set for a three-month voyage to the Pentelain Moons. If those bastard Carcarrions hadn't been so fixated on destroying the planet, I very much doubt I'd be here talking to you now. Sometimes, I wish I wasn't. Let me tell you, witnessing the destruction of your home planet is something no man, woman, or child should ever have to endure."

The three men sat in silence for a time. Cal's brain was reeling with the information. None of it made any sense.

"Have there been any sightings of these Carcarrions since?" Jumper asked.

"No. I've heard rumours of attacks on larger colonies and some of the military bases at about the same time that Earth was destroyed, but they're only rumours, nothing trustworthy. All I know for certain is that they destroyed Earth, and no one I've talked to has seen them since. The fear still remains though. People arriving from other colonies say there's a lot of paranoia, even panic, that the attackers might return to finish the job."

Cal could understand such fears. But for the invaders to attack and destroy all human colonies would be one hell of a task. Since the Federation had been formed over three hundred years ago, thousands of life-supporting planets had been colonized, and thousands more terraformed.

"What about the military? Any messages from them? Strategies? Re-grouping?"

Nick let out a humourless laugh and shook his head. "You guys really are out of the loop, aren't you? All long-range communications are dead. The tech has just stopped working. Nothing coming in, nothing going out. I've heard no one give a convincing reason why, and I've heard a lot of very smart people discussing it. The only thing they seem to able to agree on is that the transmissions went down around the same time as the attack. Certainly no coincidence." Nick scooped the last few nuts out of the bowl.

Cal rubbed his head in frustration. "What about the military starships or bases? Has anyone had any *physical* communication with them?"

"Just more rumors, I'm afraid. Impossible to confirm."

"Indulge us."

Nick shrugged again. "Word's going around that all military bases and starships are abandoned. Some say they've spotted the starships clustered together, crew-less, drifting aimlessly through space. If you ask me, it's probably just lies from people who get a kick out of spreading fear. There's plenty of those types around here."

"You mean the crews abandoned the ships?" Jumper asked.

"Who knows? Like I said, they're just rumors, unconfirmed."

"There's no way entire military crews would abandon their ships. Some would rather die," Cal said. "Being clustered together makes sense though, especially with long-range transmissions down. Protocol would be to converge at certain prearranged points—strength in numbers."

"I hope you're right," Nick said solemnly. "We're going to need people like that to stand a chance at getting some order back. Even with the threat possibly gone, things are spinning out of control fast."

"How d'you mean?" Jumper asked.

"Criminals taking advantage is what I mean. With the military dead in the water and the communication problems, we've got ourselves a perfect environment for chaos, and chaos feeds chaos. It's exponential. Most residing on the colonies are decent folk, but there's countless others roaming space with pirate ethics. From what I hear, they're already taking advantage, and it's only likely to get worse."

Cal shot Jumper a concerned glance. The so-called facts concerning the attack on Earth didn't add up. But he couldn't deny the likelihood of civilization spiralling out of control very quickly. Pirates had proved a serious problem even before the chaos had begun.

"You want my advice," Nick said, pushing the empty bowl of nuts away, "get the hell away from this hole and search out another colony. This place will eat up your body, then your mind, then make a start on your soul."

"We need no convincing," Cal replied. The man didn't seem the type to over-dramatize.

"Why do you stay here?" Jumper asked.

"Because I was a fool. My crew and I were conned into giving up our ship."

"Conned?"

Nick gave a quick scan of the surrounding booths then leaned forward before continuing. "Listen to me: If you've got a decent-sized ship, the guy that owns this place, I mean the whole damn city, he's going to want it, an' he'll probably do near anything to get it."

Cal glanced again at Jumper. None of this was shaping up well, and he had a bad feeling that time wasn't on their side. "Don't worry about us; we won't be staying long. We appreciate your help. If you need a ride out of here, we can take you to the next decent colony."

"Thanks, but no," Nick said without hesitation. "Forty-nine crew and three hundred and ninety-eight passengers are stuck here because of my foolishness. They were my responsibility, and I failed them. Thanks for the offer, but I'll be taking no easy ticket out of here."

Cal answered with a silent nod. He admired the man's dedication to his passengers and crew. He wished he could give them all an easy ticket out of the city, but it would be impossible. *Big Blue* was certainly large enough to hold that amount of people, but with the slow engines, the next colony would be weeks of travel away. Even if they could somehow get enough supplies, the huge cargo ship simply wasn't designed to cater for more than a handful of crew.

Before the conversation could continue any further, Nick swore under his breath and became noticeably paler. Cal followed the man's line of sight to see two brutish men approaching the booth. From the black clothing they wore and the shock sticks nestled in their meaty fingers, Cal guessed them to be bouncers.

Twisting in his seat, Cal shot the two brutes a wide smile. "Three Alvorian ales, and another bowl of these delicious nuts if you would," he said, sliding the empty bowl towards them. One of the brutes looked amused at that, or possibly, he was just looking forward to what was to come. The more fierce-looking of the two men gave his bald head a quick scratch with the end of his shock stick before pointing it menacingly at Cal and Jumper. "Gonna have to come with us," he grunted, his expression suggesting he was hoping for some sort of refusal.

Cal glanced at Nick; the man's eyes were full of warning. He answered the warning with a shrug. "Well, I guess our time's up then, eh?" he said cheerily, offering Nick his hand. "Best of luck, old friend. Always good to catch up."

"Yes, best of luck to you too," Nick replied, gripping Cal's hand and giving it a firm shake. "Mind how you go, old friend."

Giving their new acquaintance one last nod of thanks, both Cal and Jumper stood and calmly stepped from the booth. As they did so, Cal pondered the possible nature of the con that had stranded Nick Rail, his crew, and all of his passengers in this violent pit. He had the distinct feeling that he'd soon be finding out whether he wanted to or not. Giving Jumper a casual slap on the back, the two of them followed the brutes out of the seating area and off through the parting crowds.

With its combination of dented, blood-stained walls and its overwhelming stench of urine, Cal decided that the corridor he and Jumper were being led down was the least pleasant he'd ever witnessed. In front of them, another heavyset bouncer opened a side door, through which he shoved a reluctant drunk. As they approached, Cal saw the words *Waiting Room* printed across the door, which, intentionally or not, had been underlined by a long smear of blood. With some assistance from their brutish escorts, he and Jumper followed the path of the reluctant drunk.

The room they found themselves in was less a waiting room and more a prison cell. The majority of its occupants were unconscious, sprawled on the floor amid sticky cocktails of blood, urine, and sick. Of those who were conscious, some busily paced back and forth, fists clenched, perhaps unsatisfied with the conclusion of a recent fight. Others simply stared into space, various parts of their anatomies in spasm—possibly the result of one too many days nestled in a pleasure pod. Two of the occupants, however, sat quietly in the corner, doing nothing more than looking solemn: Eddy and Toker.

Cal and Jumper made their way over to the sorry looking pair.

Jumper shook his head. "Get lost?"

"Idiot spilled his drink on some big fella," Eddy mumbled, nodding at Toker, who was sporting an impressive black eye.

"Yeah, an' I was trying to apologize to the guy when this one," Toker said, nodding sharply back at Eddy, "went and launched herself at him."

"I was backing you up, you ungrateful sod. The bloke was obviously lookin' for a fight. I just thought I'd get in there first, element of surprise, an' all that."

"Backing me up!" Toker blurted. "Granted, the guy was a little overly pissed off at having a drink spilled on him, but I get a hunch it was you breaking his nose that started the fight."

"You gotta be kidding. If I hadn't got in there first, he'd have planted *you* one in the face, idiot. Reckon you owe me a drink for that."

"A drink! Jeeze, girl. Don't you think I'd have preferred one punch from him than ten from his mates? Guys, she's nuts," Toker replied, desperately looking at Cal and Jumper for some acknowledgement of the fact.

"Ungrateful git. Won't back you up next time then."

Toker turned back to her, his eyebrows set in a high arch. "That would be great. Would you do me that favor? And while we're on the subject, exactly what part of your brain is it that's missing? The guy you popped was bloody huge, and so were his mates. Wasn't there even one tiny little alarm bell in that empty noggin of yours? Maybe a faint little tinkle suggesting that punching an angry bloke three times your size might not be the brightest of ideas."

"He wasn't *that* big, an' he slept like a baby after I knocked his lights out."

"He was a flippin' *giant*, and he bloody well knocked *himself* out. The poor bugger tripped and reshaped a table with the back of his head. And damn lucky he did too."

"Maybe, but it was my rock-solid punch to his honker that made him trip in the first place," Eddy countered. "So it was me who knocked him out."

"Alright, granted, you managed to somehow break the guy's bloody great nose, I'll give you that. But it was bewilderment that made him fall. Even a lion might take a pause if it was suddenly turned on by a little psycho gazelle."

Cal realized he was grinning. The thought of the tiny Eddy getting the better of some giant thug was pretty amusing. He kind of wished he'd seen it.

"We were damn lucky that those bouncers were nearby too," Toker continued, seeming eager to get his point across. "The guy's mates would've flattened us otherwise. This one punch," he jabbed a finger at his black eye, "could've turned out to be fifty. On top of that, any one of them could've been shoved in this cell with us. Did you think about that? Damn lucky, I tell you, don't you reckon, Cal? Jumper?" Toker looked up at them, nodding as if it was already unanimously agreed. Then his nod slowed, and his line of sight drifted past them. Something had caused his already low expression to fall quite a bit further.

Cal had a strong hunch of what that something could be. In his experience, the powers that be—or whatever mysterious forces guided the sequences and events of life—had the uncanny ability of throwing things back in your face often instantly. Following Toker's line of sight, he turned towards the cell door and saw a huge man on the other side of it. The man's height was so great, it was necessary for him to bow his head before lumbering under the door frame. He even dwarfed the hulking bouncer, who was roughly attempting to guide him inside. The giant man raised his head to reveal a particularly aggressive pair of eyes, beneath which was a large, blood-soaked bandage haphazardly stretched over a recently broken nose.

"Bugger it to hell," Toker mumbled.

Those aggressive eyes had only scanned the room once before resting in Toker and Eddy's direction.

Bending around the man's hulking form, the bouncer was now peering into the cell. "You'll be pleased to see that your friend here has regained consciousness," he said, directing an amused grin at Toker and Eddy. "I've decided to grant him his wish to be reunited with you kids, that way you can get to finishing up your business." Before the heavy cell door was slammed shut, Cal spied a silver credit protruding from the bouncer's meaty fist, undoubtedly a bribe from the mean-eyed brute.

Cal regarded the big man. He suspected that any pain caused by the broken nose paled into insignificance next to the crushing blow to the man's reputation. He'd suffered the ultimate humiliation in front of his friends and all at the flying fist of one petite girl. Unfortunately, the man looked dangerously sober and wickedly pissed off.

"That nose was your handiwork, Eddy?" Cal asked, not taking his eyes off the man.

"Yep," came the girl's nonchalant reply.

"Quite an achievement. I'm impressed."

Remaining at the closed door, the new arrival raised one of his long arms and extended a thick finger towards Toker and Eddy. "Unfinished business," he grunted in a deep voice that sounded unused to forming words.

"Round two, eh, fat head?" Eddy snarled before leaping off the bench and bolting towards the man. Fortunately for Eddy—or possibly the man, Cal couldn't be sure—Jumper was as quick as ever and hooked an arm around the girl's waist, holding her at bay. The brute remained at the doorway and stared menacingly but also with a hint of astonishment as the pint-sized girl struggled in Jumper's arms.

Cal stepped forward and blocked the man's line of sight. "I don't know the full story here," he said calmly, "but it seems you received a punch, and my friend Toker here received a punch. That sounds about even to me."

"Ain't nuffin even, an' it ain't none of your business." As the big man spoke, the almost comical sight of the bobbing nose bandage did nothing to detract from the aggressiveness in his eyes.

"He's right, Cal," Toker blurted. Hopping off the bench, he shuffled around Jumper and the still-struggling Eddy and came to stand by Cal's side. "You're right, big guy, it's not my friend Cal's business, and it wasn't my friend Eddy's business to step in and throw punches either. It was just an accidental beer spillage though, right? I didn't get a chance to apologize for that before the fighting started. She...my friend Eddy, that is...she was just trying to stick up for me, you see..."

The big man clenched his massive fist, causing his knuckles to crack.

"Okay, I admit it," Toker continued. "She's a little misguided in her methods, but come on, man... I'm sure an honourable bloke like you would've done the same for one of your pals, am I right?" Toker offered one of his best, pacifying, white-toothed grins but only got some sort of animalistic snarl in reply. "Come on, violence isn't gonna get us anywhere, is it, eh?"

The man snarled again.

"So, we call it quits, yeah?"

Snarl.

Putting away his white teeth, Toker sighed. Cal thought he may have even detected an uncharacteristic twinge of anger in his young friend.

"Dude, look at yourself," Toker continued in a somewhat harsher tone. "I mean, check out this situation. What's violence gotten us so far, eh? I'll tell you what it's gotten us: one black eye for me and one broken nose for you. Not to mention your total humiliation getting knocked out by a little girl in front of your mates."

Cal raised an eyebrow. It seemed his young friend had reached his apologetic limit and decided the man wasn't worth any more of his kind words. The response was pretty swift. A look of rage morphed onto the man's brutish face, and with a deep grunt, he took two surprisingly fast bounds forward and swung his great fist like an axe, Toker's head being the log.

Having briefly turned to see Eddy's reaction to his clever jibes, Toker didn't register the fist until it was mere inches from his nose. Thankfully, it was at that point that Cal managed to pluck it from its plotted course and, in one smooth motion, redirect the brute's arm until it reached an unnatural angle behind his wide slab of a back. There was a loud crack accompanied by a bellow of pain. Keeping the arm twisted, Cal used the big man's momentum to spin him towards the cell's heavy door then gave him a shove with his palms followed by a forceful boot to his backside.

The stumbling giant did his best to protect his face with the one hand that wasn't tangled up behind his back. Unfortunately for him, his best wasn't good enough. The sound of his forehead connecting with the solid, steel door was loud enough to stir even the most inebriated of the cell's occupants.

Much to Cal's disbelief, the big man didn't go down. Instead, he somehow managed to turn himself around—skittering slightly on the sick-slick floor as he did so—and stare with pure hatred in Cal's direction.

Shit. Cal stared right back at him, doing his best to hide his surprise that the man wasn't already unconscious on the floor. "I'd prefer you didn't try to punch my friend."

The man scowled, causing a few beads of blood to emerge on the angry red mark that had appeared on his forehead and trickle down into his nose bandage.

"That was one seriously kick ass move," Toker whispered over Cal's shoulder. "But I think you've just gone and made him all sorts of crazy."

"Uh huh, thanks for pointing that out," Cal replied, glimpsing back briefly. "You think I should apologize?"

"I'm not sure that would work."

"No shit. You better back up."

Toker barely had time to heed Cal's advice before the big brute charged forward. Cal noted, with some relief, that there was some lasting damage to the man's right arm, which now flapped pathetically at his side. Unfortunately, the left arm was still very much intact and was stretched forward, a huge clawed hand on its end eager for something to crush. Cal didn't let the hand get near enough. The power of his perfectly-timed front kick combined with the lumbering oaf's considerable forward motion caused the big man to double up instantly, the foot in his gut causing a torrent of beer-infused breath to whoosh from his gaping mouth.

Still bent double, the man stumbled sideways, desperately trying to refill his lungs. Cal's mouth twitched a smile as the stumbling man tripped on the prone form of an unconscious drunk and fell heavily into said drunk's far-reaching excretions.

"Cal, that was awesome!" Eddy squealed, having finally stopped squirming in Jumper's grasp.

"Beautiful," Toker agreed, shaking his head in awe. "Brutal, but beautiful."

"Thanks," Cal replied without turning from his opponent. "You wanna take a turn?" Already, the big man had regained control of his lungs and was successfully, albeit clumsily, getting to his feet. With the help of a nearby bench, he heaved his great bulk upright and stood on remarkably steady legs. Cal sighed. The guy seemed freakishly robust, possibly the sort who could withstand this sort of battering all night—a body well used to high levels of abuse.

He came at Cal yet again, carefully this time, looming closer with slow, steady strides while clenching and un-clenching his big left fist. The beating had simmered the man's rage, and Cal wasn't overly keen on his newfound caution. People made fewer mistakes when they were cautious.

"You're not much of a fighter, are you, big fella?" Cal said, attempting to rekindle a bit of that previous rage. "I guess size really doesn't matter after all."

The man remained silent, but Cal took encouragement from the scowl that re-emerged on the man's face, which squeezed another trickle of blood from his wounded forehead.

"I fear this is a bit of a mismatch. Perhaps I should rouse one of those drunks for you to tussle with, eh?"

Another bead of blood trickled from the wounded forehead.

"I would have suggested putting you up against my little friend Eddy here, but I guess she's already put you on the floor once today...and only one punch too, as I hear it."

Another trickle.

"I feel for you, big fella, I really do. Being knocked out by such a delicate young thing must've caused quite a crack in the ego not to mention your reputation."

Trickle.

"Still, it's not all bad. At least your mates got a good laugh out of it, eh? Probably be talking about it for years."

That about did it.

The big man roared and, launching himself forward, put every ounce of his considerable weight into a wild hay-maker of a punch. Whistling harmlessly over Cal's ducked head, the punch only served to throw the man hopelessly off balance. Taking full advantage, Cal moved swiftly forward, slamming his elbow into exposed ribs and causing a satisfactory *crack*. The big brute howled part in pain, part in frustration. Cal slid under another punch, this one backhanded and slow. Popping up behind the disorientated man, he issued two strikes to his kidneys. There'd be no backing down now. The guy was an angry bull, the sort who wouldn't relent until he was, quite literally, incapable of doing so.

As he dodged and swerved the continued attacks, Cal suddenly felt a pang of anxiety as pain flared in his own back. That bloody injury again. Would he ever be free of it? Losing his focus for just a moment, he suddenly found himself only narrowly avoiding another wild haymaker. *Shit, keep it together.* He was under no illusions as to what would happen if even one of those punches made contact. Similarly, if his back went, the giant would have no trouble making mincemeat of him. He'd have to finish this quick, but the man's great height was proving problematic.

In a moment of inspiration, Cal thrust his booted foot into the back of the man's tree trunk of a leg and managed to bring him to his knees. He then proceeded to wrap his right arm around the brute's thick neck while carefully avoiding the massive left hand, which was clawing desperately at the air. Leaning forward, he braced the man's head with his other arm and applied all the pressure necessary and no more. Soon, the giant's clawing hand became a flailing hand and shortly after that a limp hand.

Finally, the big bastard lost consciousness.

"I've never seen such an ass kicking," Toker blurted, staring at Cal with a ridiculously wide grin. Eddy's grin was equally ridiculous and seemed to be disabling her speech.

Cal let the sleeping thug flop to the ground, showing him far more kindness than was deserved by ensuring his head bounced off his boot instead of the hard floor.

"Well done, Cal," Jumper said simply.

Could have turned out very differently, Cal thought as he rubbed at his burning back. He looked down at the thug and shrugged. "I thought the bastard would never go down."

Before anything else could be said, the cell door slid open again. The sound almost caused Cal to wince; the way things were going, if it wasn't the friends of the unconscious giant, then he half expected

Viktor and Melinda to be led in. He was relieved to see it was neither. Instead, a thin, smartly suited man glided partway into the room. Cal knew immediately by his immaculate appearance and the respectful distance that the bouncers were keeping that he wasn't a new cell mate.

In an almost machine-like way, the thin man scanned the room and quickly fixed his gaze on Cal. Carefully stepping over numerous puddles of excrement, he approached without paying the least bit of attention to the unconscious brute at Cal's feet. "I understand you're the captain of the large cargo ship…" The thin man whipped a pic-slip out of his suit pocket and studied it. "Named '*The Big Blue*.'"

"Abandon the *the,* and you'd be correct," Cal replied coolly.

"Good. I'm Randall Meeks." The man shot out a hand at Cal. Cal silently shook it.

"My sincere apologies for the conditions of this waiting room. I can guarantee you won't have to wait amongst this filth a moment longer."

Cal found Randall Meeks' words polite enough, but his expression was that of boredom and indifference.

"Please follow me."

"May I ask what this is concerning?" Cal asked as Meeks began to negotiate a sick-free route back to the door.

The thin man paused and turned back. "Of course," he said with obvious irritation. "Mr. Hogmeyer, the man we have to thank for this wonderful city, wishes to meet with you."

This time, there was sarcasm. Cal suspected that Meeks had about as much love for this city, and the man responsible for it, as he did for the puddles of sick he was so desperately trying to avoid. Meeks continued on towards the exit and, upon reaching it, turned once again to see that Cal had no intention of following. With a sigh, he elaborated, "Mr. Hogmeyer has, shall we say, a certain *admiration* for your ship."

Cal nodded. "Well, that's wonderful. I'd love to come and natter all about cargo ships with Mr Hogmeyer," he replied. "Unfortunately, I couldn't possibly accompany you without my crew," he said, indicating Jumper, Eddy, and Toker.

The man smoothed his jet black hair with a thin, pale hand. "Very well, bring them along."

"Two others are still enjoying the pleasures of the Lucky Deuce."

Meeks shot Cal a thin smile. "Granger," he barked. The big, bald bouncer who had herded Cal and Jumper to the cell looked up. "You know who these other two crew members are?"

"Sure do. That's my job," Granger replied with a shrug. "A hot blonde and some scrawny kid."

"Well, go and fetch them, idiot, and don't dilly dally."

The bouncer grunted and headed for the door.

"Hey, Granger," Cal called out as he stepped over the drooling head at his feet. "Careful not to touch the scrawny kid; the hot blonde is a little…over protective."

Granger snorted a laugh as he departed the room. Cal sighed as he watched him go. The next time he saw the bouncer, he was fairly certain that at least one part of his body would be smashed, snapped, or severely dislocated, maybe all three, at the hands of a certain hot blonde.

Chapter Sixteen
HOGMEYER

Cal and the rest of the gang soon found themselves in the back of a wide, black hover car. Meeks looked decidedly uncomfortable as he sat facing them. The car was travelling at great speed down one of the many exterior roads that snaked around the metallic peaks and troughs of the vast, jagged city. The particular road on which they travelled was a good ten lanes wide—lanes that were rarely being adhered to by the multitude of other vehicles hurtling along around them. From tiny, one-man racing pods to huge, missile-shaped tankers, no matter their size, they all weaved and dodged at dizzying speeds. Above them, hovering billboards, similar to the one that had guided *Big Blue* to Lucky Deuces' docking port, buzzed through the mass of structures like giant, flying pic-slips. They were advertising everything from holographic enhancement bras to pleasure pod sustenance pills guaranteeing two extra days of uninterrupted pleasure or your credits back.

Cal was paying little attention to the scenery; his mind was too consumed by the news of the apparent Carcarrion involvement in Earth's destruction. The information Captain Rail had supplied them couldn't possibly be true. During the centuries of deep space exploration, humans had discovered many life forms, of which the

137

Carcarrions were undoubtedly among the most advanced. This, however, was not saying a great deal. Most of the alien races discovered thus far held little more intelligence than the average four-legged pet. Even being at the top of that pile, the Carcarrions were still residing in caves and crafting crude tools and weapons from soft metals. To place them at the controls of an interstellar space vessel was ludicrous.

The Carcarrions didn't even qualify for the bottom rung of the military's threat ladder, a ladder that really only consisted of human rebels and pirates. Cal remembered having had a good laugh with one of his sergeants when they'd been informed of the Carcarrions' lack of threat rating. They'd mused over what that particular rating would have been had a fully grown Carcarrion been towering over the military adviser's desk at the time of assessment.

Cal still clearly remembered his first time seeing a live Carcarrion. It had been during a brief stopover at Delta Point 3, one of the military's major alien research bases. Cal's encounter, although brief, had made quite an impression. It had been an adult female of average size seen through a hefty sheet of protective smart-glass. He'd been quite taken aback. It hadn't so much been the stature of the alien that had made it so striking; it was, after all, more or less human in shape and size, albeit a very tall, particularly well-muscled human. It was more the appearance of the creature's strange skin—if it could be considered skin at all—that had taken his breath away. Until the alien had moved, Cal had thought he'd been looking at a statue, a figure flawlessly carved from jet black rock. It had such a solid appearance that he'd been surprised it could move at all. When it finally had moved, however, it was fluid, even graceful.

Equally striking had been the Carcarrion's, feline-like facial features. It had a flat, triangular nose that met a wide, lipless mouth, through which gleaming white fangs could be seen. The fangs had offered a stark contrast against the jet black skin but not half as much as its pale, silvery eyes. The hands had also been of note with three thick fingers and a thumb, each ending in a lethal point. More like powerful talons than fingers.

Pound for pound, Cal had thought the creature the most formidable he'd ever laid his eyes upon. He shuddered at the possibility that such a physically lethal alien had somehow adopted a level of intelligence to match. If such a thing were true, it would be ill news indeed. Particularly as they seemed hell-bent on destruction. Still, Cal allowed himself some hope that the reports and word of mouth had somehow become distorted, resulting in some serious misinformation.

As the car continued on, Cal became vaguely aware that Viktor was shooting questions about the construction of the city at Meeks. Rather than listening to the thin man's reluctant, monotone answers, he decided to take his mind from the Carcarrion mystery by staring out at the strange sights whizzing by. The car was moving faster than any non-flying vehicle he'd ever been in. The fact that the magnetic force of the road was the only thing preventing them from spinning off into space was a little disconcerting. Occasionally, the road would intertwine dangerously close to trains and exterior tube lifts, so close in fact that Cal could see the faces of the smartly suited hordes inside. The expressions ranged from bored to miserable. In fact, he was having trouble spotting one smile.

"So, this is the financial district of the middle class sector..." Meeks droned on.

"I don't get it," Viktor interrupted. "Why can't everyone just live together? How come you've divided the city up?"

"Because, young man, not everyone is created equal. We can't very well have the scum mingling with the upper class, or even the middle class for that matter. It simply wouldn't do."

"But who decides who's scum?" Viktor pushed.

Meeks sighed and rubbed his forehead. Cal had a feeling Viktor was annoying the man on purpose; he'd taken an instant dislike to him when he'd suggested putting Melinda in restraints after the bouncer, Granger, had been carted off to the Lucky Deuce medical wing. Cal didn't like to think what would have become of the poor soul given the job of trying to apply the restraints to the tall blonde. Fortunately, he had managed to persuade Meeks that Melinda was simply a shy girl who, after growing up on a fringe space colony, was understandably a little jumpy and uncommunicative. He'd gone on to explain that she'd probably just struck a lucky punch, and Granger had most likely dislocated his arm and broken his ankle as a result of the fall. Cal didn't believe for a second that Meeks had fallen for his spiel, but fortunately, he'd seemed too tired to argue the point.

"Whoever it was obviously thought we were scum," Toker added. "That Lucky Deuce place definitely wasn't upper class."

"Well I reckon they realised their mistake," Eddy chimed in. "That's why we're in this tarted-up car. Right, fancy pants?"

Meeks understandably flinched as the girl leaned forward and slapped him hard on the thigh.

"Something like that," Meeks mumbled in reply while brushing his trouser leg with a spotlessly white hanky.

Cal continued to stare out of the window, smiling a little as he listened to his friends taunt the man. The journey was proving a bit of a blessing. The car was a smooth ride, and the comfortable seats gave his aching back some much-needed support. The pain that was ignited during the fight was rapidly dispersing, but that fact did little to encourage him. Was this the way it would always be from now on, crippling pain whenever he did anything too strenuous? He'd always been blessed with good physicality, something he'd taken for granted until it began to fail him. Cal had never been one to dwell on problems over which he had no control, but he had to admit, this problem was starting to get to him in a big way. Rubbing the back of his head, he refocused his attentions on the sights through the window.

It wasn't long before they arrived at what Cal guessed to be a checkpoint for the upper class sector. As they slowed to pass through it, some construction work in the distance caught his eye, in particular a large ship maybe a third of the size of *Big Blue*. It had been upended and attached, skyscraper-like, to a mass of at least three melded freight ships. As the car once again reached its full, dizzying speed and swooped closer to the construction, huge, mechanical work spiders came into view. They were crawling up the side of the upended ship, busily spray painting over the word *Queen*. Cal had little doubt that he was looking at what was once Captain Nick Rail's ship, *The Swan Queen*. The sight was a harsh reminder that he'd have to stay sharp. Fellow humans or not, losing their ship and becoming stranded on this floating monstrosity of a city was the last thing they needed.

Eventually, the car slowed again. Veering off the main thoroughfare, it slipped onto a single-lane track that was free of other vehicles. Moving at what now seemed a snail's pace, the car passed under a grotesquely lavish golden arch. Cal felt the familiar electric buzz of a halo scanner pass through the vehicle. Although the halo scanners supposedly caused no harm, Cal never liked being subjected to them. Anything that made the hairs on your arms dance about in such a weird fashion surely couldn't be good for the body.

Tall, pristine trees, brilliant green against the blackness of space—and obviously fake due to the lack of atmosphere—were neatly lining the track. The sight of the trees surprised Cal. They seemed so out of place in a city that had so far ranged from tacky to garish with not a hint of taste or beauty in between. Impressed by their realism, he leaned closer to the window to get a better look at the lush foliage and the elegant, twinkling lights buried within. Closer inspection, however, revealed that the pretty lights weren't the only things buried within. Protruding from every tree were the unmistakable hexagonal rims of Jago cannon blasters. Considering the amount of trees they had already passed, Cal estimated a heavy artillery nearing that of a midsize military attack ship. This man, Hogmeyer, was either incredibly unpopular or seriously paranoid, quite possibly both.

Many more trees later, the track came to an abrupt end. Two hefty blast doors slid open, allowing the car to slip in between. Leaving behind the starry vista of deep space, the vehicle entered a featureless, box-like room. Cal heard a subtle hum and a series of thumps, which he guessed was the artificial gravity activating. The box-like room opened up to reveal a third and final door, this one crafted from glass embedded with elaborate swirls of gold. The look of relief on Meeks' gray face as the car passed through the glass doors and came to a halt rekindled Cal's grin.

Cal stepped out of the vehicle into a space so large it almost felt as though they were still outside. The area was contained by shimmering walls of white marble that soared as high as cliffs and were lined with giant, round pillars that looked fit to support the heavens. At the top of these pillars, an immense ceiling made from glass and supported by thick, golden struts arched its way across the vast space. Through that glass, the blackness of space offered a stark contrast to the bright interior.

In the distance, an ever-increasing line of sleek hover vehicles were coming to a stop outside a series of golden archways. Uniformed drivers were busily opening doors, allowing richly garbed men and women to spill out onto long, crimson carpets. Even from this distance, it was obvious the men and women were ludicrously wealthy. But what was wealth now? Surely, it relied on the Federation banking system, a system reliant on long-range communications. Possibly, the Federation could eventually recover from this disaster. After all, Earth had been the hub, but it hadn't been the be all and end all; there were hundreds of large, well-established colonies. But what if the rumors of the military were correct? And what if they couldn't re-establish communications? What then?

"This way." Meeks was irritably waving aside two heavily armed guards to indicate a small entranceway in the marble wall before them.

"Taking us through the back entrance, Meeks," Cal commented, nodding towards the rich guests in the distance. Meeks simply sniffed in reply and led the way through the door with his freakishly precise steps.

Once inside, the little man did his best to herd them along a spotless corridor. By the time they neared its end, however, his attempts had begun to fail. Eddy and Toker had broken away, becoming distracted by a wide glass panel that ran the length of the corridor.

"Check this out, Cal. You ever see such a big bunch of rich stinkers in one room?" Eddy asked, her grubby forehead pressed against the window.

Cal walked over and took a peek. Far below, he could see a swarming mass of lavishly dressed men and women—more of the same he'd seen streaming through the golden arches a few minutes earlier. "Not sure I have."

True to the city's form so far, the area below was huge, more a grand hall than a room. The walls and floor were crafted from the same gleaming white marble that Cal had seen earlier complete with the golden swirls of the glass doors. The people were swooning around a myriad of gambling tables and drinks bars, all of which were constructed in gold. In fact, practically everything non-living was either made from gold, marble, or glass, including the tentacle-like tube lifts, which spiralled up to countless pleasure pods adorning the high ceiling. In essence, the hall was the absolute antithesis of the Lucky Deuce.

"No amount of money can buy good taste, I guess," Jumper muttered in Cal's ear as he peered over his shoulder.

Cal smiled without taking his eyes from the view. Weirdly, he found himself feeling sorry for all those people. All those privileged lives, which, in all likelihood, would soon be flipped upside down. They all seemed to be doing a good job at turning a blind eye to the situation. The chaos hadn't reached them yet, but it would. And if it continued, power would then revert back to the fittest and the strongest and probably the most aggressive.

Next to him, Eddy peeled her head off the window and proceeded to bang her bony fist against the glass while flashing a grin at the unaware—or possibly uninterested—crowds below. "Finally got us to the right class level, eh Meeky," she said without bothering to turn to see if the man was even listening.

"Yeah, thanks for the upgrade," Toker added. "Now don't you go punching anyone around here, little chick," he said, jabbing a finger at Eddy.

"You're the only one I'll be punching anytime soon."

Toker chuckled. "Hey, you might want to consider keeping this one under lock and key, Meeks, my man," he shouted over his shoulder.

Cal turned to look at Meeks. The little man was standing at an open door at the end of the corridor, his expression as bleak as ever. "This way," he said in a tone that suggested more words were simply too much effort.

Cal indicated the door. "Shall we?" he said, knowing full well that the rest of them were unlikely to obey a man like Meeks.

The room they entered was, for once, not all that big. Almost immediately, Cal recognized it as the interior of a small ship. The consoles had all been removed, but the room's overall shape, coupled with the large, cockpit-shaped window to his right, left him in little doubt. The window had the subtle tell-tale sheen of smart-glass, and through it, he could see the same lavish gambling hall they'd seen from the corridor. There was a vast, polished desk in the center of the room. On the other side, a tall man was busily heaving his bulk out of a spring-backed leather chair.

"Welcome. Glad you could make it," the man said in a deep, overly jolly voice. Reaching over the desk, he held out a sweaty hand laden with gold rings. "Captain Harper, I presume."

Cal gave the man a firm handshake and a silent nod.

"Aaron Hogmeyer. Welcome to my city," the big man said, seemingly unperturbed by Cal's silence. He then proceeded to turn his wide, yellow-toothed grin to each of the gang in turn. "Welcome, welcome," he continued, stepping partway around the desk to grab Viktor's reluctant hand and give it a rough shake. Lastly, his eyes fell admiringly on Melinda's face and shortly after, her ample bosom. The big man's smile faltered slightly as he made an unsuccessful attempt at raising Melinda's hand. Looking a little confused, he aborted the attempt, his seemingly naturally ruddy complexion turning a shade darker. "That's quite an arm you've got there, missy," he mumbled as he shuffled back behind his desk.

"This is an unusual office, Hogmeyer," Cal said, deciding it best to draw the attention away from Melinda.

"That it is, Captain—"

"Call me Cal."

Hogmeyer nodded. "Well, believe it or not, Cal, this office used to be the interior of a ship. The Golden Nugget, I called it. A great ship it was too: a Corrin cruiser."

"A Corrin Type Three if I'm not mistaken," Cal replied. "A rare but admired ship."

"I'm impressed," Hogmeyer said, genuinely seeming so. "You must—"

"There's not much I don't know about ships," Cal interrupted.

The man's grin twitched.

Cal was pleased to see that the gang was embracing their naturally inquisitive natures and were spreading themselves about the office, an act that was clearly irritating their host. Jumper was standing motionless in the far corner while Toker and Eddy loitered before the huge window, giggling and pointing at something in the gambling hall far below. Meanwhile, Viktor was studying some technological device near the entrance door, Melinda close by his side.

Meeks, having never ventured far inside the room, was also standing by the door. Cal noticed the slightest hint of amusement in the man's sharp features, perhaps triggered by the increasing annoyance of his employer.

"On the subject of ships, that's quite a ship you have yourself—" Hogmeyer's voice faltered as something over Cal's shoulder distracted him. "Er, young lady, I'd appreciate it if you didn't press your mouth up against my viewing panel."

"Right you are, hog man," Eddy replied gruffly.

"Yeah, where's your respect, young lady?" Toker said with a snigger.

Eddy swung her combat booted foot at him, narrowly missing his crotch.

Cal did nothing to simmer the pair.

Hogmeyer cleared his throat and turned his eyes back to Cal, his smile now closer to a baring of teeth. "As I was saying, that's a fine ship you folks came in on—"

"You're right, it is a fine ship," Cal cut in. "It's done us proud during the recent troubles."

"Indeed, indeed. Terrible business," Hogmeyer replied with a shake of his balding head.

Cal briefly considered quizzing the man on the situation but, not wanting to reveal how out of the loop they were, quickly dismissed the idea.

Hogmeyer thrust his belly forward and stretched his lower back. "Some might say it's dangerous to be roaming with such troubles. And if you ask me, they'd be right. Especially if you're lumbering through space in a big old ship like yours. A ship that size could easily attract unwanted attention. My advice would be to settle somewhere…much safer."

"Others might say it's the settlers on their static planets and space stations who are facing the greatest risk," Cal said without hesitation. "If accounts are to be believed, I think we're much safer on the move."

"Well, everyone's entitled to their own opinion, I guess, even if it is completely misguided." Hogmeyer eased himself into the spring-backed chair. "Still, you have to admit, it's a big old ship for such a small crew."

"Not so," Cal replied. "Certainly not when you're a creative bunch like us. All that extra space comes in handy from time to time. We're even throwing around a few business ideas. Such a huge ship could become quite the big earner, isn't that right, J?"

In the corner of the office, Jumper cracked a grin and nodded. "Yes, we're really quite blessed."

"Maybe, maybe," Hogmeyer replied absently. He'd been

distracted again, this time by Viktor, who had wandered over to a small drinks bar at the back of the office and was tinkering with a strange-looking dispenser. "That's not for kids, sonny," the big man said, his face now completely devoid of a smile. He followed Viktor with hard eyes as the boy sniffed and meandered back towards the door. "Meeks, maybe you want to supervise the kid." He shot Meeks a look that promised pain if he didn't comply.

"So you agree?" Cal said.

"Agree? 'Bout what?" Hogmeyer mumbled, turning his attention back to Cal.

"Our ship. *Big Blue*. We were agreeing on what a fine and valuable vessel it is."

"*Valuable?* Not sure about valuable, certainly not to someone like me." Hogmeyer replied, scratching the bulbous flesh under his chin.

Cal laughed. "A huge cargo ship of no use to a man with a city almost entirely built from the things? Come now, Hogmeyer, let's not make fools of each other. If you found someone willing to part with such a ship, a businessman like you would be cracking open the credit safe without a second thought."

Hogmeyer returned the laugh. "Takes a lot for me to crack open the credit safe, Harper, that much I can tell you right away. Certainly not for an ugly hunk of cargo ship. Space stations, that's where my interests—"

Hogmeyer was distracted yet again. This time by a rapid thumping behind Cal's back. "Would you tell that damn brat of a girl to stop banging her fists against my window? She'll do some bloody damage." The big man slammed one of his meaty palms on the desk.

Cal grinned. "We have a somewhat relaxed chain of command, I'm afraid. Orders don't sit all that well with us," he replied, taking note of the man's short fuse that was attached to a rather explosive temper. He turned to look at Eddy. She seemed totally unperturbed by the man's sudden rage.

Also seemingly unbothered by the man's temper, Viktor strolled over to perch on the end of the huge desk. "I wouldn't worry," the boy said casually. "There's no way fists could get through that window. If I'm not mistaken, which I never am, that's T4 smart-glass. Even a ten-click pulse rifle would have trouble damaging that."

Hogmeyer peeled his eyes from Eddy to glare at Viktor instead. He opened his mouth but seemed unable to find a suitable reprimand. Before he could formulate his words, Viktor casually plucked a control wand, which had been lying idly on the desk, into his nimble fingers and began to study it.

Hogmeyer was up and leaning over the desk as fast as his long legs could manage under his bulk. "If you know what's good for you, boy, you'll hand that back immediately."

Cal took a step forward and braced himself, not to protect his young friend—he knew there was no need—but to try and prevent Melinda from doing some irreversible damage to their bad-tempered host should he attempt to lay a hand on the boy.

"An old model," Viktor sniffed, still quite unperturbed by the big man's new outburst. "You wanna upgrade, get yourself a Wizard Poker 3000, twice as many functions and a far superior range."

Hogmeyer looked in danger of bursting something vital. He was obviously unused to such lack of control over those around him. The longer the boy ignored his outstretched hand, the more the rage seemed to build. Eddy and Toker's continued giggling wasn't helping it any.

"Perhaps you ought to give our host his little stick back, Viktor," Cal suggested. "You wouldn't want to upset Melinda with all the commotion, would you?"

"Right you are, Cal. All I was saying was that the range on these things sucks." Viktor tossed the control wand back towards Hogmeyer.

Dropping well short of the big man's reach, the wand clattered awkwardly on the desk, and a green light sprang to life on its end. Instantly, the view through the office window disappeared and was replaced with a huge grid of multiple images. Each image contained a different view of the city, ranging from sweeping, action-filled shots of the bustling arenas where spikeball games and gladiator rumble ring tournaments were taking place to mundane, static views of vehicle parking sectors and hotel lobbies.

"Some interesting surveillance you have there, Hogmeyer," Cal remarked as he turned and scanned the grid. His eyes quickly came to rest on the rotating image of a docking hangar filled with numerous small to mid-size space cruisers. "And that's an impressive collection of ships in that hangar," he continued, indicating the square a third of the way up "I can even see a Star Splinter nestled in there." He turned to look at Hogmeyer, who was straining his bulky frame over the desk in a clumsy, somewhat desperate attempt to retrieve his control wand. "The new Harper 7 series if I'm not mistaken."

"And if *I'm* not mistaken," Toker added loudly, "that's a bunch of naked chicks."

"Where?" Viktor asked a little too eagerly.

"Right up there," Toker replied, stretching up on his tiptoes and jabbing a finger at a square halfway up the grid, which was filled from corner to corner with naked females glistening amid sauna steam. "Who's been a naughty boy then?" Toker continued, coming down off his tiptoes and turning his wide grin towards Hogmeyer.

The big man, having finally retrieved his control wand and fumbled it the right way up, wasted no time flicking away a good three or four of the images. "Purely security measures," he mumbled, the color of his face suggesting otherwise. With a twirl of his wand, he singled out the view of the hangar in question and enlarged it so it filled the entire window. "Yes, quite right, a brand new Star Splinter, Harper 7," he said in a swift, clumsy attempt to divert attention. Any trace of his previous rage seemed to have dwindled. "Only three of the Harper 7 series were made before Earth saw its end, and I own the best of the three. I splashed out on every upgrade on offer plus a few bespoke ones from the very best of designers."

Cal heard a snort from behind him, which he guessed was Viktor's response to the comment.

"How's about enlarging the one with the naked chicks?" Toker suggested, his tone half mocking, half hopeful.

Fingering his control wand, Hogmeyer did his best to ignore him.

Cal continued to look up at the screen. "Yes, not a bad ship. A craft like that would certainly ease the blow should we decide to part with a ship such as *Big Blue*." Cal didn't believe for a second that Hogmeyer would even consider such a trade. Even if he was a fair man, which Cal knew he wasn't, it would take at least four cargo ships to warrant such an exchange. The Star Splinter ships were the very best credits could buy, and this was a brand-new Harper 7.

As suspected, Hogmeyer reacted to the comment with an explosion of mirth. "Your ship for my Star Splinter Harper 7? A fair trade indeed, assuming your big, ugly hunk of metal is filled to the brim with Casgorian diamonds."

The big man's laugh eventually simmered to a humorless grin. "Just because you share a name with a thing, Captain Harper, doesn't necessarily make you worthy of it. I'd like to help you and your friends out, I really would, but I'm just not in the market for another big cargo ship."

Cal smiled at the man. "I hate to repeat myself, Hogmeyer, but believing that an enormous ship such Big Blue isn't of considerable value to a city like this, that's a tough one to swallow. You only have to look at those images of yours to see that this city's bursting at the seams. You don't strike me as the type to be turning potential custom away. Besides, I'm afraid your man here," Cal nodded towards Meeks, "has already let it slip that you're interested."

Hogmeyer shot a venomous look at Meeks. Surprisingly, the thin man seemed relatively unfazed.

Turning back to Cal, Hogmeyer drew himself up to his full, considerable height. "I can assure you that Meeks was mistaken. I simply invited you here because you're first timers to my city…simple manners. Besides, I prefer to know firsthand who's visiting and residing in my city." Hogmeyer planted his hands on his desk and leaned forward. "Now, Mr Harper, I too hate to repeat myself but, as I was saying before the commotion caused by your unruly crew, space stations are where my interests lie at this particular time. Unlike hulking cargo ships, they give the city a certain *finesse*. Too many cargo ships are cumbersome, ugly even, and to be quite honest, I'm already satisfied with the size of my city. I believe in quality, not quantity, a concept that you and your crew are perhaps not all that familiar with."

Having recognized the failure of his nice guy façade, Hogmeyer had now abolished it entirely. Unfortunately, in doing so, he seemed to have regained a good deal of his composure. But the words spilling from his flapping mouth didn't fool Cal for a second. A man who donned such a gross multitude of gold rings didn't know the meaning of too much or too big. From everything Cal had witnessed, he had little doubt that Hogmeyer was obsessed with excess. It was worthless beating around the bush with such a man.

"Space stations… Well, I'm afraid I can't help you there," Cal said with a shrug. "I don't think I know of anyone with a station.

Not one they're willing to part with, in any case. Thanks for the warm welcome, Hogmeyer, but seeing as we've got nothing to offer each other, my crew and I will be on our way." Cal turned and slapped Toker on the back. "Right then, gang, I think we've taken up enough of our host's time—"

"Now, now, let's not be hasty," Hogmeyer interjected. He smiled, but it was nothing more than a poor imitation. "A good-natured man such as myself could hardly allow his guests to up and leave his city in such troubled times as these. Certainly not without first offering an act of kindness."

Cal didn't miss the threat that simmered in the man's words. He suspected, however, that carrying out that threat would be a last resort to a man like Hogmeyer. The man was a scam artist. Violence and force took the skill and fun out of it.

"I suppose," Hogmeyer continued, "with the recent troubles in mind, your cumbersome ship could be made use of. A little extra space for those poor souls in need of safe harbor." Hogmeyer pondered for a moment or at least pretended to. "In exchange for your ship, I'll stretch to offering you some fine quarters, a safe home for each of you. Of course, for fit, young bucks such as yourselves, I'd make sure you were put in the heart of my city—the liveliest, most exciting areas."

Cal smiled and shook his head. "Well that's a very charitable offer, Hogmeyer. Unfortunately, we'll have to decline. I have a feeling that the areas of the city you're referring to are probably a little *too* lively, even for those as young and fit as us. Besides, as I said before, we're travellers at heart. Adventurers if you like. And we're rather fond of our ship. Staying in one spot for too long is not an option for us."

"Is that so?" Hogmeyer leaned back into his chair and drummed his long fingers on his chest. After a few moments, he continued.

"Well then, if I can't manage to convince you of the dangers of space travel in these dark times, how's about I offer you a faster, more *maneuverable* ship. At least give you a chance to outrun any trouble. It will of course be a much smaller ship than you're used to but far more suitable and easy to manage for a crew of your size."

This was what Cal was hoping for. However much he hated to admit it, the fat man was right; travelling in a ship as large and as slow as Big Blue was perilous even in times of peace. He still didn't trust him an inch, but at least the conversation was moving in the right direction.

"Again, a very generous offer," Cal said. "An offer that may well be of interest, especially seeing as you're clearly a man with an eye for quality. I don't believe you'd ever dream of offering a ship of *substandard* caliber."

Hogmeyer let out a throaty chuckle. "Despite being totally misguided, Harper, you're at least a good judge of character."

"Yes, I am. We would of course need to give the ship in question a thorough, physical inspection."

"You don't trust me?"

"I don't know you. And, if nothing else, we'll need to ensure the ship's suitability to our personal needs. I'm sure you understand."

Hogmeyer sniffed and pointed his control wand at the viewing panel. Sweeping the view of the Star Splinter ship aside, he zeroed in on its neighbor, a ship of similar size. "A Delta Pinpoint, series II…in excellent condition of course."

Cal turned to look at the image. The ship filling the screen did indeed look in good condition, nowhere near as sleek in appearance as the Star Splinter but still an impressive-looking craft.

"You realize I'm being particularly generous here, Harper. The Pinpoints are damn fast ships."

"I'm familiar with them," Cal replied, still studying the image.

"Nice," Toker said. "Reckon we could get away from anyone in that little monster."

'Hey,' Eddy blurted. "We don't run from no one."

Toker snorted. "Suppose with you on the crew, we won't have to; we'll just press your ugly mug up against the cockpit window. They'll abandon the chase in no time."

Cal continued to stare at the screen in silent thought. The offer was particularly generous. *Too* generous. The Delta Pinpoint was a basic ship—far from a Star Splinter in quality, but it was still a decent vessel: swift, reliable...in short, perfect.

"No messing around with credits," Hogmeyer said gruffly. "A handshake and a straight swap. I'll let you have your little inspection, and once my honesty and generosity has been proven, you can thank me and be on your way."

Cal looked over at Jumper. His old friend was staring at the screen looking just as troubled as he felt. The ship appeared intact, and Hogmeyer seemed confident in its condition. The offer of a straight swap was more than fair, but therein laid the problem: Every fiber of his being was telling him that this man was incapable of being fair. He turned to face Hogmeyer. "I'm in total agreement that there should be no messing around. But with that in mind, an *immediate* physical inspection would be preferable."

"Fine by me," Hogmeyer replied a little too quickly. "I'll even take time out of my busy schedule to give you and your little crew the tour myself. Meeks, contact officer Dalton down in the hangar 14. Inform him that I'll be down shortly to escort a crew around the Pinpoint, dock 32." Heaving himself out of his chair Hogmeyer shot Cal a smile that not even a loving mother would trust. "So let's go."

Chapter Seventeen
STURDY SHIP

Hangar 14 was gargantuan. A brightly lit dome of shiny metal and glass that housed a multitude of similarly shiny ships. Sitting neatly in docking bay 32, the Delta Pinpoint, like the rest of the ships, seemed tiny within the cavernous space. Cal sat alone at the base of the Pinpoint's loading ramp. So far, the vessel had proven to be in the excellent condition that Hogmeyer had promised: a simple, sturdy ship that would no doubt do him and the gang proud. Right now, however, he wasn't paying the adequate little ship any attention. Instead, he was staring thoughtfully at its neighbor.

The Star Splinter, Harper 7 gleamed almost supernaturally under the hangar's bright lights. Cal had always loved the Star Splinters. This Harper 7 was a brand new model, and he was pleased to see that the beautifully sleek design of its predecessors still remained. It was streamlined to the extreme, a silver hull shaped like a shard of glass, so seamless it could have been molded from liquid mercury. Even the huge Vortex engine thrusters, which protruded from the rear like the gaping maws of two giant, chrome fish, had a certain grace. The sight of the ship triggered a cascade of childhood memories.

"You're staring at the wrong ship, Cal." Toker came bounding down the Pinpoint's loading ramp, hopped off its side, and took a seat next to him. "Not that I blame you, bro. That Star Splinter's one hell of a looker."

Cal smiled. "She's a beauty."

"So they name a ship after you or what?"

Cal's smile turned to a grin. "Not quite."

"Just coincidence then, huh?"

"No…not quite."

"You're not gonna divulge, are you?"

"Maybe later."

Toker shook his head but grinned back all the same. "And speaking of not divulging, you still haven't told me how you got that posh English accent. I always thought my family was rich, but your folks must've been filthy rich for you to grow up in old England."

"Actually, I never knew my parents, and I was brought up about as far from old England as you can get."

"Oh yeah?"

"Yep. Remind me to tell you about it sometime," Cal said, giving his young friend the usual slap on the back. "For now though, I'm going to need your expert opinion on all things fast. This hunk of metal we're sitting under will likely be our new home and transport soon." Cal stood up and, before Toker had a chance to dig any deeper, he strode off towards the Pinpoint's rear thrusters.

"Dude…you're so damn mysterious," Toker shouted. He then hurried after him.

The Delta Pinpoint was similar in size to the Star Splinter. That, however, was where the similarities ended. Its hull was copper colored and, despite being smooth and structurally sound, had an unfortunate rusty appearance. The design was straightforward, and its construction was cheap but solid. When it came down to it, the Delta Pinpoint was an economic ship for those who needed speed. That speed came from its deep space thruster: a P-blast 33. That was where the ship's value lay, and that was where Cal and the rest of the gang now stared. Far above them, the thruster protruded from the back of the ship like some sort of monstrous cannon.

"So those are the cruising thrusters?" Toker asked, pointing to the ten small thrusters that circled the main, cannon-like one.

"Exactly," Cal replied. "They're for economy. They're powered by a separate, less power-hungry engine."

Hearing loud footfalls, Cal brought his gaze down to see Hogmeyer coming out of the ship, the loading ramp bending in protest with each step.

"What do you think of those cannons, eh, girly?" the big man asked, his tone almost cheery as he strode over to join them. He seemed to be making another attempt at his nice guy façade although this time, it was decidedly half-arsed.

"Not bad I 'spose," Eddy replied, not bothering to look where Hogmeyer was directing his long, gold-ringed finger. "Reckon this big fat one stickin' out the back could dish out some destruction."

"I'm afraid that's not a cannon, Eddy," Cal informed her, "it's the main thruster, used for deep space travel."

"There, girl...*look*," Hogmeyer said, attempting to point more accurately at two neat little cannons mounted high on the side of the ship. "Those babies'll punch a hole through near anything."

Eddy squinted and wrinkled her nose. "Ya reckon? I don't reckon."

Hogmeyer rubbed what little hair he still had left on the back of his head and eyed the girl in annoyance. "They'd look pretty damn big if I got your blinkin' nose up real good 'un close to the barrels," he growled quietly.

"How loud are they?" Eddy asked, oblivious to the man's annoyance.

Hogmeyer sneered but managed to hold his temper at bay. "Bloody loud. How's about this then?" He dug a small device out of the back pocket of his tight jeans. Pointing the device theatrically at the ship, the big man proceeded to press a button that caused the ship to all but disappear before their eyes. If you studied the space very carefully, a transparent, jelly-like impression could be seen, but it was far from obvious. "State of the art cloaking device. Your enemies won't see a thing."

"That ain't so good," Eddy scoffed, unimpressed. "It's old. I've seen kiddie toys that can do that disappearin' stuff."

Giving up on the girl, Hogmeyer turned stiffly towards Cal. "Harper, I'll give you three more minutes. Then, I want an answer." Red-faced, he turned and strode off toward Meeks. The little accountant had remained at a distance during the inspection as if allergic to the whole affair.

"What do you think, Cal?" Jumper asked once Hogmeyer was out of earshot.

"I think that short of a long-distance test flight, we've inspected the ship as thoroughly as time and equipment will allow," Cal replied, looking up again at the pinpoint. "Something's not right with this ship, that much I know, but I'm damned if I can spot the scam." He shook his head. "I tell you, Jumper, I don't trust this fat man any further than I can throw him."

"Maybe we should get Melinda to throw him?" Jumper suggested. "That might get us some answers."

'Tempting, but he's damned careful, or possibly paranoid. There're guards everywhere. Even with Melinda backing us up, we're seriously outnumbered on this one."

"Aren't we always?" Jumper said.

"Fair point."

A moment later, Viktor sauntered over and joined them. The boy looked a touch aggravated. "I've done a diagnostic on the ship's systems, Cal, just like you asked. Everything looks good, but to be honest, it wouldn't be difficult for someone to jiggle around with the ship's computer, especially a cheap one like this. Could take me quite a while to dig deeper."

"Thanks, Viktor, I—"

"Er, sorry to interrupt," Jumper said, sounding puzzled. "But is everything okay with Melinda? I hate to be rude, but she's looking a little...*flat*."

Cal and Viktor turned in unison to look at Melinda. At first glance, the synthetic looked her usual self, standing a few paces away, her expression serene. Then Cal realized that her luscious blonde locks—usually so full of technologically enhanced bounce—were hanging limply off her head and down over her square shoulders like thin, damp curtains.

"Wha... That's weird," Viktor mumbled with a frown. "Better take a look."

Cal watched as the boy went over to inspect her, confident that whatever the problem, Viktor would have it fixed in no time.

Jumper put a hand on Cal's shoulder. "I guess our three minutes are up," he said, nodding to his left.

Hogmeyer was striding back towards them, a hard look on his face that suggested negotiations were well and truly over. "That's time enough, Harper," he barked, coming to stand next to them. "I think my honesty and generosity has already been proven enough. So are you ready to honor our agreement and thank me?"

Cal looked the big man in the eye for a few moments then turned his back on him to face the rest of the gang. "What are your thoughts?" he asked, looking at each of them in turn. "Would you all be happy leaving here on this ship?"

Eddy stood up from the box crate she was slumped on. "Cannons are a little weedy, but at least it's got some. Reckon they could be good for a laugh, so yeah, it's all good with me, Cal."

"I'm in too, Cal," Toker added. "This hunk 'o junk certainly isn't as pretty as I'd like, but I gotta admit that I've got a soft spot for that bloody great engine thruster."

Cal nodded. "Viktor, what's your vote?"

The boy was perched on the back of Eddy's crate box, busily rummaging his fingers through Melinda's limp hair like a monkey hunting for ticks. "Whatever you say, Cal," he replied distractedly.

Cal looked to his old friend. "And you, Jumper?"

Jumper took one last look up at the ship. "I guess I'm in agreement," he said with an air of reluctance. "At least it'll be good to have a bit of speed to get us away from this place."

Cal nodded and turned back to Hogmeyer. "We'll need decent-sized transport to move our belongings between ships and of course access to the hangar tonight and tomorrow to get it done. We'd prefer to load it personally. You understand."

At that, a smile appeared on Hogmeyer's face. "That can be arranged. Officer Dalton, my head of hangar security, will make sure such things are provided."

"Then I believe we have a deal."

The big man's smile spread into a fully-fledged, yellow-toothed grin. "Of course we have a deal. You're a half smart man, Harper, and only a fool would turn down such a generous offer." At that, he held out his right hand to reveal a long gold chain. On the end was a hefty, oversized golden die. "And while we're on the subject of my generosity, I always like to close a deal with a gift. It's an Aaron Hogmeyer lucky gold die, my gift to you and your crew."

"Nice." Eddy snatched it out of the big man's outstretched hand.

Hogmeyer laughed with seemingly genuine humor. "Something to remember me by, girly. Tie it up in the cockpit of your lovely new ship, an' it'll bring you guaranteed luck on your travels."

"Dunno about that," Eddy replied, swinging the gold die wildly and almost planting it in Hogmeyer's face in the process.

"Charming little thing, isn't she?" Hogmeyer mumbled, taking a couple of steps back and chuckling softly. Cal didn't like the man's sudden good humor now that the deal was closed. It only acted as further proof that the deal was rotten.

"Well, that's enough charity work for one day." The big man looked over at Meeks, who was watching the proceedings without an ounce of interest. "Meeks will introduce you to Officer Dalton so you can sort out your needs."

Cal nodded.

Hogmeyer went to stride off then paused and turned back. "Oh, and Harper. I of course won't be letting you leave without a personal send off. Once Dalton has approved your departure, rest assured, I'll be here to see you gone."

Again, the threat wasn't lost on Cal. The guy was really starting to piss him off, his yellow-toothed grin looking more like a target by the second. But aggression wasn't going to help them at this point. He needed time to think. Something was sickly about this deal. Unfortunately, there was only a day and night for a diagnosis and remedy.

Chapter Eighteen
CON

Meeks pressed the shiny silver button and looked at the comm.

"Damn you and your bloody timing, Meeks."

Bored of explaining that he'd once again arrived at precisely the time instructed, Meeks wordlessly entered the office. Being careful not to block the big man's view through the smart-glass window, he set his little holo-cube on the edge of the huge, empty desk.

"Believe it or not, Meeks, I'm still not in the mood for your dull graphs."

"I see. In that case, may I ask how else you wish to use up my time?"

Hogmeyer sneered, but it was only half-hearted. "If you can manage to keep your bloody smart arse comments to yourself, I shall endeavor to explain to you the details of my latest piece of art."

Meeks smoothed back his hair. "By art, I assume you're referring to the scam involving Captain Harper and his motley crew? To be honest, I was under the impression that it hadn't gone all that well so far."

Hogmeyer twiddled his control wand and gave him a hard look. "That's because you don't have the skill set, Meeks. Your dullard, number-obsessed brain doesn't recognize the subtleties of my performance. It's truly unfortunate that the manipulations I utilize are utterly lost on you."

"Must be," Meeks replied, allowing his sarcasm free reign. He really wasn't in the mood for this today. *Civilized society's on the edge of oblivion, and the bastard is still obsessed with his little scams.* "It looked to me like Harper's companions just kept triggering that substantial temper of yours." Recognizing that very same temper surging again, Meeks quickly continued. "A reaction I completely understand, of course. I had to travel here all the way from the lower class with those brats of his… Close to unbearable."

Fortunately, the big man's temper simmered just as fast as it had risen.

"Yes, I must admit, those kids buzzing about made for a difficult crowd. And that dark man didn't move an inch the whole time. Seeing him staring at me out of the corner of my eye…would've been distracting to a lesser man."

"Not to mention the tall blonde," Meeks offered.

"Yes, her too. Certainly off-putting." Hogmeyer shook his head and sniffed loudly. "But that just goes further to proving my talents. Not only have I managed to acquire another huge cargo ship, but I've even saved some accommodation spots."

"Accommodation spots in the lower class slums," Meeks wasted no time in pointing out.

"It all adds up, Meeks," his boss replied testily. "And of course, there's the icing on the cake. That Pinpoint ship I'm sending them off in is almost worthless. Plus, it's set up to eradicate any potential mess."

"Mess? I'm not sure I follow." Meeks knew what was required of him. The words left his mouth with little thought, as if reciting from a script he'd read a thousand times before. "I'm no expert on the subject, but that ship looked half decent to me."

"Of course you don't follow, Meeks. And you're right, you're not a bloody expert—certainly not in anything outside of your dull numbers. Now, if you can manage to quit your interrupting, I'll try to spell it out in a way you might comprehend." Leaning back in his chair, Hogmeyer sniffed once again and continued. "I understand people, Meeks. I can see right through them, see how their minds work. When it came to my exchange with Harper, it rapidly occurred to me that the man is a troublemaker. And by troublemaker, I don't mean the sort who gets his backside slung up above a stage in the Lucky Deuce. No, what I'm referring to is the worst type of troublemaker, one with half a brain. One who can think." He pointed his control wand at Meeks. "Such a man isn't welcome in my city, Meeks. Not even in the Tin Slum jail."

Meeks tried to stifle a yawn. "So why not shoot him and be done with it?"

"Damn it, Meeks," Hogmeyer barked, sitting up and glaring at him. "We've been through this. Do I have to spell it out every bloody time? Any fool can have someone shot. There's no bloody skill in it."

Meeks nodded, and after a moment, the big man leaned back and continued. "Besides, the sad fact is that if you shoot enough people, word eventually gets around. With a city like mine, I can't afford a bad reputation. Especially when it comes to my more sophisticated clientele. Believe it or not, Meeks, rich people don't like to risk getting shot."

The way things are going, they won't be sophisticated much longer, Meeks thought, *and when that happens, they'll likely try and shoot someone themselves.* He gave the big man an automatic nod of agreement.

"I knew almost immediately that Harper wasn't going to take the bait on my accommodation offer," Hogmeyer continued, still twiddling his wand. "I drew the talk out however, played with him a little to give myself time to get a measure of the man. And that measure turned out to be that I didn't want his type anywhere near my city. But, of course, I couldn't let him leave with such beautiful, big, blue ship. That would be a crime to me *and* my city."

"Indeed."

"So, Meeks, how to dispose of such a man without attracting attention while simultaneously keeping hold of his ship?"

The big man was clearly enjoying the sound of his own voice. Meeks was enjoying it less so. "How indeed."

"The trick is to always have a plan B, a *backup plan* if you like, something that is already organized and ready to go. My pinpoint instantly came to mind. That ship that you so expertly analyzed as being half decent, Meeks, is actually half dead. It's been sitting down in docking bay 32 of my best hangar for a while now, nestled amongst my finest ships, just waiting for an opportunity to serve its purpose." Hogmeyer snatched up his control wand and, giving it a wave at the huge window, brought up an enlarged the camera view of hangar 14.

Meeks turned stiffly and took in the image. "I see Captain Harper already has the ship on the launching pad," he observed dutifully.

Hogmeyer's brow creased. Grunting an inaudible reply, he pressed a few buttons on his wand that bought officer Dalton's face onto the screen.

"Do you not like being the head of my hangar security team, Dalton? Want to get yourself demoted, is that it?" The security man began to blurt an explanation, but Hogmeyer cut him short. "What the hell am I seeing? I told you to inform me the moment Harper and his crew were ready to launch."

"Yes, sir, I was just about to contact you and let you know. In fact, I've just come off the comm to Captain Harper this very moment. He wanted to check personally that you were aware of their departure."

"Did he now?" Hogmeyer's brow creased a little further. "You make sure they don't move an inch before I get down there, or you'll be scrubbing Lucky Deuces' holding cells for the rest of your days. You understand me, Dalton?"

"Loud and clear, sir. They're not—"

Hogmeyer whipped the image of the still speaking man from the screen with a swish of his wand. He looked back at Meeks. "I'm surrounded by incompetent morons."

Meeks knew the feeling.

"Where was I?"

"Backup plans," Meeks offered, "plan Bs."

Hogmeyer grunted and nodded. "What makes a man like me truly great at what I do is that I leave nothing to chance. I make plans, and then I make backup plans; therefore, I can be flexible simply because I'm *prepared* to be flexible. That dodgy little Delta Pinpoint is one of hundreds of backup plans that I've got readily prepared about my city. The craft may look intact even to someone like Harper, who seems to know his ships, but I know differently."

Hogmeyer zoomed in on the launch pad and beamed a green laser pointer from his wand directly at the image of the Pinpoint. "You see, Meeks, Delta Pinpoints would be ranked pretty poorly were it not for their one redeeming factor: the P-Blast 33 thruster."

Meeks tried his best to keep his eyes alert as he watched the green laser pointer hover over the huge, cannon-like thruster that was sticking out of the ship's rear.

I acquired this particular craft from a crew of colonists who'd narrowly escaped a pirate attack shortly after Earth saw its end. The P-Blast thruster was damaged in the attack, and the poor buggers had to crawl through space relying entirely on the ship's cruising thrusters." Hogmeyer indicated a line of smaller thrusters poking out from the lower portion of the ship's rear. "Those thrusters rely on a secondary, much weaker engine. So weak, in fact, that it took them over a month to get here. The ship's main engine is still intact, but without the big P-Blast thruster, it's absolutely redundant."

"Ah," Meeks replied and managed to turn to his boss and raise an eyebrow.

Hogmeyer grinned. If it weren't for the yellow teeth, the grin might've almost had a schoolboy edge to it.

"You see, Meeks, that P-Blast thruster you see there doesn't actually exist. It was blown almost clean away during the attack."

This statement caused Meeks' other eyebrow to rise unforced.

The big man chuckled at the sight. "You're confused? Unsurprising. Let me explain. A man of my intellect understands the importance of acquiring useful contacts in many different fields. A few of my contacts are deeply involved in advanced technologies— technologies that are still far from being revealed to the public at large, the little people that make up ninety-nine percent of the population…little people like you, Meeks." Hogmeyer stood up and snatched the holo-cube off the desk. "What you won't be aware of is that the technology involved in your little holo-cube here took a rather substantial leap forward shortly before Earth was destroyed. That big P-Blast thruster you're looking at is actually the very latest in hologram technology."

Meeks took a couple of steps towards the screen and peered at the image. He couldn't deny that a spark of interest had been piqued within his bored brain.

Hogmeyer chuckled again. "Good, eh? There's not a hint of flicker like you see in those graphs of yours. You could have your nose right up against that bloody great thruster, and you'd never know that it didn't actually exist, not until you got close enough to pass right through it, that is." Hogmeyer barked a laugh and sat back in his chair. "And it's all down to a wonderful piece of technological wizardry that's not much bigger than your little cube here."

Meeks continued to peer at the image, not entirely sure that he wasn't the one getting conned. On the screen, the big thruster looked so real.

"Looks even better in the flesh," Hogmeyer said as if reading his thoughts. "And there's more icing on the cake. These new hologram devices are cheap...not cheap like your suit, Meeks, but cheap enough."

Meeks turned to see that his boss was beaming now.

"In fact, they're so cheap, I went and stuck two of them in that little Pinpoint. You know why, Meeks?'

"A backup?" Meeks suggested, turning back to the screen.

"You're catching on. What if one of them were to malfunction and that big thruster was to suddenly disappear? I leave nothing to chance, Meeks, and that's what makes me great at what I do."

"Forgive me," Meeks said after a moment's thought, "but with the main engine and the rest of the ship intact, wouldn't it be better just to replace the big, um...*P-Blast* thruster and keep the ship for yourself?"

"You insult me with you dumb questions," Hogmeyer replied, his grin faltering slightly. "Don't you think such a thing would have occurred to me? The technologies and materials used in the construction of that thruster are extremely unique and costly. Like I said, the thruster is what gave the ship its impressive speed. It's worth ten times the rest of the ship, engines included. Added to that is the fact that the factory where the bloody things were made was on Earth. Even if it had been worth replacing, it would have been impossible." Hogmeyer paused for a moment, contemplating the image. "Still, it's a shame to let that main engine go even if it was only worth a pittance. But it served its purpose and satisfied Harper's physical inspections—had his grubby hands all over the thing. I'm fortunate that the P-Blast thruster isn't more accessible else that thorough bastard might have tried running his hands all over that too."

Meeks finally turned from the screen. His boss was mumbling now, more to himself than his one-man audience.

As if using the act to clear his thoughts, the big man once again leaned back in his chair and sniffed. "Now, I know what you're thinking, Meeks…"

Meeks hoped to God that wasn't true; he'd just been thinking what a pathetic and idiotic amount of effort the whole scam was.

"…You're thinking, 'Very clever, but what happens when they try and use the main engine and it fails due to the lack of thruster?'"

Just shoot the bloody lot of them and get it done. "Yes, sir, you snatched the thought right out of my mind."

His boss let the sarcasm slide, perhaps too caught up in his own genius.

"Yet another thing that an ignorant little man like you is probably unaware of is that there's a far-reaching field that emanates around my entire city, a safety bubble if you like. This safety bubble, among other things, prevents the activation of deep space engines within its borders. It helps minimize dangers of kamikaze or just plain incompetent pilots. Harper will have to wait until they've flown the ship out of that bubble before they get a chance to utilize the main engine and its non-existent thruster. The bubble provides plenty enough distance. They'll be well away from my city and out of the view of my more *sensitive* clientele."

Meeks nodded then realized his boss was looking at him expectantly.

"Any questions, Meeks? Isn't that dull brain of yours even slightly curious as to what's going to stop them turning back around when the thruster turns out to be a dud? What if they come back here for some half-arsed attempt at revenge?"

All Meeks could manage was a shrug. That made the big man sneer in disgust, but it was all the encouragement he needed to continue.

"There's a rather interesting result when one attempts to activate a deep space engine—such as the one nestled in the back of that Pinpoint—when the ship's thruster isn't functioning or indeed when there *is* no thruster. I once witnessed the result myself a few years back, and I can assure you, Meeks, it's something akin to activating a rather spectacular bomb. All I'll lose will be one near-worthless ship. What I'll gain is a huge blue ship and Harper and his band of idiots disposed of nice and neatly. All achieved in a way that keeps my clientele none the wiser, my reputation intact, and my artistic mind pleasantly satisfied."

"I'm impressed," Meeks said, still not feeling anywhere near. The hologram looked impressive, but his boss could hardly take credit for that. "And how does your little gift, the chained golden die that the grubby girl was swinging about her head, fit into your master plan?"

"Ah, very perceptive of you, Meeks. Another of my little backup plans. It's entirely possible that Harper could play it safe and hold off using of the deep space engine until he's given himself time to do a more thorough inspection. God forbid he might unravel my little deception before he's gone and blown himself up. It would be a shame to have a man like that lurking in space with revenge on his mind. So, in answer to your question, that rather beautiful gold die has a clever little sensor and activator hidden in it. As soon as the Pinpoint craft leaves the city's safety bubble, the sensor will

automatically activate the ship's deep space engine. *Boom!*"
Hogmeyer bellowed the word with a theatrical wave of his long
arms.

Meeks couldn't help but flinch a little. "Sounds like you've
thought of everything," he said flatly.

"I have thought of everything," the big man snapped. Getting to
his feet, he pulled hard at his jeans even though his protruding belly
prevented them from shifting an inch and glared at Meeks. "So now
that you know all the details of my little piece of art, do you fancy
accompanying me down to the hangar? Witness the grand finale first
hand?"

"Do I have a choice?"

"No, you bloody well don't."

Chapter Nineteen
BACKUP

Meeks knew a scared and desperate man when he saw one, and officer Dalton was meeting the criteria with flying colors. Even remaining at the very rear of the hangar's security room, Meeks could see the sweat dripping from Dalton's neat, blond beard. Upon entering the room, the man's obvious panic had instantly wiped Hogmeyer's grin away. Since then, the big man's face had remained a stony mask even after Dalton had recounted the moment when the main security control panel had malfunctioned, comm units and all. Without the comms, it had been impossible for Dalton to contact Captain Harper down at the launch bay. It had also been impossible to contact any of the guards that were posted within the hangar itself.

Meeks doubted whether Officer Dalton's panic had truly kicked in at that point. After all, with the launch bay shield still up, Captain Harper and the Pinpoint ship wouldn't succeed in going anywhere. No, Meeks would have laid a substantial bet that the panic had started when Harper had looked directly up at one of the security cameras. Meeks was no expert on technology or the workings of the city's security systems, but even he knew that the cameras within the hangar were all but invisible to the naked eye.

"He looked directly at it?" Hogmeyer asked, his voice flat.

There was a small nod from Dalton.

"Coincidence," Hogmeyer mumbled to himself then asked, "Tell me, Officer Dalton, why are you not out in the hangar talking to Harper and instructing your guards in person?"

Meeks was impressed by the steadiness of his boss' voice. But he wasn't fooled by it. There was anger lurking there. He knew the tell-tale signs only too well: the reddening of his already ruddy face, the constant opening and closing of his gold-ringed fingers. The longer the build-up, the greater the rage. If Meeks had given a damn, he might have feared for the poor, sweating security officer.

"I tried that, sir. As soon as the comms failed, I went straight for the entrance to the hangar, but…" Dalton's panicked eyes drifted over to the heavy, steel door to his left. "The door, sir…the opening code…well, there was a strange hissing sound…and some smoke around the edges… That's when Paulter here," Dalton nodded at his second-in-command, "well, Paulter came over to inspect the door."

Paulter was hunched nervously over his control panel on the far left of the room. On hearing his name, he hunched a little further as if the panel held some sort of protective field.

Meeks almost smiled. If officer Dalton was trying to divert Hogmeyer's attention over to his colleague, he was failing miserably.

"And what did Paulter discover with this inspection?" Hogmeyer asked, his hard eyes not deviating from Dalton for a second.

"It…er…well, the door seems to be sealed shut, sir."

"Seems to be?"

Dalton visibly squirmed. "*Is* sealed shut."

Meeks did smile at that. It was very brief and small, but it was a smile. He had found himself physically repulsed by Harper and his crew, and he was bored to death with having to play along with his boss' pathetic little scams. But he couldn't deny that this one was shaping up into something interesting or at the very least amusing.

Hogmeyer finally turned his gaze from the sweaty officer and glanced at the sealed door. Then he nodded and turned to stare out of the security room's viewing panel. In a similar fashion to the big man's office, the panel was constructed from smart-glass, and through it, the entire hangar could be seen.

"You...Paulter."

The second-in-command flinched.

"Use camera eight to zoom in on the launch bay."

"Right away, sir."

The man hammered at his controls with nervous fingers, and within seconds, the viewing panel was filled with the image of the Pinpoint ship. Captain Harper was still standing at the base of the loading ramp, but none of the rest of his crew were visible.

Officer Dalton cleared his throat. "Sir, I was just about to—"

Hogmeyer shut the man up by firmly grabbing his shoulder and shoving him aside. He then strode up to the viewing panel. "What the hell you up to, Harper?"

The words were mumbled, but Meeks heard them well enough. The big man's left fist was still opening and closing. But with his right, he tapped against the smart-glass, closing in on Harper and enlarging the image until it was practically life size. "What the hell is your game?"

At that very moment, as if hearing the words, Harper looked directly at the camera, causing both Hogmeyer and Dalton to stumble back in surprise. Then he shot them a smile, causing them to stumble a little further.

Meeks' thin lips twitched. This really was beginning to get interesting.

For a few silent moments, they all stared at the screen. Even the guard standing at the back of the room, who until this point had seemed a bit of a non-entity, shifted forward to get a better view. Meeks tore his eyes from the screen to glance at the guard. He was a big man, even bigger than Hogmeyer, and had a dumb, oafish face that he was using to openly smirk at the turn of events.

The oaf better be careful; the rage is coming.

Captain Harper was still smiling—a smile that seemed to have paralyzed Hogmeyer. Then Harper proceeded to pull a small device from his pocket and, turning back to the Delta Pinpoint behind him, theatrically pressed a button.

The ship disappeared.

"He's activated the Pinpoint's cloaking device, sir," the second-in-command informed loudly.

"I can see that, you dolt," Hogmeyer spat, turning to glare at the man. "You think I don't bloody see that?"

The man shook his head and quickly went back to studying his controls.

Here comes the rage.

Meeks was doing his best to keep his amusement in check, but the oaf of a guard next to him was having less success. His deep, nasal sniggering eventually seemed to pull Hogmeyer from his paralysis. Whipping around, he shot the guard a look that would've made a more sensitive employee wet themselves.

"You think this is amusing, idiot?"

Meeks, who was standing a little too close to the idiot in question, took a few steps away.

"No, sir," the guard replied, managing only a partial stifle of his snigger.

Hogmeyer strode over to the man and, gripping him roughly by the front of his armored jacket, swung him towards the sealed door—quite a feat considering the man's size. "Get that bloody thing open before I end your smirking for good."

"And you," Hogmeyer thrust a hammy finger at the second-in-command, "get locked onto that Pinpoint and deactivate its cloaking device."

"Already on it, sir."

"So why the hell am I still not seeing it?" Hogmeyer bellowed. "All I can see is Harper's cocky bloody grin."

"I can't deactivate it, sir...and it doesn't make sense. My readouts...they're saying it's been cloaked for the past three hours already."

Meeks watched as his boss rubbed his forehead with sweaty palms. Even through the rage, his confusion was evident. The big man was used to creating mysteries, not solving them.

"Don't worry, sir," Dalton said in a failed attempt to sound confident. "Whatever they're up to, they're not going anywhere with the launch bay shield still up."

The veins on Hogmeyer's neck began to swell. He turned to the man, his expression suggesting he might commit cold-blooded murder right then and there. Meeks wouldn't put it past him.

"I think I've done it, sir," the second-in-command blurted triumphantly. "The ship's uncloaking now."

All eyes went to the screen.

In the large space on the launch bay, where the Pinpoint craft had disappeared moments earlier, the gleaming form of a Star Splinter, Harper 7 was taking shape.

"That's odd. Looks like your Star..." The second-in-command abandoned his statement upon seeing Hogmeyer's face.

A little unsteady on his feet, Dalton stumbled forward and, with a few taps and swipes of his finger on the smart-glass, opened up a wide-angled view of the entire hangar. "This doesn't make sense. Your Star Splinter's still in its docking bay. I can see it clear as day."

"Lock onto that bloody ship," Hogmeyer growled. "Deactivate

all its functions."

"You mean the Pinpoint?" the second-in-command asked desperately.

"No you bloody imbecile, my Star Splinter."

The second-in-command hesitated. There were clearly two Star Splinters in the hangar: one on the launch bay and one in its docking bay. He looked frantically to his superior officer for assistance. Unfortunately, Dalton appeared the most bewildered of them all.

Hogmeyer threw his arms up as he took in their blank expressions. "*The one on the Goddamned launching pad, you slack-brained morons,*" he roared.

Meeks remained at the very back of the room as if the big man's crimson face was emanating a scorching heat.

"So where'd the other Star Splinter ship come from?" asked the guard. He was still working on the sealed door. "And what happened to the Pinpoint ship?" Both were questions dominating the heads of the other men in the room, but the oaf was the only one willing to take the risk of asking. Meeks thought him either incredibly brave or completely blunt of mind.

Ignoring him, Hogmeyer continued to stare at the screen. "Hologram," he muttered, more to himself than for the benefit of the others.

"Damn good hologram," the guard pointed out recklessly. "Where'd they get a hologram like that from?"

"I wonder," Meeks said, briefly losing hold of his controlled silence.

Hogmeyer ignored him too.

The second-in-command was still hammering away at the controls of his console. "I'm having trouble locking onto the ship, sir." He ceased his hammering for a second to shake his head. "These controls, they're all messed up."

Dalton rushed over and sat next to him. "No, it isn't a hologram," he called out after a few moments. "I can confirm that the ship on the launching bay is the real Star Splin—"

The security officer was cut short by two gold-ringed fists clamping onto his collar and hauling him up out of his chair. "Not the Star Splinter," Hogmeyer snarled, his crimson face an inch from Dalton's. "The Pinpoint...the Pinpoint was the hologram, you snivelling maggot of a man."

"So where'd the real Pinpoint get to?" The guard asked, not bothering to look up. He was being showered by a stream of sparks from his pulse rifle's laser cutter as he continued his work on the sealed door.

As if it were Dalton who'd asked the question, Hogmeyer bodily dragged the limp-legged security officer over to the viewing screen and pressed his face against the cold, hard smart-glass. "If even one of you incompetent morons had been doing your job properly and observing the hangar, you'd have noticed that Harper and his crew performed a ship swap. That Star Splinter," Hogmeyer dragged Dalton's face across the glass screen until it reached the image of the Star Splinter in the docking bay, "is a bloody hologram. The ship over here," Dalton's face squeaked against the glass as Hogmeyer maneuvred it mercilessly over to the Star Splinter in the launch bay. "That's the real ship...my Goddamned, top-of-the-range Star Splinter. They used a second hologram to make it look like the Pinpoint. And now, because of you bloody fools, Harper and his friends have got their filthy mitts all over it." Hogmeyer swung Dalton and sent him crashing awkwardly back into his chair.

"Captain Harper is entering the ship, sir," the second-in-command shouted.

Hogmeyer spun and peered through the viewing screen, slamming his big fists against it. "Why aren't those dim-witted guards doing their rounds? They're just standing around like a bunch of limp fools."

"Don't worry, I'll have this door open in just a minute," the oaf assured him in a tone that suggested they would all have a good laugh about this later. "So they've got two holograms then, eh? Always good to have a backup I suppose."

Meeks felt an overwhelming urge to make a comment at that moment, but the look on Hogmeyer's face snuffed it out almost instantly.

"So that would explain why the Pinpoint ship's cloaking device has been activated for the past few hours then, eh?" the oaf continued in his conversational tone. "I guess it's still sitting there in its docking bay, but we just can't see it. That's pretty damn clever." Deactivating his laser cutter, the guard looked up as if expecting some sort of praise for this insight.

Definitely blunt of mind.

Hogmeyer lunged forward and yanked the pulse rifle from the witless guard's grip. Grunting with surprise, the oaf tumbled back into the corner, his hands raised.

"I'm not gonna shoot you, you mindless fool," Hogmeyer barked. "Although I bloody well should. I want you to use the gun's sights. Shine the aiming laser into the eyes of those guards out there. Get their bloody attention."

"But you could blind a man doing…" The guard stopped short, finally realizing the benefit of a closed mouth. With a shrug, he took back his weapon and moved to the window.

"Don't worry, sir," the second-in-command said confidently, "they won't be going anywhere with the launch bay shield up. I'm activating the backup shield too, just in case."

Hogmeyer glared at the screen. Meeks was fairly certain that any last remnants of patience had well and truly seeped out of the man.

Then the main launching bay shield began to deactivate.

"What the hell are you doing, man?" Hogmeyer shrieked the words in a way no man his size should have been capable. *"You're deactivating the Goddamned main shield."*

"It's…it's these controls, sir," the second in demand stammered. "They're all mixed up. They keep doing the opposite of what I want."

Panic suddenly overruling his rage, Hogmeyer looked desperately to the guard, who now had his weapon pointed through the viewing panel. "Any response?"

"No, sir. I'm shining the laser right at um, right in their eyes, just like you said, but they're not even flinching. It's like they're a bunch of zombies or something."

Hogmeyer raised his clenched fists as if to punch something. *Anything.* "Get back to opening that bloody door," he spat. "Dalton, who the hell has been at these controls?"

"Not a soul, sir, I can assure you."

"What about that kid?" the oaf pointed out.

"Kid?"

"Yeah, the skinny kid with glasses," he continued as he reactivated his laser cutter and directed it once more at the sealed door. "The little runt was tapping around on those controls for quite a while."

Meeks noticed Dalton gripping his chair, knuckles white as Hogmeyer turned his eyes back on him. "Maybe he…he looked at them for just a minute." The security officer released his chair to scratch rigorously at his beard.

There's a tell if ever I saw one, Meeks thought, surprised that a man who resided in a gambling city didn't have more control over such things.

"But he's just a kid," Dalton reasoned, still scratching away. "I kept a close eye on him the whole time—"

"No you didn't," the guard interrupted, pausing with his cutting laser to give a little chuckle. "As I remember it, the both of you were flirting your asses off with that tall blonde. Like a couple of giggling schoolboys you were."

The second in command shot Dalton a panicked glance before returning his attention to his screen.

"You let one of Harper's kids monkey with these controls?" Hogmeyer closed in on Dalton.

His amusement rising to levels he'd not felt for years, Meeks watched on, not even risking a blink lest he miss something.

"But he's just a kid," Dalton managed to repeat lamely before receiving a backhanded strike to his face that sent him tumbling from his chair.

"They're starting up the engines, sir," the second-in-command informed tentatively. Meeks could tell the man was scared to say the words but was more scared of the consequences if he didn't.

"*What?*" Hogmeyer had been about to plant one of his boots into the floored security officer's gut. But instead, he half roared, half moaned and staggered over to the viewing panel. "My ship, that's my bloody ship." He pressed his sweaty palms against the smart-glass as his beloved Star Splinter slipped smoothly from the launch bay and cruised effortlessly out into open space. "*Cannons...*the external cannons...blow the bloody thing to smithereens, Goddamn it." He turned, wild-eyed, to the second-in-command. Not having the courage to inform the big, crazed man that the cannons had also been monkeyed with, the man simply looked up and shook his head.

"Got it, sir," the oaf said, looking up as the door juddered open.

Hogmeyer whipped around, looking a little unsteady on his feet as he did so.

Meeks remained silent. In fact, an eerie silence had descended upon the entire room as Hogmeyer stared, almost dumbly, at the open door. Then, as if a starter gun had gone off, he launched forward, violently kneed the crouched oaf of a guard aside, and bolted through the door and out into the hangar.

"Where's he off to?" the guard asked, picking himself up and brushing down his uniform. "He's certainly not catching them now."

Dalton heaved himself back into his chair and dabbed at his bloody nose. "He's not going after the ship, you idiot. He's going to hammer his fists into your fellow dim-witted guards out in the hangar."

Silently agreeing with the security officer's assessment, Meeks gave into his curiosity and ran through the door after his boss.

Meeks scuttled along the metal floor in a futile attempt to catch up with his boss. The big man was setting quite a pace considering his size, but there was no mistaking his destination. As he neared the Star Splinter's docking bay, Meeks felt quite taken aback by the life-size hologram looming above him. Surely, Hogmeyer was mistaken; it seemed so real, so solid and heavy, with lights and detailed reflections bouncing off its hull. It even cast a shadow, for Christ's sake.

Meeks slowed his pace. Ahead, Hogmeyer had skidded to a halt beside one of the ship's bulky rear landing supports. Deciding to observe from a safe distance, Meeks watched as the big man took a swipe at the support, his fist passing clean through as if by magic. Wheezing, Meeks risked stumbling a little closer before catching sight of his boss' face. It was hideously contorted with rage. *Christ, he's really bloody lost it.* Not wanting to get too close to such a face, Meeks stopped dead in his tracks.

Seconds later, the big man was off again, but this time, Meeks didn't follow. Instead, he bent over and clutched at the stitch in his side, all the while straining his neck in order to observe. Anger-fuelled, Hogmeyer was running full tilt to the very center of the ship's phantom shadow. Then, barely missing a step, he swung his booted foot at a small, pyramid-shaped device that was nestled on the floor. Meeks almost fell over with surprise as the little device went spinning across the docking bay, taking the large, silver hologram of a ship with it. He sucked in a sharp breath as the ship passed harmlessly through numerous loading vehicles as well as one of the hangar's massive support pillars.

Once the hologram had spun out of view, Hogmeyer turned and came striding back towards him. Meeks felt the last of his amusement melt away to be replaced by a spark of fear. The big man's expression suggested that any power for rational thought was now hopelessly overwhelmed by unadulterated, animalistic rage. Meeks felt a sudden urge to turn and run. But then the big man's wrath-filled attentions turned towards the nearest guard, a man with the terrible misfortune of being posted in the closest proximity to the Star Splinter's docking bay. Tentatively, Meeks pursued. His amusement might have been bullied away by fear, but his curiosity lingered.

Strangely, the guard was grinning. Without a word, Hogmeyer clamped an unforgiving hand around the man's neck, causing his head to slam nosily against the pillar at which he was standing. Stranger still, the guard's grin remained.

"My ship, my bloody ship," Hogmeyer snarled, spittle firing from his contorted mouth. "I'm gonna rip your worthless head off, you pathetic, useless scum." The big man's crimson, sweat-beaded face was practically touching the guard's, which in stark contrast was rapidly turning blue. *"Why are you still fucking grinning?"*

Meeks suddenly felt an urge to be helpful, purely to remind his enraged boss whose side he was on. "He looks drugged," he suggested quietly, making sure he remained a good ten feet from the violence. "I'd be willing to lay a bet they all are."

Hogmeyer ignored him or possibly wasn't even aware of him. Removing his hand from the man's neck, Hogmeyer proceeded to strike the guard with all his considerable might. Rather than collapsing to the ground, as would have been expected after receiving such blows, the guard simply sagged and began to giggle, a little blood bubbling from his still-grinning mouth. Meeks winced and backed up another couple of steps. The guard's pulse rifle looked to be hanging at an awkward angle, and there was a length of white cord dangling from his left wrist.

Hogmeyer looked at the cord. "What..." His rage began to subside to confusion. Roughly grabbing the guard's arm, he lifted it to see more white cord binding the man's right hand to his weapon's grip. "What..." he repeated dumbly as he pulled at the guard's shoulder. Numerous large, metal pins were clamping the man's armoured vest to the pillar, holding him more or less upright. Hogmeyer's eyes grew wide as the full realization of the situation took hold, the sheer disbelief seeming to burn away the last of his adrenalin-fuelled rage. Meeks curiously shuffled forward. He wasn't quite sure whether to run, laugh, or maybe even offer a few words of consolation.

His rage now dissipated, Hogmeyer began to pant like a fat, overheated dog. Releasing his grip on the giggling guard, he stumbled back a few steps and simply stared as he tried to regain his breath. After some time, the panting finally eased, and the big man's face turned from bright crimson back to ruddy.

Feeling uneasy in the silence that followed, Meeks opened his mouth to speak, but his boss beat him to it. "No one's to hear about this, Meeks." His voice was little more than a whisper. "Not a word uttered."

"Of course, sir."

"Not a bloody word," he repeated, turning to face him. His usually cold, hard eyes looked tired and bloodshot.

"Not a word, sir. I swear it."

Seemingly satisfied with his sincerity, Hogmeyer nodded and turned to stare at the distant launch bay and the black, star-studded space beyond. "That's the very last time anyone takes something from me."

Feeling a little confused by the situation, Meeks felt his curiosity getting the better of him. "Forgive me for asking, sir, but I'm still a little lost. What exactly happened to the Delta Pinpoint ship?"

The big man exhaled heavily, seemingly too exhausted to be angry or annoyed. "It's cloaked. The heap of junk is still in its bloody docking bay with its cloaking device activated."

Meek's stared in the direction that Hogmeyer was lazily waving his limp fist. He could just about make out a transparent, jelly-like blur in the opposite docking bay. "Yes… I think I see it."

As if lobotomised, Hogmeyer remained silent and continued to stare through the opening of the distant launch bay.

"One more question, sir, if I may?"

"What, Meeks?" Hogmeyer rasped, finally tearing his eyes from the launch bay to eyeball him. "What is it that your pathetic little brain can't grasp?"

Feeling a surge of annoyance, Meeks smoothed his hair and went on regardless. "That backup plan of yours, the golden die that the girl was whirling about her head." Meeks was about to inquire as to the range of the remote trigger when the sudden look of horror on Hogmeyer's face killed the question in his throat.

Before the little accountant knew what was happening,

Hogmeyer was barging him aside and bolting back across the hangar. Meeks stumbled over and hit the deck in a clatter of limbs. Suddenly aware of the danger, he wasted no time picking himself up and scrambling off as fast as his smooth office shoes would permit. Neither he nor the big man had run very far, however, before a deafening explosion erupted behind them. The force was so great that the reverberating tremble was felt throughout the city from the peaks of the first class viewing domes to the sewers of the lower class slum pits.

The shock wave that rippled out from the exploding Pinpoint ship treated Hogmeyer and Meeks equally. Lifting the two men off their feet, it launched them several meters through the air then sent them sliding painfully across the smooth, metallic floor.

Moments later, the hangar was still. Not a sound could be heard other than the crackle of burning ships and loading equipment. His vision blurry, all Meeks could see was his boss' prone form next to him. The big man wasn't moving, but he was swearing enough for the both of them. As his vision cleared further, Meeks' attention moved past the curved horizon of the big man's belly to focus on another guard who was hanging almost horizontally from a nearby vertical pillar. Despite the guard's painful looking position, the nature of his expression was absolutely clear. He was a man experiencing complete and utter bliss.

Chapter Twenty
THE JOYS OF A STAR SPLINTER, HARPER 7

"Cal, I swear this thing just beeped at me."

"Beeped?" Cal turned briefly from the Star Splinter's flight console to look at Eddy. She was leaning back against one of the cockpit's rear chairs, closely studying her large, golden die. The girl had been swinging Hogmeyer's gaudy gift about her head ever since swiping it from the big man's hand. "You sure?" he asked distractedly before turning back to the flight console. He wanted to check that no ships were attempting pursuit and that the Star Splinter's deep space engines were performing correctly now they'd cleared the city's restriction zone. Viktor, Melinda, and Jumper were busying themselves elsewhere on the ship, but Eddy and Toker had decided to remain in the cockpit to witness firsthand the Star Splinter's capabilities. The flight, however, was smooth, and the expanse of deep space offered nothing to give any sense of speed, so the pair had soon lost interest.

Satisfied they weren't being pursued, Cal turned back to Eddy. The girl was still peering at the large, golden die, her expression quizzical. He'd all but forgotten about the odd gift from Hogmeyer. He should have chucked the bloody thing out of the airlock the first chance he had.

"I vote we chuck that thing out the airlock," Toker suggested as if he'd the power to read minds. "She's nearly slammed it into my face three times already." He shot a pleading look towards Cal.

"Shut it, blondie. This thing makes a decent weapon. I ain't never lettin' go of it."

"You mean that? Then I definitely vote we lob it out the airlock!"

"Bloody hilarious, you are," Eddy spat. "I can keep it, right, Cal?"

Not for the first time, Cal began to feel a little more like a parent than he would have liked. "Well, I'm not sure, Eddy. It is a little lethal when you swing it about like that."

Eddy huffed. "But I got it under control."

"Yeah right." Toker scoffed.

"Yeah, bloody right," she snapped, scowling at him. "Who's to say I wasn't actually *aiming* for your fat head those times. Reckon I'd be doing us all a big favor."

Cal blew out a breath and rubbed his palms into his eyes. The unravelling of the potential scam over the last couple of days hadn't left much time for sleep, and he was starting to feel it. They all were. "How's about a test to decide?" he offered after a moment. "You could prove how accurate you are by swinging it as hard as you can at say…the circular plate on the end of that console." Cal indicated the area with a pointed finger. He knew the girl wouldn't do any damage except, with any luck, to the hideous golden die. On a ship as well-crafted as the Star Splinter, even the thin data screens and the sleek, silver consoles were made of the strongest materials. Nothing short of a ten-click pulse rifle could cause much damage.

Eddy shrugged. "Piece of cake. I could give this thing a full swing and whack a flea off Blondie's nose."

"No chance," Toker said with a chuckle and a few precautionary steps back.

"I could hit that little circle plate blind," Eddy persisted.

"Okay." Cal got to his feet. "You've got to swing it hard though," he said as the girl wrapped the end of the die's long chain around her fist and lined herself up to the target. "It's no good hitting hard if you're not accurate, and it's no good being accurate if you can't hit hard."

"It'll be hard, don't worry 'bout that. I hate to bugger up our new ship, but if it's what I gotta do..." Gripping the chain tight, Eddy swung the golden die, lasso style, three times around her head then, to Cal's surprise, sent it hammering with impressive force directly into the center of the metal plate. There was a loud, explosive bang as the die disintegrated on impact.

Toker dove for cover, squealing a little as he did so. Cal didn't blame him. Twisting away, he had to bring his arms up to shield his head from the flying fragments.

"What the hell," came Toker's muffled voice a few moments later from under a navigation console.

Cal lowered his arms to see Eddy staring a little dumbly at the metal plate. The disintegrated die had left a paint mark dead in its center, a golden bullseye. That paint and the fact that the cube had smashed apart to reveal tiny bits of tech, proved two things: the gift should have been shown the airlock long ago, and it certainly wasn't crafted from real gold.

Toker crawled out from beneath the console. "I told you that thing was bloody dangerous," he grumbled, standing up and brushing himself down. He looked ready to complain further when the look on Eddy's face stopped him short. She was on the verge of tears, the chain hanging limply from her hand. "Hey...you okay?" he asked tentatively.

The girl looked up, and the tears spilled out. "I miss my brothers."

So unexpected, the statement hit Cal harder than any punch. No such words had been uttered by any of them for months, and to say they took him by surprise was an understatement. In that moment, his young friend looked painfully innocent and small. Sometimes, it was easy to forget that she was little more than a kid.

"An' I miss my pa." The tears began to drip off her chin, and her shoulders shook as she sucked in loud breaths. "He was gonna move the workshop, my pa was. He was gonna move it to some colony. Should've bloody done it. They'd all be safe if he'd bloody done it."

Cal suddenly felt guilt course through him. He hadn't really talked to any of them about loved ones lost. He'd thought they'd all wanted to mourn in silence, but suddenly, that sounded a lame justification. But what would he have said? It was a lousy excuse, he knew, but somehow, he hadn't felt qualified. He'd lost many friends over the years, but he had never known a family, had never *lost* a family. Was it any different to losing friends? Feeling awkward, he started to walk over to the girl, his mind reeling over the best way to comfort her.

Toker beat him to it.

"Hey, I miss my folks too," Toker said as he gently put an arm around her. "Real bad. And my sisters and grandparents."

Toker too had lost so many. He should have asked them, should have talked to them about it. To add to his guilt, Cal felt an odd pang of envy, that old orphan envy that he hadn't felt for years— not since he was a child, truth be told. It was strange that it kicked in now. But it was gone as fast as it arrived. Gone when he realized that maybe his family was right there: the two young people before him. And Jumper and Viktor. Even Melinda. Why not? An unusual bunch, but what more of a family could a man ask for? Already, he couldn't imagine a life without them.

Eddy's words became almost incoherent as her sobs took over.

Even more so as Toker cocooned her in his arms and began to gently rub her back.

Cal watched on, impressed by Toker's tenderness. The sight was heart-breaking but also strangely calming. He knew they'd always be there for each other no matter how hard things became, no matter how crazy. They all had their talents. His was keeping them safe.

"Sorry. Stupid, eh?" Eddy said, breaking partway out of Toker's embrace to give her face a rigorous wipe with her sleeve.

"There's nothing stupid about it," Toker assured her. "It's natural to have a good cry. I've had plenty."

"S'pose," she said, giving him a little shrug to show she was all done.

Toker retracted his arms then looked at Cal, his expression seeming to seek his approval. *Even in this, they think I know it all. How had he been put on such a pedestal?*

"Can't believe I bust it." Eddy was looking down at the limp chain in her hand. Her tears had stopped, and her breaths were slowing.

"I guess you just had too strong an arm for it," Toker suggested. "Better it bust to pieces now instead of in the middle of a fight...right, Cal?"

"Couldn't agree more."

The girl turned her red eyes towards him. "What d'ya reckon of my aim?" she asked with a sniff.

Cal smiled and nodded approvingly. "Hard and accurate."

The girl gave a little smile back then rubbed at her face again. Despite her red eyes and dishevelled appearance, she suddenly looked lighter. Walking to a nearby console, she set the chain carefully upon it. "Jumper's still the best though, I reckon," she continued after a moment. "You see how quickly he shot all those guards back at that flight hangar?

"Yeah," Toker agreed with a smile. "He's pretty incredible with that bliss rifle of his. Those poor buggers 'll have one hell of a hangover by tomorrow."

Eddy nodded and wiped her nose.

"I still don't quite get how you knew the Pinpoint ship was bust up though," Toker said as he walked over and perched next to Cal on the smooth edge of the flight console.

Pure blind luck, Cal thought, while trying not to think of the consequences if they hadn't been lucky. "To be honest, we have Melinda to thank for that. There was an energy field coming from a hologram in the back of the ship that disrupted her nano technology. Screwed up her hair for a time."

"I knew that crappy old ship was a hologram," Eddy murmured with another sniff.

"The ship wasn't a hologram," Toker pointed out, his tone less mocking than usual.

"How d'you know?"

"Well, we were standing inside it for a start."

"Actually Eddy, it was only the main thruster on the back of the ship that turned out to be a hologram," Cal explained. "A hologram projected from a little device we found attached to the main engine. Two actually. Hogmeyer obviously didn't trust his own technology. Luckily, Viktor figured out how to reprogram them. He scanned both ships and came up with two seriously convincing holograms. I doubt you'd ever get him to admit it, but I think our little boy genius was pretty damned impressed with those devices."

"Lucky we found 'um then, eh?"

Cal had never heard Eddy hold such a quiet conversation. She was still wiping at her eyes, but she was definitely much calmer, relaxed even.

"Luckier than you think. Without the main thruster, that

Pinpoint ship would have been a disaster waiting to be triggered." Cal glanced at the fragments strewn across the floor. "That Hogmeyer was a major prick."

"Wish I could have seen the look on his ugly face when he figured out we'd nicked his best ship," Toker said with a grin.

"Best ship!" Eddy remarked. "Dunno 'bout that. I s'pose it's fast an' all that. An' it looks kinda decent if you're into that sorta thing. But what if we wanna fight?"

Cal gave her a crooked grin. "Perhaps it's time I showed you both what a gem of a ship we've swiped."

Eddy shuffled over to the flight console as Cal sat himself in the primary piloting chair, its smart-gel swiftly molding to the shape of his body. Running his hands across a wide, shiny black section of the console, he activated the touch-sensitive controls that immediately illuminated in sharp blue and red lines.

"I'll set these controls so that they respond to our touch. And when I say our touch, I mean *our* touch. Anyone else tries, and they'll have a lifeless ship on their hands." Cal considered for a moment then turned to look at the pair. "If you want, I could set aside some time each day to teach you how to operate and fly the ship."

"Sounds good to me," Toker said, sounding enthusiastic.

"I guess," Eddy added, sounding less so.

"You're not overly keen, Eddy. Maybe this will change your mind." Cal tapped at the controls, and a large screen emerged smoothly from the back of the console. The screen was crafted from such fine, clear material that it would have been barely visible were it not for the image upon it. "This shows the exterior hull of the ship," he explained as the image began to rotate. "As you know, this ship is seriously fast, and we could probably outrun just about any threat we're likely to meet. But inevitably, there comes a time when you need to turn and fight." A red, palm-sized circle began to pulsate in the center of the console. Cal tapped it with a single finger.

Four aiming targets immediately lit up on the wide smart-glass of the cockpit window: two red and two blue, bright against the blackness of space. At the same time, six cylindrical devices sprang seamlessly from the armrests of the three front-facing seats, the middle one being the piloting chair in which Cal sat.

"Notice anything different about the exterior image of the ship, Eddy?"

The girl's eyebrows shot up as she spied the multi-barrelled swivel blasters that had ejected out of the front and rear of the ship. Two monstrous cannons had also protruded from each side of the hull.

"They real, Cal?" Eddy asked.

"Yep." Cal patted his hands on the two cylindrical controls that had emerged from the armrests of his chair. "This chair is the piloting chair, and these two control devices are used to pull off the maneuvering during combat. I've flown a shit load of ships in my life, but I can assure you the Star Splinter's are easily the most fun and without doubt one of the best ships to be in if you're ever caught in a dogfight."

Jumping up, Cal moved into the chair to his right. "This is a combat seat. There's three others: that one the other side of the piloting chair, and those other two at the back of the cockpit.' He jabbed his thumb back over his shoulder. Then he slipped his hands inside the two cylindrical devices protruding from the seat's armrests. Toker and Eddy eagerly huddled around him as the devices closed firmly around his forearms. "These combat controllers do exactly that; they control all of the exterior weapons and defenses. They're the same design as the ones on the piloting chair but have different functions. The controllers are extendable and flexible, and once you place your hands inside, the smart-triggers automatically adjust to your grip." Cal began to move his arms and nodded at the cockpit window. "See how any movement I make moves the two red targets? The right hand moves one and the left the other." Cal swirled his hands in exaggerated loops, and the two red targets looped about the right side of the window. "The other combat seat controls the blue targets. Once you're homed in, you can blast away with the triggers." He contracted his right index finger, causing a torrent of bright red blasts to streak diagonally across the window before fading into the blackness of space.

Eddy laughed. The sound was music to Cal's ears.

"If there's enough people in the cockpit during combat, the two rear seats can also be manned using the image screens to cover the back of the ship. Also, it's a little gimmicky, but some people find it helpful to activate the acoustics whilst firing." Once again, he squeezed off another couple of rounds. This time, the cockpit filled with explosive noise.

By the time the sound dissipated, Toker was laughing too.

"Of course, there's not really any sound out there in the vacuum of space, but some find it useful. Gets the blood pumping."

"Can I have a blast, Cal?" Toker asked.

"Yeah, me too," Eddy blurted.

Cal grinned and shook his head. "Afraid not. It's a hard and fast rule of space combat; no one can operate a ship's weaponry until they're fully schooled in the piloting of that ship. As to who goes first...well, that depends which of you is the most dedicated. Don't blame me," Cal said, taking in the look on their faces. "Ask any space veteran. It's not my rule, it's just the way it is. Like I said, I'll be willing to teach you both...that is, if you're keen on eventually manning the weapons."

"Count me in, Cal," Toker said quickly. "I'll be flying this thing and hammering out cannon blasts in no time."

"Not before me, dimwit," Eddy countered, a little of her usual confidence re-emerging.

"Sounds like we've got a bit of a competition heating up," Cal said as he slipped his hands out of the controls.

"There won't be any competition, Cal," Toker said with a self-assured grin. "By the time I'm blasting stuff apart with those cannons, you'll still be teaching this little monkey how to sit in the pilot's chair properly."

"Watch it, mush nut." Eddy retorted, her voice fully reverted to its usual pitch.

Cal took that as his cue. Jumping up, he left Toker defending his face from Eddy's elbows and wandered over to one of the rear consoles. There were still no pursuers. Not one ship or tracking drone. He grinned. They were away scot free.

"So where we going, Cal?"

"Huh." He turned to see that Toker had survived Eddy's attacks and had managed a retreat.

"Yeah, Cal, where we goin' to?" Eddy asked.

Cal got as far as opening his mouth before he realised he had no answer. "You know what, I really don't have a clue."

Part Three:

Chapter Twenty-One
THE FATHER AND THE SON

Laurence Decker softly cradled his father's emaciated body in his trembling arms. It seemed like an eternity since he'd been a captain of a Class One Military Starship and his father had been one of the most respected admirals in the fleet. Of course, now there was no fleet, not anymore. Now, all that remained of a once-great military force lay helpless on the dark, desolate planet known as C9. The planet was a prison of sorts—a prison that relied on an inhospitable, food-less landscape as its lock and key. Like suffocating fish at the bottom of a dried-up lake, a multitude of broken men and women— once strong-bodied and mentally tough soldiers—lay weak with despair and starvation. Decker looked around at some of those broken souls now. As far as his stinging, dry eyes could see, bodies were scattered and slumped among the vast expanse of black volcanic rock. Many of them were dead. The rest were close to joining them. Months previously, when he'd still had the strength to walk and the will to do so, Laurence had learned from his nearby comrades that hundreds of thousands of soldiers and military personnel were spread across the planet surface, all living this hellish nightmare.

Laurence looked up as a shadow passed over his father's limp body. One of the tall, dark aliens, who occasionally stalked among them, passed by, its menacing, silvery eyes sending an unstoppable shiver down Laurence's spine. The creature was a Carcarrion, one of the very same creatures that had brushed aside their military defenses so easily, and taken them all from their starships like babes from their cots. What a horrifying day that had been. Laurence remembered it with disturbing clarity. He'd been in the starship's hospital wing. Lieutenant Harper had punched one of his front teeth out a week previously, and he was having it surgically repositioned. Upon waking from the rather unpleasant dreams of the surgeon's anesthesia, he found himself facing a true nightmare: a fully grown Carcarrion warrior baring its cat-like teeth just inches from his face. Seconds after, the beast had used its great fist to send him back into unconsciousness.

Shifting himself slightly on the black rocks, Laurence watched, his head half bowed, as the Carcarrion strode away. It walked with an air of supreme ability and confidence, a creature that had never felt threatened a day in its life. It had clawed hands, which looked powerful enough to crush bone, and its jet black, muscular body looked as hard as the sharp rocks that it stalked among. To Laurence, the Carcarrion seemed a gross, unnatural melding, a nightmarish hybrid of human and demon. On occasion, the passing creatures would throw down metal canisters containing something almost resembling water. Very occasionally, they'd scatter scraps of a dried, plant-like substance. It was a poor excuse for sustenance but food nonetheless. Much to Laurence's dismay, this had not been one of those occasions.

"They're weeding out the strong, father, killing off the weak. Why else keep us alive?" Laurence's voice was little more than a hoarse whisper.

His father didn't answer; he didn't even hear. The fever had all but taken over his mind.

Laurence shifted a flat, slate-like rock by his side and pulled out a canister of the gritty liquid along with a morsel of the plant-like substance that he'd managed to eke out since it was last thrown at his feet. "You're one of the strong ones, father. You've always been one of the strong ones."

The only reply was an incoherent moan. Laurence looked away. He found it almost impossible to look upon the skeletal form of his once broad-shouldered, athletic father. Laurence had never been athletic. In fact, not all that long ago, he'd been nothing short of obese.

For the first couple of months on the ominous planet, Laurence had considered his extra body weight a blessing, something that would help assure his survival. But now, that extra bulk had mostly gone, and it had been far from a blessing. It had kept him alive long enough to witness the countless deaths around him and the wasting away of his father. Now, all he felt was an anguished bitterness towards that extra flesh and the fear and agony that it had prolonged.

He slipped the morsel of dried plant into his mouth and slowly began to chew. After a moment, he carefully spat it into his hand and gently pushed the green pulp between his father's quivering lips. "You have to be strong again, father. I need you. We all need you."

As if in spasm, Laurence's face suddenly screwed up as he tried to fight back an uncontrollable bout of tears, tears that had constantly plagued him since this nightmare had begun. Deliriously, his father coughed and automatically spat the chewed offering from his contorted mouth.

"*Damn it*," Laurence rasped, his anger overshadowing his self-pity. He did his best to scrape the pulp from the rocks beneath him and feed it back between the man's feverish lips. "You *will* eat, you *will* become strong again, and we'll both get off this bloody planet." Laurence's voice had become as near to a shout as his raw throat would allow. The only response he got was a deep rumble from one of the distant volcanoes coupled with a trembling of the hard ground beneath him. It was as if the planet itself was mocking his words. He stared miserably to the horizon and wondered if the ash and lava ever stopped spewing, if the smoke-filled, orange skies ever became clear.

"Son?"

The word was little more than a breath, but it was enough to shock Laurence out of his misery. He looked down to see his father's eyes fixed upon him, a sight he hadn't witnessed in weeks.

"Father?" he whispered disbelievingly. He wanted to say more, but all he could do was bring his head as close as possible to his father's softly moving lips in order to discern the faint words.

"Strength, Laurence. You must find strength."

"There's no need, father. You've come back. You're strong enough for the both of us."

His father weakly shook his head. "No, I'm dying, my boy. I'm sorry; there's no stopping that now… Soon, it will be only you."

Laurence shook his head, the need to shed tears once again threatening to overwhelm him.

"I've failed you, my son…in so many ways." The admiral's eyes were wide open now. "Stay close, son, and listen carefully. There's much I need to say."

Chapter Twenty-Two
DESTINATION

Cal couldn't help but grin as Toker bellowed with everything his lungs could muster. "Shoot, Eddy. Blow the bloody great thing to smithereens."

The girl answered his cries with an explosive torrent of cannon fire.

The Star Splinter's cockpit boomed, crackled, and rumbled as if a ricocheting thunderbolt was imprisoned within its smooth walls. Eddy then watched with obvious delight as the blasts streaked towards the giant asteroid and blew it, as Toker had requested, to smithereens. Not wanting to be outdone, Toker followed her efforts by accelerating the ship on maximum thrust to spiral it expertly through the careening shards and spinning fragments of disintegrated space rock. Throughout his fancy maneuvering, the young, blond man complemented the cockpit's dissipating rumble of cannon fire with howls of triumph.

Cal could have laughed, but he didn't want his two young students to get cocky—or at least not overly so. Eddy and Toker had met his challenge well, spending almost every waking hour of the last two months tirelessly studying and practicing the ship's flight controls. During that time, Eddy had achieved a level of piloting competency that Cal felt earned her a position in one of the combat seats. Toker, however, had voiced no further interest in the ship's weaponry. He'd become far too addicted to piloting the ship, and as far as Cal was concerned, he was damn good at it. It was clear the pair loved their new ship. Indeed, they loved it to the point that it had turned into yet another competition as to who loved it the most.

"Very good, guys. I mean it," Cal said happily. He turned to Jumper, who was looming behind Eddy. "You agree, Jumper?"

Eddy spun in her combat chair and looked up at the tall man.

"Absolutely. I'm no expert in flight combat, but they seem like a crack shot and an ace pilot to me."

"Thanks," Toker said with a flash of his white teeth.

"Yer, cheers, J," Eddy added. Standing up, she unsheathed the huge combat knife from her skinny thigh and spun it around her finger.

Jumper winced.

"Relax, old man. I'm just gonna give myself a hair chop," the girl said before hopping up onto one of the side consoles and hacking into her hair with a wild sawing motion.

"Bloody hell, Ed," Toker exclaimed. "Why don't you save some time and start at the neck?"

Eddy ignored him and continued to hack away. The rest of the gang had put their faith in Melinda's steady, cybernetic hands to keep their hair from becoming too unruly. But until now, Eddy had let her buzz cut sprout freely into a finger-length mass of grungy black spikes.

"So, Cal," Jumper said, trying not to look at Eddy's reckless grooming, "you mentioned earlier about having another destination in mind?"

Cal rubbed the back of his neck. "Er, yes," he said with a crooked grin. So far, his destination choices hadn't been all that successful.

Viktor, who until that point had had his eyes glued to one of the cockpit's rear consoles, looked up. "Another colony, Cal?"

"No, not exactly." During the last eight weeks, they had visited seven colonies, all of which were at least partially occupied. It had been a relief to find and converse with humans other than those residing in Magnet City, but frustratingly, they'd gleaned only scraps of information regarding the invasion, and most of that was conflicting. During these visits, however, three things had remained constant: First, long range communication remained worryingly unachievable. Second, other than the rumours of empty, drifting starships, the military remained completely absent. And third, people were scared out of their wits.

Other than paranoia of further attacks from the invaders, fear was bubbling up from many sources, and lack of military enforcement was already causing civil unrest. Whether trouble was brought about through desperation or through opportunistic crime, the effect was often the same: chaos. Some felt lost, some felt free, and some felt it was time to take matters into their own hands. The pirates were growing bolder of course, and there was even talk of cults rising up. *The end of days is upon us. Embrace your new masters. Your sins have brought this wrath. Repent for mercy.* Etcetera, etcetera. Cal had even heard rumours of human sacrifices on one planet. They'd decided not to stay.

"The way I see it," Cal explained, "we have two options. Option one, we continue to search out occupied colonies or possibly other ships and space stations. Basically wander around and see if we can gather more information about what's been going on…"

"And option two?" Toker asked, not sounding overly keen on option one.

Cal paused, a little unsure of the wisdom of his words. "We go and find out about this strange new enemy first hand—"

"Now you're talking, Cal," Eddy interjected.

"Really, Cal?" Viktor said, paling slightly. "You really think we should go and seek them out?"

"No, not all...just one."

"One?" Eddy asked, sounding deflated.

"I assume you all know of the Krill Strip?"

"Course, Cal," Viktor snorted. "Everyone knows about the Strip. Toddlers learn about it in school." Seeing the expressions on Eddy's and Toker's faces, the boy continued. "It's that section of space. Somewhere near the fringe boundary. Three thousand and eighty-four planets and twice as many moons all packed up tight. Home to eighty-one percent of all alien life discovered so far." Viktor suddenly paused then paled a little more. "You think we should go to C9, Cal? That's in the Krill Strip, right?"

"C9?" Toker asked.

"The Carcarrion home world," Cal informed him. Then he shook his head. "But no, that's not what I had in mind. A few years ago, I paid a visit to another planet in the Krill Strip. It has a military research base on it called Deltapoint Three, a place where they collect and study alien life forms...thousands of specimens all under lock and code. Assuming they haven't gotten rid of it or dissected it into a million pieces, one of the specimens was a pretty formidable female Carcarrion. Of course, without communications, there's no way of knowing if she's still there or even if the base is still operational. But it might be one of the only places to find people who really know what they're talking about, a place to get some real answers. Otherwise, we might have months, even years, of useless rumors."

Toker shrugged. "If these specimens are under lock and code, then I guess it sounds like a good plan to me. They *are* under lock and code though, right, Cal?"

"As far as I know. But a visit to Deltapoint Three wouldn't be without risks. We'd have to travel to the near side of the Krill Strip, a good two months' travel from here, maybe more. And once there, we'd only be a stone's throw from the Carcarrion home world, maybe two weeks from it in a ship like this. Personally, I don't believe the Carcarrions can be responsible for all this mess, but there's a link there somewhere. Could be risky getting so close."

"Maybe too risky," Jumper said.

Cal almost nodded in agreement. It *was* too risky. In fact, he'd almost not suggested it at all, but he hadn't been able to get the idea out of his head. He was pissed off not knowing what the hell was going on. And he was pissed off being bounced around like a pinball. If he was on his own, the route would already be programmed in. But he wasn't on his own. "Yes, it could well be too risky. But then, everything's going to be risky now. Pirates, raiders—"

"Human bloody sacrifices," Toker interjected. "Crashing ships, feasting monsters, fat frickin' con men. I agree with Cal; trouble's getting worse, and we're bloody trouble magnets. No matter where we go, it's gonna find us. If it's going to a vote, then I vote we head to Cal's base and try and work out what the hell's going on…an' I reckon we should do it before things get any worse."

"Bravo, blondie," Eddy said, sliding off the console and brushing clumps of black hair off her shoulders. "I'm with him. Let's go get our hands on one of these Carrion things and work out the best way to bust them up."

Cal nodded. "Okay, that's two votes. What about you and Melinda, Viktor?"

The boy's attention was back on his console screen. Always hungry for knowledge, Cal guessed he was probably studying up on the Carcarrion home world of C9, or the research base of Deltapoint Three.

"We're in, Cal, Melinda and me," he mumbled with a wave of his hand. "Whatever you decide."

"Okay," Cal said with a shrug. He wasn't sure how he felt about the ease at which his young companions were agreeing to the plan. Part of him had been sure that Toker and Viktor's vote would have been no. Then they wouldn't go. Then he could get the bloody idea out of his head. "Jumper?"

Jumper rubbed and scratched at his smooth chin. "Like you say, it could be the best way to get some facts," he said after a few moments. After a moment more, he added, "I think we should be especially cautious though."

"Agreed," Cal said, slapping his old friend on the shoulder. "Caution it is."

Chapter Twenty-Three
THE PERFECT PRESSURE

Laurence Decker's arms were limp with exhaustion. Every muscle in his starved, pathetic body was now utterly defeated by sickening fatigue. The previous evening, he had made a solo attempt at burying his father, a task that had utilized every last scrap of his withering energy. He'd then spent the longest night of his life slumped, almost paralyzed, among the black rocks. Unfortunately, the overwhelming fatigue had never quite reached his brain, and his dying father's last words had run on a continuous loop in his mercilessly active mind. To make the waking nightmare worse, great sheets of hot rain had fallen, hammering rain that had stung his skin and abused his ears as it noisily pounded the rocks around him. The torrent had finally dissipated sometime just before the crimson dawn. Now only sparse, heavy drops fell, plopping loudly in the deep puddles that had collected in the crevices of the jagged landscape.

Slumped against a smooth, angular rock face, Laurence shifted his head in an attempt to look about at his fellow survivors. Of the scores of prisoners who had once filled the desolate landscape, maybe a third now remained. Laurence had remembered thinking that their alien captors were, for some unfathomable reason, weeding out the strong. Now, he wasn't so sure. Every single one of those supposedly *strong ones* were now in a similar state to himself, and it was far from strong. He had no doubt that every one of them, himself included, would soon be dead, and for what? He'd probably never find out.

The Carcarrion aliens remained a mystery to Laurence. A far greater number of them had begun to stalk among the surviving captives. They continued to dish out stale water and scraps of dry plant, but they also picked their way through the rocks, peering menacingly at each of their prisoners, systematically carrying away the dead. Monstrous gardeners ridding their land of weeds. Laurence wanted to cry out to them, wanted to let them know they'd made a mistake. He wasn't one of the strong ones, he'd just been a fat one. Maybe in realizing their error, they'd kill him quickly. But it was no good; even if he had the energy to cry out, he still couldn't bring himself to do so. He'd lasted this long, hadn't he?

No, he would see it through.

Feeling almost in a trance, he stared into a pool that had formed in a small hole before him. The hole was there as a result of his excavations the previous evening. He had eventually succeeded in lifting enough rocks to cover his father's body, but only just. He was damned if he was going to let those monsters take it from him, not as long as he still had breath. No, his father would rest in peace. He deserved it. What a shame there would be no one to do the same for his own corpse when his turn came. But perhaps he didn't deserve it.

Waiting helplessly for that inevitable turn to come, Laurence caught sight of a strange-looking insect. The creature was no bigger than his thumbnail and was struggling desperately on the surface of the newly formed pool before him. *Why bother to struggle?* he thought bitterly. *Life and death is oblivious, uncompromising. Far easier to let it do with you as it pleases.* As he continued to witness the little insect's futile struggle, his father's final words flashed again into his mind and brought with them their usual dose of shame. Fearful that the torturous mind loops might restart, Laurence quickly, almost desperately, pushed the thoughts aside. He felt like crying, but this time, he held back the tears. He'd had enough of crying.

The little insect's efforts slowed, and Laurence found himself wondering where those *gods* were—any one of those all-powerful, all-forgiving gods that countless people seemed so fond of. "If God's real, then I guess you and I aren't in his line of sight, eh, little feller," he whispered, letting a somber chuckle escape his lips. "Or maybe we're just not worth the effort."

"How do you know God is a *he*?"

The voice was loud, high-pitched, and so unexpected that it almost made Laurence leap to his feet. Had he the strength, he just might have. "What the…?" he gasped. For a ridiculous moment, he almost believed the struggling insect had been the one to address him. Forcing his head up, his eyes fell upon the strange sight of a skinny, deeply tanned man standing just a few meters away. The man was barefoot and wore tattered gray clothing. His long hair and beard were as white as snow and close to becoming dreadlocked.

"I must apologize for startling you, my friend," said the strange man in a cheery tone. "The voice has a tendency to amplify in this rocky terrain."

With great effort, Laurence straightened himself and rubbed his face with a grubby hand. "I'm hallucinating," he muttered.

"Possibly, but who's to say your whole life hasn't been a hallucination, eh?" The little man let out a quick, bird-like laugh.

Laurence rubbed his face again.

The man walked—almost skipped—towards Laurence then squatted down on the opposite side of the little pool. Closer up, Laurence could see deep lines mapping his face. *If he's real, he must be pretty old*, he thought. But the spring in his step and the glint in his bright eyes suggested otherwise.

"Now I *know* I'm hallucinating," Laurence said. "No one could negotiate these razor sharp rocks with bare feet. It's hard enough in military boots."

"Well observed, my friend. It's true, the black rocks are far from forgiving on the old feet. Twelve years of hopping around on them though seems to toughen up the sole. There's no lie."

Laurence stared at the man. "Okay, perhaps you are real. But I have to tell you your brain is playing tricks on you. It might seem like twelve years, but I can assure you, we've only been here a handful of months."

The man smiled and gave his nose a quick scratch. *There are hidden depths in that smile*, Laurence thought. Profound wisdom or possibly a deep-set madness.

"You're nuts," Laurence decided.

"Indeed, my friend. I concur, I'm as nutty as a heap of Leepan squirrel dung, but then, surely a mad person would probably think themselves sane, would they not?"

Laurence had no answer for the odd little man, so he remained silent. He wondered how someone so small and old had survived the ordeal of the past few months. He concluded that the man must have been of ample proportions just as he'd once been. Where his energy and enthusiasm was coming from, however, was a mystery. Laurence mused over what role such a man might have played in the military. He certainly wasn't a soldier. Far too old. He finally settled on military intelligence. The smartest ones always had a tendency to become the craziest in times of high stress.

"I say, what have we here?" The little man's eyes had fallen upon the insect struggling in the pool.

With the odd stranger's arrival, Laurence had all but forgotten about his little partner in death. He watched in silence as the man leaned forward, dipped a finger into the pool, and lifted the tiny creature from its watery doom.

"Why bother?" Laurence asked glumly.

The man smiled at him—that same strange, all-knowing, all-mad smile—and began to gently blow on the sodden little creature. Once dry, he set it on a nearby rock and watched happily as it scampered away.

"You and I are the equivalent of gods to that little bug." The man jabbed a skinny finger at Laurence. "You even had a hand in creating part of its world when you excavated that hole." He straightened up and casually leaned back against a tall, jutting rock. The relaxed manner in which he moved gave Laurence the impression of someone enjoying a sunny vacation rather than a prisoner of war.

After a moment of careful beard-smoothing, the man said, "I guess I'd like to think that if I were adrift in a vast, perilous ocean, a god might take pity. Make the effort to scoop me to safety, maybe even give me a little blow dry, eh!"

Laurence was about to scoff at the man's words but held his tongue. Perhaps they made sense. "How do you know that I dug that hole?"

"Because I watched you dig it, and I commend your efforts. Was the man your father?"

Laurence nodded.

"I thought so. It seemed you were having quite the father-son talk before his new journey began."

Laurence couldn't decide whether he should take offense at the man's strange comments or for the fact that he'd obviously been spying on him. But he was too tired to be offended. "My father told me many things: some painful and some that have done nothing but tie my brain into knots." He pulled a face of unconvincing anger. "I wish he hadn't said anything."

"Brain knots, eh? You want to share any? Maybe I could help you untie a few."

Despite his odd appearance and his queer way of talking, Laurence was finding himself strangely comfortable in the man's presence. Maybe voicing out loud some of what his father had said was a good idea. Maybe it would help put an end to those damned mind loops. Still, Laurence remained sceptical. "I doubt you'd make any sense of it. Most of what he said was probably gibberish. He was pretty feverish towards the end."

The little man shrugged. "You know, you'd be surprised about that. Sometimes, fevers can squeeze quite a bit of truth, even wisdom, out of people. Sometimes stuff that's been locked away for a lifetime. Imminent death also has a habit of inducing, shall we say, high levels of confessional bravery."

Laurence wasn't sure he knew what the little chap was spouting on about, but he continued the conversation anyway. "He confessed all right. Quite a few things in fact. Some confusing stuff came towards the end. He was mumbling plenty by then. Some of it sounded like a foreign language or, like I said, just a bunch of gibberish. Some I made out though. Talk of how he hadn't pushed me enough. He'd prevented my development, denied me the challenges of life."

The little man nodded, his all-knowing, all-mad smile returning. Laurence raised an eyebrow. "You understand his meaning?"

"Of course. And I'd wager that a not unsubstantial part of you does too. Isn't that right, Laurence?"

Laurence felt a sudden pang of anger. The old man seemed to know every bloody thing, even his name. He wanted to tell the crazy old git that he was nuts and to forget it, but again, he held his tongue. "Okay, okay. I understand it…at least some of it," he blurted after a long, uncomfortable pause. He hoped the confession might redirect the little man's gaze, which seemed to be boring a direct path into his brain.

The old man didn't shift his gaze and remained silent.

Feeling annoyed, so did Laurence.

In a partially successful attempt to compose himself, Laurence took a few dry, rasping breaths and eventually broke the silence. "I guess I would appreciate your take on what he said. Unless, of course, you're too busy saving bugs or birds or some other little critters."

The little man let out a big laugh. "Very good, Laurence. Critters, yes. Very good. I do enjoy a good joke."

Much to Laurence's bemusement, the man seemed genuinely amused.

"Very well. Seeing as you've given me a good laugh, I shall attempt to return the favor by sharing my take on your father's words." Pushing himself off the tall rock, the old man skipped forward and scooped up a fist-sized stone from the ground. "I believe your father was referring to the application of perfect pressure."

"Application of what now?"

"Perfect pressure, Laurence. It's one of nature's grandest laws." The glint in the little man's eyes grew. "Have you ever pumped iron, Laurence?" Seeming to take Laurence's blank expression as an indication to continue, he said, "As you know, there are people out there who like to build big muscles. I'm assuming you've heard of, or have possibly even seen, a gymnasium?"

Laurence nodded. "You mean a power gym. Of course I have," he mumbled, uncomfortably aware of the dumb confusion in his voice.

"Good. Then you'll know that gymnasiums are among the perfect places to build muscles. To pump iron, as the old saying goes." Holding the stone in his right palm, the old man began to pivot his skinny arm at the elbow. "To make muscles stronger and bigger, one has to put strain on them or, if you like, *pressure*. If one puts too little pressure, then not a lot's going to happen. The muscle will remain weak and small. You must watch for the danger though, Laurence, for trying for *too much* pressure will overwhelm the muscle, causing it injury." The little man's arm trembled as he feigned a difficult curl of the rock. "So you see, one must find the perfect amount of pressure to reach an optimum rate of growth. *That* is the application of *perfect pressure*."

Laurence shifted uncomfortably. "Very insightful, but I'm guessing my father's dying words weren't a plea for me to venture forth and build bigger biceps!"

The little man let out another big laugh. "Congratulations yet again with the wit. I thank you. Yes, in my opinion, your analysis is correct. I believe that what your father was referring to was the application of the perfect pressure in conjunction with raising his son. Would you agree, Laurence, that you were…how to put it…*mollycoddled* as a child? Would you agree that you missed out on some of the harsh realities of youth? Bullying for example? Perhaps you even had your grades plumped up? Maybe a career boost to boot? And a—"

"Okay, enough," Laurence interjected testily, his throat burning under the strain. He was angry. Not at the old man and his damned uncanny insightfulness but at his own ignorance—Ignorance that had apparently consumed him his entire life. "I'm sorry," he said after a moment. "I didn't mean to shout at you."

"I know you didn't. I believe you meant to shout at yourself. Possibly even at your father too, eh?" the little man said calmly. "It seems your father didn't apply enough pressure, perhaps even no pressure. He likely shielded you from any outside pressures too.

218

Maybe you feel a little bitter towards him. He denied you that chance to grow into a strong-minded, strong-bodied man. Your father took all the weight of your God-given dumbbell, and you remained a flabby, underdeveloped bicep."

Laurence thought the words a little harsh, but they shone light on a truth which, if he was honest, he already knew full well. Of course he knew it. He'd known it most of his life, but he'd ignored it, pushed it aside. He was angry at his father, but at the same time, he didn't blame him one bit. He knew all his father's acts had come from a deep-seated belief that he was doing right by his son.

"Of course, your father's no longer with you, is he, Laurence? He's busy experiencing whatever delights that mysterious afterlife offers. For the first time, you are your own man, and no one can deny that you now have the mother lode of pressure on you. Is it going to be too much, Laurence? Or is it going to be the perfect pressure?'

Laurence gazed at the man, feeling almost hypnotized. It was as if his odd little friend was reaching inside him and plucking at a chord. There was a good chance, of course, that he'd become delirious during the long night. Maybe this strange man was no more than a projection of his subconscious. He didn't feel delirious though. Far from it. In fact, his mind was perhaps clearer and more focused than ever. He was probably close to death, and his current situation should be considered impossible. But strangely, the impossible suddenly seemed altogether possible. Was it *his* turn? His turn to become a man of worth? That plucked chord was resonating, giving him strength. Not physical strength. He could still barely lift his head. No, a nameless strength that, in truth, had been building all night...or perhaps for months now.

Questions began to form in Laurence's mind like soda bubbles in a bottle. Every one of those questions suddenly burst, however, as his little friend stood bolt upright and began peering over the rocks.

Seconds later, he'd ducked down again. "It's been a pleasure conversing with you, Laurence," he said as he stretched forward over the pool and extended an open palm. "Tarquintin Matisse." He smiled. "Friends call me Tark."

Laurence managed to raise a weak arm and slapped his limp hand into the open palm. He marvelled at the strength in the old man's grip as his hand was rigorously shaken. The little fellow was most definitely real.

Tark released Laurence's hand, which promptly fell back into his lap. "I'll see you soon, my friend."

Before Laurence could enquire as to where the little chap was off to, a familiar sound came from beyond the rocky ridge behind his head—the chilling footfall of one of the Carcarrions. Laurence shifted his head in an attempt to see the approaching menace.

"They're coming…" Laurence said as he rolled his head back towards his white-haired friend. But the man was gone. Laurence had little time to puzzle over the disappearance before the large, jet black alien crested the ridge. It slowly stalked around him to stand exactly where his little wiry friend had been perched just moments before.

The alien peered down with its lifeless, ice-gray eyes. Determinedly, Laurence craned his neck and stared right back, his own eyes emanating his new-found bravery and defiance. For a long while, their eyes remained locked. Despite every fiber of his being fighting him, Laurence was determined not to break. He wouldn't lower his gaze, not this time.

Then the creature moved, reaching a heavily muscled arm behind its back.

So this it, Laurence thought as he watched the creature pull out what was sure to be some sort of death-dealing weapon. *At least I got to be brave once if only for a few moments.*

But he was mistaken. Instead of a weapon, the creature pulled out what appeared to be a large chunk of raw meat and tossed it at his feet. Laurence's eyes widened as he stared at the glistening flesh. He looked back up at the creature, searching for some sign of deceit, a clue that the offering was rotten, or for it to be snatched away from him in some cruel game. But he could see no such sign. There was something though. Just before the creature turned to stride away, a hint of something on the smooth, feline-like face: yes, an unquestionably sadistic smile.

Once the beast was gone from sight, Laurence turned back and stared disbelievingly at the food before him. He couldn't be sure what kind of meat it was, but he didn't much care. It was food. Life. Strength.

He was still staring dumbly at the flesh when the familiar tanned face, framed with white hair, appeared from behind a rock to his right.

"Looks tasty, Laurence. If I were you, I'd start filling my belly."

Then, the face was gone again.

Laurence didn't need his little friend to tell him twice. With an incredibly painful effort, he levered himself forward to seize the hunk of raw flesh in his trembling hands. Then, with dark blood flowing between his knuckles, he brought it to his salivating mouth.

Chapter Twenty-Four
LIGHTS OUT

Cal watched in disappointment as the huge, snake-like creature reared up, parting trees as it did so, and opened its massive, multi-fanged mouth.

"It's gonna strike," Toker blurted, taking a fearful step back from Cal and the others.

"Where you off to, bloody wuss?" Eddy chided him. "It can't hurt you."

"I know," Toker said tetchily. "You think I don't know that?" He took a tentative step forward and forced himself to look up at the twelve gleaming white fangs—not an easy thing to do considering each was as long as a man's arm and looked strong enough to pierce metal.

Then the creature did indeed strike.

"There goes another spy drone," Viktor mumbled as the smart-glass of the Star Splinter's cockpit went black. "Don't reckon it'll be working too well after passing through that thing's gut." The boy tapped a couple of controls, and the cockpit window reverted back to its real-time view: star-studded space and a distant, green planet.

Cal stared at the planet for a time, trying his best to hide his frustration. The alien research base, Delta Point Three, had been their best chance at getting some real answers. Unfortunately, the lack of communication from the planet surface suggested the base was unoccupied. And now, the fourth of the Star Splinter's spy drones had been eaten but not before revealing that the base actually was occupied though not by anything even closely resembling a human. He'd had friends on that base. He wondered where they were, what had happened to them. If things stayed the way they were, he'd probably never find out.

Everyone remained silent.

Eventually, Jumper laid a hand on Cal's shoulder. "I guess it wasn't meant to be."

Cal nodded. "Maybe." He rubbed the back of his neck and considered for a moment. "But I'm still going down there."

The words made Toker choke on thin air. "You can't be serious, bro," he said once he'd recovered. "We can't go down *there*. The base is all bust up. There's bloody beasties everywhere, worse than bloody Mars."

Cal put up a placating hand. "Not we, Toker. *Me*."

"But why? What's the point?" Toker argued, an edge of annoyance in his voice. "If *you* go down, we *all* have to go down. That's the way we operate."

"Well, maybe that needs to change," Cal replied, feeling a little annoyed himself. He didn't need them, not this time. "Not all of those buildings were breeched. There might be survivors. It will only take one of us to find out."

"Survivors? Down there? No chance, bro."

"Looks like the base was attacked," Jumper suggested, "just like Mars. I think Toker's right, Cal. You'll not find anyone down there."

Toker nodded. "Nothing but man chompers."

"Is a lot of beasts," Eddy agreed. "Reckon any survivors would'a got et up."

Toker turned and glared at her. "Jeeze, little chick, d'you always have to point out the grizzly bleeding obvious."

"Shut it. I'll go down there with you, Cal."

Cal shook his head. "No, not this time, Eddy. I'm the one that dragged us here; I should be the one to take the risk."

"But why take the risk at all?" Toker persisted.

"Because, Toker, even if there's no survivors down there, there might be information. We *need* information." *Or maybe it's just me who needs it,* Cal thought, but his growing irritation pushed the thought aside.

Toker nodded at Viktor. "So get little genius here to get the info remotely."

"It doesn't work that way, idiot," Viktor said harshly, his tone suggesting he'd said it a hundred times before.

"So send down another of your little spy drones."

"We've already sent four. We haven't got an endless supply, you know," Viktor spat back. "I don't wanna risk anymore. We've only got three left."

"So we should let Cal risk himself then, should we?" Toker said, raising his voice and turning on the boy.

"I didn't say that," Viktor shouted back.

"Okay, easy, easy," Cal interjected. "No one's saying that. But I'm going alone. The choice is mine." This was rapidly becoming one of the rare times he missed his military rank and the simplicity of orders.

"Right, Cal," Eddy agreed. "An' I'll be goin' too…to watch your back."

"Are you deaf?" Toker said. "He's already told you no, Ed. Besides, if you go, that definitely means I have to go."

Cal stared at the pair. "I'm going alone."

Eddy screwed up her face, her eyes still on Toker. "Wot you on about? We don't need you slowin' us down and givin' away our position with your flippin' squeals."

Jumper moved in and put a hand on Eddy's shoulder. "If anyone should go down there, it should be me. I've got the most experience with dangerous beasts."

"I have plenty of experience," Cal said, looking at Jumper. "Besides, you taught me everything you know." The words sounded lame in Cal's head, and he suddenly felt a teenage boy again, justifying his recklessness to his tall, all-knowing hunting mentor.

"You can't teach everything, Cal."

"You taught me enough," Cal replied, trying his best for a firmer, more *adult* tone but probably overcooking it a little. "And I'm the one best qualified to assess any information."

"*None* of you need to go," Toker said, throwing his hands up in exasperation. "It's too bloody dangerous."

A part of Cal agreed with his young friend, but for the moment, that part was smothered under frustration, annoyance, and an overwhelming need for information. He had to find out what the hell was going on. To come all this way and not even get a piece of the puzzle... He was starting to feel out of control, and it was only going to get worse the longer he remained ignorant.

"Unless..." Toker said. "Maybe Melinda should go."

Viktor whirled on him. "*Huh? Why the hell should my Melinda go?*"

"What d'you mean why?" Toker shouted back. "Cos she's quicker and stronger of course." He shook his head. "And you call me idiot. Besides, she's not alive like the rest of—"

Viktor lunged at him, tears springing from his eyes. "*Shut up. She is alive.*"

Toker stumbled back, narrowly missing the boy's bony fist.

"Hey, watch it, squirt."

"Take it easy, kid," Jumper said as he reached out and restrained the boy.

For a moment, Cal thought Toker might try and strike back, but then his shoulders dropped and he held up his hand placatingly. "Okay, *okay,* I take it back."

Cal rubbed his face and eyes. This was getting ridiculous. *They're just stressed. I'm bloody stressed.* Maybe he could drop them all off on some colony for a bit. Do some detective work unimpeded. *Alone' I could get some answers.*

Seeming oblivious to the tension, Eddy took a step forward. "If Melinda's goin', I'm definitely goin'."

Toker turned on her. "Bloody hell, chick, it's not a competition."

"Just cos you're too flippin' scared."

Seeming unable to retort, Toker glared at Eddy, his expression caught between exasperation and anger. Fists clenched, he shook his head and stepped away towards the flight console. "Okay, you know what, you lot bloody decide between yourselves who goes down there and gets munched. I've had about enough teeth and frickin' claws for one lifetime. Bunch of bloody madness."

Cal rubbed his eyes again. *I could be down there by now.*

"Coward," Eddy barked at Toker's back as he turned to stare out of the cockpit window.

Sniffing loudly, Viktor shrugged Jumper off and turned to bury his tear-streaked face in Melinda's ample bosom.

"Okay, everyone just calm down," Cal said, his own voice still far from calm. "We've come too far to just turn back now. I've made my decision. No one else need take the risk."

"An' I've made my decision too, Cal," Eddy persisted. "I'm comin' with you."

"No, Eddy."

"I ain't lettin' you go down there without me watchin' your back."

"Hey guys, what the hell's that?" Toker asked.

Cal barely registered his young friend's question and easily ignored it. "I'm going alone, Eddy, and that's final."

Jumper sidled up to Eddy. "She's right, Cal. You don't have to be the lone hero."

"*D'you guys hear me?*" Toker called out.

"I'm not trying to be a hero, Jumper, I'm trying to save lives."

"*Guys,*" Toker persisted, louder this time.

Jumper shook his head. "And at what cost, Cal, your own life?"

"*Bloody hell, will you lot bloody listen to me?*"

"*What, Toker?*" Cal shouted, finally losing his composure.

"Yeah, what you flippin' whinin' about?" Eddy snapped.

"*Look.* What the *hell* is that?"

They all turned to see that Toker had climbed onto the flight console and was now on his tiptoes, staring at something through the cockpit window. "That there...what is it?'

With a sigh, Cal stepped forward and peered up through the window. He could see nothing but stars. Even the green planet had moved out of view due to the slight twisting drift of the ship.

"What's what?" Eddy asked, nudging past Cal to get a better look. "Oh... What the hell is that?" she exclaimed, planting one of her knees on the console and stretching towards the glass.

Cal stared at the window, still seeing nothing but stars.

Giving in to curiosity, Viktor peeled himself away from Melinda. "Hey, you don't have to clamber all over the consoles, dummies," he said with a sniff. "It's smart-glass, zoom tech built in." The boy shuffled over to a combat-boot-free console and tapped at the controls.

Shit. Cal's gut lurched as he caught sight of the thing in question.

A ship…possibly. It was a long, silvery block, glinting in the light of a distant sun, little more than a sliver. "Anything on the scanners, Viktor?"

"Nothing. According to this console, it's not there."

"Course it's there," Eddy spat, "an' it's bloody well getting closer I reckon. See, it's getting bigger." The girl slid off the console and hopped over to one of the combat chairs. "It'll be in cannon range soon. Then we'll see how real it is."

"Hold off, Eddy," Cal said, not moving his eyes from the fast growing object. *Fuck. This isn't good.*

"What do you suppose it could be, Cal?" Jumper asked quietly.

"I've no idea. I've never seen anything like it."

Still standing atop the flight console, Toker briefly turned to look at Viktor. "Thought you said you could zoom in on it."

"I can't zoom in on something that the scanners say isn't there," the boy replied defensively.

With nothing to compare it to, Cal couldn't easily judge its size, but he had the distinct impression that it was large. Not Big Blue large but big nonetheless. The lurch in his gut had turned to waves of adrenaline that were joined by alarm bells clanging ten to the dozen. In all his years in the military, he'd never seen a ship like it, if it even *was* a ship. Its design was smooth and featureless, alien in every sense of the word. And Eddy was right, it was approaching fast. "This is no time for attack, Eddy. This is a time for running." Swinging himself into the piloting chair, he quickly powered up the ship's Vortex engines. "Viktor, the cloaking device if you would."

"Just tried it, Cal. It's…it's crapped out. Everything's going haywire." There was fear in the boy's voice. "Someone's hacking into the ship's systems…it shouldn't be possible. No one could hack through this level of security. It can't be done."

As if mocking Viktor's words, the Vortex engines died.

Cal looked back at the strange craft. It was almost out of view due to the Star Splinter's slow, twisting drift, but he could see enough to know that it was getting damn close.

"My cannon doesn't work, Cal," Eddy pointed out in a tone that suggested that the looming threat was nothing more than a toy-breaker.

"Viktor, try—" Cal's words caught in his throat as the cockpit's lights went out. *What the hell?* His thought was supported by a chorus of swearing from the others, most notably Toker.

Fortunately, the cockpit wasn't in complete darkness; a block of light, emanating from the distant sun, was falling through the main window. The light offered just enough illumination to see Toker tumble off the flight console. Cal sprang out of the flight chair but wasn't quick enough to prevent his young friend from hitting the deck with a sickening thud. "Toker, you okay?" he asked, kneeling by his side.

"Shit...*shit*. I think my arm's bust up."

Helping him into a sitting position, Cal did his best to inspect the arm in the dim light. Sure enough, it was achieving an improbable angle at a point with no benefit of a joint. "Don't worry. We'll get you fixed up in no time," Cal said, trying his best to sound optimistic. "For now, it's probably best if you stay sitting."

Eddy shuffled over and stared down at Toker's arm, her expression part disgust, part genuine concern.

"You okay, Eddy?"

"Yep," she said without taking her eyes off Toker's arm. The disgust was already fading, leaving behind only concern.

"Nothing's working," Viktor called out. The boy was frantically tapping at one of the lifeless consoles. Cal suspected that the absence of technology to one such as Viktor was akin to a loss of sight. "We're adrift, completely dead in the water."

"Keep trying," Cal said as calmly as he could manage. Striding over to the side viewing panel, he leaped up on the console beneath it. Pressing his head against the panel, he just about made out the edge of the giant, cylindrical threat. It was still closing in fast and was beginning to dwarf the Star Splinter. "It's almost on us," he said, still managing a calm tone despite his rising fear and anger. He should never have brought them here, not so close to the Carcarrion home planet. He shouldn't have even suggested it.

"*Who,* Cal? *Who's* almost on us?" Toker asked, clutching his broken arm.

Cal looked down at him but said nothing. There was no need; they already knew the answer. He dropped off the console, strode purposefully to the rear of the cockpit, and began running his fingers along the back wall like a blind man searching for a door.

"It's circling us, I think," Viktor said.

Cal briefly turned to see that the boy had scuttled over to Melinda, his eyes fearfully locked on the main window. Sure enough, the huge craft had begun to maneuver around the Star Splinter and, like a boulder rolling across a cave mouth, it was slowly blocking out the light of the distant sun. Swearing under his breath, Cal turned back to the rear wall. "Melinda, I need your help."

Without a second's hesitation, the synthetic was by his side.

"Do you think you can get this open?" he asked her, indicating the edge of a large panel that was neatly inset within the wall. Melinda remained silent as she wedged her fingertips under the panel's bottom seam. After a moment of strain, the cybernetic woman succeeded in forcing the panel open. The sound was not a pleasant one.

The inky black shadow had almost leaked its way over the last section of the cockpit floor as Cal ducked down and snatched a bag from the exposed compartment. He was hurried but efficient as he pulled night vision glasses from the bag and passed them around to the rest of the gang. As they put them on, the last sliver of sunlight was swallowed by the predatory mass looming over their paralyzed ship.

With the benefit of night vision, Cal delved back into the compartment then remerged with a five-click pulse rifle gripped in each hand. He looked at the wide eyes staring at him through the night vision glasses. They seemed to be seeking reassurance that was not in his power to offer. The anger he felt at himself gnawed a little deeper. "Obviously, we're in deep shit here. I'm sorry for getting you all into this."

"Wasn't your fault," Eddy said without hesitation.

Jumper nodded in agreement. "We each had a vote, Cal."

"Unanimous as far as I remember it, bro," Toker said from his seated position. "We're all—"

Whatever Toker was going to say was interrupted by a loud, metallic clang, the echoes of which reverberated through the ship's smooth walls. There was a moment of silence, then the ship lurched, sending the lot of them—bar the ever-steady Melinda and the seated Toker—stumbling. Another moment, and the ship was once again still and eerily quiet.

Viktor broke the silence with a whisper. "That sounded like a magnetic grasper."

Cal took a moment more to listen before he replied. "They mean to board us."

"So hand out the big guns, Cal." Eddy didn't bother to keep her voice low. "Reckon it'll be them that'll be in deep shit, they try hoppin' on *our* ship."

Cal would have been heartened at the girl's infallible bravery were it not for the fear he could see in her eyes.

"At least they didn't blow us to smithereens like they did Earth,"

Toker pointed out. "Could be a good sign."

Cal nodded. "I think it's time for one more vote. Toker's right; they haven't destroyed the ship, which is no doubt within their capabilities. That could mean we're to be kept alive."

"Kept alive for what?" Viktor asked, his voice still not much more than a whisper.

Eddy sniffed loudly. "Could be we're kept alive, or it could be that we're blasted with our hands up and our pants down."

"Or experimented on," Toker suggested.

Eddy sniffed again. "I vote we give 'um all we got with these pulse rifles."

Jumper smiled at her, fatherly and infused with pride. Picking up his Long Eye rifle, he calmly checked that it was loaded and turned to Cal. "You know my vote, my friend; I've never been one for prisons."

"Well if we're gonna fight, you better get me up off the bloody floor," Toker blurted, reaching up with his good arm.

Eddy walked over to him, slapped a hand into his outstretched palm, and hoisted him to his feet with surprising strength. "Always knew you weren't a complete wuss, blondie."

He winced as his broken arm fell to his side, then he managed a small shrug. "Don't fancy getting probed."

Another haunting clang echoed through the darkness, and the ship lurched again.

Viktor took a deep, wobbly breath and did his best to stand straight. The panic on his young face tore painfully at Cal's heart. *Damn it.* He could barely look at the boy. What a fool he'd been leading them here. This is why he'd left the military: that damned responsibility for the fate of others. He couldn't bloody take it. His resignation seemed so long ago now. He'd punched out Captain Decker's tooth that day because of his foolish orders. But was he really any better? He was too reckless. He'd always been too reckless.

He forced himself to look Viktor in the eye. It was the least he owed him.

"Melinda and me will fight, Cal," the boy said, managing to raise his voice above a whisper. "Isn't that right—" his words died in his throat as he looked up at Melinda.

Cal looked at her too. The cybernetic woman seemed even more still and silent than usual. Instead of giving Viktor her usual loving smile, she simply stared dead ahead without so much as a twitch of a cybernetic finger.

"Something wrong with her?" Toker asked.

"*Yes*," the boy cried. "Something's *seriously* wrong with her."

Before Viktor had a chance to elaborate, there was a deafening bang. Cal and Jumper instinctively thrust their weapons towards the source of the sound. It had originated directly above their heads, but there was nothing to be seen.

Eddy moved to Cal's side. "You mind, Cal?" she asked, finally lowering her voice.

Without taking his eyes from the ceiling, Cal handed the girl the second pulse rifle. "Remember Jumper's top tip," he whispered.

"Don't worry. I'll make 'um count."

Melinda remained completely unresponsive as Viktor desperately worked his nimble fingers in a section he'd opened up at the base of her spine. The boy didn't get a chance to do much, however, before there was another defining bang, this time followed by a loud hiss emanating from the very same spot above their heads. Cal could see something now: a metallic probe with an arrow-shaped head that had pierced the ceiling and snaked its way into the cockpit. Before he had a chance to decide whether or not to fire his pulse rifle, a fine, red mist burst from the end of the probe and rapidly started filling the cockpit.

"Should I blast it, Cal?" Eddy bellowed over the sound of the hissing probe.

Cal didn't reply—to do so would allow the red mist to enter his mouth.

As his friends dropped to the hard, metal floor around him, Cal had about ten seconds to come up with an idea, a plan to execute before the red mist penetrated his shirt, which he now held over his mouth.

Unfortunately, ten seconds simply wasn't enough.

Chapter Twenty-Five
THE EARNING OF TRUST

All things considered, Laurence felt pretty damn good. It seemed impossible that only a week before he'd had little more strength than a premature newborn. But a lot had changed in that week. Reaching up to the dusky orange sky, he flexed and stretched his muscles. Having always been concealed under thick folds of soft flesh, the muscles seemed strangely new. He held the stretch for a time then brought his arms down and stared at his biceps. They were far from large, but he could *see* them, and they *worked*—a near miracle considering the hell his body had been through.

Over the past week, he'd been consuming the raw meat offerings with ravenous vigor. He had no idea what animal the flesh originated from, but it was rich and restored his strength fast. He found himself filled with gratitude. Not towards the Carcarrions who kept throwing the meat at his feet, but towards the animal whose life had ended to ensure that his could continue.

Taking a seat on a rock, Laurence took some time to look about him. Thanks to the meat offerings, most of his fellow survivors had also rediscovered some of their past strength and were now ambling about the dark landscape, re-educating their emaciated bodies and conversing with their fellow captives. Despite this new turn of events, Laurence could still recognize desperation within each of their faces. They questioned reasons behind their continued survival. Were they simply being set up straight in order to be knocked down again? Was this all a game? Laurence could see that leadership was needed, and he was finding it within himself to offer just that. A few weeks previously, a chord had been struck deep within him, and now, that chord resonated louder than ever. As his mind and body grew stronger, so did his will.

But Laurence knew that hope would never be brought about with specifics—there were none—but instead with a show of strength and defiance. As soon as he had been able, he'd begun to introduce himself and converse with as many of the men and women around him as possible. At first, it had taken him a great deal of time and physical effort. They were, after all, scattered far and wide across the jagged landscape. But then, remaining consistent in their mysterious ways, the Carcarrions had set about herding them together like sheep into a pen, the pen in this case being a large, rocky expanse of noticeably flatter terrain. There were still rocks—some large enough for even a big man to conceal himself—but in general, the contour of the land was relatively level with little in the way of ridges. Being in closer proximity to his fellow captives, Laurence had been better able to converse and estimate their numbers. Over the months, they had been reduced from hundreds of thousands to maybe ten thousand at most. Still, ten thousand was a good deal of men and women, and they were getting stronger by the day.

Looking beyond the flat expanse, Laurence focused on something which, despite not being the first time he'd laid his eyes upon it, still seemed to play tricks on his brain. Some sort of monstrous vessel was firmly planted on the planet surface far in the distance. The vessel was like none that Laurence had ever seen. Huge and featureless in its design, it had come to his attention on waking a few days previously. It was quite a shock as it certainly hadn't been there the night before. The speed of its arrival left Laurence with no doubt that it was a ship as such a colossal structure could never have been constructed in so short a time.

He wondered if it was the same craft that had overwhelmed his starship. Having been under a dental anaesthesia on that day, he'd never seen the attacking ship. Then, upon waking, he'd only had a few moments of terror as the Carcarrion looming over him sent him straight back into slumber. The next thing he'd been aware of was this hellish landscape.

On first inspection, the huge vessel appeared to be a simple, silver cube, its gleaming surfaces reflecting the deep, orange skies and black, volcanic peaks. As Laurence had examined it longer, however, he'd seen that it was made up of thousands of smaller cubes, some of which would occasionally twist and move and in doing so change parts of the vessel's structure. Occasionally, one of the cubes would detach itself and fly solo towards the horizon, eventually disappearing from sight into the volcanic dust clouds or vertically into the dark, fiery sky. Laurence could only speculate as to their destinations.

Despite its simplistic design, the vessel oozed technological superiority. Whoever or whatever had engineered it were certainly more advanced than humans. Although Laurence knew little of the Carcarrions, the thought of them achieving such a technological feat was a tough one to swallow. He saw undeniable intelligence in the eyes of his captors, but for them to be responsible for such engineering wizardry seemed an absurd stretch of the imagination. He had considered the possibility that the Carcarrions were simply slaves, somehow bent to the will of a higher force. But he had a hard time believing that too. For one, the tall, dark aliens appeared far too willing, too full of malice towards himself and his fellow captives to be sharing in their fate.

Pushing his thoughts aside, Laurence crouched down and picked up a few fist-sized rocks, testing each of their weights in turn. The rocks must have been incredibly dense; even the small ones were surprisingly heavy. Making his choice, he straightened up and, holding the rock in his right fist, began to repeatedly curl his arm.

"How you getting on finding that perfect pressure?"

Without looking up, Laurence smiled. His mind was now calm enough that his new friend's, stealthy approaches no longer startled him. "I'm getting there."

"Glad to hear it," Tark said, his long, white dreadlocks bouncing almost comically as he hopped over the rocks to perch nearby. For a moment, the little man just sat and stared at Laurence with his strange smile. Laurence glanced up and smiled back, all the while continuing to curl the rock.

"I'm afraid time is running short," Tark said eventually.

Laurence gave him a questioning look.

"I've just been to the North border of your new little pen. Your captors are driving metallic spikes into the ground. My guess is they'll soon be activating them: a pretty little force field to keep you *truly* captive."

Laurence swapped the rock to his left fist and began to curl. It didn't escape his attention that his strange friend always referred to the captives as if he wasn't a member of that particular group. But he *was* real. Laurence was now of sound enough mind to know that the little man wasn't simply a figment of his imagination, a subconscious mentor, or a manifested guide to bring him back to sanity.

"A force field? Maybe they're fearful," Laurence suggested after a moment. "Now, we're regaining strength and starting to communicate."

Tark gave a little shrug. "From my observations, I'm not sure that *fearful* is a word they're all that familiar with. Not in respect to their own emotions at any rate."

Laurence nodded. "Maybe you're right. Just keeping their pets in a smaller, more orderly cage then." He strained on his last few arm curls then let the heavy rock thud to the ground. "Of course, sometimes, pets can escape. And on occasion, they bite their owners...sometimes even fatally."

"Getting strong and quick, Laurence," Tark said with a wide grin. "Seems that perfect pressure is really working out for you, eh?"

Laurence grinned. "I've a way to go yet. My arms still feel like wet spaghetti."

The little man let out a squeal of a laugh. "Spaghetti arms, very good, young Laurence." He popped off his perch with the gusto and nimbleness of a child. "Of course, I think you know that I wasn't referring to your muscles."

Before Laurence could reply, Tark spun to his left and straightened up in his usual meerkat fashion. "I'm afraid I must be off."

"No, wait. What did you mean by running out of time? Time for what?"

Tark stared at him with those soul-seeking eyes. "Do you trust me, Laurence?" he asked, his tone turning serious.

"Of course," Laurence replied without hesitation.

"You mustn't. Not yet. Trust has to be earned. And these people, these soldiers," he swept his skinny arm over the far-reaching group that surrounded them. "They have to learn to trust *you*."

"Why...? Why me?" Laurence asked the question even though he already knew the answer.

"Because they're already starting to look up to you. You're a leader, Laurence. Even under all that molly-coddled flesh, there was always the potential for great leadership. It's coiled up in your genes, just waiting to be sprung."

Laurence stared back at him. "You seem very sure of yourself…very sure of *me*."

The little man just smiled again.

Unsurprised by the lack of answer, Laurence continued. "So how do you and I go about earning each other's trust?"

"Simple," Tark replied. He extended a deeply tanned arm to point a knobbly finger. "You see that large, triangular rock? The one protruding near the western border of the flatland?"

Laurence's eyes followed the finger. "I see it."

"Meet me there in twenty minutes," he said. Without waiting for a reply, the little man turned and strolled off, whistling a jolly tune.

It took Laurence a good deal longer than twenty minutes to work his way westward to Tark's triangular rock. Many of his fellow captives had stopped him en route, wanting to talk, seek advice, or simply shake his hand. Laurence was unused to such attention. His fellow soldiers seemed to recognize something in him, something in his words and actions that inspired them. He wasn't sure where these words and actions were coming from. They just came, and he was grateful to let them. His growing strength felt good, but it scared him a little too. What if it failed him at some crucial moment? The thought was a flash, and Laurence didn't allow its effects to linger. Perhaps that was strength in itself: the ability to push such thoughts aside, to overrule them.

Circling the rock, Laurence eventually found Tark casually leaning against its far side. The little man was gazing into the distance. At first, Laurence assumed he was staring at a cluster of large volcanoes that had been particularly angry for the past few days. On closer inspection, however, he saw that the little man's gaze was directed above the spewing black mountains and directly at the shimmering red sun.

"Careful of your eyes," Laurence said, his tone light but only half-joking.

Tark didn't drop his gaze. "Don't fear for my peepers, Laurence. There's plenty of ash in this sky. Besides, there's an abundance of free energy just begging to be borrowed from that big fiery ball, and I'm happy to accept it."

Laurence replied with a non-committing nod. For all he knew, the old man was right. He was certainly getting his boundless energy from somewhere. He looked back at the large, triangular rock. "So I'm intrigued. What's the big deal with this rock? Something special about it?'

"No," Tark replied, dropping his skyward gaze to shoot him a grin. "At least no more special than the rest of the rocks on this beautiful planet."

Laurence chuckled. Surely, the use of the word *beautiful* was sarcastic one.

"Okay, maybe that's not strictly speaking true," the little man admitted. "It might be that this particular rock *is* a little special. Allow me, if you will, to demonstrate." He pointed a finger to the horizon. "You see there, in the distance."

Laurence's eyes followed the knobbly digit and, after a moment of peering, said, "I don't understand what you're pointing at. All I see is black rock and spewing lava."

When he didn't get a reply, Laurence glanced again at the pointing finger, but the finger was no longer there. Turning around, he found that his little friend had gone. "What the..." Laurence knew that the old man was ridiculously fast, something he'd witnessed many times, but the speed of this vanishing act seemed nothing short of miraculous, supernatural even. If he hadn't felt so dumbfounded, he might have become irritated. He turned about for a few moments then did a couple of loops of the triangular rock. "A bloody magician," he mumbled under his breath. "Tark? *Tark…?*" He shouted towards the horizon for lack of a better direction.

Eventually, an answer came in the form of a high-pitched giggle. The sound seemed distant yet close, and it had a definite *echo* quality to it. Laurence turned back towards the triangular rock and saw one of the oddest sights he'd ever witnessed. One of Tark's wrinkled, sun-kissed hands was protruding from the almost vertical rock face. It was as if the rock was made from a smooth, black liquid from which the hand was emerging. Suddenly, as if sucked back into the rock, the hand disappeared and was quickly replaced by the little man's grinning head.

"Don't look so spooked, young Laurence. I can assure you, it's not voodoo."

Laurence shook his head.

"What you're seeing is nothing more than an optical illusion combined with a bit of weird science. It has something to do with tiny particles that hover between certain rocks and the way the light on this planet falls across them. Strange, I know. I could never quite grasp the physics behind it myself, but it's quite common. There's quite a few of them about."

"There's more?"

"You're surprised? Don't be. Too many people are far too reliant on their gift of sight. Sight can easily be manipulated."

Laurence took a step forward to get a closer look at the rock that had devoured all but the head of his little friend. "My God, would you look at that," he said as he tentatively reached forward and allowed his hand and forearm to be enveloped by the blackness.

"I think you'll find that God already knows about it," Tark replied with another giggle. "Come on then, Laurence, time's a wastin'," he said as he playfully rocked his disembodied head from side to side.

Taking a couple of deep breaths, Laurence shrugged and stepped forward. Wide-eyed, he allowed himself to be completely enveloped by the blackness. Suddenly, he couldn't see a thing, which he knew shouldn't have come as a surprise, but it did. Never before had he experienced such complete darkness. Before his rising panic forced him to step back out into the light, a strange *pop* sounded, followed by a *fizz*, which was accompanied by a blue glow. Laurence suspected it was a dim light, but after such blackness, it felt more like a blinding flare. His eyes adjusted to see Tark standing before him, his skin blue under the light and his long, white hair appearing almost luminous. In his right hand, he held a round, translucent pouch within which was the source of the blue light.

"Fizz worms," Tark said, giving the pouch a little squeeze. Seeming to react to his touch, the little bugs inside glowed brighter still and *fizzed*. Laurence almost laughed out loud. With the strangeness of the experience, coupled with the sight of his little blue friend, laughter seemed the only fitting reaction. He suddenly felt like a schoolboy who'd just found the ultimate hiding place.

"I'm reliably informed that they enjoy a good tickle," Tark said, giving the worms another squeeze. Laurence considered asking who it was who had informed him of such a thing but then decided that he'd only get some riddle of an answer, so he didn't bother.

Holding the pouch out to his left, Tark nodded in the same direction.

Laurence peered into the darkness. "Tunnel?" he asked, his eyes vaguely discerning a passageway that dipped downwards at a treacherous angle.

"Indeed it is."

The tunnel walls were incredibly smooth, and Laurence couldn't decide whether the passageway had been carved or was simply another natural phenomenon of this strange planet. A chill ran down his spine when he thought about what might be at its end. He began to formulate the question, but expecting another riddle, he once again didn't bother. Besides, a part of him—the newly awakened schoolboy part—was enjoying the mystery.

"Shall we?" Tark said, indicating the tunnel with an open palm.

Laurence began forward then stopped.

"Something wrong?"

Laurence gave him a blue-lipped, white-toothed smile. "You said it yourself, Tark. You've got to *earn* trust."

Tark chuckled. "Quite right, Laurence. And once you've remained safe after leading us down this dark, ominous tunnel, I'll have earned your trust, yes."

Laurence raised an eyebrow then sighed and tested the tunnel with one cautious foot. Satisfied the smooth floor had sufficient grip, he began the downward journey.

The tunnel felt as though it went on for miles. Laurence was glad that he didn't have a fear of enclosed spaces. The tunnel wasn't that small, but the darkness made it seem so. Thankfully, Tark remained close behind him the whole way, the fizz worms held over his shoulder for illumination.

"How far does this go?"

"Not much further."

But the descent went on.

Laurence's legs became increasingly pained, and soon, they began to shake uncontrollably. Despite his newfound strength, his body was clearly not yet up to the task. Despite his efforts to fight through the pain, he thought it likely he might collapse at any moment.

Perhaps if he did, he might simply slide the rest of the way. It was a prospect that wasn't entirely unappealing, and only the fear of what speed he might achieve stopped him from giving in to it. Gritting his teeth, he increased his efforts. After all, what other choice did he have? It certainly wouldn't be any easier going back up.

Much to Laurence's relief, Tark eventually called a halt. "Well done, young Laurence. This is it."

Breathing heavily, Laurence peered at the dimly lit walls. "But there's nothing here. The tunnel hasn't finished."

"There's plenty here. Try looking directly to your left."

Laurence did so and just about made a slight change in the blackness of the smooth wall: a door-sized area that failed to reflect the dim, blue light. He reached forward, and his hand passed straight through. "What's through there?" His voice was a whisper.

"You'll find out," Tark replied, a little less humor in his voice than usual.

Laurence turned to look at him, but the little man's face was in shadow. Turning back to the dark entrance, Laurence sighed and decided to take another a leap of faith. With his hands out before him, he once again ventured blindly into the darkness. After only three steps, he met with another blue light, which caused him to raise his hands up over his face until his eyes adjusted.

Then he froze, his blood turning to ice.

He was standing at the entrance of a large cavern, its ceilings and walls covered with thousands of glowing pouches just like Tark's. Under their light, spread throughout the cavern, stood hundreds of tall, dark figures. They remained completely still—so still, in fact, that Laurence initially mistook them for statues. But of course, they weren't statues. They were Carcarrions, hundreds of Carcarrions, all of whom were gazing directly at him, their pale eyes shining icy blue in the light.

Laurence couldn't move. His mind screamed at him to run, to flee back through the black space and scramble back up the tunnel as fast as his exhausted legs could manage. Unfortunately, his legs wouldn't obey.

Then the chance to run disappeared as the nearest of the tall, demon-like aliens lunged forward, like a nightmare made real, and seized him by the shoulders. As the creature's steely talons lifted him off his feet, only one thought formed in Laurence's mind.

So much for trust.

Chapter Twenty-Six
CAPTIVES

Cal woke. It was a sluggish awakening. So sluggish, in fact, that it took a few moments for his eyelids to catch on and scrape open over his dry eyes. His vision was full of blonde curls, a sight that wasn't helping his pounding head and near delirious state. Eventually rustling up the will to prop himself onto one elbow, he saw that Melinda's cybernetic form was lying limp on the floor next to him.

"You have a headache too?"

Cal knew the voice well. "*Ache* isn't a strong enough word," he replied as he turned to face his friend.

Jumper sat a few feet away against a white wall, his long, lean arms resting on his knees and an unconvincing smile on his face. "I guess we should count ourselves lucky that our thumping heads are still attached."

"Maybe," Cal replied. With a stiff turn of the head, he looked past Melinda's prone form to see that Viktor, Eddy, and Toker were also sprawled unconscious on the floor.

"I don't have the expertise to diagnose our synthetic friend, but the rest of them seem fine," Jumper said quietly. "I thought it best to let them come around in their own time."

Cal nodded and, with a grunt, struggled to a standing position.

His head wasn't the only part of his body in pain, not by a long shot.

"That old injury playing up again?"

Cal nodded and pressed both his palms into his lower back. The area felt like it had become home to a set of kitchen knives. "I'll live," he said, trying not to wince as he did so. He attempted a gentle, upward stretch, but a spasm of searing pain forced him to abandon the effort. Swearing under his breath, he carefully and slowly turned about to take in the surroundings. There was nothing to see but a small cube of a room, its walls, ceiling, and floor constructed from a smooth, flawless material that was somehow emanating a soft, white light. The room was completely enclosed and featureless without even a hint of a door or window. It was disorientating to say the least. He looked back at Jumper. "Clean as a whistle."

"That it is," Jumper agreed. "There's some hairline fractures around the floor and walls, but you practically have to press your nose against them to make them out." He pointed to his left. "There's one in the center of the wall behind you. It's about the size and shape of a door."

Trying his best to ignore the agony in his back, Cal approached the wall and ran his fingers along it until he'd found the line. "I've got it."

Jumper rubbed at his temples. "I gave it my best shove."

Cal looked at him with a raised eyebrow.

"Hey, you never know until you try, right?"

Cal nodded and tried for a grin. "I guess we'd feel pretty damn stupid if after a few days, we discovered that all we had to do was *push*." He turned from the wall and looked down at his unconscious friends.

Jumper got to his feet. "What do you suppose happened to Melinda? Pretty weird the way she just…turned off like that."

Cal raised an eyebrow again. It was one of his few parts he was having no trouble moving. "Turned off just like the Star Splinter," he pointed out, still staring at Melinda. Limp on the floor, she seemed more human than ever. Maybe it was the vulnerability. "I guess we'll have to wait for Viktor to wake before we get any answers."

"We didn't really stand much of a chance, did we, Cal? I would have said that we were outmatched, but outmatched seems a bit of an understatement."

Cal couldn't have agreed more. "I should never have brought us here. I have a nasty habit of tackling problems head-on. These kids trusted me, Jumper, and I let them down in a big way."

His tall friend shook his head and, quiet unexpectedly, chuckled. "Always the protector, Cal. You've got to face the fact that you can't keep everyone from harm. And you can't always take the blame when things go wrong. These *kids,* as you call them, are more capable than most adults. We all had a vote, including me. You're not responsible, and you're not to blame."

Cal looked down feeling unconvinced.

"I know it's hard for you to accept, Cal. It's part of your nature to be the protector. It always has been." Jumper grinned. "They even briefed me on that when I was nominated as your hunting mentor. Told me to pay close attention, make sure you didn't try jumping between me and a charging T-rex, fists raised or something. Apparently, you kept getting yourself beaten to a pulp in the orphanage, picking fights with boys twice your age and size. They thought you had a couple of screws loose at first 'til they realized you were just sticking up for your younger, smaller pals. They wanted me to try and teach you a bit of self-preservation. I guess I didn't do too good a job."

Cal wasn't sure how to respond. His memories of the orphanage were a little hazy to say the least, though he did remember getting punched an awful lot. He certainly never thought of himself as different to anyone else when it came to looking out for his friends. Of course, he wanted to protect them. Wouldn't *anyone*? He opened his mouth to reply but, still unsure of what to say, shut it again.

"Looks like Toker's stirring," Jumper said before the conversation could continue any further.

Cal turned to see his young friend rubbing his face but making no attempt to sit up. On the floor next to him, Eddy too had started to squirm. Yet again, Cal found himself amazed by the spooky synchronicity of the pair.

"Who spiked my drink?" Toker mumbled, his eyes still clamped shut.

Eddy's eyes were wide open, and her hand was slapping at her thigh. "My knife."

Cal walked stiffly over to them. He made an attempt to help Toker up, but his back quickly overruled him. Fortunately, Jumper soon had them both on their feet. Despite the situation, Cal couldn't help but feel a hint of amusement at the bemused look on Toker's face as he took in the surroundings. The strange, white cube of a room had an odd effect on the eyes and the brain—perhaps akin to finding yourself in a big fish tank hovering within a bright cloud.

Finally, the young man's bloodshot eyes met his. "Heaven?" he mumbled in confusion.

Cal grinned. "If this were heaven, do you really think your head would be feeling the way it does?"

"Huh." Toker gave the top of his head a slow rub. "You know, my head actually feels pretty good. Everything feels pretty good."

Lucky bugger. Cal's own head was playing an increasingly intense duet with his throbbing back. He was also starting feel rather hot, which was unsettling as he suspected the room was actually quite cool.

Toker looked down at Viktor and Melinda. "They okay?"

"Viktor'll be fine. As for Melinda...who knows?" Cal looked at Eddy. "You good, Eddy?"

"Course, Cal," she replied almost breezily then reached both hands down to her toes and began to stretch.

"Does your head hurt?" he asked her.

"Yep, kinda." She straightened up and attacked the air with a series of jabs. "But it ain't gonna stop me from bein' prepared."

"Prepared...for what?" Toker asked, retaining his bemused expression.

Eddy paused in her routine and shot him an exasperated look. "You really are a thickie, ain't ya? You believe this guy, Cal? Jumper?" she said, turning to them, then back to Toker.

Toker shrugged.

"Prepared to fight, dimwit. We've been taken by hostiles. Who knows when they might show up."

Toker still looked bemused although Cal caught a hint of a smile tweaking the corner of his mouth. "So what's being prepared got to do with aerobics?"

Eddy ignored him.

Toker took another look about. "So I guess this weird little room's a cell then, eh?"

Cal nodded. "A cell...or some sort of observation room."

Toker again rubbed his head as if he were trying to warm up his brain. "Now I remember. Yeah, that bloody great tube of a ship. What the hell was that? And the red mist... Didn't leave us much of a fighting chan—" the young man suddenly stopped short and yanked up his sleeve. "*What the fuck? My arm's healed!*"

Cal looked at Toker's right arm in surprise, not least because he hadn't remembered it had been broken in the first place.

Abandoning her limbering routine, Eddy turned and roughly

grabbed the arm in question. "*No way*. It was totally bust up. I remember." She gave the arm a good, hard twist to make sure that it definitely wasn't broken.

"Hey, ease up. You'll bloody break it again if you keep that up." Toker yanked his arm out of the girl's grip. After flexing his fingers a few times, he jiggled the arm about. "Man, that's bloody weird. It doesn't even hurt. Feels good, just like the rest of me."

"Mind if I take a look?" Cal asked.

"Knock yourself out," he replied, thrusting the exposed arm under Cal's nose.

Jumper also leaned in for a closer look. "There's no mark, no bruising."

Cal turned the arm over and saw no hint of the injury. It had been dark in the Star Splinter's cockpit, but the arm had definitely been broken, and it had been a bad break at that. He found himself inclined to agree with Toker; it was bloody weird. "A miracle," he said, feeling a brief moment of envy that the miracle hadn't reached as far as his own back.

"Maybe I got exposed to some weird space rays," Toker theorized. "Went and got myself some super healing abilities."

No one replied.

"Right…probably not."

"How about that red mist stuff?" Eddy said. "Maybe it like…knocked us out for ages. Like a year or somethin'. Enough time for the arm to heal up all on its own."

"Good thinking out of the box, kid," Jumper said, "but there's no sign of hair or nail growth and no tech for life support."

"Whatever the cause," Cal said, "I think we should take it as a good sign. Whoever our captors are, it seems they want us healed and healthy." *Maybe they just overlooked my back.*

"I'm not so sure, bro," Toker said, pulling his sleeve back down and looking about the room. "I mean, this cell. Sure it's all nice, bright, and clean, but it's not all that friendly."

"How so?"

"Let's just say that I've been in a few cells in my time. Trouble seems to seek me out," he said with a half grin. "Even the very worst cells had at least, shall we say, *facilities*. Even the jails on JuJu beach have the basic life sustaining stuff, an' JuJu's on one of the crappiest of back worlds. I mean, this cell sucks. My mouth feels like a Casgorian desert. We don't even have anything to drink—"

Without the slightest of warnings, a tall, white, cylindrical tube ejected vertically from the floor in the very center of the room. Toker stumbled back in surprise to land in Eddy's arms. "Watch ya self," she growled, shoving him roughly aside.

"What the hell?" Toker grumbled, making sure not to take his eyes off the strange new cylinder.

Tentatively, Cal approached it, although it didn't appear in any way threatening.

"Careful, Cal. Could be some sort of alien naughtiness."

"I don't think so, Toker," Cal replied. The cylinder was about eight feet in height, and as he approached, a thin tube sprouted, branch-like, from its side at the level of Cal's head. "You might just be getting that drink you were after, Toker. I think your voice has activated some sort of drinking fountain."

"It did?"

Cal moved his lips towards the thin tube.

"Careful," Eddy warned. "What if it poison or somethin'?"

Cal shook his head. "If they wanted us dead, it would have happened already. They want us in good shape.' He sucked on the tube. "Water." He took another sip. "Damn good water!"

Within seconds, the rest of the gang were moving forward to relieve their parched throats. As they did so, more thin tubes sprouted, each convenient for the height of their mouths.

"This is all well and good," Toker eventually said, using his sleeve to wipe some watery dribble from his chin, "but sooner or later, one of us is gonna need to take a leak, and I ain't seeing a toilet—" The words had barely left his mouth when a white, seat-sized cube with a round hold on its top slid out from the floor in the corner of the room.

"No frickin' way. Did I just order a *toilet*?"

Cal walked stiffly over to the cube and looked down through the hole. All he saw was a curving tube of slightly grayer white. After a few moments, the cube, having obviously detected no use, slid back into the floor.

"That's pretty damn clever," Toker said, sounding truly impressed. "What else d'you think we could order?"

"Let's find out," Cal replied. "Door…"

Nothing happened.

"Exit…"

Still nothing.

"Viewing panel," Jumper tried, followed by, "control panel…"

Still nothing moved or appeared.

"*Pulse blaster*," Eddy bellowed, causing Toker to jump in fright.

"Yikes, Ed. What the hell is up with your volume control? And your brain for that matter. *Pulse blaster,* really?"

"Worth a try, wasn't it? Don't hear any smart ideas comin' outa your gob."

Toker frowned, then said, "Bed." A long, low cube slid a little way out from the wall nearest him. "Not much of a bed, is it?" he muttered.

"Try stepping back a bit," Cal suggested. "I think it senses that you're in the way."

Toker did just that, and the long cube immediately slid out

further until it was the size of a single bed.

"Whoever built this place sure has a fondness for white," Jumper said.

"Too right," Toker agreed as he stared at the bed. "And hard lines. Doesn't look too comfy." He sat himself down and looked pleasantly surprised as he partially sank into it. "Wow, who'd have thought? Looks hard, but it's as soft as a plump bottom!" He swung his legs up, laid back, and slid his hands behind his head.

"Lazy git," Eddy said with a loud sniff, then shouted, "*Combat knife.*" She gave a disappointed huff when nothing happened.

"Maybe we should get Viktor off the floor?" Jumper suggested and moved to scoop the still unconscious boy up. Somewhat reluctantly, Toker shifted himself off the bed, allowing Jumper to lay the boy down.

Cal was tempted to try ordering a chair. The water had helped reduce his rising temperature, but his back still felt like it was slowly killing him. After some deliberation, he decided to remain on his feet in an attempt to keep the blood flowing.

"Do you think they're watching us, Cal?" Toker asked as he leaned back against a wall.

"It's possible," Cal answered after a moment. "But these little pop-out cubes seem automated to me. Too quick to be manually activated."

"So what do we do? How do we get out?" Eddy asked.

Cal looked at her for a moment as he thought things through. The girl was unsuccessfully trying to scuff the pristine white floor with the black heel of her combat boot. If she was scared, she wasn't showing it. None of them were. "I'll be honest with you, Eddy, I don't think escape is going to be all that easy. Jumper's already found what looks to be a door seal on that wall—"

"So let's give it a good kickin'," she suggested excitedly. "Bust it open."

Cal shot Jumper a wry smile. "Jumper's already used his considerable skill and cunning to get it open."

"No luck, eh, J man?" Toker said as he located the door seal and took his turn in giving it a good shove.

"Afraid not."

Toker gave up on the door. "So unless our captors have a change of heart, all hope of getting out of here is in the hands of our little sleeping wizard and his lovely lady."

All eyes fell on Viktor and Melinda. The smaller of the two was snoring quietly.

After a few moments of staring at the boy, Eddy said, "Couldn't I just give him a nudge with my boot, Cal? We could be waiting forever."

Tempting. "Best to let him come around on his own, Eddy. He'll be disorientated enough." Cal looked down intently at the boy, willing him to wake. The way he was feeling he'd be on the floor himself if they didn't get out of here soon. *Maybe we could give him just a little nudge—*

"You reckon he'll be able to get us out of here, Cal?"

"Huh. I'm not sure, Toker. I don't see anything for him to crack open and jiggle."

Eddy wrinkled up her nose, "Well if he can't bust us out, he could at least wake up miss bimbo there. She's dim for a robot, but she'll be good in a tussle."

"She's not a robot." The words were barely audible.

All eyes went back to Viktor. The boy still appeared unconscious, but it was undoubtedly he who had spoken.

"Viktor?" Toker said, leaning over the boy. "Rise and shine, bro. We need your brain…"

Chapter Twenty-Seven
ESCAPE

"Can I help in any way, Viktor?" Cal asked, looking down at the boy. "Maybe we could get Melinda up on the bed?"

Almost two hours had passed since Viktor had regained consciousness. He was now crouched on the floor with one leg splayed at an awkward angle as he leaned over Melinda's prone form. His hands were buried deep within in an opening in the cybernetic woman's back.

"No worries, Cal. This is kinda tricky with her horizontal, but I think I'm almost done." The boy reached in further still, his tongue poking out of the corner of his mouth as he concentrated. Cal heard a series of clicks that caused the boy to frown then two more clicks, which turned the frown into a smile. "Besides," he continued, "I think we'd have a hard job lifting her. She's pretty damn heavy. I tell you, who or whatever dragged her in here must have been seriously strong. She'd probably sink straight through that bed anyway."

Toker, who'd wasted no time reclaiming the bed, looked happy to hear that. Over on the far side of the room, Jumper was attempting to keep an irritable Eddy occupied with some hand-to-hand combat instruction. Cal might have joined them if it weren't for the crippling pain in his back. During the last hour, it had taken all of his will just to stand up straight and not pass out. With the situation already dire enough, he'd tried to hide his worsening condition. But his temperature was steadily rising, and the sweat was getting excessive.

"You think you can wake her up, Vik?" Toker asked.

"If you mean can I reactivate her, then of course I can. I practically *built* her."

"Oh, so you know what caused her to switch off then?" Toker persisted.

Viktor huffed in irritation. "Obviously, I don't know *who's* done it, and...and...I don't really know *how* they've done it." The words were leaving the boy's mouth with some reluctance. "But I do know *what* they've done. I know *exactly* what they've done. But I also know that *what* they've done shouldn't be possible—definitely *isn't* possible—which is why I don't know *how* they've done it. You see what I mean?"

"Man, you're twisting my brain with your nonsense talk."

Cal had to agree.

Viktor sighed and stopped his tinkering to look over at Toker. "Okay, I'll try and talk slow and clear, and you go ahead and stop me if your mushy little brain can't keep up."

The boy sounded testy, but Cal guessed he was just disguising his fear and frustration.

"When they were first created, which wasn't all that long ago," the boy continued, "all synthetics were fitted with a Gata V-Tech safe switch, a trigger that could be remotely activated in case the synthetic malfunctioned. It puts them into a sort of temporary paralysis, for safety's sake, just in case they got out of hand— something that could never happen, by the way, if they went ahead and implanted a behavioural chip like the one I developed. Anyway, it seems that someone went ahead and activated Melinda's safe switch, even though it's impossible."

"Why is that impossible?" Cal asked.

"It's impossible, because they, whoever the hell *they* are, would have had to have gotten hold of Melinda's unique V-Tech frequency code from deep inside the military's mainframe system, which in itself is kinda impossible seeing as how that mainframe and its three backup systems were all on Earth. But, for argument's sake, let's say that they did somehow manage to get Melinda's code before Earth was destroyed. *Even then,* it's still impossible."

"What d'ya reckon, Cal?" Toker said, leaning up on his elbows, "Think he's ever gonna get to the point and tell us why it's impossible?"

"It's impossible, smart arse, cos I bloody well removed Melinda's safe switch sixteen months ago."

Cal rubbed the back of his sweating neck. "Could there be another explanation, something other than the safe switch?"

Viktor frowned and shook his head. "It's the only thing that I'm aware of that could disable every single one of her systems like that— simultaneously and completely." The boy looked frustrated as he bent down to resume his tinkering.

"Can you reactivate her without your tools?"

Viktor looked up again, his frown disappearing. "Course, Cal. I wasn't lying when I said that I practically built her. After I rescued her from those tech dummies on the starship, I replaced a good seventy percent of her internal workings."

"There's a surprise," Toker said.

Viktor ignored him. "I tell you, Cal, I don't know what the hell those Federation scientists were thinking with their design work. I mean, she's supposed to be a combat soldier. *Combat.* That suggests to me that she's gonna spend most of her time off on some distant planet kicking ass, right? Well, I'll ask you what I asked them; what if somethin' got damaged or went haywire during that combat? I'll tell you what, their shoddy designs would mean that you'd have to drag her back to a full-tech engineering workshop to fix even the smallest fault. Bunch of idiots. So anyway, with my design, I can actually do most of the diagnosing and fixing with my eyes, ears, and fingers, see?" The boy sucked in a deep breath. "So anyway, there's a few things that can't be done by hand, so I've got a couple of small, purpose-designed tools stored in here: a couple of replacements for her smaller, more delicate components too. Just as well too, cos one of them's been irreversibly disabled. Weird, I tell you. Hold up a sec. This bit's kinda tricky." Again, the boy's tongue poked out of the corner of his mouth. There was a loud *pop* followed by a faint *whir*. "Got it." He pulled his hands free from Melinda's back, and the gap sealed over immediately with a metallic matrix that began oozing a skin-colored liquid.

Toker was upright now, perched on the edge of the bed as he peered with fascination at the new skin rapidly forming on Melinda's back. "So you've fixed her then?"

Pulling Melinda's clothing back in place, Viktor grinned and nodded. "Yep. Might take her a bit of time to do some self-diagnostics and adjustments though."

"Hey, tell her to take her time, little bro," Toker said. "And when she's ready, it'd be great if you could ask her to break us out of this damn white box."

Cal used his already damp sleeve to wipe his forehead. "I second that."

"She'll get us out, don't worry about that," the boy replied confidently. Then, he leaned over the cybernetic woman. "Melinda? Wake up, honey. We're gonna need your hair…"

Twelve minutes later, Cal was relieved to see Melinda standing tall.

"So come on then, V," Eddy said gruffly.

Viktor looked at the girl quizzically.

She huffed and sharply nodded to the white wall in front of them. "Tell yer big blonde chick to kick the door in."

Viktor looked at the girl as a disappointed parent might look at an underachieving child. "You really have no concept of the technology we're cocooned in, do you? Or the likely strength of the materials used to form this cell? Just because Melinda is incredibly strong in comparison to a puny thing like you doesn't mean she can just go charging through sealed metal doors. Besides, even if she could, it's a crude means of escape."

"Whatever," the girl replied impatiently, "just bust us the hell outa here." She turned to Cal with an exasperated look. "Cal tell—" She stopped mid-sentence, her look of exasperation turning into one of concern. "Hey, you okay? You look kinda rough."

Cal gave her a weak nod. For the last ten minutes, he felt as though he'd been chopped in half then crudely been put back together. "Fine, Eddy. So what's the plan, Viktor?" *Please, God, let there be a plan…a bloody good one.*

"Well I can't guarantee that it'll work, Cal."

Shit.

"But it should. Melinda, a nano lock if you please?" Melinda reached up and took hold of a single blonde hair from her head. The hair came away easily, and Cal could just about see it squirming in her grip like an incredibly thin snake. The boy took hold of it between his thumb and forefinger and, moving to the seam in the wall, laid the hair against it. A second later, it had disappeared. "A lock of hair to pick the lock!"

"How the hell does that work?" Toker asked, moving forward and peering at the point where the hair had wriggled into the seam.

"It's simple," Viktor replied. "Melinda has full control over every single lock of her hair even if they're disconnected from her head. She'll be able to explore around in the internal workings of the wall and will hopefully be able to manipulate the locking mechanism. I came up with the idea after the shit we went through on Mars."

"Huh, simple." Toker grinned.

"That really is very clever, Viktor," Jumper added.

"Will she be able to disable any alarms?" Cal asked, trying his best to keep his head in the game.

"Don't worry, Cal, she knows what she's doing."

They all fell silent and stared at the wall, occasionally glancing at Melinda's face, which remained blank and unreadable. Cal wanted to offer advice as to the best action to take once the door opened— assuming it did open—but his head felt fuzzy and, without knowing what was waiting for them on the other side, giving advice was a tricky thing. Not that he felt capable of action anyway. In his current state, it would be all he could do to just walk out of the cell. Fortunately, his adrenalin had started to rise, bringing with it a little strength.

"You okay, Cal?" Jumper had come to stand by his side. "You're looking a little...hot."

Cal turned to him and did his best to grin. "I'll take a cold shower once we're back on the Star Splinter."

Jumper nodded but didn't look convinced by the bravado.

A few minutes later, the door still hadn't moved. Cal took a deep, slow breath. His ribs hurt. *Open, damn it.* Sweat trickled uncomfortably down his neck. He looked at Viktor and was relieved to see that he still appeared confident. Next to the boy, Eddy looked ready to burst. And next to her, Toker kept looking back and forth between Melinda and the wall.

Then, the door slid open.

The few muscles in Cal's body that weren't already tensed suddenly became so. Beyond the open door lay a white corridor. *Empty. So far, so good,* he thought, feeling himself relax ever so slightly. Melinda moved silently forward to retrieve her hair, which was somehow clinging to the side of the newly formed exit.

The long, white corridor was eerily quiet. Cal took a couple of deep, steady breaths and did his best to push his pain aside as he silently led them out of the cell. Continuing tentatively forward, he saw numerous open doors lining the left hand wall. His relief was palpable when Melinda moved up alongside him and stayed by his side.

Feeling as though his heart could breach his chest at any moment, Cal peered around the first door. He saw a modest-sized, white room, which, judging by the setup, he guessed to be living quarters. The room was devoid of life. Not only that, but he had a feeling it hadn't been occupied for quite some time. It was clinically clean with not a single personal artifact. Turning back to the others, he gave them a nod then continued to the next door. Peering in with caution, he saw a room exactly the same as the last. Seven doors later, all that had been revealed were the exact same lifeless living quarters.

Cal paused to take another couple of deep, steadying breaths. The deathly silence was beginning to get to him. Not that he was hoping for one, but he couldn't deny that a face-to-face fight was far easier on the nerves. He continued on, Melinda by his side and the others still close behind. The eighth door finally revealed something different: a much larger space, possibly a canteen. There were numerous white tables with matching chairs, but still, the room was eerily quiet with no signs of life. *A damned ghost ship.* Deciding that the canteen was unlikely to lead anywhere, he continued on.

Only one door remained before the corridor came to an abrupt end. The door in question was on the opposite side of the corridor, and Cal approached it with his usual caution. Peering around its edge, he saw a room radically different to the others. It too had pure white walls, floor, and ceiling, but it was much larger than even the canteen, and it was far from empty and featureless. Consoles and workstations filled the large space, and in its center, Cal could see a series of large, block-like tables on which sat coils of glass equipment holding liquids of varying colors and consistencies. Some of the liquids gave off gasses that either rose towards the high ceiling or poured over the edges of the tables to settle, fog-like, on the floor.

Other than the gasses, Cal could sense no other movement. "Looks clear, but stay alert," he whispered.

As he moved into the room, he saw huge screens set high on the wall to his left. Some displayed complex charts and equations. Others showed images of numerous alien species and what he took to be microscopic views of blood and perhaps tissues. Below those screens, sitting on white platforms that protruded from the walls, were glass specimen tubes. Some of the tubes were fist-sized, and some towered higher than a human adult. Each tube contained at least one life-form either submerged in preservation liquid or suspended and rotating in a frozen state. Below these specimens, he could make out rows of dissection blades and laser cutters, all lying on desks with built-in, snake-arm microscopes.

"What the hell is this place?" Toker whispered.

"It's a laboratory, idiot," Eddy said in remarkably hushed tones. "What's goin' on, Cal? Where is everyone?"

"Yeah, it's not as populated as I thought it'd be," Toker said. "Kinda feels like the whole place has been abandoned."

"I don't think they'd have left all of this equipment on before leaving," Cal replied as he moved further into the room. He couldn't see any obvious doors other than the one they'd entered. "Let's make a quick search. See if you can spot any exits or a lift."

Eddy and Toker continued on into the center of the room while Viktor and Melinda moved over to what appeared to be a control console.

"Strange place," Jumper said quietly.

Wiping his brow and his eyes, Cal continued to scan the room. "Somehow, *strange* doesn't seem to cut it."

Jumper nodded. "Is it me, or does this place seem distinctly…"

"*Human?*" Cal offered.

"Yeah, human."

Not keen on standing still, Cal stiffly pointed to his left. "Looks like there might be a concealed door or viewing panel over there. Fancy joining me whilst Viktor does his thing?" More than anything, he wanted to distract himself from his failing body.

Jumper nodded and indicated for him to lead the way. As they wound their way between consoles and equipment, Cal spotted a pile of fairly hefty metal clamps strewn on the surface of a workstation. Grimacing as his back strongly disagreed with the move, and picked up one of the clamps. He weighed it in his hand and, feeling satisfied with its weapon-like quality, offered it to Jumper, who accepted it gratefully. Painfully picking up another one for himself, he moved on, the crude weapon doing little to boost his confidence.

"You wanna press it, or shall I?" he said to Jumper as they arrived at the concealed panel and stared at the touch pad on the wall.

"You spotted it, Cal," Jumper said with a half grin, "I think it only fair that you get to open it."

Cal paused. Now that they were closer, he could see that the panel was a heavily armored barricade of sorts. He took a moment to check on the others; Viktor was still working at the control panel while Toker and Eddy were continuing their search on the far side of the laboratory. Turning back to the armored panel, he opted for a mental shrug rather than a physical one and reached for the touch pad. The result was instantaneous. The barrier retracted so fast it was almost as if it had magically disappeared. Suddenly, he and Jumper were staring at two dark, alien figures, both baring bright white fangs and glaring at them with menacing, ice-gray eyes.

Cal grunted and stumbled back in alarm. He tried to raise his heavy clamp in defense—or attack, he hadn't entirely decided which—but searing pain flashed through his spine and froze him on the spot.

"*Hell*," Jumper cried. He too had recoiled back in shock, almost swinging his clamp into a nearby container in the process.

After a moment, Cal dropped his weapon, breathing hard. "Don't worry. We're safe," he said and walked forward to press his hand against a thick smart-glass panel. Even the toughest of aliens would never penetrate it.

"Carcarrions?" Jumper asked, slowly lowering his clamp and peering at the two tall figures behind the glass.

"In the flesh," Cal replied. There were smart-straps binding the two Carcarrions to horizontal supports. "It seems they're as much prisoners as we are."

Jumper tentatively moved forward to get a closer look. "You really weren't exaggerating when you said they were fearsome," he said with a soft chuckle of relief. "There's not many things able to give me a fright, but the unexpected sight of these guys just made the list. What the hell is this place, Cal?"

Bloody good question. Cal could feel theories and suspicions turning in the back of his mind, but with the state he was in, none of them were making it to the forefront intact. Even though he knew the two aliens posed no threat, he felt compelled to once again tap the touch pad, bringing the heavy metal barrier back into place. "I've no idea, Jumper, but I think it's best we leave that closed, yes?" He blinked as sweat ran into his eyes a set them stinging.

Looking at him with growing concern, Jumper nodded in agreement. "Don't worry. We'll be out of here soon enough."

Cal did his best to grin. Judging by Jumper's expression, it had come out more as a grimace.

"How's about we find out if Viktor's having any success?" Jumper suggested.

Cal looked back across the laboratory. Apparently, none of the others had noticed the unveiling of the two dark aliens. "Sure."

The boy was still tapping away at the console when they approached. Cal felt the need to lean against it for support and almost fell as his clammy hand slipped on its edge. Fortunately, Melinda shot a cybernetic hand under his arm and set him straight. *God bless her.*

"You okay, Cal?"

"Fine, Viktor, just a little under the weather. Any, um…luck?"

After shooting a worried glance at Jumper, the boy returned his gaze to the console. "I'm almost into the system. This is weird though, guys. This system, this whole ship, it's human…definitely human. Even the—"

Viktor's words were cut short as a figure briskly entered the room via the very same door that they'd crept though just a few minutes earlier. Cal froze, as did the others. Eddy and Toker, who had been making their way back across the laboratory, were now standing motionless near its center. Cal watched, his heart pounding, as the figure walked keenly toward the central tables. A human. A female. She had her head turned towards the huge screens as she walked and seemed completely unaware of their presence. She was even softly humming to herself, an act that sent a strange wave of relief through Cal. *Bad people don't hum, do they?*

Still not taking her eyes from the screens, the woman arrived at the central tables just metres away from the statue still forms of Eddy and Toker. Distractedly, she set a drink canister and a small box down on a table.

How the hell has she not noticed them? Cal looked at Toker, who was staring at him with wide, questioning eyes. Eddy, on the other hand, had her eyes firmly fixed on the oblivious woman and looked ready to pounce. Fortunately, she glanced towards him first. Cal slowly shook his head and raised a finger to his lips.

With her back to them and her eyes still studying the big screens, the woman remained unaware. Cal couldn't see her face, but he guessed she was young. She had a slim build, was of average height, and had long, almost white-blonde hair that was tightly pulled back into a ponytail. Her attire was strange: a pale blue, close-fitting suit perhaps designed for physical activity.

Turning to Melinda, Cal pointed towards the exit. She immediately moved stealthily towards it. Hoping to come close to matching that stealth, he began moving towards the center of the room, his eyes remaining fixed on the woman.

Finally looking away from the screens, the young woman turned and picked up her drink. After taking a few sips, she placed it back on the table then leaned forward and began tapping on one of the glass contraptions that held a bubbling green liquid. She then picked up the small box, opened it, and jabbed two small sticks inside. *Food*, Cal realized. She must have been in the canteen kitchens as they'd crept by. It had seemed so deserted, but a silent, single person...

Suddenly, whether by sound, peripheral vision, or a tardy sixth sense, the woman detected that she wasn't alone. Spitting out a mouthful of noodles, she spun around, her eyes growing large with fright as she saw Toker and Eddy. Toker immediately raised his open palms in a gesture of peace. Eddy, on the other hand, exploded forward in a vicious attack.

"Eddy, wait," Cal shouted, but he doubted she could even hear him over her battle cry.

Jumping back and throwing the remainder of her noodles in Eddy's snarling face, the woman dashed around to the opposite side of the tables. Cal tried to hurry towards her but immediately regretted it as his back exploded in pain. All he managed was a wordless grunt as his legs collapsed beneath him, and he crashed to the floor. Colored dots filled his vision as he clutched at his back.

Unlike the pain, the dots soon dissipated, and Cal looked up to see Eddy and Toker circling the tables in an attempt to herd the woman. Extremely efficient in her movements, the retreating woman thrust her right hand into her hip pocket, pulled out a device not much bigger than a pen, then pushed it against the side of her neck. Seconds later, she was throwing the device down and looking defiantly at Toker and Eddy as they closed in.

"You okay, Cal?" Jumper was suddenly kneeling by his side.

"Make sure she doesn't get out of the room."

Jumper leaped up to begin circling the woman.

Seeming to decide that Toker was less of a threat than the tall Jumper or the snarling Eddy, the woman made a dash directly in the young blond man's direction.

"I got her," Toker cried, his arms wide to intercept the woman.

Cal attempted to push himself upright. The attempt failed, and his face hit the cold, hard floor. Trying a different tack, he rolled himself over, grunting loudly in pain as he did so. He then looked up just in time to see Toker literally flying backwards through the air, arms wheeling before landing with an almighty crash into a tower of sample racks.

As the lightweight racks skittered loudly across the smooth floor, the woman bolted passed Cal at an incredible speed. She was heading straight for Melinda and what was perhaps the one and only exit. Even with her unnatural speed, Cal very much doubted that she'd succeed in dodging past the cybernetic woman. But as it turned out, no dodging was intended and Cal turned just in time to see her barrel directly into the tall blonde. To his amazement, Melinda was jolted by the hit and was even forced back a little way. Coming to a halt, the two seemed locked in a stalemate. Face to face, their arms braced. Melinda's face was a blank mask, giving nothing away. Cal couldn't see the woman's face, but her posture gave the impression of incredible strain. This seemed to be confirmed as Melinda quickly and easily gained the upper hand. Forcing the smaller woman's arms down, the cybernetic woman turned her around into an immobilizing embrace.

Gritting his teeth against the pain, Cal finally made it to his feet. "Don't hurt her, Melinda," he said as he shuffled towards them like a man three times his age.

As if somehow annoyed by the implication that she'd been defeated, the woman began to struggle in Melinda's embrace, kicking her feet in the air and back at her captor's legs. Melinda seemed unbothered by the desperate attacks.

"Calm down," Cal snapped as he hobbled nearer. "We don't want to hurt you."

The woman paused in her struggles for a moment, dropping her head forward as if realizing the futility of her struggles. Then she brought her head up, slamming it hard into Melinda's face. Cal winced at the sound of the contact.

The move was seemingly one too many for Melinda, whose long blonde hair quickly snaked around the woman's slender neck.

"Melinda, don't—"

Viktor intercepted Cal with his hand raised. "Don't worry; she won't hurt her. She's just gonna put her to sleep for a bit."

Cal watched as the woman's struggles slowed then eventually

stopped. Her head flopped forward as Melinda retracted her hair and lowered her to the floor, leaving her limp form at her feet much like a gentle dog might a soft toy.

Cal felt lost for words. Bewildered didn't even come close, and he obviously wasn't alone. For a time, they all looked at each other in stunned silence. Everything had happened so fast.

"You okay, Toker?" he asked as his young friend limped over to join them.

"Sure, Cal," he replied even though he didn't sound it or indeed look it.

His adrenalin dissipating, Cal began feeling increasingly dizzy. With great effort, he crouched down over the woman's prone form, and thankfully, the dizziness eased. Satisfied that he wasn't about to pass out, he moved the woman's white-blonde hair aside and laid a couple of fingers upon her neck. "Pulse is a little fast but strong," he said, looking up at the others.

Toker slowly wheeled his right shoulder around, wincing as he did so. "So she's not a synthetic like Melinda?"

Cal could understand his thinking. "No, most definitely flesh and blood."

"But she was so fast," Toker insisted.

"And strong," Eddy confirmed. "She certainly sent you flyin'."

"Too bloody right she did," Toker conceded. "Felt like I got hit by a damn hover train."

"Maybe we should be checking if there's any others around?" Jumper suggested.

Cal nodded. "Viktor, do you think you can find out what and who the hell we're dealing with here?"

"Sure, Cal." The boy tore his nervous eyes away from the unconscious woman and scuttled back to the console he'd been working on.

Instinctively, Cal leaned forward to pick the unconscious woman up. *Damn it.* What the hell was he thinking? He could barely pick *himself* up. He needed to rest his body *and* his brain. He gave Melinda a look. Without hesitating or making a sound, the cybernetic woman seemed to read his thoughts. Crouching down, she scooped the unconscious woman into her arms and looked at him for further instructions.

"Thanks, Melinda. I owe you one."

Chapter Twenty-Eight
CAUTION...AND PAIN

Cal was regretting having sat down. His entire lower torso felt as though it were filled with molten lead, which was burning through his skin and fusing him to the chair. He had a talent for pushing pain aside, but those talents were fast failing him. He had searched the huge laboratory for pain patches, but it had been like looking for a fusion coil in a military junkyard. He was hot, too damn hot, to the point that his t-shirt had become soaked with sweat. Where the hell were the others? They were supposed to be bringing a med kit from the Star Splinter, and if they didn't arrive back soon, Cal had a nasty feeling that he'd never stand up again. Ever.

He stared at the unconscious figure on the bunk. The woman with the white-blonde hair had been out cold for a good thirty minutes now. He'd been right about her age: She was young, maybe late twenties or early thirties. Her skin was pale. Flawless. Cal wondered when she would wake so he could get some answers and some merciful distraction. He took a few, grating breaths and allowed himself a little experimental stretch. All he achieved was an agonized groan. Aborting the stretch, he stiffly glanced to the doorway of the living quarters, where Melinda stood. The synthetic woman remained still, silent, and apparently untroubled by his obvious pain. If he was honest, he felt like crying. If he wasn't so afraid of how much it would hurt, he just might have done. Every ten minutes that passed felt like a new lesson in the nature of true agony. He was glad that no one else was in the room to witness him in such a state unless, of course, that someone possessed a dozen pain patches.

He did his best to bring his attention back to the unconscious woman. How the *hell* had she launched Toker through the air like that? And how could she possibly have challenged the cybernetic strength of Melinda? He'd seen her inject herself. Possibly a muscle stim of sorts to give her a huge physical boost. But he'd personally experienced muscle stims as part of his military training, and even the very best fell far short of the strength increase this woman had displayed. Besides, muscle stims left you drained, looking and feeling like an addict at their worst. This woman looked nothing short of radiant.

He closed his eyes tight and had an overwhelming urge to shake his head. Where the hell were the others? He was sure they'd be back by now. Earlier in the lab, Viktor had partially managed to access the strange ship's systems. The boy had been animated about it too. So much so that he spent a full two minutes gushing its praises before revealing that—bar a collection of suitably contained live alien specimens—they were the only living souls on board. A one-person crew seemed extremely unlikely considering the ship's complexity, size, and living quarters, but Viktor had been adamant.

Viktor had also managed to locate the Star Splinter down in a docking bay, and it was there that Cal had sent them. He had decided that from now on, "Caution," would be his new motto, so the first thing he wanted to ensure was that the Star Splinter was intact and fit for a quick launch. Secondly, he had requested a fistful of pain patches. And thirdly, thinking it best the woman woke up without them all looming over her, he'd sent them off to complete the first two tasks. Now that he thought about it, this last decision was possibly a very early deviation from his new motto. His decision to leave her unrestrained to avoid her panicking was most definitely a deviation. He really wasn't thinking straight. That angelic, beautiful woman could probably break him in half with very little effort. Still, Melinda was nearby—something Jumper had thankfully insisted upon before they'd left.

What the hell was in that injection? Trying his best to keep his breathing steady, Cal continued to ponder the woman's strength and speed. Strangely enough, it was during that very ponder that the woman leapt from the bunk and wrenched him violently from his seat. With a forearm pressed hard into his neck, she slammed against the rear wall. More than a little shell-shocked, Cal stared into the woman's pale blue eyes that were now only inches from his own. A sudden new appreciation for her strength kicked in not to mention for the importance of his new motto.

After what felt like an eternity but was likely only an instant, Melinda was tearing the woman away, leaving Cal to drop to the ground in a ball of agony. "Melinda, wait," he managed to rasp between desperate attempts to suck in some air. He tried to hold out a pacifying hand towards the cybernetic woman but failed miserably. "Let her go," he managed before a coughing fit sent more searing pain through his spine.

Melinda released her arm from around the woman's neck but didn't back away.

"Please," Cal said, looking up at the woman. "We don't want to hurt you."

The woman turned her wide eyes to him as she backed away from Melinda. "Why should I believe you?" She sounded almost calm but didn't look it. There was definite fear in those pale blue eyes.

Cal crawled over to the chair that he'd been sitting in and, remaining on his knees, managed to push himself almost upright. "Because I think this is a military craft," he reasoned, "a damned advanced one like I've never seen…but military. And if I'm right, then we're on the same damn side."

The woman had backed up into a corner of the room. She was shaking her head. "You're pirates."

If he didn't feel as though he was being pounded by a giant meat hammer, Cal might just have laughed at that. "We're not pirates. My name's Cal Harper. I was a lieutenant."

The woman appeared far from convinced.

Even the act of talking was causing excruciating pain, but Cal forced himself to continue. "The tall, black man is Jumper Decoux, a Big Game hunter. The girl's Eddy…I mean, Edwina. Edwina Cole, military private. The blond guy is…" Cal realized that he had no idea what Toker's surname was. Or maybe he just couldn't recall. Was Toker even his real name? "Well, he's Toker, and he's a…well, he's…" *He's a what? A celebrity?* Cal was fast regretting this approach. "The boy is Viktor, and…well he's…" *Military too?*

The woman's doubt didn't seem to be diminishing.

"Look, we're not pirates. We're… We're…" *What the hell are we?* Cal desperately needed to clear his thoughts. He wanted to shake his head, but his spine would likely come apart. "You healed…my friend's arm," he said in an attempt to change tack.

"It was an opportunity, an experiment. I needed a broken bone and didn't fancy breaking one of my own."

Cal could feel a shit load of sweat trickling down his face and neck. "I don't suppose…you have a…a pain patch?"

The woman ignored the question. "That Star Splinter, it's a stolen ship," she said accusingly. "As, no doubt, is this synthetic." She glanced at Melinda and shook her head as if in disbelief. "Who the hell modified her?"

"The boy," Cal managed weakly. The words didn't seem to want to leave his throat. It was as if they were being sucked back down by a vacuum in his lungs. He was pretty sure that elaboration was necessary, but he had nothing. Words had become a lost art. The pain had seeped up his spine and was burning the nerves in his brain. There was a loud thumping in his ears and high-pitched ringing. His vision swirled, and through those swirls, he thought he could see the woman staring at him in an odd fashion. Even Melinda was staring at him now. He tried to take some deep breaths, but he didn't even manage shallow ones. His ribs seemed to be shrinking. The chair he was leaning on was scraping across the floor, and some small part of his brain realized too late that he was toppling forward. That same part of his brain thought about throwing his arms out in order to break his fall.

Unfortunately, a thought was all it was. He was unconsciousness before he hit the floor.

Chapter Twenty-Nine
THICK AIR

Cal woke up. At least, he thought he was awake. There was a possibility that he was asleep. Either way, he didn't much care. He felt strange, like his brain had been dipped in honey. He was feeling slow and sort of…distant. He was shrouded in darkness and floating in midair. Of this, he was almost sure. His arms and legs were gently swaying but not in a loose way. More slow and sluggish, just like his brain. It was as if the air all around him was thick enough to float in. He tried moving one of those swaying limbs but was unsure which one. In the end, it really didn't matter. None of them obeyed. The lack of control didn't bother him; he didn't feel like moving anyway.

He briefly wondered whether he was experiencing some sort of delirium, but the thought didn't have much impact, and it soon faded away. The next thought was a realization; he was naked…well, mostly. This really didn't bother him either.

Despite the dark all around him, Cal could see his body clearly. He briefly considered whether he was floating in space, but he could see no stars. Somewhere right at the bottom of his mind, he suspected he should be experiencing panic. This should be scary, shouldn't it? Being suspended in a strange, dark place, unable to move. Yes, it probably should be scary. But it was hard to feel scared when you felt good. And he did feel good. Weird, but good.

As he continued to float in the nothingness, there came a gradual awareness of something to his left...possibly his right. He couldn't say for sure. Two pale snakes writhing in his peripheral vision. He thought about turning to take a proper look, but it seemed like a lot of effort. He probably couldn't move his head anyway.

He floated a little longer. Five minutes. Possibly an hour.

Now, there was something else. Something new. Even paler than the snakes. A kind of white smudge far above him, possibly below him, maybe even in front of him. He decided that it didn't really matter. He stared at the smudge for a while—not that he had much choice; not even his eyelids obeyed.

The white smudge was getting bigger. Definitely bigger...maybe closer. Also less smudge-like and more solid, and it was wobbling. *A fish*? Was the thick air liquid? Yes, liquid. It seemed obvious now that he thought about it. Perhaps the depths of some dark ocean? Maybe the white fish was a shark: one of those big, demonic ones, the ones with big, black eyes and rows upon rows of sharp, triangular teeth jutting from a downturned mouth. He'd had nightmares about those big, white sharks before. But this wasn't a nightmare. He was feeling good. Happy. Peaceful. If he'd been able, he might even have laughed.

He was sure he was awake now but not completely sure.

Closer, clearer. The white thing wasn't a shark. Not even a fish.

Closer, clearer...

Cal knew what it was now. It was an impossible thing. It looked just right, just how he'd imagined they should. He was feeling confused, but he didn't much care. The mermaid glided closer. Shining white skin, long hair flowing...beautiful. Then, she was beside him. Dealing with the writhing snakes...protecting him?

Something occurred to him, a strange, dull something that grew slowly brighter in his mind—he was breathing. He shouldn't be able to breathe, not underwater...should he? It was all becoming a little confusing. More confusing. But that was okay; he didn't much care.

The mermaid was hovering over him now, her body and tail a blur, but her beautiful face as clear as day. Blue eyes: incredible, pale blue eyes. She was cradling his head in her hands. Delicate but strong fingers. Was she to guide him to the surface? Free him from the dark depths?

But he was breathing. Must be air, not water. He stared at the mermaid. How could such a creature survive in such a place? But the answer was out of his reach.

He really didn't mind overly much.

Did I die? That thought came quicker and sharper than the others. Was this an angel? Perhaps here to guide him back to life or onward to heaven? Or maybe to hell? After all, he'd killed. He'd killed many—always in defence of himself or another—but it was still lives taken.

No, he decided after some time—or perhaps no time at all—that this beautiful creature had nothing to do with hell.

Her face was close. Long, shining hair slowly curling, bright white against the blackness. Such blue eyes. Cal could feel her hands lightly pressing against the sides of his face, firm but tender. She was looking directly at him. He thought maybe there was an expression on her face. Sadness? Seriousness? Yes, a little seriousness but not entirely. *Concern?* Yes, possibly concern. Concern for *him*?

He wasn't keen on the concern.

He tried a smile to remove the concern from that beautiful face. Had he managed it? He really wasn't all that sure.

He felt suddenly strange...stranger than before. He felt as though he was drifting...suddenly drifting...but without moving. He didn't mind—the blue-eyed angel was still with him.

His vision began to fade, but with an edge of defiance, he continued to gaze at the beautiful, pale face.

Then the concern was gone. And just before his vision went completely dark and his conscious mind faded away, the blue-eyed angel returned the smile.

Chapter Thirty
KAIA

"Calie boy… Wake up, bro. The day is a wastin' away."

Cal was lying down, that much he knew. He blinked open one eye and saw a face looming over him. The face was deeply tanned and dominated by a white-toothed grin.

"Man, I *knew it*, I *knew* you were awake. I think I might be psychic."

With an effort, Cal blinked open his other eye. "Toker?"

"Yes, bro, it's me. You okay?"

"Yup…at least I think so." Cal brought his hand to his face and rubbed his eyes. "Toker, I've been meaning to ask you…"

Toker gave him an encouraging nod.

"How the hell d'you keep such a tan in deep space?"

Toker showed even more of his white teeth. "Ha, knew you'd be fine. I told them there ain't much that can keep Calie boy down; that's what I told them." He reached out a hand.

Gratefully accepting it, Cal pulled himself to a sitting position and was surprised to find that, apart from a little disorientation, he actually felt pretty good. Pretty *damn* good. He looked about. He was sat on one of five bunks set along the straight back wall of a large, high-ceilinged, D-shaped room. Seeing monitoring equipment to the rear of each bunk, he guessed he was in some sort of medical facility. Just like all the other rooms he'd found himself in of late, it was almost entirely white. There was a high viewing panel stretched across the entire length of the curved wall through which he could see other white rooms housing more equipment.

Cal had been in more than his fair share of medical facilities in his time, and despite the obvious advanced nature of the facility, nothing he saw was particularly unusual. Nothing bar one exception. A large, round pool was set within the circular-shaped portion of the room that was filled almost to the brim with an eerie-looking, inky black liquid.

"Weird, eh?" Toker said, having noticed the direction of his stare. "Kinda spooky looking."

Cal agreed with a nod. "What...er..."

"What the hell is it?" Toker offered. "That's a good question. Some kind of healing juice. There was a lot of science talk to be honest, bro, which kinda shot over my pip. Whatever it is though, it healed you up good un proper. The very same stuff that fixed up my arm apparently."

Cal could feel confusion settling in. "What about the woman?"

"Woman... You mean Kaia? What a lady, eh? Gorgeous."

Cal rubbed at his face. "I think you might have to fill me in a bit here, Toker. I'm feeling a little out of the loop."

"Sure, yeah. Sorry, I'm not being all that helpful. The woman's called Kaia. She's a scientist. She thought we were pirates. You believe that, Cal?" Toker smiled. "Took us a while, but we managed to convince her that we were good 'uns. Well, Viktor and Jumper did most of the talking. I think Eddy and I were kinda making things worse. I tell you, Cal, it's a pretty damn amazing ship, this. Some sort of research vessel. We had a good look round yesterday, real advanced stuff. I didn't really get most of it, but it had Viktor grinning from ear to ear. Like a pig in the finest slop he was."

"*Yesterday*? How long have I been out?"

"Oh right, let me see… Er, a good few days. Three, no, three and a half I think. You were in pretty bad shape. It was kinda scary for a time. You've been sleeping like a baby for most of today though."

Cal took a moment to get his head around what Toker had said. Three days? What the hell had happened to him? He sighed and followed up his face rubbing with a bit of habitual neck massage. "How are the rest of the gang? They about?"

"Sure, Jumper should be here soon. We've been taking it in turns sitting here, waiting for you to wake up."

"Appreciate it."

"Course," Toker said with a wave of a hand. "I think Viktor's off with Melinda doing tech stuff. And Eddy…" He shook his head. "Well, Eddy is off searching for clues."

"Clues?"

"Yep, she still doesn't trust Kaia even after she saved your life. Crazy little nitwit's sneaking round the ship trying to find something to incriminate her. Personally, I think she's still pissed off at having noodles chucked in her face." Toker shrugged. "She'll calm down eventually. Anyway, how's the back feeling?"

"My back?" Cal instinctively reached his hands behind himself. Of course, his back. How could he have forgotten? He stretched, slowly and experimentally at first, then more rigorously, even throwing in a couple of twists from side to side. "It feels…well, it feels fine. It feels…*great*. That's incredible."

Toker nodded enthusiastically. "Uh huh, it's that pool. The black juju juice. It's crazy stuff. You were scratching at death's door when you went in that pool. Kaia had you at the bottom of it for a full day and night."

Cal looked again at the inky black liquid and shook his head in confusion. "What the hell happened to me?"

"We found you crashed out on the floor. I gotta tell you, pal, I thought you were a goner. You looked like death on a stick. There was a bit of a crazy tussle at first. Kaia was kneeling next to you with some sort of zapper device when we turned up. Looked like she'd done you a mischief. Found out after that it was a medical scanner but not before Eddy had launched herself at Kaia. Used all of her limbs and her head to pound on her. Let me tell you, bro, after we got Eddy under control, there was a shit load of arguing and confusion. My head still aches from it. Eventually, she convinced us that you'd croak for sure if we didn't let her help you."

"*Die*? From a *bad back*?"

"Not just the back. You had a fever too. A bad one. Goon goo or garn gar fever. Something like that." Toker grinned again and shook his head. "Man, you gotta have some guardian angel looking over you. If we hadn't ended up on this particular ship when we did…" He continued to shake his head, but the grin left his face. "Sorry, kind of a morbid. Anyway, none of that matters now. All is good."

"I guess so," Cal murmured. He had a ton of questions in his head and more flooding in by the minute. And his back, it felt completely normal. *Better* than normal. Nothing short of a miracle. "I'd like to talk to her, er…Kaia. Is she about?"

"Yep, she's actually closer than you think," Toker replied, nodding towards the inky pool.

Cal raised an eyebrow. "She's in there? Right now?"

"Uh huh, she went in a few minutes before you woke up. Said she had to do some maintenance."

"How deep is it?"

"Fifty feet apparently."

"*Fifty.*"

"Yeah, seems a bit excessive, right?"

"What's she using for a breathing apparatus?"

Toker chuckled. "That's the weird thing; she's not using any."

"Some sort of breathable liquid?"

"Nope, she had to put a bubble mask on you when she took you in."

Took me in. "Huh. A small gum breather then."

"That's what I thought. I use a gum breather when I surf the big waves. Damn clever bit of kit. Thing is, she swears she doesn't need one. An' you know what, I believe her. She's one hell of a lady, Cal. Capable. She's probably fixing the tubing on the bubble breather mask. There was a bit of a malfunction the first day you were down there. You should have seen her, bro. She was pretty scared for you. Stripped off and dove in there like some kind of mermaid."

"Huh. Mermaid?" Cal narrowed his eyes at his young friend, a strange feeling that he was being mocked creeping in.

"Yeah, you know, part chick, part fish," Toker continued. "Tell you what, Cal, I wouldn't mind another go in there myself."

Cal slowly nodded. He didn't blame his young friend one bit. Despite his confusion, he really was feeling pretty damn good.

"It can get quite addictive," came a female voice.

Cal turned to see that Kaia had surfaced in the center of the pool. Only her head was above the surface, her pale skin and white-blonde hair offering a striking contrast to the black liquid.

"It's the particles in the liquid, they charge up the cells in the body."

"Oh yeah," Toker exclaimed.

Cal thought his friend's voice a touch higher than normal.

"How d'you even see when you're down there?" Toker asked.

Kaia swam to the pool's edge before answering. "It's like when you're in a cloud, Everywhere you look is white, but you can clearly see yourself. Except, of course, in this case, it's black." Placing her hands on the white floor, she nimbly pulled herself out of the pool. Cal was surprised to see that the black liquid looked almost clear as it ran off her body.

"I'm glad you're awake," she said, giving Cal a radiant smile as she walked towards the bunks.

"Er, yes. So am I," he replied and returned a smile albeit an awkward one. "It sounds as though I might not have woken at all if it wasn't for you. Thanks."

Kaia frowned. "Please, you don't owe me any thanks. Certainly not after disabling your ship, knocking you all out, and dumping you in a cell," she said, the guilt plain on her face. "Then, of course, there was that wall I slammed you against."

Cal shrugged, hoping he came across more composed than he felt. "Just mistaken identity." He reached out an open palm. 'I'm Callum, but um...I guess... Well, I guess you probably already know that." *Pull it together, Cal.* The woman's radiant smile seemed to have disrupted the coordination of his mouth and brain.

"Kaia. Dr. Kaia Svensson," she said, taking his hand and shaking it.

"Hey, Doc," Toker said, seeming unsure where to direct his eyes. "Can I, um...a towel. Can I get you a towel or something?'

Cal smiled at his young friend's awkwardness. *Not just me then.*

"I'm fine thanks, Toker," she replied, tipping her head and giving her hair a twisting squeeze with her hands. She seemed completely unaware of the effect she was having, which to Cal only made her more attractive. "To be honest, you'd be hard-pressed to find a towel on this vessel anyway," she continued. "There are tiny micro pores in the floor that sense damp skin and direct warm air at you wherever you walk."

"No kidding?" Toker said, his awkwardness fading a little. "That's pretty frickin' clever."

She nodded and squeezed her hair again. "Great for your feet, not so great for your head."

Toker chuckled. "Mind if I give it a go?"

"Knock yourself out."

Grinning, Toker perched on the edge of the bed, yanked off his boots, and made his way barefoot over to the pool.

Cal enjoyed the amused expression on Kaia's face as she watched Toker hop away. Unfortunately, it turned to one of guilt as she looked back at him. "I really am sorry, Callum—"

"Just Cal is fine."

She nodded. "The way I treated you all. I was confused and, well, scared."

"Understandable. These are crazy times." He glanced at Toker. "And we *are* a bit of a weird bunch."

Kaia smiled, but the guilt lingered in her eyes.

"You were just being cautious," he added.

"Too cautious."

He shrugged again. "Maybe you could give me a few tips. I'm trying *caution* as a new motto."

She laughed at that then turned to look at Toker, who now had his trousers rolled up and was sitting with his legs immersed in the black liquid. "You've got some good friends there. I saw real fear in their eyes when I explained what was wrong with you."

"I couldn't hope for better," he replied honestly. "Can I ask what exactly *was* wrong with me?"

She indicated the end of the bunk. "You mind if I sit?"

"Please do."

She perched on the corner of the bunk and after a moment asked, "Have you ever been to the Guan islands on Fili Dett?"

Huh. Now that really did confuse him. "Actually, yes. I was on Fili Dett about five years ago with my squad. We spent about four months there, most of it on the islands trying to protect a group of scientists from the local wildlife."

Kaia raised her eyebrows. "Bet that was a tough job?"

He nodded. "Eventful. Quite the lethal planet."

"Yes, and most of its dangers you can't even see."

Ah. "Parasites?"

"I'm afraid so."

"But that was five years ago."

"There's a parasite called the *guan gara*. A nasty little critter, and it's all but impossible to detect on scans—at least whilst it remains dormant. It waits in hiding until the host body is subjected to suitable level of stress, then it strikes hard. It's strange, really. Why it would kill its host, its home? But that's what it does, and it does it quickly."

Cal took a moment to absorb Kaia's words. "I guess I was pretty stressed. This ship of yours is...*unusual.* I was convinced for a time that I'd offered my friends up on a plate to...well, who knows."

"The problem was physical too. Your lower back was in a complete state."

"Yes, I er...had a bit of a tumble off a cliff a little while back."

"Why didn't you get it fixed?"

Cal felt his cheeks warm. *Jesus, what am I, a schoolboy?*

Kaia suddenly reddened a little too. "Sorry, that was a bit abrupt."

He laughed. "No that's fine. I really should've had it seen to, but I never seemed to find the time." The reason sounded lame, but that didn't make it any less true.

"Probably for the best," Kaia replied. "Military doctors would have only made it worse. I'm sorry. If I'd paid more attention, I could have fixed it when I saw to your friend's broken arm."

Cal looked over at Toker, who was still sitting at the edge of the pool, sporting a wide grin as he waved a wet left foot over the floor. "Well that black liquid seems nothing short of magical; my back feels stronger and healthier than ever. As a matter of fact, my whole body does."

Kaia smiled with a knowing nod. "It's a safe bet that neither the parasite nor the back will trouble you again. I wish I could tell you how it works, but truthfully, we don't have a clue. All I can tell you is that the deeper you're immersed in the liquid, the more powerful the effect."

"Where's it from?"

"The northern mountain ranges of the planet Alvor. There are entire lakes full of it."

Alvor. That planet again. He still had a clear visions of the Alvorian oak that Jumper had led them to on Mars. The mammoth tree had been a wondrous treat to the eyes just as its fruits had been to the taste buds. "You know, even though I've never stepped foot on it, Alvor is fast becoming my favourite place."

Kaia smiled. "Yes, it's an incredible planet. The discoveries we've made there are spectacular, and we've only just brushed the surface."

"We?"

"Sorry, Cal, you must be pretty confused right now."

"Just a bit." He turned to gaze at the black liquid. His mind felt as full as the pool and then some. "That was some pretty impressive breath holding you did down there?"

She recognized the complement as the question it was intended to be. "I have certain…abilities."

"So I've noticed," he said, looking back at her. "You're the first person I've met who's managed to tackle and surprise a synthetic. You gave Melinda a little run for her money for a moment there in that lab. I'd love to know how you…" He dropped his head and suddenly found himself chuckling. "I think maybe I'm getting ahead of myself. I have so many questions for you, Kaia, but I really have no idea where to start." *And I can barely look at you without feeling like a jabbering teen.*

Kaia nodded, her blue eyes full of understanding. "I know the feeling; I've been firing questions at your friends pretty much nonstop for the past couple of days." Sitting up straighter, she shot him another of her ridiculously radiant smiles. "I guess I've had my chance to get ahead, so how's about I help you catch up?"

"I'd appreciate that. Thanks."

"Okay," she said, using her hands to brush back her hair. It was almost dry now, and its wavy length was beginning to form into ringlets at its ends. "This ship is *The Orillian,* one of three scientific research vessels. It has eighteen departments, including motion physics, cybernetics, biological upgrading, and alien study. I'm the head of biological research."

"One of three? What happened to the other two?"

Kaia shrugged. "I wish I knew."

"What happened to the rest of *The Orillian's* crew?"

Kaia paused for a moment, the smile faltering ever so slightly. "Fear happened," she said. 'There were three hundred and ten of us on board originally. People started getting scared when the long-range communications went down."

Cal nodded his understanding. "Isn't it amazing how much we rely on communications to feel safe? The mind starts to fear the worst when the lights go out."

"Yes. I guess this time, the worst *had* happened. Eventually, word *physically* reached us of Earth's destruction."

"Oh?"

"It was a private vessel. They'd witnessed the attacking ships firsthand before they fled. The state the crew was in, I wouldn't be surprised if they're still fleeing now. We spent a few weeks trying to confirm it. Visited a lot of colonies. A few months after that, I was the only one left on board."

Cal detected bitterness in her voice. "What happened?"

"The majority of the crew bailed early on. Roaming through space with the threat of an advanced, aggressive alien race just proved too much. Then, there were rumors that military starships and bases had been attacked and overrun. Those rumours turned out to be true; all the bases we visited were empty and in ruins."

"Like Delta Point Three?"

Kaia nodded. "During that time, we didn't cross paths with any starships, but we all feared the worst. The remaining crew didn't want to risk staying on board a ship with military connections. There were arguments, of course. Dr York argued that *The Orillian* was one of the safest places in known space. He was the scientist responsible for our ghosting net technology."

"Ghosting net?"

"A new stealth and cloaking technology. So new that only *The Orillian* and a few other ships had been fitted with it before the invasion. The crew still didn't feel safe though, and eventually, they all jumped ship."

"Where did they jump ship to?"

"Most to Alvor. We have three large research bases there."

"They hadn't been attacked?"

"No, but Alvor's quite a distance." She looked lost in thought for a moment. "Also, they're not listed as military..."

"You didn't fancy Alvor? Seems it would make a nice home."

"I had my reasons to stay. I wanted to learn more about the threat. So did Dr. York and some of his team."

"What about military personnel, soldiers, security detail? They didn't feel it their duty to stay on board?"

"*The Orillian* isn't a military vessel. It's part of Sync Corp."

Cal shook his head.

"You're unlikely to have heard of it. They didn't exactly advertise. They develop advanced technology—or at least they *did*. They often supplied the military but were never owned by them. We did have a sizeable security detail on board, but none of them felt any great loyalty. They weren't soldiers, just hired muscle to keep order among the crew. She gave Cal a half smile. "Scientists have a habit of heatedly disagreeing from time to time. The truth is that threats from outside forces were never really considered a potential problem. *The Orillian* is a stealth ship. And with Dr. York's ghosting net system, we relied on never being detected in the first place.'

"Well, it certainly worked on us. We didn't have an inkling of your presence until you came into view."

"If I'd had the ghosting net on full, you wouldn't have seen a thing. You'd have been none the wiser until the ship's clutchers had grabbed hold and the knockout probe burst through. Sorry."

"You disabled our Star Splinter like it was a child's toy."

She gave him another half-smile. "Might as well have been. Sync Corp designed and built every Star Splinter ship on the market."

"Really?"

"Yep."

Cal detected a hint of pride in that *yep*.

"They don't exactly advertise the fact, but they're behind most of the best tech out there—all of the *smart* technology: smart-straps, smart-glass. They had a hand in nearly all of the military's technology. Even the computer systems that big starships operate on were designed and built by Sync Corp."

"Huh." Cal suddenly felt a little stupid. He'd never given much thought as to where those technologies had originated. In truth, he'd always assumed that the military had been responsible for their own tech. "And the synthetics?"

"Yes, those too. In fact, many of Melinda's counterparts were built here on this very ship."

"Really? Viktor's going to love that."

Kaia laughed, and Cal felt his heart skitter. "Your young friend is *already* loving it. He's practically set up home down in the cybernetics department. That kid is incredible."

"Yes, there's some brain in that head of his," Cal replied, surprised at the swell of pride he felt. "So I guess that explains how you managed to disable Melinda too."

Kaia nodded, that touch of guilt peeping out again. "Sync Corp never likes to completely relinquish control of their products. Every one of them contains what's called a *TCW, a Transparent Control Worm*. I'm not convinced even the military knows about it. Any major Sync Corp computer can detect their products within a particular radius. Then they can hack into it and take control. That's how I discovered your ship."

"Strange," Cal said after a moment's deliberation.

Kaia looked at him questioningly.

"Sorry, it's just that, after what you just told me, I was wondering how in the hell a man like Aaron Hogmeyer could ever manage to get hold of and keep a stolen Star Splinter. Hogmeyer is—"

"Yes," Kaia interjected, one corner of her mouth curling. "Your friend Toker over there has already told me about Hogmeyer and how you *acquired* his ship. The reasons for him having it are probably simpler than you think though. It's just deception on the part of Sync Corp. They take steps to hide the presence of the TCWs by allowing a certain percentage of their products to get stolen. In fact, I wouldn't put it past them to *employ* a man like Hogmeyer to help arrange such deceptions."

Cal nodded and scratched his head. "So, um, we seem to have strayed a bit. What happened to Dr York and his team? If they were so confident in their new stealth tech, why didn't they stay?"

"They took a ship and headed to Alvor just over a month ago."

"They finally got cold feet?"

"Yes, but it had nothing to do with alien invaders. Pirates scared them off."

Pirates. How the hell could pirates manage to threaten such a ship? Cal decided to put that particular question on the back burner. Something else had begun to dominate his thought process. "Forgive my snooping, Kaia, but I couldn't help noticing the two rather large Carcarrions in your lab."

"Yes, sorry if they gave you a fright. Your friend Jumper was quizzing me about those yesterday. I'm studying them."

"They're just specimens then?"

"Specimens...*and* prisoners."

"So the rumors are true? The Carcarrions are involved in this threat?'

"Yes, they're involved, but not in a way that you might think." She looked down and gave her head a little shake. "I've learned a lot in recent weeks. A hell of a lot." She looked up at him. "But I think it would be easier to show you rather than tell you."

Cal suddenly felt a wave of hope, excitement even. Kaia's words were like music to his ears. He might finally get some answers, some *real* answers. Time to stop being bounced around...he hoped.

"Looks like you have a visitor," Kaia said, pulling him from his thoughts.

Cal looked up to see Jumper strolling towards them, a broad grin stretched across his face.

"Maybe it's best I give you two some time to catch up," Kaia suggested, pushing herself up off the bunk. "How's about I meet you in the specimen's lab when you're ready?"

"Sounds good," he replied, his smile finally losing its awkward edge.

"Jumper knows the way."

"Okay. And, Kaia, thanks again."

"You're welcome." She turned and headed off towards the exit, exchanging a friendly greeting with Jumper as she went.

Cal took some deep breaths to oxygenate his overtaxed brain. So much had happened, so much had been learned, and he'd bloody well slept through it. He was glad Jumper was finally here to help set free the cacophony of questions battering his skull. Jumper would help get him back on track, and he didn't fancy his old friend in the least.

"Good to see you awake and looking fit," Jumper said as he approached the bunk.

"Well, my feet haven't touched the floor yet, but I guess *looking* fit is a good start."

Jumper stood at the end of the bunk for a moment, something strange in his smile.

"You okay?" Cal asked hesitantly.

Jumper didn't answer; instead, he walked around the bunk, leaned forward, and gave him an embrace. Cal was taken aback; Jumper had never been one for openly showing emotion. So much so, in fact, that when Cal was a boy, it had taken him quite a while to recognize his subtle expressions.

Jumper continued the embrace. "Damn it, I thought I'd lost you for a time there, kid," he said before releasing him and straightening up. His smile had turned to a deep frown.

"I'm...I'm sorry to have scared you, Jumper."

Jumper noisily cleared his throat and just about managed to lose the frown. "Yes, well, just don't go doing it again."

Cal nodded. "I'll try."

"See that you do." Jumper rubbed at the back of his neck and had a look around the room. "Everything alright with Toker?" he said after a moment.

Cal looked towards the black, shimmering pool. Toker was on his hands and knees, directing his long, dripping wet hair towards the floor.

"He's…just experimenting."

Jumper sighed. "You know, Cal, it was far easier when I was going solo, only having my own hide to worry about. Having people that you're fond of is…well, it's pretty damned stressful."

"Uh huh." Cal nodded. 'You know, if you wanted, we could always drop you off on some jungle planet. A good one with plenty of big, nasty beasties to stop you from getting bored."

Jumper chuckled. "You know what? All the stress in the world wouldn't make me abandon you lot." He was still watching Toker, who was now making his way around the pool in a sort of sumo wrestling stance, his rapidly drying hair still flopping forward. "Being on your own is peaceful, sure, but it's bloody difficult to keep yourself amused."

"I'm glad to hear it."

Jumper nodded. "Besides, who the hell else would make sure that you lot ate properly?"

Cal grinned, and the two men sat in silence for a few moments. His old friend's exceptional zen had somehow quietened the questions within him. But it couldn't last… "So, our new friend Kaia's been filling me in on a few things."

"Kaia, yes. She's something, eh? She's like a magician, and this ship's her box of tricks. Beautiful too. And brave. It must take a lot of courage to go solo on a ship like this. Quite a woman."

Cal grinned. *Definitely not just me.*

Chapter Thirty-One
CATCHING UP

"Man, that's weird looking."

"What? Where is it?" Eddy's nose was practically touching the smart-glass barrier as she squinted and peered through it. "I don't see it. Do you see it, Cal?"

Toker sighed, exasperated. "Of course Cal can see it. It's right there." Toker stabbed his finger forwards. "On the back of its neck."

"More parasites?" Cal asked, turning to Kaia.

"Of a sort," she answered. "To be honest, they're like nothing I've ever seen before, and I haven't had them here long enough to study them in full."

Cal nodded and continued to stare into the chamber. Nothing had changed within since he and Jumper had first seen it; two Carcarrions on separate platforms although Kaia had turned one of the aliens in order to view a parasite-like creature on the back of its neck. The other Carcarrion was glaring at them, its silvery eyes bright and its white fangs bared. Both aliens were propped upright, their muscled forms bound by restraints that seemed disturbingly flimsy. Cal wasn't worried; the real protection lay in the huge slab of smart-glass that made the viewing possible. It would take nothing short of a severe act of God to break it.

Cal could understand why Eddy was having trouble seeing the critter in question; even though it was the size of a large hand, it was as jet black as its Carcarrion host and was attached to the back of its neck almost seamlessly.

"You lot are havin' me on," Eddy grumbled. "There ain't nothin' there."

"I can make it more visible if you'd like?"

Eddy turned to look at Kaia with hostile eyes.

With an uncomfortable smile, Kaia picked up a control wand and used it to activate a slim, robotic arm within the chamber. Smoothly moving it up and forward, the arm expelled a fine mist towards the strange parasite. The moment the mist made contact, the little critter jerked in spasm, and its jet black form burst into color—a mottled mass of vibrant blues, greens, and yellows that wriggled back and forth across its length.

"*Whoa...* Man, now *that* really is weird," Toker exclaimed, taking a step back in surprise. "Tell me you can see it now, Ed."

"Course I bloody do."

Toker turned and raised an eyebrow at Kaia. "So the little beastie's not keen on your spray, eh, Doc?"

"It's a rilium acid, not particularly strong, but for some reason, the parasite reacts to it. The mist does no harm to the Carcarrions. At least, it wouldn't if they were alive."

"Not like that mist you sprayed at us then?" Eddy commented.

"No," Kaia said, her uncomfortable smile turning to an apologetic one.

"Jeeze, Ed, hold a grudge much?"

With a sour face, Eddy mumbled something inaudible and turned back to glass.

Using the control wand, Kaia stopped the acidic mist and retracted the robotic arm. Almost instantly, the parasite stopped its wriggling and rapidly darkened until it once again matched the color of its host.

"They're dead?" Cal asked after a moment.

Kaia looked at him questioningly.

"The Carcarrions. You said that even if they were alive the mist wouldn't hurt them. They seem pretty alive to me."

"You'd be forgiven for thinking so. I thought the very same thing not all that long ago until I began my studies and ran some scans. To all sense and purposes, the Carcarrions in there are most definitely dead. Their brains are completely offline. Those parasite-like creatures are running the show. They've inserted minute tendrils through the neck directly into the spinal cord, probably killing the host instantly. Through those tendrils, they control the entire body. The Carcarrions are nothing more than drones now. Vehicles."

"So they've basically killed the mind and hijacked the body?"

"Exactly. They're much more than parasites though; they don't require their hosts to be alive to assure their own survival. In fact, they insure that the host *doesn't* survive—"

"It kills them, then it nicks the body! Oh man," Toker said, turning to Cal and Kaia with a disturbed look. He shook his head and, seeming unsure of what else to say, simply turned back to look back through the glass.

"'Oh man' *what,* idiot?" Eddy spat.

Toker looked at her. "Well, it's… Well, it's just…bloody evil, isn't it? How can a little thing like that *do* all that?"

"I wish I knew," Kaia answered. "Their biology is completely baffling. To be honest, I've never seen anything like it, and trust me, I've studied an awful lot of species."

"*Trust you,*" Eddy exclaimed, her voice somewhat muffled by the barrier in front of her face. "That's a laugh."

"You know what, Ed," Toker interjected, "you need to start

being a little more polite. I've a good mind to put you over my knee."
He flashed Cal and Kaia a quick grin. "And what is it with you and
glass? You just have to press your face against it, don't you?"

"Shut it, blond—"

Eddy's glass muffled retort was interrupted by a loud bang as one
of the Carcarrion drones snapped forward, slamming against its
restrains and issuing a strange, alien hiss as it did so. Taken by
surprise, Eddy fell back and landed heavily on her backside.

Toker's grin widened. "Is there a lesson learned?" He wagged a
finger down at her. "You don't press your face against the glass."

Eddy shot him a look that Cal wouldn't wish upon his worst
enemy. A second later, Toker was dashing off across the lab, Eddy
hot on his tail, fists clenched.

"She really doesn't like me much," Kaia said as she placed the
control wand on a nearby desk. "I guess I can't really blame her."

"Don't worry about Eddy. She'll come around,' Cal replied as he
watched the pair battle their way around the lab. "Sorry for any
damage."

"It's fine," Kaia said with a wave of her hand. "The only things
of any real importance are the two—well, *four* creatures behind this
glass."

Cal turned to stare back into the chamber. "Where did you find
them?"

"We came across their wrecked ship shortly before Earth was
destroyed. They'd fallen victim to the Kalloth drift."

Cal nodded. He knew the K drift well; he'd had to navigate it as
part of his training. The physics of it was way beyond him,
something to do with the close proximity of multiple planets,
moons, and asteroid fields. Ships passing through the area had a
habit of suddenly and quite severely being pulled off course, often
resulting in a crash. "They were shipwrecked?"

"Yes, on one of Serros' moons. There wasn't much of their craft left. It was incredible these two remained so intact. Just shows you how tough the body of a Carcarrion is."

"There were only two of them?"

"As far as we could see, yes. The wreckage suggested the craft was small. Scouts maybe. I'm no engineer, but their technology seems just as baffling as their biology. We gathered the wreckage for study."

"I'd like to see it."

Kaia shook her head. "Sorry, Cal. The technology engineers kept hold of it. They took it to Alvor for further study."

Cal shrugged, feeling a little disappointed. Lost in thought, he approached the glass to get a closer look at the neck critter. The other Carcarrion drone hissed at him and slammed against the restraints. Cal ignored it. *What the hell are you?* The critter itself was completely motionless, but he could see the gentle rise and fall of the alien drone's heavily muscled shoulders as it breathed. He formed a mental picture of the tendrils that Kaia spoke of and could imagine them worming their way through the Carcarrion's neck into its spinal column.

"Things are starting to make sense," he said, turning to look at Kaia. "But at the same time, they're becoming more confusing. I've never known a great deal about Carcarrions, but I know enough that the thought of them flying planet-destroying vessels is pretty ludicrous. These parasite critters are the start of an explanation, but where the hell do they come from? And what the hell are they? Any theories?"

Kaia frowned and gave a small shrug. "Theories are pretty much all I have in that regard. They're obviously not from our little section of known space. Not even close. The advanced nature of their technology certainly suggests that they're capable of travelling extreme distances. Also, the biology that I've studied over the past ten years is hugely diverse, but these creatures… Well, it's like their biological structure is governed by a whole different set of rules: rules that have evolved very differently to any ecosystem that I've ever studied. Looking at them in the scans…they almost seem too simplistic, too *basic,* not enough there to control an entire body like they do, let alone hold the intelligence to design and build their technology. To be honest, I don't think these creatures are our enemy. I mean, not our *true* enemy."

"I don't think I follow."

Kaia let out a small, frustrated sigh. "Sorry, I'm not explaining myself very well. I don't think they're a complete living entity. They're more like a remote receiver, a *biological* remote control receiver. Controlled by something else, somewhere else."

Cal looked back in the chamber with a frown. "It's just a theory," Kaia finished with a shrug.

"But if that were the case, wouldn't they try to locate this ship and retrieve their…drones?"

"Perhaps…" Kaia looked down, seemingly lost in thought.

Despite the questions filling his head, Cal tried to do her a favor by staying silent until she continued.

"There's more I have to tell you," she eventually said, looking up and fixing him with her blue eyes. "Much more you have to see. What I'm showing you here is only the tip of what I've discovered." She looked back through the glass and went quiet again for a time. "Maybe if their controlling signal is biological in nature," she suggested, "perhaps it would function completely differently to a technological counterpart. If that was the case, whoever or whatever is controlling these two drones might not know anything other than what can be seen, heard, and felt through the drone's physical senses—" Kaia's words were cut short by high-pitched alarm. "*Damn it,*" she exclaimed quietly before hurrying over to a nearby console. "They're bloody relentless," she said, sounding annoyed as well as a little scared.

Bemused, Cal followed her to the console and looked up as she activated a large, holographic screen.

"Do you see them?" she asked, sounding stressed as she pointed up at the screen, which revealed a view of deep space. There was a distant planet with multiple moons, but that wasn't what she was pointing at. With a movement of her hand, she enlarged a view of an approaching ship. Cal recognized it immediately as a pirate ship purely because every pirate seemed compelled to adorn the hulls of their ships with custom weaponry. Such modifications often made them look ridiculous but not this particular case. This ship looked nothing short of deadly.

"Pirates."

"Yes, they've been tracking *The Orillian* for months now. I don't know how or why. They shouldn't be able to. They shouldn't even be able to see us, let alone track us. Twice, they've almost commandeered the ship. They're the reason that Dr York and his team left."

"I take it you can't disable them like you did the Star Splinter?"

"Not a chance. That's a black market ship built from scratch on some back world most likely."

"What weapons and defenses does this ship have?"

Kaia shook her head. "None."

He looked at her in surprise.

"It's a research vessel," she said a little defensively. "It relies solely on speed and stealth. The ghosting net is—or at least *should* be—its real protection."

"So how are they beating the system?"

"I have no idea. I wish I knew. Somehow, they're managing to track us even through the ghosting net. They keep locking onto *The*

Orillian's flight signature. It shouldn't be possible. Not even our new alien invaders are capable of that."

This last statement took Cal by surprise, but the questions would have to wait.

"Luckily, their ship's nowhere near as fast as *The Orillian*," Kaia continued. "They'll never catch us, but it certainly hasn't stopped them trying."

"Maybe they're hoping to catch you with your pants down…if you'll excuse the expression."

"Probably. Especially if they somehow knew I was alone."

"Well, they've got seven of us to deal with now."

Kaia briefly turned from the holographic screen to smile at him. It was a smile that said a lot; finding yourself alone in space, even in peaceful times, was trying for even the bravest of souls. Cal suspected that Kaia was deeply grateful for the company.

"Have you managed to scan their ship?"

"Yes, just basic sweep scans that I've run each time before fleeing. They have a crew of seventy-eight, and energy scans suggest multiple weapons."

"A large crew for pirates."

Kaia cast her eyes down to her console and nodded. "Yes and, by all accounts, an unusually sophisticated ship," she said, her hands dancing over the console's controls. "I've set *The Orillian* at full speed on a random escape vector. It will shake them off our trail. But it means it'll take us longer to reach our destination."

Cal watched as the lethal-looking ship rapidly faded into the distance. Soon, it was nothing more than a distant blip on the scanners. Satisfied that the threat was well and truly left behind, he turned to Kaia, "Our destination?"

Chapter Thirty-Two
INSIDIOUS MUSHROOMS

Cal stared at the gleaming white table, his brain spinning like a defective gyro detonator, just as it had been all night. Despite his sleeplessness, he was still feeling pretty damn good. Whatever that magical pool of black liquid had changed within him was lasting in its effect. He was grinning – something he'd been doing periodically since the previous day. He felt ten years younger, better even. There wasn't a hint of pain where his old injuries had been. It was as if they'd never existed, nothing short of a miracle. He looked over at Jumper, keen to discuss the miracle for the hundredth time, but his old friend looked to be at a crucial stage in his cooking process. The scrambled eggs in Krasien herbs and salted taka sausages smelt divine, a little miracle of their own.

Cal looked to the opposite side of the canteen table. Toker was slumped in his chair, head back, eyes closed, and snoring softly. Eddy sat next to him, intently tying a fistful of his long, blond hair to the frame of his seat. Viktor, Melinda, and Kaia were yet to arrive. Cal hoped they wouldn't be long; he wanted to talk things through, plan things out. He wanted to *chat* and not just about the magical black elixir. Not by a long shot, not after the previous evening's discussions.

Kaia knew where at least some of the invaders were. Not only that, but she'd observed them for five full days. Cal shook his head, still not quite believing she'd managed it. Her discovery of the huge alien ship on the surface of the Carcarrion planet C9 had been the start. A giant block of a ship and close to it a prison camp revealing the terrible plight of thousands of military personnel. She had also seen the battle class starships those prisoners had once crewed. Perhaps a third of the Federation's military fleet now empty and drifting aimlessly among C9's many moons. Cal could scarcely believe the truth of it; how could so many heavily gunned starships have been overpowered and so many soldiers taken captive, even if they were technologically outmatched? Fortunately, it seemed Kaia had some answers.

Despite knowing her for less than a day, Cal's admiration of Kaia had continued to rise exponentially. Of *The Orillian's* substantial crew, she'd been the only one with the dedication and courage to stay on board and then some. She'd put her faith in the vessel's unparalleled technology—its highly advanced ability to remain unseen and undetected—and taken a bold risk. He could barely imagine the fear she must have faced and subsequently conquered when she'd set the ship on a course into what was possibly the heart of the alien invader's territory. Fortunately for Kaia, and quite possibly the rest of the human race, the gamble had paid off. Even orbiting the conquered Carcarrion planet in close proximity, the cloaked vessel had remained undetected.

Still lost in his musings, Cal scooped his mug of tea in one hand and looked up to see Melinda entering the canteen. She was wearing a close-fitting body suit similar to Kaia's, and he could have sworn her hair was a shade lighter. He slurped at the hot beverage as she approached with her long strides and sat at the end of the table.

"Good morning, Cal, Eddy."

Almost spilling the steaming tea over his lap, Cal suffered a small coughing fit. Not once during his time spent in Melinda's company had the cybernetic woman ever addressed him directly. In fact, he'd never seen her talk to anyone other than Viktor. Wiping his chin with his sleeve, he tried to clear his throat. "Yes… Morning, Melinda."

She smiled at him and then relaxed back in her chair. A little confused by this turn of events, Cal looked over to Toker and Eddy. Toker was still snoring, and Eddy was slouched back, grinning as she glanced at the huge blond knot she'd tied around the chair. Cal wasn't all that surprised that Eddy had missed the unusual event; she wasn't the most observant of girls. He'd have to remain confused on his own. But then, he'd been confused a lot of late. At least Kaia was helping to clear some of that confusion now.

"Is, um…is Viktor on his way, Melinda?"

"Yes, Cal, six seconds," the cybernetic woman replied, turning to smile at him again. *Still not quite human, but close.*

Moments later, Viktor entered the canteen. He was walking side by side with Kaia, deep in conversation. Bar Toker, who slept on, and Eddy, who was busy staring at Kaia suspiciously, morning greetings were voiced by all. Cal didn't believe for a second that Eddy's glaring held any real malice. He suspected the girl had already accepted that Kaia was on their side but was reluctant to lose face. He also suspected a little jealousy.

"How did you sleep?" Kaia asked as she took a seat next to him.

"Fine, thanks," Cal lied.

Viktor sat himself on the other side of Kaia. "Melinda talked to you yet, Cal?" he asked eagerly.

"As a matter of fact, she has."

The boy beamed. "Did she come across as natural?"

Cal nodded. "Very," he replied a little generously.

Viktor continued to beam. "Kaia's been helping me. You should see the tech lab down there. All the kits and spare parts you could dream of. New stuff too. I can help myself, right, Kaia?"

She nodded. "Anything you need."

"That's very generous, Kaia."

She gave a little shrug. "It's just good to have someone down there who really knows what they're doing."

The boy's cheeks turned pink.

"Oh, bloody hell," Eddy suddenly snapped, glaring at them from the other side of the table. "Don't tell me you bloody fancy her too, Vik."

"Shut up," Viktor hissed, his face turning from pink to red.

Cal looked at Kaia; unlike Viktor, she'd barely reacted to the comment at all. So much so that Cal thought her oblivious to Eddy's meaning.

"No arguing at the breakfast table," Jumper said without turning from the stove, "else you'll be getting nothing but long life protein blocks to chew on."

The calm threat even managed to silence Eddy, but the peace was brief.

"*Arrrgghh.*" Toker had finally woken and attempted to sit up. "What the...?" He reached up with his hand to find the large, tangled knot of hair. First, he looked shocked. Then, he grinned. "Very bloody funny, Ed."

Eddy's sour look had been replaced by silent racks of laughter adorned with an occasional uncontrolled snort.

"Yeah, laugh it up," Toker encouraged. "Don't forget though, little pipsqueak, you don't get one past ol' Toker without it coming back at you...threefold." He was standing now. At least, he was attempting to stand; the chair dangling from his head was forcing him to bend over as he desperately dug his fingers into the tangled knot. "I can't undo it. I can't bloody untie it. Seriously, guys, I'm not joking. Okay, new rule, Ed, not the hair in the future, okay? Or the face. Agreed?"

Eddy was too busy fighting for breath to answer.

Cal looked at Kaia; her eyes were bright with amusement. The lonely existence she'd endured had well and truly been disrupted, and she looked very glad of it. She turned his way smiling. Realising he was staring at her a little dumbly, he returned the smile. "Never a dull moment."

Jumper approached the table, a huge bowl of eggs in one hand and a tray filled with sausages in his other. "Breakfast is served," he said with a wide grin. Leaning over the table, he placed the bowl and tray down then walked over to the still-struggling Toker. Casually pulling a gleaming chef's knife from a sheaf on his hip, he flicked his wrist and sliced through Toker's hair just above the knot, causing the chair to crash to the ground. "Take a seat, Toker, we don't want the eggs to get cold."

Toker held the clump of shortened hair before his eyes then turned to shake his head at Eddy. She was too busy wiping the tears from her face to notice. "I was going ask Melinda for a haircut anyway," he mumbled, picking up his chair and sitting himself down.

"That would be my pleasure, Toker," Melinda replied.

A little startled, Toker looked across the table at Melinda. "Who the hell are you?"

"It's Melinda, you dolt," Viktor snapped.

"I know, but since when does she speak?" Toker asked, looking around at everyone, "I mean, to anyone other than her little man?"

"I've been upgrading her programming," the boy replied with a sniff. "Been meaning to do it for ages but haven't had a decent enough tech lab. The military can be damn stingy with their gear."

"You programmed in any new moves?" Eddy asked casually, reaching over and grabbing a handful of sausages. "I mean, she's strong, but her fightin' technique is a bit off if you ask me. Guess I could teach her a few things before we get to facin' these alien critter things."

"You're kidding," Viktor snorted. "Melinda's combat programming incorporates the best of one hundred and twenty-one proven fighting disciplines."

"Uh huh, so program in my fightin' discipline, an' she'll have a hundred an' twenny-two."

"*Ha!*" Toker blurted as he leaned over the table, scooped up a huge portion of scrambled eggs, and dumped them on his plate, "You haven't got a fighting discipline, Ed; you bloody make it up as you go along."

"Right," Eddy agreed. "That's the best kind. It's *instinct* fightin'. Better than squealing like a little girl and runnin' away."

Toker looked at her, an egg-filled fork paused partway to his mouth. "Little girl! You do realize that you actually *are* a little girl, don't you?'

Eddy snorted. "We'll soon see… When we face up to them neck critter things, then we'll see who's the biggest little girl."

Toker put down his fork and grinned at her. "You know, I wonder sometimes if even *you* know what the hell you're going on about cos sure as hell no one else does."

"I know what I'm sayin'," Eddy said defensively then filled her cheeks with an entire sausage. "Cal, when we gonna get to them neck critters?" she mumbled between chews.

Cal winced inwardly at the question. His *caution* motto had lasted all of one day. In his defense he'd originally voted against heading to the planet C9. In fact, he'd argued caution for a full hour or near enough. But then Kaia had convinced him otherwise. Even if she'd been wrong, she'd still probably have convinced him with that smile of hers. But, he had to concede, she had it right. Risking the lives of a few for the lives of many may be a cliché, but it didn't make it any less true. Of course, it didn't help when those few were your friends, your family.

But it was a mammoth task. Surely, the rescue of thousands required at least hundreds and not a few? Again, Kaia had shown her worth. She'd already proved the effectiveness of stealth over force, and she'd devised a plan that utilized the best of that stealth. There would be an inevitable point where force was needed, but the supporting numbers were already there. What better fighters than those fighting for their own freedom? All they had to do was give the imprisoned soldiers that fighting chance, something that the seven of them might just be able to pull off.

"We'll arrive at C9 by tomorrow, Eddy. Then at least a week of prep, right, Kaia?"

"I think a week will be enough," she replied, looking a little worried. Uncertain. Cal knew the feeling. He'd come up with a fair few military strategies himself over the years, and doubt was a constant partner. The bigger the plan, the bigger the worry, and this plan certainly wasn't small.

"The plan is a good one," he said, hoping to take the edge off her unease. "And if all goes well, we won't actually be facing the enemy at all." *The prisoners will have that privilege.*

Eddy looked on the verge of protest but instead pushed another sausage into her mouth.

"I think we need to come up with a name," Viktor said after a moment. "None of us know what to call these, alien critter parasite thingies."

Toker nodded. "He's got a good point."

"Carcarrions, ain't they?"

Toker shook his head. "No, Ed, they're just drones, the poor buggers who ended up dead and hijacked," he said, scooping up another huge portion of eggs even though his plate was still half full. "It's the evil little hitchers on their necks that need to be named."

Eddy nodded thoughtfully and after a moment of chewing blurted out, "Wormoids. No, Sluggoids."

Toker screwed up his face. "We'll save those as backups I think."

"Don't see you comin' up with any good 'uns."

"I think Kaia should name them," Toker said, turning to Kaia. "What say you, Doc? You kinda discovered them after all."

Eddy huffed, letting a few bits of chewed sausage fly free to land on the shiny white table.

Kaia hesitated then gave Cal a quick glance before saying, "Actually, I think Eddy was pretty close with wormoids; there's a species called the hairworm or *Spinochordodes tellinii*, a parasite sometimes found in grasshoppers. The nasty little things like water, so they control the grasshopper and get it to drown itself."

"Grim," Toker muttered.

"Yes," Kaia agreed. "There's also *Paraponera clavata,* an insidious fungus that takes control of the brains of ants."

"Huh, parapona clavituh, an' you thought my names were bad," Eddy protested.

"Ease up, Ed."

"No, it's fine, Toker," Kaia said quickly. "Eddy's right. I don't have a creative flair for names. Too much dull science going on in my brain."

"How's about puppeteers?" Viktor offered.

"Not bad, bro. Maybe a little bit on the cute side though, eh?"

"Cal?"

"Huh." Cal tore his eyes from Kaia and looked around. "Sorry, Toker. Um, what?"

Toker eyed him with an amused glint. "Any ideas for names?"

"Er, no. Coming up blank, I'm afraid."

Eddy scooped up some eggs. "Vampoids."

Toker shook his head. "You got a thing about the 'oids, don't you?"

Eddy dumped the eggs clumsily on her plate, then said, "Insidions."

Toker went silent for a moment. "Huh. *Insidions,*" he said, his eyebrows raising.

"That's what I said, Insidions. Like lady doc over there said, '*insidious mushrooms,*' or somethin'."

"Insidions," Toker repeated the word, rolling his tongue around it. "You know, I reckon that's actually…well, that's actually pretty damn good, Ed. Insidions, yeah, I like it."

Eddy grinned then shrugged nonchalantly.

"What thinks the rest of you?" Toker said, looking around the table.

"Sounds fitting to me," Kaia said.

The unanimous nodding seemed to settle it.

Baffled, Cal watched Toker and Eddy consume the last two sausages. He didn't doubt the two of them were way beyond full but, just like most things, eating had turned into a competition between the pair. Letting out a contented sigh, he stood up and reached over to take the bowl of eggs, now scraped clean.

Melinda stood. "Please, allow me, Cal."

Cal smiled and nodded his thanks as the cybernetic woman reached over and picked up the empty bowl and sausage tray. Melinda had included herself numerous times in the various conversations over breakfast, but it was still taking him by surprise whenever she spoke.

Kaia passed her plate along. "Jumper, I think that was the best meal I've had since…well, ever."

"I'm glad you enjoyed it," Jumper said with broad smile. "A fit, healthy young woman like yourself can't live on rehydrated noodles alone. Especially with a scientific brain to feed, isn't that right, Viktor?"

The boy, who was still nibbling on a sausage, quietly nodded in agreement.

"I've given cooking a pretty good try in the past, but it's not really my forte, I'm afraid."

"Well, I'm here to cook for you now. We can't have you starved of nutrients. In fact, I'm eager, if you don't mind that is, to dig into that huge collection of Alvorian herbs. I couldn't help noticing the culinary section in the botany lab. I imagine there's some real gems in there."

"I don't mind at all. You'd be wise to stick to the blue vials though. We've found some pretty strange herbs on Alvor that have…*odd* effects on the body."

"Yes, I've tried some myself back on Mars," Jumper said with a chuckle. "Well, if you don't mind, I think I might go poke around in a few now."

Gladdened by his old friend's enthusiasm, Cal watched as he briskly made his way out of the canteen. "He'll be like a kid in a candy shop sifting through all those herbs."

Kaia smiled then shook her head. "How are they all so calm and relaxed? I mean…with what we're about to face."

"They're a brave bunch."

"I wish I could feel braver. I wish I could *relax*."

Cal smiled. "Trust me, you *are* relaxed, I've seen battle-hardened soldiers biting their nails when there's no nails left to bite before a mission. You'll be fine. Besides, if all goes to plan, those…*Insidions*…won't even know we're there until it's too late for them."

"There's a lot riding on my plan, Cal. Makes me nervous. After all, I'm hardly a military strategist!"

"You *could* be. It's a damn good plan." He wished he could take some of her burden, but the fact was, it was one hundred percent her plan. "If it makes you feel better, we'll double and triple check each step together."

"I'd really appreciate that," she said, pushing away from the table and getting to her feet.

"Now?" he asked, looking up at her with a grin.

She nodded. "Yes please. Last night, it was all talk. Maybe it's time I actually showed you a few things."

Cal's grin widened. "I thought you'd never ask."

The Orillian's hanger was a stark contrast to the sleek appearance of the rest of the ship. It was all blocks of unpolished metal, grated floors, and heavy launch doors built for practicality rather than style. Bar a few particularly advanced-looking cranes and loaders, the hanger itself didn't appear much different than any other. As well as the Star Splinter, there were three other ships present: two simple dropships and a very small craft that Cal didn't recognize.

With Kaia by his side, they strolled towards the Star Splinter. As he neared, he couldn't help but let out a long, impressed whistle. "Kaia, this is incredible. You did all this yourself?"

"Yes. Unfortunately, I didn't have much choice. Viktor and Melinda have helped a lot over the past couple of days though."

Sitting neatly in front of the Star Splinter's loading ramp were rows upon rows of large crates, each one filled to the brim with handheld weaponry. Cal could see everything from slimline pistols to big, ten-click pulse blasters. Looming tall behind the crates were masses of multi-level racks holding meticulously neat rows of syringes, each containing a bright green substance. Neither the racks nor the crates held Cal's attention for long, however. Instead, his eyes were drawn to a tall figure standing, statue still, next to the loading ramp. A fully grown Carcarrion.

Cal's heart felt as though it took a momentary pause. He gestured towards the alien figure. "I assume that fellow is the infiltrator, not one of your drones escaped from its cage?"

"Sorry, I forgot to warn you about that. Yes, that's the infiltrator," she assured him as she walked towards the tall, menacing figure.

"Glad to hear it," he replied, his heart seeming to start up again and indulging in a couple of extra beats. His mind felt so overstuffed that he'd almost forgotten this particular element of Kaia's plan. As he approached, the realism of the Carcarrion astounded him. But then it stood to reason that if a synthetic combat soldier could be made to look human, the same technology could be used to create a realistic, synthetic Carcarrion.

"What do you think," Kaia asked, "will it pass as one of the enemy?"

It better. The plan'll go to hell if it doesn't. He nodded. "It certainly fooled me." *And if the plan goes to hell, all these rifles will make damn expensive clubs.* During her observations of the enemy, Kaia had discovered the reason for the military's failure to put up any sort of fight: a disrupter signal emanating from the Insidion vessel that rendered pulse weaponry inert. Unfortunately, pulse-based weapons were a clear favorite of the military from the huge starship cannons to simple pistols. Without a weapon, what sort of a fight could a human put up against a Carcarrion drone? Cal could scarcely believe the simplicity of it. One single, disrupting signal becoming the ultimate weapon, devastating in its effect. Fortunately, Kaia had managed to pinpoint the signal's source. Unfortunately, that source was deep inside the Insidion vessel.

Kaia let out a long breath. "Well, it better fool them. If we don't manage to disable that signal..." She shook her head. "There's so many unknown elements."

Cal silently agreed. It was most definitely the riskiest part of the plan but also the most crucial. Moving around the synthetic alien, he peered closely the black lump attached to the back of its neck. "The Insidion looks real too: suitably slug-like."

Kaia frowned. "To be honest, both the Carcarrion and the Insidion looked pretty awful before you all arrived on the scene. Constructing the chassis was fairly easy. It's just bigger than the norm. The equipment down in the tech lab practically built it for me. The musculature and the flesh though...my attempts were pretty laughable. It wouldn't have even gotten close to the Insidion vessel let alone inside it. Fortunately, your young friend Viktor is nothing short of a genius. He's been working nonstop on it since I told him what I had planned."

Still staring at the synthetic Carcarrion, Cal nodded in agreement. "He's a good lad. Brave too."

"He'd have to be to hang around with you lot," she said with a brief laugh. "He's also upgraded the cloaking technology on the Star Splinter with a ghosting net system. It'll be as undetectable as *The Orillian*."

"I must say, Kaia, this really is pretty damn impressive considering the amount of time you've had."

"I just hope I'm not missing anything."

Cal shook his head. "Even the best-laid plans have weak points. If problems arise, we'll adapt. There's only so much planning you can do. The rest is left to chance." He shot her his best lopsided grin. "Don't worry; we'll pull it off."

"I hope so. I can't stop thinking about all those people held captive. It looked like hell down on that planet, Cal. Even if we can only save some of them, we've got to do it, right?" Kaia looked at him with an expression that longed for reassurance.

"We're doing the right thing, and the sooner we do it, the better." His words were full of confidence that he didn't really feel. But Kaia needed and *deserved* the reassurance. He wanted to comfort her. He wanted to take her in his arms, but then, in all honesty, he'd been wanting to do that since he'd seen her emerge from that pool.

Seeing her relax a little, he turned to the crates. "Quite the collection."

"Yes, we had a few guns on board, but the majority I salvaged from one of the drifting starships. It was pretty spooky, Cal, walking around on a completely empty ship of that size, especially when all the lights and equipment had been left on. Imagine just leaving them to drift among the moons like junk. It's as if they're collecting them, like some damn hobby."

Cal nodded. "Or trophies."

"Cocky bastards," Kaia said angrily.

Cal turned to her with raised eyebrows and a grin. "*Cocky bastards?*"

Her anger quickly dissipated. "Sorry, just venting," she said with an embarrassed smile. "It's frustrating though. If only they'd invaded us twenty years down the line, ten even, then they'd have had far less reason to be cocky. We've got some incredible technology here, stuff that would have given us the chance to put up one hell of a fight. *The Orillian's* ghosting net alone has proved that, not to mention all the new biological agents we've discovered on Alvor. We just needed more time. Time to implement all this stuff into our military."

Cal put a hand on her shoulder. "Don't worry. The fight hasn't even begun yet. If we—*when* we—pull off your plan, that will be the start. These Insidions are going to find out a thing or two about guerrilla warfare. And I wouldn't worry about their cockiness. It's a blessing. From everything you've told me, it's because of their arrogance that you've already found a way in. They're overconfident; they've left gaps wide open." Cal turned and looked over to the thousands of syringes lying neatly in the racks. "The Alvorian serum you told us about?" he asked, nodding at the racks.

Kaia's face brightened. "Inside every single syringe."

Cal stared at the multitude of little, bright green tubes. This is what he'd been itching to see. This was the part of Kaia's plan that had kept him most intrigued through the night. As they made their way over, he could see pride in her expression. Unlike the clunky weaponry in the crates, the contents of these syringes well and truly fell within her area of expertise. This was her arena.

"It's known as Xn-4283-p61."

"Huh."

Kaia smiled "One of technicians began calling it *Xcel,* so maybe we're better off sticking to that. It's extracted from one of Alvor's deep sea algaes."

"It'll make us stronger?"

"And faster. You'll heal far more rapidly too."

"Sounds…well, it sounds pretty damn wonderful."

Kaia smiled again, and Cal didn't miss the mischievous glint in her eye. Every new expression only made him want her more.

"You want to try one?"

Cal shrugged, hit by a wave of unexpected nerves. "Now?"

"Of course."

He shrugged again, trying to look calm. "Why not?"

Kaia nodded her approval and, not giving him a chance to

change his mind, plucked one of the syringes from the nearest rack and passed it to him.

"How long does it take to kick in?" he asked even though he already knew the answer. He'd seen Kaia use it only moments after he first laid his eyes on her in the lab.

"It's fairly instant. Then, the effects will eventually start to fade after about three or four hours."

"That long?" He held the little glass tube up to the light. "It's um… It's an interesting color," he said, still attempting to look and sound nonchalant.

"It's okay, Cal. It won't hurt, and it certainly won't do you any harm. Quite the opposite in fact."

Cal laughed.

"What's funny?"

"Nothing." he answered with a shake of his head. "It's just that you seem to be able to see straight through my bravado. I'm usually pretty good at hiding my nerves."

Kaia's lips curled in amusement. "Don't worry. Your record's still intact. It was more of an educated guess. The stuff *is* bright green. Who the hell *wouldn't* be nervous?"

Cal twiddled the syringe in one hand and used the other to rub his jaw. "I still remember those damn muscle stim drugs they made us test in the military. I thought I was going to explode with adrenalin overload. To be honest, I wasn't overly keen on the experience."

Kaia shook her head. "Those stims relied on sloppy science, Cal. They concentrated only on the effects without a moment's thought for the consequences. I can assure you, there's nothing that your body will benefit from more than the liquid in these syringes."

"Something like the black pool?"

"Consider it a close relation, a kind of bigger brother."

"Okay. I'm sold." Taking a deep breath, he put the syringe against his neck then took another breath and pressed the button.

The effect was immediate.

A warmth spread out from the injection point and suffused through his entire body, seeping into every muscle. Pure, liquid energy. He grinned uncontrollably, and as the warmth faded, he felt his head become clearer than it had been his entire life. His thinking suddenly felt sharper and more focused, all mental debris purged. "My God... This is incredible." He looked at Kaia wide-eyed, feeling sure his grin must be stretching from ear to ear. It felt as though his body were a solar-powered machine that had been moved from a lifetime under cloud into dazzling sunshine.

Kaia was beaming back at him, her eyes full of knowing.

Looking down, he experimentally began to move his arms and legs. Every muscle felt relaxed but at the same time spring loaded. *Charged up.* He looked at his hand and wiggled his fingers then clenched his fist, feeling incredible power within the grip. It was as if his tendons were enhanced by cybernetics. "I feel like I could lift a horse!"

Kaia laughed, obviously amused by the look on his face. "You probably could! That crate full of guns looks pretty heavy, wouldn't you say?" she said, indicating the crate to his left.

Cal grinned and moved over to the nearest corner of the container. It was at least three square meters and, with the amount of weapons loaded in it, probably weighed a good eight or nine hundred pounds. Feeling like a little kid trying out a pair of hover boots for the first time, he grasped the corner and couldn't help but laugh out loud as he easily tilted the huge box.

"I'd say that right now, your strength isn't all that far off that of a fully grown male Carcarrion, and you're possibly a touch faster."

"That's good to know," he replied as he slowly lowered the crate to the floor.

Kaia shook her head. "Of course, Carcarrions have lethal claws, and their flesh and skin is a hell of a lot tougher. Unless you had a weapon, I'm afraid my money would still be on them if it came to a fist fight."

"Well, let's hope that it doesn't come to that."

"Also, be aware that your body can be a little too fragile for its newfound strength. The Xcel serum does seem to toughen up the skin and harden the bones after long-term use, but you can still do yourself damage. For instance, you'll now have the strength to crush certain hard objects in your hand, but your skin and flesh wouldn't enjoy the experience."

"I see your point."

"That caution motto of yours might be worth remembering," she said, her mischievous glint returning.

God, she's beautiful.

"What are you thinking?"

"I um…how long can I hold my breath?"

She gave a little laugh. "Long enough to dive to the bottom of the healing pool for a time."

He nodded, and an image of her pale face and swirling hair surrounded by blackness flashed through his mind. *A dream?* Their eyes met and lingered. *We're having a moment,* he thought, feeling a little mesmerised by the blue of her eyes and the curve of her smile. He'd known beautiful women in his time, but there was much more to this attraction. A blend of emotions unlike any he'd experienced before.

Eventually, those beautiful eyes looked down, and Kaia's smile became almost shy.

Definitely a moment.

Suddenly feeling a little shy himself, Cal looked about the

hangar.

"Now what are you thinking?"

Cal laughed. "Haven't you found a serum to help you read minds?"

"Not yet, but you never know."

He continued to look about the hanger. "I was actually trying to think of a good way of testing this *speed* that you mentioned."

"Oh. I could help with that," Kaia said and plucked out another syringe from the rack. Pressing it to her neck, she gave him another mischievous look as the bright green liquid disappeared from the tiny glass tube. "Think you can catch me?" she asked and barely gave him a chance to laugh before spinning on the spot and vaulting easily over one of the weaponry crates to run towards the hangar's exit.

Deciding to leave the crate vaulting until he'd gotten a little more used to his newfound strength, Cal skirted around it and took off at a speed that threatened to make the ridiculous grin on his face a permanent feature.

Part Four:

Chapter Thirty-Three
C9

Cal stood alone in the center of *The Orillian's* observation deck. Lost in thought, he twiddled a control wand between his fingers and stared through the huge exterior viewing panel that stretched out a good twenty-five feet to his left and right. Directly in the center of that viewing panel, and amid the array of distant stars was the Carcarrion planet of C9. Despite the effectiveness of *The Orillian's* ghosting net systems, he and Kaia had decided not to get any closer than necessary, and from this distance, the planet appeared little more than a blip.

Just as he had every day for the last week, Cal raised the control wand and activated the zoom capabilities of the smart-glass until the planet filled the viewing panel. The planet was a black orb broken up by veins of red magma and streaks of gray ash cloud. Its tectonic plates were in a constant, extreme state of convergence and divergence, resulting in an extremely unstable planet. The only vegetation that managed to thrive was a thick, vine-like plant that tightly wound its way around the entire landscape as if desperately holding it together. There were also huge oceans made fierce by the earthquakes and as dark as the rocks they pounded against.

Cal manipulated the control wand and brought up a view of the planet's moon cluster. Zooming in further still, he focused on the collection of drifting military starships. Kaia was right in her estimations: The ships seen here only represented about a third of what had once been the Federation's military fleet. Cal could only speculate as to what had happened to the rest. Perhaps in a similar state, drifting aimlessly around some other conquered planet.

He focused in on the starship that Kaia had chosen to execute the plan. All appeared normal. It was distressing that only one of the ships would be needed to transport the surviving prisoners. The numbers within the camp were only a fraction of those that would have once crewed that portion of the fleet. It seemed only the very strongest had survived. Or perhaps the enemy was simply killing at random. Such thoughts only served to strengthen Cal's resolve that time was of the essence.

Bringing up the view of the planet surface, he activated the preset close-up of the prison camp. True to historical form, the invaders hadn't been satisfied keeping their prisoners idle. The expanse of black rock within the boundaries of the camp's force field had been turned into a mine of sorts. Cal didn't imagine for a second that these Insidions needed humans armed with crude, handheld machinery to excavate the rock; such work could be done in a fraction of the time with basic mining drones. Subjecting them to such unnecessary slave labor was more evidence that these alien invaders were sadistic to their core. Fear and despair were effective weapons, and it seemed the Insidions knew it only too well. The fact that they'd begun their invasion by destroying an entire planet only served to strengthen this theory. Perhaps the disabling of long-range communications was further proof, a calculated decision that caused fearful rumors to escalate and inevitable chaos to ensue.

Cal studied the image. Though it wasn't easy to see from this birds-eye view, every one of the prisoners appeared strong and able.

He allowed himself a humorless smile. When the time came, those men and women would get the opportunity to put up one hell of a fight, a fight they'd been denied when the enemy had disabled their weapons. Despite his anxieties, he couldn't help but look forward to that part of the plan.

Shifting the view, Cal homed in on the Insidion base. Five huge, gleaming blocks sat in a circular pattern upon the dark landscape. When Kaia had last viewed the planet, those blocks had made up one monstrous vessel, quite possibly the very one that had destroyed Earth. Now, that vessel had broken apart, perhaps to make a more effective base, the circumference of which dwarfed even the prison camp. There was a pale line connecting the two. It was a massive conveyor belt, ten times wider than the average hover track, which was slowly transporting cut rock into the center of the alien's base. Once there, unmanned machines were manipulating it further and constructing structures. Cal peered at the image. Were they buildings? Were the invaders building a home?

"Hey, that's a good look for you, Calie boy."

Cal used the control wand to brighten the overhead lighting and turned to see Toker, Eddy, and Jumper entering the observation deck via an elevator that had emerged from the ceiling. The three of them had been loading the multitude of crates containing handheld weapons into the Star Splinter's cargo hold. He shot them a grin, which they probably couldn't even see under the big, shaggy beard he had seamlessly stuck to his chin. Kaia and Viktor had somehow managed to make the beard in the lab. He didn't like to think what materials they'd used. He was also wearing a military uniform salvaged from one of the starships. He'd made good use of the rock dust and dirt samples in the biology lab to make the uniform suitably filthy before proceeding to tear it ragged.

"Think it'll do the job?" he asked, holding his arms out and doing a three-sixty turn.

"You look like crap," Eddy said, wrinkling up her nose. The girl's mood still hadn't improved.

"I'll take that as a yes."

Toker nodded. "Yep, reckon you'll blend right in."

"Um… I'm not so sure," Jumper said, frowning as he approached. "The beard's nice and bushy, but it really is pretty damn filthy in that prison camp."

"You don't think I've made it dirty enough?" Cal asked, looking down at himself.

"Sure, the uniform's dirty enough, but um…" Jumper rubbed his fingers into a particularly heavy patch of grimy, black rock dust on Cal's shoulder and smeared it across his face. "There. Perfect."

Eddy interrupted her bad mood with a quick snort of a laugh.

"Nice touch, J man," Toker said, walking over and giving Jumper a slap on the shoulder. "So the doc and her little skinny sidekick are all ready for you up there, Cal. You really sure you wanna risk it?"

"It's not too late to go with the synthetic Carcarrion option." Jumper added.

Cal shook his head. "Those people down there need a face they can trust, one without fangs." He had run through Kaia's plan countless times in his head and, despite a few weak spots, couldn't fault it. All of those weak spots were unavoidable except perhaps one. To set the plan in motion, contact had to be made with the prisoners, their trust gained and their cooperation agreed. Kaia's original plan had been to send down the cybernetic Carcarrion and use it to infiltrate the camp unnoticed. The body of the Infiltrator could be controlled within a specially designed sync sphere on board *The Orillian* and used as an avatar to communicate with the prisoners. Cal was unconvinced, however, that they would give their full trust to one who looked exactly like their captors. Explaining the situation and convincing them would take a great deal of time, and the more time they took, the more likely they'd be discovered. Also, he wasn't keen to risk the infiltrator; they were going to need it later in the plan. After a fair amount of discussion and reluctance, he'd convinced them that venturing into the camp himself was a better option.

"Okay, let's get this plan underway," he said with a cheery confidence that he suspected, with the possible exception of Eddy, wasn't fooling anyone.

Cal had seen the craft briefly on his first visit to the hangar but hadn't taken the time to study it closely. He'd never seen such a small, *weird* looking ship. Standing a mere ten feet high and being only four feet in width and depth, the *Mosquito* was most definitely a one-man craft. True to its name, it was bug-like in design—all bubble curves of smooth, dark metal. The tiny craft had been designed for the unique purpose of sneaking up on an enemy ship and scanning for the weakest area of its hull where it would attach itself. It would then utilize an incredibly powerful piercing needle to punch through the ship's outer hull, allowing thousands of nano threads to wriggle their way in and begin extracting information from the ship's systems or steal power from its energy reserves all the while going unnoticed.

The *Mosquito* had not gone into production before the invasion had hit. In fact, the ship that Cal was about to climb into was really only a concept model. Kaia assured him, however, that the little craft had been tested to the hilt and had already been put to use on numerous occasions. It was the perfect ship for the job.

The entire gang, Kaia included, was now huddled around the ship, looking a little on edge—all except Eddy, who just looked irritable.

"You sure I can't fit in there with you, Cal? What if you need backup?"

"It's okay, Eddy. I appreciate the offer, but I'll be down and back again in no time. The enemy will be none the wiser."

"It should only take about half an hour for you to reach the surface," Kaia said as Cal climbed into the snug, standing cockpit.

"You won't have to do a thing," Viktor assured him. "I've programmed it to land behind a big bunch of rocks close to the northern end of the camp. There's plenty of cover once you leave the ship's cloaking net."

Cal nodded as numerous smart-straps snaked their way around him and secured him in place. Viktor held out his hand. "Here, Cal." A small cube sat on his open palm.

Cal took the cube and gave it a brief study. It was crafted from a copper-like metal' and he was amused to see the words "Little Lock Pick" engraved into its topside. "Smaller than I thought." It seemed that on this mission' size really wasn't everything.

"It's packed full of nano threads," Viktor explained. "Before you enter the prison camp, just place it on any one of those posts emitting the energy force field. Don't forget to pick it up again on your way back though. By then, it'll have learned the best way to disable it.'

Cal smiled at the boy's confidence and placed the cube in his pocket.

"Speaking of the force field, I think you'll be needing these," Jumper said as he brought over two large disks. They were made of black metal, not much more than an inch thick, and about two feet in circumference. "Two pop platforms as requested." He slid them into the little space that remained at Cal's feet.

"Thanks," Cal replied, suddenly wishing he'd spent a little more time practicing with them.

"And these," Kaia said as she passed him a few syringes filled with the bright green Xcel serum.

Cal took them with a grin. "Feels like Christmas!"

"Not much of a place to spend Christmas," Kaia replied.

Cal tried to shrug, but the smart-straps denied him the motion. "Perhaps we'll have better luck next year."

Kaia smiled. "One other thing: I've been going through the SS recordings—"

"SS?" Toker asked.

"Don't interrupt, idiot," Viktor snapped.

"Hey, bright spark, we're not all tech geeks."

Kaia turned to the disgruntled Toker. "Sound Snatcher recordings. It's similar to a visual zoom function on smart-glass, but it's for audio instead of visuals. I've been collecting sound samples from the prison camp."

"You've discovered something?" Cal asked.

"Yes, it might be of help. A man's name keeps cropping up in conversations. It seems the other prisoners consider him a leader. It might be worthwhile trying to seek him out."

"Sounds sensible."

"He's called Decker."

Cal's eyes went wide, a wave of hope flooding through him. "Admiral James Decker?"

"No...I don't think so. As far as I can gather, his name is Laurence. Laurence Decker."

Cal's heart sank, the flood of hope instantly draining away. "*Laurence Decker*. You're sure?"

"Pretty sure. You know him?"

Cal nodded, trying to hide his disappointment. *A leader.* The situation must be more desperate than he thought.

"The name keeps coming up time and time again. It sounds as though they really look up to him."

Surely, that couldn't be right. *Laurence Decker*. The man was an incompetent idiot, not to mention a bona fide coward. If it had been his father… "Okay, thanks, Kaia. I'll find him." He dug his fingers into the fake beard and scratched. "So, I guess it's time to blast me out of the cannon."

Kaia took a deep breath and gave him a confident smile. She was clearly doing her best to hide her nerves, and Cal was grateful for her efforts. "We'll keep track of you visually and listen in with the Sound Snatcher as best we can."

Cal nodded. They had agreed to forego any short-range communications at this point to minimize the risk of detection.

Toker casually ran a hand through his blond hair. "We'll see you soon, Calie boy."

"Yeah, kick some arse, Cal," Eddy added.

"Hopefully, I won't need to."

As the doors to the *Mosquito* slid closed, Cal stared at his friends old and new. Viktor wore a nervous smile that made him look younger than ever. Melinda stood tall behind him, a protective hand on his skinny shoulder. She seemed more human with each passing day. The ever-optimistic Toker was grinning with an enthusiastic thumbs up, while Eddy leaned against him as if he were merely a sturdy post. As always, the girl looked tough and at the same time incredibly fragile. Next to them stood Jumper, his oldest friend, steady as a rock and expression unreadable. And then there was Kaia, wearing a gentle smile full of encouragement and eyes bright with hope.

The *Mosquito's* doors sealed shut, and the tiny craft was maneuvered toward the airlock. He was about to be blasted down to an ominous prison planet occupied by an even more ominous alien race. Strange then that in that moment, he truly felt like a blessed man.

Chapter Thirty-Four
EYE CONTACT

With the dim lights lazily blinking around him, Cal found himself almost cozy within the *Mosquito's* tiny cockpit. The soft hum of the engines was calming, and the flight was smooth. Only one small, circular viewing panel graced the craft's compact hull, and through it, Cal could see a spinning array of distant stars. A cold vastness of deep space through which he slipped alone, cocooned in a small bubble of metal and glass. He knew the experience should be frightening, terrifying even, but it wasn't. He had many fears, but this wasn't one of them. It never had been. He closed his eyes and almost reveled in the moment of peace.

Unfortunately, the peace was short-lived as the entry into C9's atmosphere caused the little craft to shake with increasing violence—an effect it seemed could never be avoided no matter how advanced the ship. When the shaking finally stopped, Cal took his cue to pull out one of the little glass syringes. He'd tried the Xcel serum many times now and, as always, its effect was close to instant; warm liquid energy, strengthening his muscles and focusing his mind. A perfect, God-given fuel.

Cal felt the ship touch down on the planet surface. He took a moment to check his positioning on the cockpit screen then, releasing his restraining smart-straps, leaned forward to have a good, old-fashioned look out of the window. Even during the daylight hours, C9 was a dark planet: orange and red skies filled with streaks of volcanic ash clouds. As the little craft's doors bowed open, he was hit by a blast of hot, sulphur-infused air—fitting considering that the first thing his eyes focused on was the bright red magma of a distant, spewing volcano.

Wasting little time, he snatched up the two pop platforms and maneuvered from the cockpit to step down onto the hard, jagged ground. The hot air swirled about him, random in its strength and direction as if confused by its purpose. Turning once to check that the *Mosquito's* doors had closed behind him and that the craft was completely cloaked, Cal set off at a run. Thanks to the Xcel, he was swift and confident over the rough terrain, the two pop platforms feeling practically weightless tucked under his arm. Huge splinters of rock jutted out of the ground ahead of him like giant, black spearheads which, as Viktor had promised, offered him good cover as he sped towards the prison camp.

As the camp came into view, he cracked a brief smile; the invaders had obviously reached a very high level of technological advancement, but mistakes were becoming more and more evident. The blue glow that emanated from the force field encircling the camp served no purpose other than to give those who might want to escape the benefit of the force field's exact size and shape. Like the huge gleaming ships that sat in the distance, it was nothing more than a showy spectacle of their power and dominance.

From his elevated position, Cal could see the countless human prisoners within the boundaries of the force field. Most were chipping away at the rock with crude mechanical tools and machinery while a handful of Carcarrion drones stalked amongst them, keeping a watchful eye. The mining machinery was definitely human by design, probably taken from one of the less-advanced fringe space mining colonies. Just as he'd seen from *The Orillian's* observation deck, nearly all the activity within the camp was concentrated in its center while the areas nearer the ridiculous glowing force field remained blessedly unoccupied. The chances of entering the camp unseen were looking good. Spying the best spot for using the pop platforms, he set off again at a run.

As he neared the blue, glowing barrier, which rose approximately twenty feet above him, Cal heard thumping pulse drills and screeching disc saws. The noise reminded him that he wasn't all that far from the activity. Fortunately, the force field was transparent enough to reveal a scattering of tall rocks on the other side that offered a good amount of cover. The rocks had been one of two reasons for picking this particular spot, the second being that it put him in front of one of the tall poles responsible for emitting the force field. Reaching into his pocket, he pulled out Viktor's Little Lock Pick and touched it to the pole's base. He hoped the boy's confidence in the little cube was justified; their plan would break apart if the force field remained up.

Setting one of the pop platforms on the ground six feet from the barrier, Cal stood on it and waited a few moments for it to calibrate his weight, topography of the ground, and the size of the force field itself. He doubted the machine would have much luck in reading the random gusts of wind, but nothing could be done about that now. Hugging the second pop platform to his chest, he crouched down and waited for the tiny green light to indicate that he was good to go. With the power of the Xcel serum coursing through his legs, he almost felt the pop platform wasn't necessary. Perhaps an unrealistic expectation, but his enhanced muscles would at least make for a far easier and less painful landing.

After one last check that no one was in view, Cal thrust himself upward. Reading the pressure applied through his feet, the pop platform added just enough aid at just the right angle to launch him up and over the twenty-foot barrier. Still holding the second pop platform to his chest, he performed a single, neat summersault, clearing the apex of the barrier by a good few feet before the inevitable fall. Despite nailing the landing, the sharp rocks cut deep into his knuckles and right knee. Ignoring the pain, he moved quickly to conceal the second pop platform. Satisfied he'd be able to find it again even in a hurry, he adopted his best casual stroll and headed towards the center of the camp.

Cal didn't have to walk far before he saw the first prisoners: ten men and three women. They were busily excavating a five-meter-wide trench, most of them operating disc saws while the remaining few manipulated clasper cranes to hoist the blocks of cut stone. He was relieved to see that they all looked healthy, well-fed, and strong. He was also glad to see he hadn't overcooked the ragged uniform and the beard.

As he neared the busy group, Cal became aware of a form moving in his peripheral vision, tall and dark against orange horizon. Forcing himself not to snap his head around, Cal attempted to retain his casual manner as he approached the group. Without missing a step, he strode directly up to one of the clasper arms of the nearest crane and began physically checking the support straps wrapped around a newly cut block of stone. The dark form was growing larger in the corner of his eye. He had no doubt it was a Carcarrion drone. He also had the distinct feeling that it was heading straight towards him. He looked at the prisoners. Despite one or two brief glances in his direction, they were paying him little attention. Either he'd succeeded in doing nothing particularly unusual, or they were being quick not to make his situation worse.

Risking a casual glance, Cal confirmed his fears; the drone was heading straight for him. His heart began to thump, quicker and harder with each beat. Had he done something wrong? Something to make him stand out from the crowd? Or was he just paranoid? He had studied the birds-eye view of the camp for many hours from *The Orillian* and had discerned no particular patterns or organized teams within the mine. On the contrary, the prisoners seemed scattered rather haphazardly. *What the hell am I doing wrong?* With the Xcel bolstering his system, Cal knew he at least had a chance of defending himself, but it wasn't just his own life at stake. Not by a long shot.

He had a distinct feeling that the drone had come to a halt just a few meters behind him. He could feel its icy gaze boring into his back. Doing his best to act unawares, he continued to tug at the crane straps. Helping to maneuver the block onto the back of a hover crate, he even decided to shout out a few instructions to the machine's operator. A couple of the other prisoners were looking at him now, anxiety clear on their faces. *What the hell?* He reached up and checked his beard; still in place. What was he doing wrong? Had he screwed up already? But surely if the game was up, he'd be feeling the force of those clawed fists by now.

Seeming to attempt the same casual indifference as Cal himself, one of the female prisoners moved around the hover crate until she stood next to him. "What the hell are you doing?" she rasped under her breath.

Good bloody question. He shot her a brief, confused look.

"Turn around and look it in the eye, damn it."

Look it in the eye! Cal looked at the woman and took in the cocktail of emotions on her grubby face: fear, desperation, and more than a hint of bewilderment. Giving one last hard tug on one of the crane straps, he gave his right shoulder a stretch, looking behind him as he did so. Then he feigned a double take. The drone was indeed only a few meters behind him, standing statue still, its eyes directed at nobody but him.

A chill ran down his spine. Deciding to trust the woman's advice, he turned and forced himself to return the creature's stare. His heart continued to hammer against his chest as the Carcarrion's pale, unblinking eyes remained locked onto his. For a worrying moment, he considered whether these Insidions somehow had the ability to read minds. Fortunately, his seemingly unread mind was soon put at ease when, instead of lunging forward to tear his head off, the drone simply snarled in what might have even been some sort of smile and turned its attentions on another distant group of prisoners. Cal could just about make out the leach-like Insidion attached to the back of its neck as it strode away.

"What the *hell* were you thinking?"

Cal turned to the voice. The woman who'd offered him the advice was glaring at him in disbelief and annoyance. He raised an eyebrow "I wasn't aware that a staring contest was necessary. Thanks for the tip."

The woman's brow creased. "You been hiding under one of these bloody great rocks or something?"

"Something. What was that about anyway…the eyeballing?"

The woman shook her head and turned back to the crane strap that she'd been unfastening. "Most think it's their way of weeding out rebels. They study your eyes like some kind of lie detector. I guess you passed. God only knows how though. Even *I* can see you're up to something."

"I need to find someone."

"Uh huh, and who would that be?"

"Decker, Laurence Decker."

Cal saw the corners of the woman's mouth twitch in response, a little smile quickly brought under control and replaced by a frown.

Cal wondered whether the smile was one of respect and admiration towards the man or simply amusement at his idiocy. He hoped to God that it was the former but couldn't help but suspect the man was still an idiot.

"What business do you have with Decker?"

"I have information he'll want to hear."

"What makes you think he'll want to hear it?"

Cal sighed, getting a little annoyed himself. "I don't think; I *know*." He turned his green eyes on the woman, his expression stern. It was a look he'd used many times in the past to subdue the more troublesome soldiers under his command. On occasion, it worked. "I'm in a bit of a hurry here. Are you going to tell me or not?"

Fortunately, she seemed to shrink a little under his gaze. "Over there," she said reluctantly, turning and raising an arm. "Head over the ridge 'til you get to the big mining belt that carries the cut rocks out of the camp. Decker will be at its loading end, somewhere near the engine room."

Cal nodded his thanks and set off without another word.

He saw only two other Carcarrion drones by the time he arrived at the mining belt. As luck would have it, both were busy intimidating other prisoners. Here, in the very center of the camp, many of the other prisoners were walking about solo, which thankfully made him far less conspicuous. Approaching the engine room, he saw a large group bunched around the loading end of the belt, busily operating the cranes. He made his way over. "I'm looking for Laurence Decker. Can anyone help me out?" he asked no one in particular. Only one of them took any notice: a big burly man with thick, hairy forearms and hands black with grime.

"I don't recognize you, friend," the man said, more as a question than a statement.

"I'm...a new arrival."

The big man looked a little confused but nodded. "Hang on here for a moment," he said before heading to the engine room.

Thankfully, it wasn't long before he reappeared. Another man was by his side. He was of average height, slim but well-muscled and, just like every other man on the planet, was heavily bearded. The slim man continued forward alone and came to stand before Cal looking perplexed, an expression that quickly turned into wide-eyed disbelief.

Cal sighed frustrated. "I'm trying to find Laurence Decker," he said, failing to hide the exasperation in his voice.

The man's shocked expression morphed into a wide smile. Then he laughed out loud, making Cal feel like the butt of some idiotic joke. "What's the matter, Callum? You don't recognize me with all my teeth?"

Cal's brow creased for a moment before his eyebrows shot up in surprise. *Holy shit!* "Decker?"

Cal braced himself as the man moved closer. After all, if this was Decker, he'd knocked the man's tooth out, and people had a habit of holding on to things like that. Suddenly, the man was lurching forward and wrapping his wiry, muscled arms around him. Cal was about to counter attack by twisting and slamming him face first into the hard ground, but then he realized he was being *embraced*!

"Damn, Callum, it's good to see you."

"Well…thanks," Cal replied, his bewildered tone not nearly doing justice to his confusion.

Eventually, Decker released him and stepped back to regard him intently. "Come with me. We've got a hell of a lot to talk about."

Still bewildered, Cal nodded. *No shit.*

Chapter Thirty-Five
THE LAST TRIBE

Callum bloody Harper. What the hell were the chances? Laurence's mind was reeling as he swiftly made his way down the steep passageway. The little pouch of glow worms he held only penetrated the inky darkness enough to illuminate his next two strides and no more. Despite the lack of light, he strode with a brisk, assured confidence. He'd been down the passageway countless times now, enough to navigate it blind if need be. Of all the individuals that could have turned up. Life certainly had a peculiar synchronicity at times. His arrival was the little miracle Laurence had been waiting for.

He came to a halt and turned to face the smooth, black wall of the passage. Then, he walked straight through it. Identifying the near-invisible entrances had been a challenge for Laurence in the beginning, but now, it was strangely easy. Striding into a large cavern, he took a moment until his eyes adjusted before having a good look around. The space was lit by countless glow worm pouches, far larger than the one he held, and most radiated an orange glow that gave off a certain warmth. Under that glow were hundreds of Carcarrions, their muscled forms scattered throughout the huge space. None of them paid him much attention; they were well used to his visits by now.

As he walked further in, Laurence saw young Carcarrions, smaller in stature than most humans, leaping from high ledges and chasing each other around the sharp, jutting rocks. Most of the adults were busily performing tasks, some crafting crude weapons out of the very rock that surrounded them while others manipulated bundles of the local weed-like substance. Rather than using it for sustenance, as he'd once been forced to do, the Carcarrions were weaving the weed into rope and clothing. As far as food went, Laurence had only ever seen them feast on massive reptilian carcasses that hung at the far side of the cavern. Not one scrap was wasted from bones to the hide to the eyeballs. They even consumed the mushy, multi-colored contents of the great beasts' stomachs. Indeed, the half-digested pulp seemed to be considered a delicacy, one that Laurence was running out of excuses to turn down.

With a grin, Laurence thought of his first visit to the cavern. His friend Tarquintin Matisse had led him down the mysterious, pitch-black tunnel and persuaded...no, *tricked* him into entering the cavern first. The little bastard hadn't even hinted a warning as to what he'd face inside. Now, Laurence was all grins and chuckles about it, but when that Carcarrion had lunged forward and grasped him in its steely claws, he'd been close wetting himself. But instead of tearing him in half, the Carcarrion had simply lifted him like a child and placed him down a few feet to the left, making room for his giggling little bastard of a friend to enter behind him.

The sight of the Carcarrions held little fear for Laurence now. Quite the opposite; being among them made him feel strangely optimistic. Despite their fearsome appearance, these *true* Carcarrions were nothing like the cruel, possessed abominations on the planet surface. At first, he'd recognized little in the way of emotion among these survivors: no fear, no anger at the tragedy that had befallen them. Except for the occasional scowl, their cat-like features seemed forever cold, almost lifeless. After time spent in their company, however, he began to recognize the subtleties of their expressions and at times caught glimpses of very real emotions, something that Tark was quick to confirm.

Coming to a halt near the center of the cavern, he looked about for Tark. It didn't take long. The little man stood out like a snowy hatchling among a flock of ravens. His long, white hair shone luminously under the warm glow, so much so it almost seemed a light source in itself. Laurence waved, and Tark was quick to spring down from his perch.

On their first meeting, Laurence had found it hard to place his new acquaintance in any particular military role. He'd even questioned whether the strange little man was simply a hallucination manifested by his own delirium. As it turned out, Tark was neither. As Laurence had eventually learned, his friend was in fact a highly regarded anthropologist, zoologist, alienologist, and a couple of other *ists* that Laurence couldn't recall. He'd been living on the planet for the last twelve years—more than a decade of communication, integration, and eventually full acceptance even friendship with the planet's inhabitants. Laurence could see it now: the way the little chap hopped deftly across the sharp rocks and weaved so casually among the tall, dark aliens. Such a confident manner could only come with years of experience.

"I just had a rather strange meeting," Laurence said enthusiastically as Tark sauntered towards him. "It was with a man who's got a half decent plan to get us off this rock. And by that I mean *all* of us. Well, all of us who survive the plan that is."

Tark perched himself on a nearby rock. "Excellent, where're we off to?"

Laurence snorted a laugh. "Where are we off to?"

Tark brushed some black rock dust off his knees and looked up expectantly.

Laurence shook his head and gave it a rub. "You're not interested in the *how*?"

Tark waved his hand dismissively. "I'm sure it's a good plan."

Laurence continued to shake his head, half amused, half bemused. He wondered whether he'd ever be able to surprise his little friend. "Alvor…the planet Alvor's the destination."

"Ah, the planet where the ingredients for that nice ale come from."

Laurence grinned. "Yes…Alvorian ale."

"Good. I like ale; count me in."

"*Really?*"

"You look surprised, Laurence. I may be small, but I can knock back the ale like a pregnant guzzle fish."

"That's not what I meant." Laurence took a seat on a rock opposite him. "I'm surprised because you seem keen, eager even. I thought… Well, I thought I was going to have to persuade you to leave. God knows why, but you seem to love this planet."

"God would be wrong, Laurence. It's not the planet I love, it's the beautiful inhabitants that hold my affections." Tark swept a hand about. "Besides, I need a change. You get as old as me, and you need to keep the body and soul toned with new experiences."

Laurence nodded. He was starting to see the truth in that.

"So, this escape plan, I hope it encompasses our tall friends here?"

"Of course," Laurence replied, smoothing his thick, shaggy beard. "I mean, I hoped they'd want to escape, but I wasn't sure they'd want to leave either."

"Yes, this is their home, and your assumption is logical. But again, it's wrong." Tark grinned. "I've discussed the matter with them many times of late. Their words are few, and my ability to hear their full vocal range is limited. But their meaning is clear; they think their planet is a crap hole."

Laurence couldn't decide whether to laugh or feel sad, so he did his best to keep his expression neutral. "I see," he said after a moment. "Well, of course they can come. I've arranged that everyone can leave." He turned to look at nearby group of Carcarrions. They were crushing a huge bone into dust then adding some sort of liquid to make a paste. "We'll need them to be distinctive...stand out from the drones up above."

"Drones? Fitting," Tark said thoughtfully, then after a moment, "Don't worry, I'll make sure they're distinctive."

"Good...that's good." Laurence smoothed his beard again and continued to watch the nearby group. "I'm glad they're coming with us, Tark," he said after a moment. "We're going to need all the help we can get to pull off this plan."

"Oh yes?"

Laurence turned to him. "It's going to involve a bit of a fight, you see."

"Terrific."

Again, Laurence found himself shaking his head in bewilderment. "Like a bit of a fight, do you?"

Tark shrugged. "You know, Laurence, no matter how intelligent or spiritually evolved a human male might claim to be, there's always a primal part of him that can't help but enjoy a good old tussle. Come to think of it, quite a few women I've known over the years enjoy it even more."

Laurence chuckled and shifted himself on the rock in a failed attempt to get comfortable. "And the Carcarrions...you think they'll be up for joining the fight?"

Tark gave a slow, thoughtful nod. "Despite their tribal divisions, they're a peaceful race. In all the time I've been here, I've witnessed very little fighting or conflict, quite unlike us humans. But just because they're not naturally aggressive doesn't mean they don't have it in them to be quite lethal." Tark looked over to the huge, lizard-like carcasses hanging at the far side of the cavern. "I've seen them take down their prey often. Quite a show. I promise you, Laurence, you piss them off enough, and they'll make sweet music with your bones."

Tark's expression was serious, and Laurence nodded his understanding. "But you don't think that maybe they'll have trouble fighting against…" Laurence glanced upwards to indicate the planet surface high above them. "They might feel they're fighting their own. They kind of will be in a way."

"I was here during the invasion, Laurence. I saw what happened. The Carcarrions aren't an easy species to sneak up on. Very light sleepers. But these slug creatures have incredible stealth, and they blend into their surroundings incredibly effectively. They came while the tribes slept. By the time the alarm was raised, most had already fallen prey, and those that hadn't soon did. I would have never believed such tiny, legless creatures could move so fast. Snakes at least have the benefit of length." Tark's eyes, which had grown distant, suddenly snapped back into focus. "It takes a hell of lot for a Carcarrion to retreat, Laurence, hence the reason you see so few survivors here."

Tark took a moment to gaze around the cavern. When he turned back, his expression had grown dark, angry even, something that Laurence had never seen in the little man. "Let me tell you, Laurence, those beasts up there, those *drones* as you call them, the resemblance absolutely stops at the physical. They are dead, their bodies hijacked, and their spirits long gone. This I know, and I can assure you that every male, female, and child Carcarrion you see around you now knows it too. This is the last…the very last tribe.

When it comes time to a fight, they won't hold anything back, and this time, they'll be prepared. You'd be wise not to get in their way when that happens."

Again, Laurence quietly nodded his understanding. He tried to imagine the battle that lay ahead. The vision sent a shiver down his spine. He'd never been one for combat; just the thought of it had always scared him witless. During his mollycoddled life, he'd never once been involved in a fight—at least not until Harper had punched his tooth out, and calling that a fight was perhaps a little generous on his part. He wondered whether his newfound courage would stand up to the battle ahead. At this moment, he felt he could face any challenge thrown at him. More than that, he *wanted* to. It was like a switch had flipped within him, a switch that he hoped to God stayed flipped.

His musing suddenly reminded him of Callum's sample. The *gift*. Reaching into his pocket, he pulled out the little syringe. Maybe it was time to give it the trial run Callum had insisted on. As he rolled it between his fingers, Tark took interest and leaned over to peer at the bright green liquid within.

"Pretty."

"Uh huh," Laurence agreed, holding the syringe up to the light of a nearby glow worm pouch. "You know what, Tark, for all our sakes, I hope it's a lot more than pretty."

Chapter Thirty-Six
THE GIBSON GUN

"Eddy, what the hell are you doing?" Toker asked in disbelief. "Seriously, that gun's bigger than you are."

Halfway up the Star Splinter's loading ramp, Cal caught sight of the girl's perspiring, red face.

Toker was laughing at her. "Oh man, your delusions of grandeur are really starting to border on insanity."

"Shut ya face," she growled. "An' stop showin' off to the doc with ya smart arse long words."

As he continued up the ramp, Cal saw the gun Eddy was wrestling with—a five-barrel rotating blaster—and he found himself inclined to agree with Toker. She was attempting to lift the huge weapon as if it were a slimline pulse rifle.

The massive gun was originally designed as a mounted weapon, and only after the battle of Greenwich six years previously had it ever been considered otherwise. During that battle, a sergeant by the name of George "Bulldog" Gibson had become a little carried away while facing an overwhelming force of pirate invaders. So it was told, the Greenwich moons had been Sergeant Gibson's boyhood colony and, possibly because of this emotional attachment, the fury of the battle had overwhelmed the man. It was rumored that he'd heaved the monstrous gun off its mounting as if it were a mere toy and led a charge while unleashing all five of the weapon's barrels in a thunderous rage. The act had apparently turned the tide of the battle, resulting in the pirates fleeing.

Word of Sergeant Gibson's herculean act had spread, and before long, others were trying to imitate the achievement. A successful attempt at wielding the huge weapon—renamed the *Gibson Gun*—had soon become the ultimate test of strength among military units. The result was nothing but a massive increase in the incidents of dislocated shoulders and torn biceps. George "Bulldog" Gibson was a giant of a man, and his feat was not something easily repeated.

By the time Cal made it to the top of the ramp, Toker's laughter had diminished, but he was still grinning widely and shaking his head. "Even if you did manage to lift it, you'd fire *yourself* further than the pulse discharge."

"I will bloody lift it, an' when I do, I know exactly which direction I'll be firin'."

Cal strode past the pair and headed towards Kaia. She was leaning back against a loading crate, watching Eddy with a mixture of disbelief, amusement, and possibly even a hint of respect.

"How did it go with the Infiltrator?" she asked as he approached.

"It's in the *Mosquito* and heading down to the planet surface as we speak. Viktor and Jumper have the sync sphere up and running in your lab."

"Good." Kaia smiled at him. "Glad to get that fake beard off, I bet?"

Cal grinned as he realized he'd been scratching at his chin. "Yep." He nodded towards Toker and Eddy. "I swear, one of those two clowns must have put itching powder in that face glue. It was worth it though; there's not a lot of personal grooming going on down there."

"I can imagine." Kaia pushed herself off the crate. "So this man, Decker. Do you think we can rely on him?"

Cal rubbed his hand across his chin, doing his best not to scratch. "If you'd asked me that a couple of days ago, I'd have said not a chance in hell. But I have to admit, the man I met down there isn't the Laurence Decker I knew, far from it, and I'm not just talking about his physical transformation. I didn't have long to judge, but yes, I think we can rely on him."

"Just as well. We're not exactly overwhelmed with alternatives."

Cal nodded and took a moment to look about the cargo hold.

"One of Viktor's self-built toys," Kaia said as she saw him do an almost comical double take at something stored at the back of the hold. "He's calling it the *silver widow*."

Cal raised an eyebrow. The silver widow looked something like a mechanical spider, about six feet in circumference, four feet in height, and sported a modified swivel blaster on its back. Lost for words, Cal blew out a breath and resorted back to scratching his chin.

"He's going to control it remotely from the cockpit," Kaia went on to explain. "Says he doesn't like to send Melinda into battle unprotected. He seems a little disappointed we've put him in charge of the ship."

Cal nodded. "It's for the best. Viktor has many talents, but fighting isn't one of them, unless of course it's a virtual—"

"How's about this one, Ed?" Toker shouted, drowning out Cal's words. "Reckon it's more your size."

Cal turned to see Toker strolling towards Eddy, holding a tiny slimline pulse pistol between his thumb and forefinger.

"Get that bloody girls' weapon outa my face, bugger lugs. I got my weapon right here. Just gotta work out a technique is all."

Cal was amazed to see that Eddy had managed to lift one end of the mighty Gibson gun, the barrel tips grinding against the metal deck while its butt rested on her trembling knee. The petite girl was still a world away from wielding the weapon, but he was still damn impressed.

"Geeze chick, give it up," Toker almost pleaded. "Why the hell're you trying to lift that bloody great thing now, anyway? We're not even on the planet yet."

"Cos, idiot, you never go into battle with an untested weapon," she replied, her voice shaking and her slim limbs clearly suffering under the command of her unyielding resolve. "I got some armor plating set up out there in the loading bay. I'll blast off a few rounds so I can get used to the gun's kickback."

"Ed, where exactly *is* your little brain at this precise moment? I'm just curious." Toker glanced back at Cal and Kaia.

"There ain't nothing wrong with my brain or my plan."

"Actually, Eddy, I'm afraid none of the weapons will work yet," Kaia informed her a little tentatively. "Even from this distance, the pulse disrupter from the Insidion base is fully effective."

Still refusing to give in to the Gibson gun's massive dead weight, Eddy risked a quick glance around. "Pulse what now?"

"The pulse disrupter…the thing I was explaining last night, remember? When we were going through the plan."

Eddy shifted her grip on the weapon a little. "What's she goin' on about, Cal?"

Cal looked at Kaia with an almost apologetic shake of the head. Eddy had been distant over the last week. When she was around, she barely listened, and when she did listen, she disagreed. She was hostile, and most of it was directed at Kaia. "None of the weapons are going to work yet, Eddy. Not until we've taken out the Insidions' pulse disrupter."

Eddy swore as the Gibson gun finally slipped from her

increasingly sweaty grip and slid harshly down her trembling leg to thud loudly onto the deck. If her leg was in pain—and Cal imagined it probably was—she didn't let it show. "So let's go an' take care of this pulse thingy now then."

Cal rubbed the back of his head, wondering if his words were actually sinking in this time. "Well actually, yes, that's the plan. Kaia and I are going to take care of the disrupter, but we'll need you to help with the escape...help keep the prisoners safe."

Eddy sniffed and paused for a moment mulling over what he'd said, then said, "Course, Cal, they'll be safe with me around, 'specially once I've worked out how to lift this bloody gun." She looked down at the huge chunk of metal with a creased brow. Cal guessed her confidence was finally beginning to wane. Still, true to her usual form, she reached down yet again and wrapped her perspiring fingers around two of the gun's thick barrels.

Cal started forward, but Kaia laid a hand on his shoulder. "Eddy, I have something that will help," she said, walking over to the girl.

"Not that bloody green stuff again."

Kaia nodded. "You missed out when the others tried it."

"Had stuff to do," Eddy said then hefted one end of the gun off the floor with a grunt. "Important stuff." Only inches from the ground, the Gibson gun once again slipped from her grasp and hammered into the deck. "Bloody, flippin' 'eck," she spat then straightened up and gave a loud huff. Wiping her sweaty hands on her combat pants, she looked around suspiciously at Kaia.

Kaia was holding out one of the Xcel syringes. "It really will help," she said encouragingly.

"Trust her, Ed," Toker said. "It's bloody good stuff. An' I really don't hold out much hope for your technique if you don't."

Eddy looked at Toker then peered at the little syringe dubiously then back at Kaia even more dubiously.

"You'll like it," Kaia persisted. "You put this end against your neck and press the button just here."

Cal gave the girl an encouraging nod as she looked his way.

After one last glance at the Gibson gun, Eddy wordlessly snatched the bright green serum out of Kaia's open hand, sniffed twice, shrugged once, and then shoved it roughly against her neck. Giving Kaia one last suspicious look, she pressed the button.

Chapter Thirty-Seven
WAITING

Laurence wasn't overly keen on this waiting business. Attempting to operate the mining machinery and acting the normal downcast under the watchful eye of the roaming drone guards was proving tricky. With the knowledge of what was soon to unfold rolling about in his head, he could barely keep the weird cocktail of fear and excitement from bursting forth onto his face. On top of that was the fact that his mouth kept suffering almost spasm-like grins that he hadn't experienced since childhood; they came whenever he thought of that weird green liquid Callum Harper had given him. Its effects had been everything the man had promised and more. Laurence could only hope that his thick beard was doing something to conceal these stupid grins because, try as he might, he couldn't stop them coming.

There were no such grins on the men and women working around him. Being told of the serum and actually sampling it were very different things. Still, their faith in him remained true. He still couldn't quite get his head around the fact that each and every one of them seemed utterly trusting in his words and judgement. The previous evening, those who had been carefully selected had intently listened to him as he'd laid out the proposed escape plan. No one had argued or questioned it. On the contrary, they'd all accepted it without hesitation, and many had even voiced their approval. Perhaps they were desperate, or perhaps they simply believed. The plan had then been relayed to the countless others, and it wasn't long before every person in the camp knew every detail. Not one negative report had been voiced. Laurence had been pleased at that, but he wished that they'd all been able to feel the miraculous experience of the serum. It would have undoubtedly removed a great deal of their fear.

Switching his disc saw off, he retracted it from the rock beneath him. As he repositioned the blade, another uncontrollable grin struck him. That serum had made him feel something close to invincible. So much so that after a whole load of running around and lifting of numerous heavy rocks, he'd gotten carried away and ended up in an arm wrestle with one of Tark's larger Carcarrion friends. He hadn't won, but he'd definitely given his big opponent something to think about. Best of all though, he'd managed to wipe that annoyingly impassive mask from the alien's face just long enough for something resembling surprise to appear in its place. Fortunately, the resulting claw gashes on his hands and wrist were healing rapidly. Laurence hoped there'd be a scar or two; he wanted to remember that glorious experience for the rest of his life, however short that may turn out to be.

Eventually, he got his grin under control. *Won't be long now*, he thought as he stretched his back and looked to the horizon. He could see distant black clouds building. They were moving towards the camp like some sort of slow-motion, soot-filled explosion. Such clouds had been common of late, seeming to form practically every evening. These, however, appeared larger and denser than the norm. He could even see bright, white crackles within their depths, which was something he'd only witnessed a couple of times before. A dry storm. If he was right, there'd be no rain, but a wind force would more than make up for it.

What the hell is it with storms? Laurence mused. So often, they'd arrive when a battle was about to commence. He'd never actually been in a battle—he'd been too precious for that—but he'd *seen* hundreds of them. Sitting comfortably in the command deck of his starship, he'd watched almost idly as the live images were relayed from the multiple buzz cams hovering above the bloody action. Sifting through his mental catalog, he could barely recall a single one that hadn't been accompanied by some kind of extreme weather: snow storms, sand storms, tropical tempests. One time, he'd even witnessed an entire squad of rebel colonists getting sucked up into a tornado on the dusty plains of Giddion III. The unfortunate buggers had been winning too.

Laurence turned his attentions from the horizon and back down to his disc saw. The approaching storm clouds were close enough now for the warning rumbles to be heard. The sound was softer, lower-pitched than that of the distant volcanoes but somehow held more menace. He shook his head. Just like all the others, this battle was going to get its storm, and it was a big one at that. Starting up his saw, he mused whether it was Mother Nature showing her disapproval of the violence soon to take place. Then, he pressed the saw down into the rock and smiled a humorless smile.

Or maybe she just wanted to join in.

Chapter Thirty-Eight
THE SYNC SPHERE

"She's all fired up," Kaia called out as she sat herself at the main control console for the sync sphere.

Cal felt clear-headed and confident as he bounded up the last few steps of the platform and approached the large, silver sphere. There had been a long night of waiting. Preparations had been completed, checked, rechecked, then rechecked a couple more times. Cal had never been overly keen on that stage, but now that the plan was underway, his mind had reached a level of focus that pushed any lingering fears and doubts aside. In short, he was feeling like the plan might actually work.

The platform on which he stood was about ten feet in height and fifteen feet in diameter. With Melinda's help, Jumper and Viktor had cleared equipment from the center of Kaia's bio lab in order to erect it. The sync sphere sat in the very center of the platform. It was a shiny, silver ball, ten feet in diameter and flawless except for a large, wedge-shaped entrance hatch in its side.

"How does the suit feel?" Kaia asked.

Cal turned to look down at her. There was an amused curl at the corners of her mouth as she busily tapped away at her controls. He was glad to see it. Now that the plan was in motion, her anxieties seemed to have calmed.

"Snug," he replied. The suit she was referring to had been specially designed for use within the sphere. It was black and silver and tightly covered every inch of his body with the exception of his mouth and eyes. He wound his arms around in a circle, testing the suit's flexibility for the hundredth time. The boy in him felt like some kind of superhero. The adult in him felt like an idiot.

"Okay, you're all good to go," Kaia said, her amused smile turning into an encouraging one. "Once you're inside and hooked up, I'll run a few tests to make sure the sphere's running smoothly."

Cal nodded and raised a fist with an extended thumb. As he turned to the sphere, he silently cursed himself. *A thumbs up?* He couldn't have come up with a less heroic gesture if he'd tried. Shaking his head, he stepped through the wedge-shaped hatch into the hollow sphere, and the hatch sealed shut behind him.

Once inside, the sphere's concave walls appeared transparent as if they were constructed from one-way glass. Taking in the surrounding lab, Cal couldn't help but feel like a bug in an upturned fishbowl. Turning his attentions downward, he located the pulsating red spot at the very bottom of the sphere that marked the point on which he was required to stand. "Can you hear me, Cal?" He heard Kaia ask as he positioned himself on the red marker.

"Loud and clear. I'm in position."

"Good. I'm activating the feelers now."

Cal gave his arms a little shake, flexed his fingers, and prepared himself with a couple of deep breaths. He'd already given the sphere a couple of trial runs, so he knew that the next few minutes would feel more than a little weird.

As if filling with liquid mercury, the transparent, concave walls rapidly began to turn silver from the bottom up, and within seconds, the sphere's interior appeared as solid as its exterior. A second later, and every inch of that interior began to sprout what looked like tiny, metallic worms, literally millions of them. Tightly bunched and each no thicker than a needle, the *feelers* wriggled and squirmed as they extended almost menacingly towards him. It was as if the sphere's interior was rapidly growing metallic hair. Indeed, just like Melinda's long locks, every one of these feelers contained a mass of highly adaptable nano threads.

Cal did his best not to flinch or squirm as the wriggling feelers made contact with every millimeter of the suit he wore and began to communicate with the nerves of his skin. They configured around his lips to allow unobstructed breathing while smooth, goggle-shaped gaps formed over his eyes to give him a liquid mercury view. *Not designed with claustrophobia in mind*, he mused as he took a few calming breaths. Then, the mass of feelers lifted him and positioned him into the very center of the sphere.

Like much of the tech on board *The Orillian*, the sphere was a military prototype, its purpose to recreate a realistic sensory experience while enabling physical control of a remote, cybernetic avatar. Kaia had explained that, unlike the highly popular pleasure pods, the sync technology avoided the need to tap directly into a person's brainstem to stimulate and trick the nervous system. Brainstem taps left the user confused, delirious even, for a good while after the experience. Cal guessed that the military considered this an unacceptable side effect. They preferred their soldiers not to be delirious under any circumstances unless under strict orders to be so. Fortunately, the sync sphere achieved similar trickery over the senses without any internal poking or probing and left the user relatively intact mentally and physically.

"How you doing in there, Cal?"

"Just peachy," he replied as he experimentally moved his body around in a series of complex movements. With every motion he made, the feelers easily and naturally obliged as if he were simply floating in water. "Did I mention what an incredible machine this is the last time we used it?"

"Twice."

The feelers obliged Cal's grin.

"I'm just starting up a few tests. Tell me exactly what you feel."

"Sure. Heat in my right thigh."

"Yes, good."

"A tapping against the back of my left hand. A sort of rippling down my upper back. Pressure under my feet."

"Excellent. Okay, I'm increasing that pressure under your feet until it matches that of your normal body weight. There, now try jumping for me."

Cal did so. The pressure against his feet felt exactly like solid ground, and when he jumped, he could even feel his feet leave that ground and meet it again a moment later. The feelers mimicked the various pressures and sensations with incredible precision and realism, even creating subtle air pressures against his skin. If it weren't for the blank, silvery view before his eyes, he felt he might simply be jumping in a park.

"Okay, Cal, movements all seem fine."

"So no making me hop on one foot for five minutes this time then?"

"I can assure you that was a valid test."

Suddenly, the silvery view before Cal's eyes disappeared, and he found himself standing in a flat, dusty desert with a deep blue, cloudless sky overhead.

"Visuals are coming though okay for me, Cal. How are they for you?"

"Perfect. You know, you really should let Viktor put some of his virtual worlds into this system; the kid's got a talent for scenery."

Sensing movement to his left, Cal turned to see the slightly unnerving sight of a fully grown giraffe plodding toward him, hoofs scuffing noisily on the hard, dusty ground. Soon, the awkward-looking beast was looming over him. Then it was bending its long neck and peering into his eyes. "Friend of yours?" he asked. The only answer he got was a wet, slurping sound as the beast opened its mouth, extended a long, purplish tongue, and licked his face. Even though he knew it wasn't there, Cal still felt the need to wipe the dripping saliva away from his cheek.

"How are the acoustics?"

"Terrific."

"Good. Well…I guess it's time."

Cal could hear a hint of anxiety returning in Kaia's voice, which he fully understood. "I guess so," he replied, hoping she found his calm tone encouraging. "Let's get to it."

The desert view disappeared, and there was a moment of darkness while the system connected to its avatar. Down on the rocky surface of C9, the synthetic Carcarrion twitched within the cramped confines of the little *Mosquito* ship. Cal blinked a few times as his eyes adjusted to the sight of the ship's cockpit. Looking down, he raised his arms to see jet black, thickly muscled forearms and large, clawed hands. He flexed them and felt the cybernetic power within. The feeling wasn't new; twice before, he had taken control of the Infiltrator while it had been on *The Orillian*. Turning his head, he directed the pale, gray eyes to the ship's readouts. Everything appeared to be in order. "Okay, Kaia, I'm hooked up. How's your screen?"

"All good. I'm seeing everything crystal clear. I've disabled the mouth feelers so you can talk without the Infiltrator's mouth moving."

Cal hit the door release and experienced déjà vu as he took in the familiar sight of the dark C9 landscape. They had landed the *Mosquito* in precisely the same location as his previous excursion, and so far, the only thing distinguishing this visit from the other was his taller stature and an inability to smell the sulphur on the gusting wind. He looked toward the distant camp and then at the Insidion base beyond. This was the first time they'd risked any sort of remote signal from *The Orillian* to the planet surface. If the Insidions were going to detect their presence, now would be that time. "Well, I don't see any cavalry yet."

"Me neither. Maybe they're lazily waiting for us to go to them," Kaia replied.

"Well, let's oblige, shall we?" Cal said, stepping the Infiltrator out of the ship's cockpit and down onto the rocky ground.

"It looks like there's a storm brewing on the horizon, Cal."

"There always is."

Chapter Thirty-Nine
LYING IN WAIT

Jumper grimaced as he looked to the horizon and saw the gathering storm clouds. He didn't mind a good storm but was unsure whether this one would help or hinder their plan. One thing was for sure: It wouldn't make his long-range targeting any easier. Bringing his longeye bliss rifle up to firing position, he directed the sights on the little *Mosquito* ship far below. It was hard to see the dark figure against the equally dark landscape, but he could just about make out Cal and Kaia's synthetic Carcarrion as it left the ship and swiftly negotiated the rocky terrain toward the prison camp.

"Cal's on the move," he called to Eddy and Toker. Both were uncharacteristically calm and quiet as they gazed out of the Star Splinter's open cargo doors. Toker sat on the deck, slouched against a weapons crate and idly rubbing his adrenalin cuff that was firmly strapped to his wrist. Eddy stood by his side, eyes hard like a boxer's before a bout as she twiddled one of the Xcel syringes between her fingers. The Gibson gun was laying at her feet.

As the Star Splinter was a much larger ship, they had decided to land it much further away from the Insidion base than the little *Mosquito*. The effectiveness of the ghosting net technology had proven successful multiple times now, but landing a ship the size of a Star Splinter would cause heat changes to the ground on which it settled—a very subtle giveaway but an unnecessary risk nonetheless. When the time came, Viktor would maneuver the ship closer to the prison camp.

As always, Jumper found the feel of the bliss rifle in his hands reassuring. He'd always disliked pulse weapons. They were powerful and effective, no argument there, but he'd never liked the complexity of their workings—too much opportunity for malfunction. Of course, now, with the Insidions' ability to disable pulse-based technology, the rifle felt more reassuring than ever.

He continued to scan the landscape through the weapon's sights then brought them into focus on the relatively flat area of ground where the dropships would be landing. Just looking at it reminded him how nervous he was about that aspect of the plan. His worries weren't concerning the functioning of the dropships; he and Cal had physically checked and rechecked all ninety-eight of them. Neither was he worried about the starship; Kaia had assured them she could take control of it as easily as she had the Star Splinter. He also trusted Viktor's ability to have successfully fitted the starship with the ghosting net technology. The aspect of the plan where his confidence waned, however, was in the fact that they'd not had the time, or indeed the means, for the individual dropships to be fitted with that same cloaking technology. As it stood, there would be a race to get all the escapees to the dropships and back to the safety of the cloaked starship before the Insidions managed to take action. It was a race he feared they could lose.

"It is time for me to go, Jumper."

The voice was Melinda's, and Jumper turned to see the cybernetic woman approaching him. She was dressed from neck to toe in black to provide as much camouflage against the landscape as possible.

"Okay, Melinda. You have the cube key?"

"Yes," she replied, holding up the tiny box between her forefinger and thumb. The nano threads within the box were already set to deactivate the camp's force field. Melinda was to make her way down to the camp unseen and await the signal.

"You want some camo cream for your face?" Jumper asked, eying her pale skin. "I've got some here somewhere," he continued, looking down and patting at the multitude of pockets on his combat jacket.

"That won't be required."

When Jumper looked back up, the synthetic woman's blonde hair had turned jet black and had begun to move, something Jumper thought he'd never get used to, until it had wrapped firmly around her neck and face. Before long, the only part of her that was no longer black were her bright blue eyes.

Jumper grinned. "Looks like you've got it covered."

"Good luck to all of you," she said as her eyes darkened until they too were black.

Before any of them had a chance to reply, she silently sped off down the Star Splinter's cargo ramp and exited the relative safety of the ship's ghosting net like a panther in the night.

Chapter Forty
INFILTRATION

The Infiltrator's long, powerful legs handled the rugged terrain well as Cal guided it across the harsh C9 landscape. As he closed in on the five gleaming structures, the scale of the Insidion base really started to sink in. He'd been aware of its immense size from studying the birds-eye views, but with the nearest cube looming over him like some sort of colossal, alien castle, he couldn't help feeling they'd bitten off more than they could chew. He took a moment to glance back at the now distant prison camp. There was no one following him, but that did little to extinguish his foreboding. The low rumbles from the approaching storm weren't helping either—they seemed nothing but growls of warning.

Bar one rather messy dive over the prison camp's force field, so far everything had gone smoothly. The pop platform had easily adjusted to the synthetic Carcarrion's extra weight, and its heavy, cybernetic form had cleared the force field with room to spare, but Cal had found controlling the Infiltrator's descent within the sync sphere tricky to say the least. He'd gone into a tumble and had landed face first. Fortunately, the avatar had remained undamaged and, doing his best to play the part by glaring at various prisoners along the way, he'd guided it through the prison camp untroubled.

Taking advantage of a fortunate opportunity, he'd then boldly followed a Carcarrion drone straight out of the camp's exit and continued to follow it as it strode parallel to the conveyor belt in the direction of the Insidion base.

Of the half dozen drones that had come within close proximity thus far, not one of them had paid the Infiltrator the least bit of attention. He and Kaia had been fairly confident that this would be the case. Three days previously, they had presented the synthetic to the two captive drones on board *The Orillian*. Their reaction had been entirely promising. On sighting the Infiltrator through the smart-glass barrier, both drones had become immediately alert, excited even, at the prospect of one of their own appearing. It had taken the drones some time to realize they were looking at some sort of impostor.

The giant Insidion cubes were constructed of no material Cal could name, a shimmering kind of metal that seemed to take on a life of its own while reflecting the surrounding landscape and skies. It was entirely fortunate that, of the five structures that made up the base, the source of the weapon-disabling signal was emanating from the closest. It was also fortunate that the drone inadvertently guiding him was heading directly for that very structure.

As they neared, Cal saw a tall, hard-edged entranceway that looked as though a block had simply been removed from the side of the structure. Bright light was pouring from it and falling across the dark rocks. He could see no guards. What would such a superior, arrogant race need to guard against?

"They're not overly keen on curves," he muttered to Kaia as he followed the drone through the entranceway into a wide, straight-edged corridor. Despite the Infiltrator's agility, he was relieved to leave behind the rocky terrain in exchange for a smooth, well-lit floor. The corridor was completely featureless with no doors or windows apparent, just more corridor that seemed to stretch endlessly straight ahead.

"Well this is a little underwhelming," he said as he urged the Infiltrator on with a confident march, making sure to stride no faster or slower than his guide, who was a good twenty meters ahead.

"Yes," Kaia agreed. "Still, I'm quite happy with *underwhelming*."

"So I guess there's not a lot of point asking which way?"

Kaia let out a small, nervous laugh. "Not yet at least." She had assured him that she'd managed to pinpoint the signal to quite an accurate degree and, assuming that they would at some point have a choice in their route, was confident she could direct him to it with ease. "It's coming from the center of the ship," she reminded him. "Eventually, we're going to have to find a way to go up, but for now, straight ahead is good for us."

Cal felt it was an eternity before he could make out any sort of end to the corridor. It started with a muffled din, then colors and lights ahead. As he continued on, it became apparent that whatever they were heading towards certainly didn't match the bland, featureless design they'd witnessed so far.

"What do you suppose is going on up there?" Kaia asked.

"I've no idea, but I've a nasty feeling we're approaching a party without an invite." Cal could feel his heart pounding against his chest and wondered for a brief moment if the sync sphere was sensitive enough to pick up on such a subtle movement.

As the corridor finally came to an end, Cal sucked in a breath and had to force himself not to sweep the Infiltrator's head up and around like some kind of awed tourist. The space was so large that no matter which direction he looked, not even the Infiltrator's synthetic eyes could see an end to it.

He hadn't been far off when he'd said "party." The area was bursting with activity. Close to chaos in fact. So much so that it reminded Cal of Vangos, the once capital city of Earth's pleasure moon. Everything he saw could easily have been human in design but was at the same time distinctly alien. There were countless establishments, all set around huge pillars, offering strange foods, drinks, and who knew what else. All were adorned with dazzling bursts of color.

There were Carcarrion drones everywhere, but the life forms didn't end there. A host of different alien breeds meandered around the great space. Most were approximately humanoid, but rather disconcertingly, the Carcarrions were among the smallest in stature. The aliens on view weren't limited to live flesh and blood either; in the distance, Cal could see crowds gathered around massive hologram projections that hovered in the air, displaying images of monsters the likes of which he'd never seen. Crowds were gathered around the holograms, hissing and screeching in what he assumed was appreciation or disappointment as they watched the monsters violently rip and grapple at each other with huge claws.

"My God, Cal."

"You took the words right out of my mouth," he replied. He was doing his utmost not to break his stride as he moved the Infiltrator directly into the throng. Looking up, he saw a high, transparent ceiling that seemed to double as a floor for the level above, and he could make out at least two other floors above that before his vision became a confusing blur of color and movement. It seemed the array of chaotic bustle was replicated on multiple levels overhead, and having witnessed the colossal height of the structure from the outside, he could only imagine how many levels that might be.

"I think we should make this visit brief," he said, trying his best to remain level headed as he continued to move deeper into the strange, internal city.

"Definitely," Kaia agreed. "When you can, start veering to your right."

Cal did so, all the while doing his best to avoid any sort of physical contact with the city's occupants. The last thing they needed was to get into a tussle. "You recognise any of these species, Kaia?"

"Not even remotely. They all appear far more sentient and evolved than any of the aliens in our little corner of space. I suspect they're from far beyond."

Cal agreed and did his best not to stare as he continued on.

"I think we better pick up the pace, Cal," Kaia suggested after a time. "There's a lot of communication going on. I don't fancy our chances if we're talked at."

"We need to go up at some point, right?"

"Yes, quite a way up."

"I might be wrong, but that huge, opaque cylinder ahead looks to be stretching through the floors. See the red cubes moving up and down it? Could be elevators."

"Looks promising."

Cal manipulated the Infiltrator carefully through the crowds and soon found himself having to skirt around an area filled with multiple aliens slouched in hanging cradles. There were brightly colored tubes entering their arms. He didn't waste any time studying or musing over the sight; everything he saw was being recorded by the sync sphere and could be reviewed at a later time. One detail he had taken the time to observe, however, was that the slug-like Insidions were attached to every neck he'd seen. So far, all seemed to be drones.

Eventually, he brought the Infiltrator to a halt in front of the massive, opaque cylinder. At closer inspection, it looked more like a wide, fizzing beam of energy. Inside were numerous static cubes all of which were blue. "What do you think?" he asked Kaia as he peered through the haze at one of the cubes, "Should I just walk on through?"

As if in answer to his question, two Carcarrion drones barged the Infiltrator aside and walked through the shaft's hazy wall until they had disappeared into one of the cubes. Moments later, the cube turned red, seeming to solidify as it did so, and took off in a rapid ascent.

"I guess that answers—"

Cal's words caught in his throat as a large, powerful hand clamped onto the Infiltrator's right shoulder. Managing to twist around, he saw no less than five bulbous eyes—all on the one face— peering down at him. The owner of the eyes was more or less human in shape but was at least a head taller than the Infiltrator. The creature had pale, yellowish skin that was stretched tightly over a particularly bony head and body and was translucent enough to reveal a network of pulsating, brown veins beneath. The creature also sported four stubby arms, the short length of which was more than made up for by long, multi-jointed fingers that protruded, spider-like, from each hand.

Cal glared at the alien, hoping the icy Carcarrion stare would cause it to reconsider its aggressive proximity. Achieving little success, he casually swiped at its bony arm in order to knock the hand away. The long fingers, however, were surprisingly strong, and the swipe did nothing more than aggravate the tall brute. All five of its eyes were beginning to bulge to the point of popping. With a stab of alarm, Cal wondered whether any of those bulbous eyes could see through the Infiltrator's synthetic trickery. As if in answer, the creature turned its bony head and began to hiss loudly, attracting the attention from some of the nearest bystanders.

"How does it know?" There was fear in Kaia's tone.

"I've no idea."

"You've got to get away from it."

Inclined to agree, Cal attempted to twist free, but incredibly, the alien's long-fingered grip remained firm. *Desperate measures*, he thought as he seized hold of the creature's lower arms and launched the Infiltrator's heavy, cybernetic form back through the energy shaft. After a few meters of awkward stumbling, the Infiltrator hit the floor with a thud, the big brute landing heavily on top of it. Fortunately, they'd landed where Cal had planned—or at least hoped. Seeming to register their presence, the lift's fuzzy blue walls solidified and turned red, and they started to ascend.

Quick to recover from its abduction, the multi-limbed alien soon had all four of its massive, spidery hands grappling in determination. Instinctively, Cal tightened his grip on the big brute's lower arms. "Christ, this bastard's strong. Heavy too," he exclaimed, shocked that the Infiltrator's cybernetic arms seemed to be struggling.

"You're going to have to finish this quickly, Cal. The lift's automatic, and it's going up fast."

Cal's vision was suddenly obscured as one of the big, spider-like hands clamped onto the Infiltrator's face and another wrapped around its neck. The alien was undoubtedly exerting immense pressure, but fortunately, any pain emitted by the sync sphere's feelers was preset not go past a certain level.

"Six hundred and fifty meters to go, Cal. Then we need to get out of this thing."

Still gripping both of the alien's lower arms, Cal was becoming acutely aware of the advantage of multiple limbs when it came to a fight. Reluctantly releasing one of his opponent's wrists, he began issuing a series of fast, powerful punches to its rib cage. Despite the crunch of bone, any pain response from the alien was worryingly absent.

"Tough bastard." Cal's voice was strained. Even with the

immense, cybernetic strength at his disposal, he was still having to work hard within the sphere.

"It's nothing but a drone, Cal. It maybe doesn't register the pain. Try going for the Insidion."

Grateful for the advice, Cal blindly reached the Infiltrator's free arm up and around and began to feel for the back of the creature's neck.

"Four hundred and fifty meters."

He felt a hard, lumpy spine then soft flesh. The Insidion wriggled as he gripped it. Then he squeezed. The reaction was immediate: a pained noise, somewhere between a rasp and a roar rushed out of the alien's mouth. Unfortunately, the long fingers around the Infiltrator's face and neck tightened further.

"Three hundred meters."

Cal squeezed again, but the Insidion had obviously activated some sort of defence mechanism and become hard as stone. Abandoning the direct attack on the slug-like creature, he forced the free arm back underneath the drone's body and pushed with all his might. Slowly, the cybernetics began to overwhelm the alien's impressive strength and forced it upwards. Feeling the positioning was right, he swung the Infiltrator's right leg up in an arc and hooked it around his opponent's head.

"Two hundred meters."

Feeling multiple eyes squashed against hard, cybernetic calf, Cal used the power of the hooked leg to twist and force the brute further back. Taking a gurgling cry and a slight loosening of pressure around his neck as his cue, Cal planted the Infiltrator's other foot on the drone's chest and pushed hard and fast. Its spidery grip finally failing it, the creature was thrust backwards, and there was a loud crunch as it hit one of the cube's solid walls. Springing the Infiltrator up, Cal slammed a knee into his dazed opponent's head.

That about did it.

"Only eighty meters left."

"How the hell do we stop this thing?"

"There, to your right. That panel."

Cal turned to the illuminated panel. "How's your Insidion?" he asked, staring at lines of obscure symbols.

"Forty-five meters…try blind luck."

He began pressing the symbols at random. "Not a lot happening."

"Damn it, only fifteen meters."

Taking a step back, Cal lifted the Infiltrator's right leg and slammed its heel into the center of the panel, cracking it straight down the middle. Instantly, the cube began to slow, and a few moments later, it came to an abrupt stop.

"Zero meters," Kaia said as the cube turned blue. "That was seriously impressive."

"Absurd luck," Cal replied as he glanced at the floored alien. Thankfully, it was unmoving.

"The target's a hundred meters or so dead ahead."

Cal took a couple of deep breaths. The cube's walls had once again taken on fuzzy haze, and he tentatively stepped the Infiltrator through, relieved that the floor remained solid as he did so. Clearing the energy shaft, he was faced with yet another far-reaching space, but it was a far cry from what they'd seen below. The few drones he could see were moving with purpose but fortunately not in his direction. There was machinery in the distance coupled with huge hologram readouts. "Looks like some kind of control deck," he said as he moved forward, keeping the Infiltrator's strides swift but not so much as to attract attention.

"Keep going straight. It's dead ahead."

Despite the pace he'd set, crossing the shiny expanse of floor seemed excruciatingly slow, every thudding footstep seeming increasingly likely to reveal their deception.

"There, Cal. The cylinder…that's it. That's our target."

Cal saw it about fifty meters ahead: a tall, clear cylinder containing a coil of fierce, pulsating white light that looked ready to burst from its glassy prison. The cylinder was protruding from a wide hole in the floor that was bordered by a simple metal railing. There were a number of consoles close by and a similar number of aliens manning them. Other than that, the way was clear.

Steadily continuing his course, Cal felt a triumphant thrill rising in his chest.

Unfortunately, the thrill was short-lived.

"No… Cal… Gods no."

Cal almost stumbled upon hearing the panic in Kaia's tone. "Kaia?"

"Christ, Cal, we've got serious trouble."

Cal slowed the Infiltrator's stride and looked about. "Where? I don't see it."

"Finish the mission. Destroy the signal."

"What? Kaia… What the hell is it? Where's the problem? Kaia…Kaia?" There was no answer. The thrill that had died became a knot of fear that sunk to the pit of Cal's stomach. He felt a sudden, overwhelming urge to disengage from the sync sphere, but the sound of heavy footfall abruptly muted the urge. He cursed, whipping his head around. In his confusion, he'd slowed the Infiltrator's pace and was now stumbling in the empty expanse like a delirious drunk. Two aliens, the same yellow-skinned, long-fingered breed that he'd faced in the lift, were bolting directly at him. Cal turned to run, but the nearest alien threw itself forwards, crashing heavily to the ground and managing to wrap three of its long, steely fingers around the Infiltrator's ankle.

Breaking his inevitable fall, Cal immediately twisted to get a better view of his attackers. The second alien had already caught up and was now looming over him, all four spidery hands reaching down. Unwilling to get into another grappling match, Cal planted a devastating kick to the inside of its knee joint. As the alien crumpled to the ground, he sent a second kick into the face of the other attacker.

Cal's fear was gone, surging adrenalin having taken its place. Lurching the Infiltrator upright, he began slamming a fist into the hand gripping the ankle. Enough bones broke for him to slip free and scramble clear. Before the two attackers had a chance to right themselves, he had the Infiltrator back on its feet and was bolting towards the cylindrical target. The time for remaining inconspicuous had well and truly passed.

A suspicion was growing in Cal's mind as to Kaia's panic, but he pushed it aside. In the next few seconds, all that mattered was the cylinder. He could sense that the two aliens he'd floored were already giving chase, but they didn't worry him. Not much could catch a synthetic running at full speed. There were, however, more ahead. Every drone within earshot had turned its attention to the commotion and, as he closed in on the target, they moved to intercept. Cal ignored them. They were nothing more than a blur. All of his focus was on the cylinder.

"Contact Star Splinter," he shouted as he thrust an open palm into the face of an intercepting drone. "The plan is a go." The strike lifted the attacking alien off its feet. "Repeat, *the plan is a go*." Cal didn't even see his victim hit the floor before he was slamming the Infiltrator's shoulder into the next interceptor.

"Engage."

His heart thundering in his chest, Cal slipped under the desperate grasp of a long-armed alien, sprang up, and in one fluid motion leaped onto the huge cylinder's protective railing. Bright, pulsating light filled his vision as he launched the Infiltrator out over the gap.

As its heavy form sailed through the air, Cal instinctively put a cybernetic hand to its torso, to the very place where the helix bomb was concealed. The very moment before the Infiltrator's head collided with the glass, Cal shouted one last word.

"Detonate."

Chapter Forty-One
THE PLAN IS A GO

"Repeat, *the plan is a go.*" Cal's voice was loud and clear within the Star Splinter's cockpit as it sounded out through the comm unit.

Jumper turned to Viktor, who sat front and center in the piloting chair. "Okay, kid, this is it," he said before leaning down to the comm. "Eddy, Toker, we're a go."

Viktor's fingers glided swiftly across the control panel before him. "Right," he said, taking a deep breath. "Firing the packs now."

Jumper nodded and opened up a view of the distant prison camp on the cockpit's window. The Star Splinter's cannons had been pre-programmed to fire the packs—each filled with thousands of Xcel serum syringes—to precise points within the camp. Already, Jumper could see the packs speeding in high arcs through the dark skies, hover stabilizers battling against the ever-increasing winds.

"That storm's coming in quick," Viktor observed, slipping his skinny arms into the ship's flight controls and shooting Jumper a nervous smile.

"Don't worry, kid. It will only help to confuse the enemy. It's a good thing." Jumper hoped he sounded more confident than he felt.

"Yeah, I guess," Viktor replied as he activated the Star Splinter's launch engines.

Laurence stood up as a deep *boom* reverberated from the direction of the distant Insidion base. "Well done, Callum," he muttered to himself.

Turning away from the noise, he looked towards the opposite horizon. After a few moments, he saw multiple black shapes arching through the ever-darkening skies. He allowed himself a grin and looked about at the men and women working around him; they were hiding their nerves well. "Okay people," he bellowed. "This is it. Eyes up."

Simultaneously abandoning their mining machinery, they all looked up and tracked the paths of the black shapes tearing through the sky.

Laurence turned his gaze to the Carcarrion drone that had been stalking nearby. As he knew it would, his shouting had attracted its attention, and it now had him locked in a deathly stare. "That's right, you son of a bitch. We're done with your little slave camp," Laurence snarled, his heart thumping madly as he crouched down and snatched up a fist-sized rock. He'd been wanting to do this for what seemed an eternity, and he couldn't help but grin as he brought his arm back. "Come on then, you big bastard." He threw the rock with all his might straight at the drone's head.

Unfortunately, the swell of satisfaction that surged through him as the rock left his hand died when the big bastard in question casually plucked it out of the air with one clawed fist. Despite this lack of success, Laurence's grin remained, faltering only slightly as the drone crushed rock and let the wind take its remains.

Laurence wanted to continue his defiant stare, but the warning voice echoing in the back of his mind was becoming almost deafening. *Time to run, you fool.*

"Clear a path," he cried as he turned and began scrambling over the rocks. He didn't bother risking a glance back. The fear in the eyes of his fellow prisoners stumbling out of his way told him the Carcarrion drone was already in pursuit.

Other than the trial of Cal's bright green serum, Laurence couldn't remember the last time he'd run. He'd certainly not done any during his time in the prison camp. Such an act would have attracted unwanted attention. And he was definitely no runner before the invasion. The experience was exhilarating but at the same time utterly exhausting. He'd spent a lot of time in the past weeks building his strength, but his cardiovascular fitness remained a joke. Sucking in ragged, desperate lungfuls of air, his arms and legs started to burn almost unbearably. If it weren't for the pissed off alien hot on his tail, fuelling his adrenalin, Laurence imagined he'd be a wheezing wreck by now.

The storm was closing in, the winds whipping up like a squall. Huge piles of discarded rock dust lay a short distance ahead. Laurence bolted straight towards them. Even over the noise of the wind, he could hear his pursuer's pounding feet and snorts of exertion close behind. In the corner of his eye, he caught a large, black shape gliding steadily to the ground. He risked a quick glance and was glad to see his fellows converging on the pack. He wished he was with them; he might have even turned to fight if he had some of that bright green liquid pulsating through his veins. Perhaps foolishly, however, he'd given Cal's extra samples to a couple of his more fearful comrades. Still, even without the serum, he was doing a good job leading the drone away from the packs. With any luck, his efforts would buy valuable time for the syringes to be distributed.

A series of particularly violent gusts of wind suddenly barrelled their way through the mine ahead, picking up large quantities of rock dust as they did so. Laurence covered his eyes as best he could.

If the winds continued like this, he soon wouldn't be able to see a thing. But he surged on, and as he did, it began to dawn on him that his pursuer might actually be struggling to catch him. Maybe these hulking Carcarrions with their formidable, muscular frames just weren't built for speed. Maybe he'd even outrun the bastard.

A savage blow to the back of his right shoulder brought the thought to a sudden and painful end. Without a hope in hell of keeping his feet under him, Laurence flew forwards and inevitably downwards. Only with the help of a particularly strong side-wind did he manage to twist his body before pounding into a large pile of rock dust.

With his breath knocked out of him, Laurence kept his arms up, shielding his eyes from the gritty, gusting air. Squinting, he forced himself to look. The dark mass of the Carcarrion drone was looming over him, white fangs and pale eyes gleaming brightly through the gray. His chest heaving, Laurence managed to regain just enough breath to mumble a curse but not a lot else.

At the very moment the Infiltrator had ceased to be, the feelers within the sync sphere lowered Cal to the floor and disengaged. Disorientated, he stood on unsteady feet for a moment, shaking his head and rubbing at his face. Having a massive bomb explode within your gut was a strange sensation to say the least no matter how fleeting the experience. He hoped to God the explosion had done its job. The plan on the planet surface would be well underway by now, and without weapons, the chances of success would be bleak.

Once he'd gained enough sense of self, Cal tore away the sync suit material covering his head and face and turned to the sphere's door release. Then he paused, his finger hovering just short of the button. What had made Kaia panic in such a way? What had forced her to disconnect the communication link? Pirates? What else could it be? He moved his finger to the left and pressed a different control. The interior wall of the sphere began to melt away to give him the same three hundred and sixty degree view of the lab he'd had earlier.

His blood turned to ice.

Only a handful of paces from the sphere's base stood a rough-looking man who was staring directly up at the sphere, directly at *him*. Cal knew the man couldn't see him through the one-way glass. All he'd be seeing was his own unpleasant reflection distorted on the sphere's shiny outer surface. Still, the fact didn't make the stranger's proximity any less disconcerting. There was an old-fashioned bolt rifle slung over one of his shoulders and a modern pulse rifle slung over the other. He wore a long coat of dark, scuffed leather, beneath which Cal could see the glint of multiple knives as well as a pair of pulse pistols holstered on his hips.

"Bloody weird, eh?" The man shouted without taking his eyes from the sphere. Hearing no response, he scratched roughly at his thick chin stubble and turned towards the lab's entrance to repeat his statement. "Oi! I said check it out. Bloody weird, eh?"

"Shut your damn face, Fallon. Get on with the job."

Cal looked toward the man who'd replied. He was older, tall, and thin with sharp, hawk-like features. Even from this distance, Cal could see that those features were twisted into an impatient sneer. Three others also lingered near the lab's entrance: another man busily tapping away at a console and two tall, bald women, one of whom had black tattoos covering her face and skull. The two bald women could easily have been twins. The sight of the pair ignited a sickening feeling in Cal. There were other intruders milling about the lab, but he couldn't tear his attention from the bald women. The one without tattoos had an arm wrapped around Kaia's neck and was brutally twisting one of her wrists up behind her back. Kaia looked to be struggling for breath and was tugging desperately with her free hand at the woman's grip. She had two long cuts across her torso, the red blood bright against her pale bodysuit.

Cal pressed his clenched fists against his forehead and swore angrily under his breath. There was no doubt the intruders were pirates. There was also no doubt that the two bald twins were not women, nor indeed were they human.

As Viktor brought the Star Splinter in to land, Jumper magnified the view of the prison camp in the cockpit's window. Of course, without a force field, it was arguably no longer a prison—Melinda had seen to that.

"There she is!" Viktor shouted, relief plain in his voice.

Through the enhanced window, Melinda could be seen speedily making her way across the rocky landscape back towards the Star Splinter. No longer concerned with going unnoticed, her face was uncovered, and her blonde hair was hanging free.

The Star Splinter's landing was less than smooth, but it did the job.

"Well done, kid," Jumper said, putting a reassuring hand on his shoulder. He looked towards the distant Insidion base; as yet, there was no obvious activity. *Maybe Cal and Kaia's explosion had thrown them into disarray*, he mused hopefully. In contrast, the once prison camp was now a hive of activity. The escaping prisoners had divided up and were converging on the hover packs. With any luck, every single one of them would receive a dose of the serum—there was, after all, a lot of rough terrain for them to cover in order to reach the Star Splinter and the weapons.

"Make sure you keep the engines fired up, kid. I've got a feeling this might be tight," he said, glancing again towards the Insidion base.

"Don't worry about me, Jumper. It's those two idiots down below you should be worrying about."

Jumper nodded. The boy had a point.

By the time he made it down to the Star Splinter's loading bay, Eddy and Toker had opened the cargo doors and activated the all-terrain shifters, which were already transporting the huge crates of weaponry out onto the dark, rocky plateau.

"Good job," he shouted to the pair, making sure his voice could be heard over the gusts of sulphur-infused air swirling about the bowels of the ship.

"No problem," Toker replied confidently. The young man looked more composed than Jumper had ever seen him, perhaps sobered by the number of lives depending on him. "Melinda's just arrived. She's opening up the crates. We'll help dish them out once the prisoners arrive."

Jumper nodded his approval and looked down the ramp at Eddy. The girl was wild-eyed and looked ready to sprint solo to the Insidion base to finish what the helix bomb had started. Turning to him, she jogged up the ramp, an Xcel syringe grasped tightly in her hand. "Time to dose ourselves up yet, J?" She asked, even though she was probably still feeling the effects of her first dose.

Jumper looked out of the cargo doors, eyes watering against the fierce wind. There was no sign of the escaping prisoners yet, but it wouldn't be long. "Yes, Eddy, it's time."

Without taking his eyes from the dark horizon, he reached for his own syringe and pressed it to his neck.

The Carcarrion drone thrust its massive clawed hands down at Laurence, grasped him by the front of his ragged shirt, and hauled him into the air. Laurence kicked furiously at his attacker's legs and repeatedly slammed both of his fists into the drone's face. It was futile. Although it was tough to see through the torrent of dust-filled air, Laurence could have sworn there was amusement on the alien's feline-like face.

Where the hell are you, Tark? he thought desperately as the beast lowered him to the ground. With one of the clawed fists still clamped to his shirt, Laurence stopped struggling and watched helplessly as the drone raised its other fist like a big, black hammer. Accepting his fate, Laurence ignored the stinging rock dust and stared directly into the cold, gray eyes before him. Then he surprised himself by letting out a loud, mocking laugh. It seemed his newfound bravery was going to stick with him until the bitter end. A shame then that the end was only seconds away.

A gust of wind erupted, so fierce that Laurence was forced to break his defiant stare and shield his eyes. When he finally uncovered them, he found his shirt had been ripped clean in half and was now flapping free. Confused, he looked about with rapidly blinking eyes. The drone was nowhere to be seen.

After a moment of confused searching, he detected movement to his right. Moving cautiously toward it, a lull in the wind improved the visibility enough for him to see his attacker lying on the ground. It wasn't alone. Two Carcarrions with gray, swirling patterns marking their skin were savagely beating the drone. *Tark's friends...my friends.* The ferocious pair were concentrating their attack on the slug-like creature clinging to the fallen drone's neck.

Despite the stinging rock dust, Laurence watched on with horrified fascination. The Carcarrions began clawing and tugging at the wriggling creature, which was now little more than a pulpy mass of dark flesh. Eventually, they succeeded in ripping it free from their long-dead comrade, its tiny, pale tendrils hanging limp. Raising the ruined creature to its mouth, one of the Carcarrions proceeded to sink its fangs into the pulpy flesh then triumphantly tore it in two. Laurence couldn't help but shudder as the two aliens raised their clawed fists to the rumbling storm clouds and let out blood-curdling roars.

"Quite a sight, don't you think?" came Tark's voice in an uncharacteristically loud tone. The little man stepped up beside him, his white dreadlocks flying like the swirling tentacles of some albino creature of the deep. His eyes were fixed on his Carcarrion's.

"You were right," Laurence shouted over the howl of the wind. "No problem fighting."

"The ash war paint's formidable, eh?"

"Yes," Laurence agreed although he found it difficult to imagine a situation when the creatures wouldn't look formidable. Attempting to study them further through the grit, he noticed tight bindings covering their necks and running down their spines, a crude but seemingly effective protection from the neck slugs.

Tark turned to face him. "Here you go." He held out a glass syringe, its green contents glowing brightly in the bleak air. The little man cracked a wide grin. "Might help you put up a bit more of a fight next time, eh?"

Laurence nodded with a half grin and gratefully plucked the syringe from his little friend's hand.

Chapter Forty-Two
BEST LAID PLANS

Fucking pirates.

How the hell did they beat The Orillian's warning sensors? A barrage of curses coursed through Cal's mind. The plan was well underway; there'd be no stopping that now. He and Kaia had just achieved a near miracle, and he had no doubt that the helix bomb had done its job. But now, fate had gone and punched them full in the face. *Where the hell did they get two synthetics? And who the hell broke their behavior inhibitors?* He took a few deep breaths. He had to calm down. He had to focus.

Turning about within the sphere, he made sure he was aware of everyone in the room. Fortunately, they were all situated in the direction of the lab's entrance. As well as the man in the long coat, who was still standing near the base of the sphere, and the two men standing near the synthetics, there were three other men idly roaming the room. Even at a glance, it was clear they were as fond of weaponry as their long-coated friend. There was also a woman, short with spiky, brown hair. She was standing apart from the others, leaning against a desk and clutching her left arm with a pained expression.

Not everyone was standing; there was a lifeless body sprawled on the floor halfway to the lab's entrance. *Kaia's handiwork,* Cal thought as he scanned back toward the consoles surrounding the sync sphere. A moment later, he saw what he was looking for: a discarded syringe. Kaia had injected a dose of Xcel and put up a good fight. Unfortunately, she'd ended up in the clutches of a synthetic, and that was where her fight had finished. No amount of Xcel could match a human to a synthetic's cybernetic strength and speed. Even so, Cal would have given anything for one of those little syringes. His eyes swept over the nearby consoles, but he saw none. There was something though. Kaia's control wand lay on the floor not far from the heavy boots of the long-coated pirate. It wasn't much, but it was something.

"Will you hurry the hell up, Finch?" The shout came from the older, hawk-faced man who was standing near the synthetics. He was aiming his small, dark eyes at the man next to him, who was tapping away at a console. "In case you've forgotten, there's some nasty fucking aliens down on that planet. Get the hell on with it."

The man at the console shrugged without looking up from the screen. "They can't see us. Besides, I've been hacked into the ship's system for a while now."

The hawk-faced man pressed his palms on the edge of the console and leaned forward. "So why the hell didn't you tell me?"

Again, Finch shrugged, seemingly unperturbed by the sharp tone.

Shaky chain of command, Cal noted. Something that could work in his favor. Again, not much, but something.

"I've been poking around," Finch replied nonchalantly, still not bothering to look up from the console. "Well, hello! What you been up to, woman?" he said, finally lifting his eyes to turn and regard Kaia.

Kaia had gone limp in the synthetic's tight grip but still appeared conscious.

"What? What is it?" the hawk-faced man asked irritably, leaning in closer to get a better look at the screen.

"Somehow, this clever little bitch has hooked into one of those starships drifting out by the moons."

Cal cursed. The sight of the synthetics and his fear for Kaia had distracted him from the dropships. They should have been en route to the planet surface by now. He could easily activate them from any one of the multiple consoles throughout the lab, but what was he going to do, step out of the sphere and politely ask for a pause until he'd seen to an urgent task?

With his eyes turned back to the console, Finch suddenly barked a laugh. "God knows what the bitch is up to, but she has the bloody great thing all powered up and ready to go. Even the dropships are prepped and programmed to—"

The hawk-faced man grabbed him by the shoulder and roughly pulled him around until they stood face to face. "Stick to the bloody mission, Finch."

Untroubled by the sudden violence, Finch simply grinned, creating a standoff, which lasted for some time until the spiky-haired woman broke the silence. "Oh, bloody well get on with it, Finch," she shouted across the lab. "I gotta pilot this frickin' vessel, and that bloody bitch has smashed my arm good n' proper."

Finch ignored her protests. "What ya gonna do, Rek? Bust me up? Don't expect any of these idiots to run the ship's systems," he said to the hawk-faced man.

"I'll bloody well run 'um', Rekvit," the spiky-haired woman blurted.

"You gotta pilot," Finch said quickly. "Ain't easy to do both at once, 'specially with that dangly arm of yours."

Finally breaking eye contact, Rekvit turned his hawk-like gaze towards the tattooed synthetic. The tall, cybernetic woman took a step towards them, her face impassive.

Finch's eyes flicked nervously towards her. Then he snorted a laugh and pulled Rekvit's hand off his shoulder. "Easy, eh? I was just screwing with you, Rek. No need to get your pet involved," he said, backing up a few steps and raising his hands. "Peace. I'll get on with it... But I'll look forward to hearing you explain to the boss why you missed the opportunity of swiping a class one military starshi—"

Finch didn't get to finish his sentence. In fact, his face slammed so hard into the console that there was very little chance he'd ever do anything again.

Cal blinked in surprise, unsure of exactly what he'd seen. The tattooed synthetic hadn't been responsible; she'd not moved an inch. Neither had it been Rekvit; the man's hawk-like face was speckled with blood, and he wore an expression somewhere between shock and anger as he watched Finch's limp body slide almost comically down the sloped console to crumple to the floor.

A moment later, Rekvit turned his shocked gaze towards Kaia. She was no longer limp in the synthetic's embrace and was once again struggling in defiance. The corner of Cal's mouth twitched as it dawned on him what had happened. Having spotted Finch backing up towards her, Kaia had seemingly kicked the unwitting man in the back. With the Xcel in her system, the kick had probably contained all the force of a speeding hover truck.

"What the...what the..." Rekvit was staring disbelievingly at Kaia. Then he looked accusingly to the face of the synthetic holding her.

"The woman seems unnaturally strong," the synthetic woman explained in a monotone voice.

"No fucking shit," Rekvit spat. He still appeared stunned as he turned towards the bloodstained console and stared at it dumbly.

His fists were balled, knuckles pure white. The commotion had attracted the full attention of everyone in the lab, including the long-coated man, who had finally turned away from the sphere.

After a few moments, Rekvit raised his head and looked about. "Okay…everyone just bloody well stay calm," he barked, his own voice completely devoid of calm. He whipped his head around towards the tattooed synthetic. "Get on this console," he shouted at her. "Activate the ship's flight controls."

"And hurry the hell up," the woman with the spiky hair added. "My arm's frickin' killing me."

The tattooed synthetic took hold of Finch's lifeless right ankle and pulled him aside like an obstructing sack of rubbish. Then she turned her attention to the blood-stained console.

"No more delays," Rekvit barked, looking around the room, his cold, hard eyes hammering the point home. "We're taking control of this ship and getting the hell out of here."

Cal pressed his knuckles into his forehead, teeth grinding, temples throbbing. *If it was just humans…but two Synthetics.* Even one would have rendered his chances impossible, but two? *Shit. Shit.* Visions flared into his mind; the faces of his friends, the countless prisoners. He could only imagine their desperation waiting for the dropships. Cal had never been one to give into despair, but as he looked across the lab again at Kaia's beautiful face strained in futile struggle, he suddenly found himself dropping to his knees. In a few moments, he would burst from the sphere. He'd give it everything he had, rain down as much destruction as he could, but…

Shaking his head, Cal steeled himself and began to rise.

Then he saw it: a bright green smudge in his peripheral vision. The syringe had been placed neatly on the sync sphere's platform, right at the foot of the exit. How the hell had he missed it? He cursed his stupid mistake then managed something close to a smile. *God bless you, Kaia Svenson.*

The sync sphere's door was little louder than a soft breath as it slid open. A couple of seconds was all it took for him to reach out and snatch up the syringe before re-closing the door. Not one of the pirates noticed, not even the long-coated man who stood a few meters away nor the synthetics with their hypersensitive hearing. They were all too preoccupied, listening—or at least giving the impression of listening—to Rekvit, who continued to bark out orders.

Still crouched, Cal wasted no time pressing the syringe to his neck. He could feel a glimmer of hope expanding within his mind. With Xcel coursing through his system, maybe there was a chance, an upgrade from impossible to poor, but he was grateful nonetheless. As the serum ignited within him, he stood and scanned the lab one last time, taking in the position of each and every one of his opponents.

"And you, you good for nothing mechanical bitch," Rekvit rasped, addressing the synthetic who was restraining Kaia, "Keep that little wildcat under control."

The synthetic stared at the hawk-faced man with soulless eyes. After a few moments' she asked in an equally soulless voice, "Should I render her unconscious?"

Rekvit paused in thought, rubbing at his angular face. "Yes," he said eventually, "but don't bloody well kill her. The boss wants her alive and intact. Got it?"

"Yes," the synthetic woman replied and immediately began tightening her neck hold. Kaia's struggles became more desperate, her expression even more strained.

Cal had seen enough. His body felt ready to explode with strength, and the sight of Kaia's desperation only fuelled it further. He had no plan, just instincts, perhaps some dirty tricks, and hopefully some blind luck.

He pushed his finger against the sphere's door release and leapt out.

Jumper stared up at the dark, red skies, disturbed by the lack of dropships. Picking up his longeye bliss rifle, he set its sights on the Insidion base. Still no activity. The helix bomb had definitely detonated; the Star Splinter's scanners had confirmed that. Then, just to be sure, he had popped off a couple of test rounds with a pulse rifle. He'd never particularly liked the pulse weapons, but his relief at its functioning was palpable. The Insidions wouldn't remain idle for long, and he suspected their reaction would be brutal when it came. That thought probably should have caused a good deal of fear, but that was a hard emotion give in to when you had Xcel searing through your veins.

Shifting the rifle's sights, he focused on the prisoners emerging from the swirling clouds of grit. As planned, they were running across the harsh landscape in droves, directly towards the plateau on which the Star Splinter sat.

"How they doing?" Toker asked. He looked energized to his core and was pacing back and forth along the rows of weapon-filled crates. "Are they on their way?"

"Oh, they're on their way alright," Jumper replied, "and they're moving fast. Shouldn't be long before we're dishing out weapons." He twisted around to his left. Viktor's large, mechanical battle spider was hunched next to him on its eight, sword-like legs. "Any sign of the dropships yet, Viktor?"

"Still nothing." Viktor's reply had a metallic shrill as it sounded from the battle spider's sound emitter. "I don't understand. They should have activated them ages ago. Something must have gone wrong."

"Ain't nothin' gone wrong," Eddy said casually. She was squatting down next to her beloved Gibson gun and staring toward the approaching storm. "Cal and the lady doc can take care of things. They're probably just hanging back a bit, give us a chance to get some fighting in, test out the enemy." She sniffed then spat on one of the gun's barrels and gave it a vigorous rub with her sleeve. "Course, the time them bloody aliens is takin', we ain't likely to see any action."

"Can't *you* activate the dropships, Vik?" Toker asked hopefully.

"No. We've already talked about this. Only *The Orillian's* systems can activate them." The boy was tetchy, obviously frustrated that a technological problem had arisen beyond his ability to remedy.

"Okay, bro, take it easy. How's about contacting them?"

"No good. We're still cloaked; so is *The Orillian*. If we start communicating, then our cover could be blown, and then the Insidions might—"

"Sure, sure, I get it."

Jumper had a bad feeling the boy was right. Something must have gone wrong on board *The Orillian*, something pretty damn serious to prevent Cal from launching those dropships.

"What should we do, Jumper?" Toker asked, stopping his pacing to look at him expectantly.

Jumper kept his face as calm and composed as ever though his mind was anything but. He wasn't keen on this new role as leader. His talents lay in survival, one-on-one combat, and making solo tactical decisions when the problem was laid out in front of him or indeed actively trying to eat him. But these decisions with multiple factors and other people involved... It wasn't his strong point. He'd spent decades on his own, ordering and answering to no one but himself. Whatever decisions he made right at this moment would affect thousands. The pressure was a little overwhelming.

He began to sift logically through his options and did his best to bring his whirling mind in line with his outward expression. Before he could manage it, however, Viktor's shrill, metallic voice interrupted his efforts. "There's something... Something's happening!"

"The dropships?" Jumper asked hopefully. But as he said it, he realized that wasn't what the boy wasn't referring to. Even the distortion of the mechanical spider's sound emitter didn't mask the panic in his young friend's voice.

"The Insidion base...one of the blocks...it's coming apart."

Laurence's eyes felt raw from all the rock dust that had assaulted them. They were watering like crazy, making it hard to see, a problem that the constant flashes of lightning wasn't helping. *Damn this bloody dry storm.* He'd been right; it seemed Mother Nature did want to join the battle. The winds were the worst he'd ever witnessed, and they seemed insistent on refusing a direction. Even with the Xcel serum feeding his muscles, he'd almost been blown off his feet numerous times already.

In two bounds, he leaped to the top of a pile of boulders and scanned the landscape.

"We're lucky the twins are in full force," Tark shouted at him. The little man had remained close by his side the entire time.

"Yes," Laurence replied, looking to the horizon. "At least something's working in our favor." The two monstrous volcanoes that dominated the northern horizon were spewing huge volumes of fiery magma into the dark skies. He and Cal had chosen the massive twin peaks as a point of reference for the escape.

Trying to ignore the temptation to rub his eyes, Laurence looked around at the scores of running bodies. At first, most of his fellows had become confused and scattered within the blizzard of rock dust, but now, as they gained distance from the prison camp's mine, the air had become clearer, and all eyes had fixed on the gap between the two massive volcanoes. If Callum had remained true to his word, a great hoard of weapons lay ahead as well as a fleet of dropships.

"Shouldn't be far now," he shouted.

"Let's hope not," Tark replied, an edge to his voice.

Laurence turned and followed the little man's gaze. He was looking at the distant alien base, ghostly pale in the gray air. Something was happening to one of the block-like structures: Multiple silver dots were breaking away from it and rapidly rising into the rumbling, black storm clouds above. Laurence felt his heart thud faster and stronger. "They're coming," he bellowed.

With Tark close behind, he leapt off his perch and joined the mass of bodies surging like a swarm controlled by one brain, their destination clear.

Chapter Forty-Three
UNINVITED

As he leaped from the platform, Cal had already decided not to go for any of the unsuspecting pirate's guns. There was no way of knowing if they were charged or even loaded, and he was unwilling to risk his element of surprise. With his back turned to the sync sphere, the man knew nothing of Cal's presence until he'd slammed into him. Wrapping an arm around the pirate's neck, Cal used his other to reach for one of his many knives. With the benefit of the Xcel, his actions were lightning fast, and before the bewildered man could register what was happening, Cal had withdrawn one of the knives and thrown it at the woman with the short, spiky hair. Whether due to blind luck or the Xcel fine-tuning his abilities, the heavy knife span through the air in a blur until the metal handle struck the woman directly on the forehead. She was unconscious before hitting the floor.

Making a clumsy grapple for one of his holstered pistols, the pirate in Cal's grasp tried to twist around, almost breaking his own neck in the process. With no intention of fighting fair, Cal slammed his forehead into the side of the man's head, knocking him out cold. Before dropping to the floor, however, the pirate's body convulsed as multiple pulse blasts tore mercilessly through his frame. Having predicted this, Cal was already throwing himself to the ground, aiming for the relative safety of the nearest console.

He wasn't quick enough.

The pulse blast spun his body in mid-air, and as he crashed to the deck, a searing pain ignited across his ribs on the right side of his body. Even with the benefit of the Xcel, the pain was excruciating. Ignoring it as best he could, he scrambled back against the console, pressing himself hard against its lifesaving cover. Pounding vibrations rocked his spine as the pulse blasts pummelled the console. He stayed put, putting his full trust in the robustness of *The Orillian's* construction.

At least the helix bomb had done its job. That was something.

Eventually, the blasting ceased and was replaced by a stony, almost eerie silence. The acrid smell of burning flesh filled Cal's nose. He looked at his torso to see that the right side of his sync suit had been scorched away, revealing a bloody mess. He winced, eyes pressed shut as he swore under his breath. Even with the Xcel, he'd not been quick enough. But he wasn't finished yet, not by a long shot. Trying to push the thoughts of the injury and its implications aside, he searched for Kaia's discarded control wand. As it turned out, he was practically sitting on the little device. Gratefully, he plucked it off the floor and slid it through a hole in his sleeve—a small piece of luck in a huge crap pile of misfortune.

A man's voice broke the silence. "Guns are working again, boss."

"No shit, you imbecile. No one fires another shot 'til I give the order, got it?"

Cal recognized the voice; it was the hawk-faced man, Rekvit. Unfortunately, he suddenly sounded far more composed than Cal would have liked.

"Do you hear that, young man?" Rekvit shouted. "No one's going to fire another shot until I give the order. Now, I won't give that order if you go ahead and stand up with your hands raised."

Ignoring the empty promise, Cal fixed his attentions on the lifeless form of the pirate who lay sprawled in a bloody mess close by. It seemed his appearance had shocked them enough that they'd accidentally shot their comrade, or maybe they just didn't give a shit. Grinding his teeth as his pain flared, Cal stretched out a leg, hooked his foot under the strap of the bolt rifle still slung across the dead man's back, and pulled the body towards him. Even with his injury, the Xcel made the act virtually effortless.

"I reckon he might be dead, Rek. I think I caught him with one my shots."

"I don't think so," Rekvit replied. "You're not dead, are you, young man? If you're unable to stand, just go ahead and yell out or crawl your way into the open, and we'll come and patch you up."

If there wasn't so much at stake and he wasn't in so much pain, Cal might have laughed at that.

"Don't waste our time," Rekvit continued. "You're sorely outnumbered. How long do you think this will last?"

Cal set about removing all of the dead pirate's guns. As well as the old-fashioned bolt rifle, there was a five-click pulse rifle and a pair of identical, needle-shot pistols, all charged and fully loaded. Ripping a sleeve from his sync suit, he folded it and, with a sharp intake of breath, pressed it against the wound in his side. Then he used the strap from the old bolt rifle to bind it. It would go at least some way to stemming the blood flow. Carefully slinging the five-click pulse rifle over his back, he took up a pistol in each hand and readied himself. He would need to let them know he was armed and most definitely dangerous.

"I'm running out of patience," Rekvit called out.

Turning to face the console, Cal raised a pistol above its edge and, careful not to aim anywhere near Kaia, fired a torrent of random shots. Confident that the occupants of the room would be taking cover, he raised the second pistol, peered over the console, and ceased his random fire. He waited. There…a raised head, one of the men near the big screens. Cal shot him and was down behind his console again before the inevitable barrage of return fire.

A little less outnumbered, he thought with grim satisfaction. He'd always been a good shot, but the Xcel made him a marksman without equal.

"Fuck! Diggs is down, Rek. Bastard shot him right in the head."

"Shut up, and stay put 'til I say."

There was a long silence.

Taking advantage of the moment of calm, Cal considered his next move. He'd be damn lucky to pull off the same trick twice. To stand any chance, he'd have to get inventive.

"That was a fine shot, friend," Rekvit shouted. His voice was still calm, but it was fast sounding forced, an underlying edge of anger and possibly fear. "Might be that you were just lucky, though, eh?"

"I'm saving my luck for a difficult fight," Cal shouted back, trying his best not to let his pain seep into his voice. "Let the girl go, and I'll allow you all to leave unhurt." As soon as he'd finished shouting the words, he began shifting himself along the floor with as much stealth as he could manage. None of the pirates would take his words seriously—no more than he had theirs—but with any luck, they'd keep their weapons trained on the spot they'd heard his voice.

The console behind which he'd taken cover was the first in a long line. They curved around the center of the lab in a wide arc, and if he stayed low, he could move alongside them without revealing his position. The fact that his left side felt as though it was being eaten away by acid didn't make stealth an easy thing to achieve. Nor did the pulse rifle slung over his back, but fortunately, any noise he made was drowned out by Rekvit's loud rambling. He was still making a feeble attempt to weed him out without losing any more men. Cal knew his type well. His concern would be for his reputation rather than the wellbeing of his comrades. He also suspected that there was a good deal of fear encouraging the man's efforts. *The boss wants her alive and intact.* Even in the pirate world, there was always someone to answer to, and when mistakes were made in that world, a shot through the head was the preferred method of demotion.

"The girl is important to you," Rekvit bellowed. "I'd hate to be forced to treat her the same way you did Diggs. She has such a pretty head. It would be a shame to ruin it."

Cal gritted his teeth. *Empty threats.* He already knew Kaia was valuable to them. Their intentions had become as clear as day. Technology was their bounty, and based on their ability to track and commandeer *The Orillian,* and the fact they had two synthetics, made it clear they were way beyond the average crew of pirates. They wanted the ship and, with it, Kaia's wealth of knowledge. Cal shook his head. The insight wasn't going to help him now. Pushing the thoughts aside, he did his best to focus on the task in hand.

"Maybe I should just have my synthetic slowly squeeze the life out of her. What d'you think about that?" Rekvit shouted.

Cal continued to drag himself along, breath rattling in his chest. Even bolstered by the Xcel, he was starting to feel his strength wane—although a conjured mental image of throwing Rekvit out of an airlock went a little way to rekindling it. Never had he felt so much hate for a man so quickly. Still, it was good of him to keep drowning out all other sounds with his constant prattle.

"I think you must like the idea," Rekvit continued. "You must, else you'd be standing up by now with your hands held high." Cal was starting to detect a desperate edge to his tone.

Finally, he reached the end of the arc of consoles. Whatever the hell his next move was going to be, he'd have to pull it off quick. Rekvit's men were likely creeping around the lab by now in order to flush him out, and it wouldn't be long before they spotted the long smear of blood he'd left across the gleaming white floor. Remaining low, he maneuvered himself around the edge of the last console until he was sat at the front end of its base. It was painfully frustrating that the means for activating the dropships was just above his head. Even to stand for a couple of seconds, however, would have been suicide.

"Maybe I'll just have to send one of my synthetics after *you*. That's right, young chap, you heard right: a *synthetic*. In fact, I have two of them here with me. Have you ever witnessed the speed and strength of a synthetic?'

There it was. Cal had been wondering how long it would take for the synthetic card to be pulled.

"What d'you think? Should I order one of them to come and pluck you out of your hiding place?"

Again, empty threats. At least, Cal hoped. He strongly suspected that Rekvit—at least for the time being—wouldn't risk a valuable synthetic while he still had expendable men at his disposal. The synthetic would very likely succeed in carrying out the order, but Cal was armed, and even synthetics weren't infallible to a direct blast from a five-click pulse rifle; a lucky shot could cause severe damage. Just in case he was wrong, he placed the two pistols on the floor and un-slung the pulse rifle from his back, feeling a little dizzy as he did so. The blood loss was starting to take its toll. If he didn't start shooting again soon, they'd be on him.

Bloody get in gear, Cal.

Pulling Kaia's control wand from his sleeve, he shifted himself to the edge of the console and made sure he had a decent view of the large, high screens on the far side of the lab. Pointing the wand, he brought up a live, wide angled view of the entire lab. With their attentions fully focused on the center of the lab, neither Rekvit nor any of his crew reacted to the screen, and despite its distance, it was large enough that Cal could easily make out their positions. Nice of them to come wearing dark clothing to a largely white lab.

Realizing the futility of coaxing Cal out with words, Rekvit had gone quiet. On the screen, Cal could see him busily directing his men with silent but rigorous hand signals. Seemingly unwilling to risk his own hide, the hawk-faced man had remained near the entrance. As Cal had predicted, Rekvit's three remaining men were cautiously inching their way around the lab and towards its center. Two of them held twin pistols while the third favored a single pulse rifle.

Cal was relieved to see that the two synthetics remained near Rekvit. One of them was still tapping away at a console while the one holding Kaia stood close behind. Kaia was unconscious now, and the synthetic had thrown her limp body over her shoulder. Cal gritted his teeth. *She's alive. That's what counts.* He brought his attention back to the human threat.

With a tight grip on the pulse rifle and finger firm on its trigger, he waited patiently for the three armed men to move a little closer. Remaining focused on the distant screen, he pinpointed the console behind which he was hiding and judged the positioning of the men. As he'd hoped, their attentions were firmly set on the spot where he'd shouted his reply. Taking a couple of quick breaths, he swiftly stood and, with a calm efficiency that came from years of experience, thrust the muzzle of his five-click pulse rifle in the direction of the nearest man. He squeezed the trigger once and was back down behind the console before the weapon's blast had even stopped echoing around the room.

"What the hell?"

"*Christ*, Borlen's down."

"Shit…*shit*. Where did the shot come from?"

"Bugger this…"

"Hold your position, Deets, or I'll bloody well shoot you myself."

Cal managed a grim smile as he listened to the panic he'd created. He peered at the distant screen—his lifeline—and watched the men cowering behind consoles and workstations.

"It's only one bloody man. Keep your shit together." Rekvit was now far from composed and had given up trying to hide the fact.

"How the hell did he aim so quick?"

"I said keep your shit together, and hold your positions."

Cal listened and continued to study the screen. Despite Rekvit's threats, one of the men was clumsily retreating towards the lab's exit.

"Damn it, Deets, I said—"

But Deets didn't hear; Cal's next shot had caught the man in the left shoulder, and he was spinning to the floor with a wail.

"*Christ*," Rekvit cried disbelievingly. Even though the hawk-faced man was all the way over the other side of the lab, Cal could see him stooping down to take cover.

The shot man was writhing on the floor, clutching at his shoulder and bellowing in pain. Cal could sympathize. If it weren't for the Xcel, he was certain that his own pain would have rendered him unconscious long ago. The man was definitely no longer a threat, which left only Rekvit and one other. Cal had a feeling that Rekvit wasn't the sort to dive into the fray. More a long-range leader armed with longeye goggles and a comm unit. Then of course there were the synthetics, but Cal was doing his best not to think of them. Not easy with the remaining pirate screaming at Rekvit to let the cybernetic women off their leash.

"I'm tellin' ya, Rek, this ain't right. This guy ain't right. No one can move that quick and shoot that easy." The man had to shout to be heard over the cries of pain from his floored comrade.

Cal kept his eyes glued to the screen, eagerly awaiting a chance to take the man out. Unfortunately, fear was keeping him well and truly concealed behind a work station.

"Please, just send the synthetics. For all we know, he's some sort of male synthetic himself."

Even with his boosted hearing, Cal could barely make out the words over the injured man's cries, which were fast becoming a shrieking howl.

"Shut your face. I give the Goddamned orders," Rekvit reminded his last man.

"What'd you say?"

"I said… *Christ*," Rekvit barked in frustration. "Can you see Deets?"

"Yeah, I can see him. His bloody arm's hangin' off. He's wrigglin' on the floor like some sort of flippin' eel."

"Take care of him," Rekvit bellowed. "I can't bloody well hear myself think over that racket."

"Take care of him?"

"Yes, *fucking take care of him*."

A few moments later, Cal heard two rounds from a pulse blast and saw the injured man shudder twice.

Again, the room became deathly quiet.

Cal clutched the five-click pulse rifle tight to his chest and shifted himself a little to get a better view of the distant screen—in particular, a better view of Rekvit. Surely, the man must have learned his lesson by now. Surely, he was ready to put the problem into the hands of his precious synthetics. Cal watched closely, trying to get an idea of the hawk-faced man's intentions. *Please let him be the incompetent prick I hope he is.*

The silence was broken by the synthetic at the console. "There's activity on the planet surface."

Rekvit whipped his head around. "What kind of activity?" There was fear in his voice. "The aliens'?"

"Yes, multiple parts of their base have detached and mobilized."

Cal felt his stomach lurch.

"*Shit.*" Rekvit spat. "Are they coming this way?"

"No, they are remaining well within the planet's atmosphere. But I have no way of assessing whether this vessel remains undetectable."

Rekvit's tone was dropping, and Cal struggled to hear what was being said. He stared at Rekvit's strained face on the screen. *What's his next move? What the hell's my next move?* Out of habit, Cal looked down and checked his weapon's charge even though he knew it was full. He squeezed his eyes shut and tried to force a solution. So far, he'd done well in disabling the threat, but his injury was serious, and unless Rekvit ordered a full retreat, the worst was still to come.

"We're leaving," Rekvit suddenly shouted, causing Cal to hold his breath in anticipation.

"*What?*" his last man cried from his hiding place. "How…how do I get to the exit?"

"That's your problem," Rekvit replied tersely before turning toward the synthetic holding Kaia. "Give me the girl. You two stay here, and once you've dealt with the asshole with the big gun, finish commandeering this ship and follow."

Goddamn it, no. Cal strained to hear every word and watched with growing trepidation as both cybernetic women nodded their understanding. Then the synthetic holding Kaia reached up and pulled her off her shoulder like a rag doll.

"We'll rendezvous back at Hex," Rekvit continued as he took hold of Kaia. Then, after a brief glance in Cal's direction, he said, "Try not to get yourselves shot. The boss will overlook a few dead idiots, but if either of you get damaged, there'll be hell to pay."

Again, the two synthetics nodded in unison. And with that, Rekvit turned to leave.

Anger boiled up in Cal as he watched the man carry Kaia off through the exit. He gritted his teeth, his head suddenly pounding. It took all of his will to not to jump up and attempt a last-ditch effort at saving her. He pictured himself unleashing everything he had at the synthetics and running straight for the bastard. Every instinct screamed at him to do just that, but he forced the feeling down. He wouldn't stand a chance. The synthetics would take him out before he got anywhere near.

He'd failed her.

Anger threatened to overwhelm him then, but he extinguished it with force of will. *She's still alive,* he reminded himself, something that couldn't be said about him for much longer if he didn't pull it together. He shook his head defiantly. He had to think, had to focus. Kaia wasn't the only one relying on him, not by a long shot. If he didn't come up with a strategy, the synthetics would kill him efficiently and without the slightest remorse. And if that happened, the fate of those down on the planet surface wouldn't be much better.

A sudden commotion made him whip his head toward the screen. Rekvit's last man was making a dash for the exit, sending lab equipment flying as he did so—maybe a desperate attempt at distraction or just plain clumsy panic. Whatever it was, it didn't matter. Cal let him go.

Doing his best to gain control over his anger and his fear, Cal watched the two cybernetic killers on the screen. They were moving slowly, skirting in opposite directions around the room. Then, in precise unison, the pair turned towards the center of the lab and began to stalk him.

Chapter Forty-Four
CHAOS

Jumper had never witnessed such utter chaos. He had climbed onto a rock to get a better view of the situation and didn't like what he saw one bit. The multitude of cube ships that had detached from the distant Insidion base were now dropping from the thick storm clouds. The ships were large, maybe three times the size of the Star Splinter, their smooth, gleaming surfaces flaring bright under the angry sky's white lightning. The ships were merciless in their descent, coming down swiftly, crushing many of the escaping prisoners beneath their huge, flat hulls.

As planned, the prisoners were converging on the crates and passing the weapons back. Unfortunately, that crowd was now far larger than had originally been intended. Only a carefully selected portion of the escaping prisoners were supposed to be arming themselves. Those selected were then to offer cover, should it be needed, while the remaining boarded the dropships. But with no dropships evident, panic and confusion had erupted, and the crates had become the sole focus of attention. Bodies were clambering, limbs were flailing. Desperate fingers clawed, searching for that cold, reassuring gun metal. Jumper, Eddy, and Toker had done their best to redistribute the crates, but too many were converging all at once.

In a desperate attempt to make room, Jumper had requested that Viktor use his mechanical combat spider to tow some of the crates further afield.

Pivoting on the rock, Jumper turned towards the Star Splinter. Despite his proximity, his eyes couldn't register it. As well as the ghosting net, he had instructed Viktor to create a temporary force field around the ship to ensure it didn't become overrun by the confused crowds. The expanse of flat ground behind the cloaked ship was still distressingly empty. He glanced up to the skies and again found them devoid of dropships. Twisting back to the chaos, he mouthed a silent curse.

Up to this point, the Xcel serum had served the escaping prisoners well; getting them swiftly over the jagged landscape to their destination in a fraction of the time it would have otherwise taken them. But now, with no dropships to converge on, the Xcel was proving a hindrance. Being their first time experiencing its effects, many of the men and women were having trouble keeping control. They were far stronger and faster, but there was suddenly no room to allow for mistakes. Further back, bodies were tumbling and crashing all over the place perhaps due to fear and confusion or maybe an over-eagerness to fight. Closer to the crates, however, the escapees had become pressed together like sardines in a can. Weapons were being fumbled as they were passed back, resulting in the occasional mistaken discharge. Most of the blasts disappeared harmlessly into the rumbling skies, but many tore into the mass of bodies, causing countless early casualties.

Trying his best to ignore the heaving chaos, Jumper took advantage of his elevated position and concentrated on the Insidion cube ships. Those already landed had opened up, one full side of their hulls dissolving away. Peering through his bliss rifle's sights, he swore—audibly this time—as he witnessed giant, crab-like creatures pouring out of the cubes in nightmarish swarms. The huge beasts had dark red bodies with dirty yellow stripes crossing their broad, flat backs. Upon each back were three Carcarrions, all crouched menacingly on the juddering mounts and ready to pounce.

"Something wrong?" Toker cried up to him.

Jumper looked down from his perch at his young friend's perspiring, grubby face. He and Eddy had been working tirelessly handing out the weapons, Toker shouting words of encouragement and reminding them to pass the weapons back while Eddy shoved weapons roughly into the reaching hands, growling at anyone whose eyes fell admiringly on the Gibson gun nestled at her feet.

"We might have unwanted company very soon," Jumper shouted down, making sure Eddy could also hear and that she was paying attention.

"The big silver ships?" Toker asked, looking skyward.

Jumper nodded. 'Remember, no heroics. We stick together and stay close to the Star Splinter at all times. As soon as it gets too hairy, we get on board. You hear that, Eddy?"

Eddy was practically falling headfirst into a crate in order to reach the last of the weapons. When she re-emerged, she looked up at him with a shrug. "Whatever you say, J." She shouted it with little conviction, and Jumper didn't believe for a second that the girl had taken his words in. He watched as she turned back to the mass of reaching hands and practically threw a rifle in the face of an escapee. "Get shootin'," she growled at the bewildered looking man.

Toker shook his head and looked up at Jumper. "I'll keep an eye on her."

Another cube ship dropped rapidly from the sky. This one was far closer than the rest, and Jumper had no need of his bliss rifle's sights to see the hull open up.

"They're getting close," Toker cried out and without waiting for a reply said, "What the hell happens if one of the bloody great things comes down on our heads?'

The words had barely left Toker's lips before a rapidly increasing roar sounded overhead. Jumper snapped his head up to see a silver, square doorway in the black, tumulus sky. It was growing larger by the second. "*Run, everyone run,*" he bellowed, and he wasn't the only one to shout it.

Leaping off his rock, he was only vaguely aware of the mass panic erupting around him; his eyes were fixed solely on Toker and Eddy. The huge Gibson gun was already in Eddy's Xcel-strengthened hands, and she was in the process of directing it upwards towards the fast-dropping ship. Toker, having wrapped his arms around the girl, was doing his best to drag her away. Seconds later, Jumper was joining him in the effort, practically lifting the girl off her feet as the cube drew nearer.

Jumper felt Eddy's tiny frame shuddering in his arms as the Gibson gun spewed out a massive surge of explosive pulse rounds. As he and Toker stumbled wildly across the hard, jagged terrain, Jumper saw countless prisoners struggling around and over the weapon crates to join them in running for their lives. It was suddenly getting very hot. He risked a glance up; the smooth, silvery hull was close, so close, he could make out the distorted reflections of pale, fleeing bodies among the black rocks. He briefly wondered how the hell the strange ship was flying. He could see no thrust jets, no boosters.

"Faster. We've got to run fucking faster," Toker screamed in his ear.

Jumper couldn't have said it better himself.

He wondered if Eddy was even aware that she would very possibly be squashed flat in the next few seconds. Whether she did or not, her finger didn't ease off the Gibson gun's twin triggers for an instant. She was even continuing her fire as he and Toker threw her through the air—even if they were crushed, she might just make it clear.

As he made his final leap, Jumper's ears seemed to filter out the thundering storm and the cacophony of guns and ships. All he heard was Eddy's unrelenting battle cry and the unique sound of Toker's half-scream, half-roar. He hoped to God that those kids would survive. He simply couldn't imagine a life without them.

Then every sound was overwhelmed by a horrendous boom: the sound of a massive ship meeting hard ground.

Laurence hurriedly picked himself up. He'd misjudged one of his Xcel-enhanced jumps and had gone head over heels as he'd hit the ground. The wind was gusting stronger than ever, and it didn't help that there were countless others running and leaping around him. Collisions were plentiful. There was blood pouring from a gash on his forehead. He couldn't really feel the injury just as he wasn't feeling the myriad of others over his body, but this one was troublesome as the blood continuously dribbled into his eyes. He dabbed at the gash with his sleeve in an unsuccessful attempt to stem the flow.

Tark landed nimbly by his side. His friend had adapted well to his new strength and speed and was wielding it with infinitely more style and grace than Laurence could ever hope to achieve. Without a word, the little man quickly tore a strip off his shirt and bandaged Laurence's head. "Should do the trick."

Laurence opened his mouth, but his thanks were interrupted by a pulse blast that ripped through the small space between their heads. He stumbled back in surprise, falling on his backside. Seeming unfazed by the pulse blast, Tark didn't shift an inch.

"It's getting pretty chaotic up there," the little man observed, looking towards the increasingly dense mass of bodies ahead. "Quite a crowd."

Laurence picked himself up and nodded. "They've got nowhere to go; there's still no dropships," he shouted back, trying to sound calm. "And those attack ships are causing a mass panic." He looked back at one of the nearest cubes. "Did you see what's coming out of them?"

Before Tark could answer, a man crashed to the ground in front of them. Laurence reached down to pick him up.

"Run. They're coming. The crabs are coming this way!" The man was young, his eyes wide as he looked desperately at Laurence.

Laurence laid a reassuring hand on his shoulder. "Go get yourself a weapon, son. We'll be barbecuing the bloody great beasts in tonight's victory feast."

The words, and the confidence in which they were said, extinguished a little of the fear in the man's eyes. He straightened up and managed a shaky salute before bounding cautiously towards the heaving crowd.

Tark shot Laurence an approving smile. "Nicely said."

Laurence nodded. Even as the words had left his mouth, it struck him that they'd sounded like something his father would have said. Even his tone of voice had begun to resemble his father's.

A distant screeching accompanied by multiple human shouts seemed to hitch a ride on the howling wind. Laurence turned to see a scramble of people surging over a distant, rocky ridge. Three of the massive, crab-like creatures stomped among them, Carcarrions leaping off their backs to land mercilessly on their victims. Some of the escapees were running as fast as their legs could carry them. Others were putting their faith in their new power and defiantly turning to fight. Laurence admired their bravery, but he could also see it was suicide.

"We should hurry. We won't stand a chance without a weapon."

Tark gave a nod of agreement, and together, they leapt off the rock.

A few minutes later, Laurence was deep in the crowd. He'd given up trying to control the direction he moved. Whether he was heading the right way, he had no idea. The dense mass of bodies was so tightly packed, they seemed one entity. A great number of weapons had already come his way, but reasoning that those nearest the attacking aliens would need them the most, he'd passed them all on and hoped to God they weren't being passed in a circle. He wondered how Tark was doing, he'd lost sight of the little man a while back.

Suddenly, Laurence's back pressed up against something that wasn't flesh and bone. He was rammed in so tight, however, that it took him a few attempts to turn around. When he eventually managed it, he found he'd been carried right to the source of the weapon distribution. Looking left and right, he could see a long line of large, metal crates. Bodies were pressed up hard against every single one, and those who were lucky enough to be facing in the right direction were reaching in and pulling out a myriad of weapons, some of which Laurence didn't even recognize. The crate he was jammed up against was almost empty, but it had never been the plan for every person to be armed.

On the opposite side of the crate, he saw a small, spiky-haired woman who was practically toppling head over heels in order to grab the last of the remaining weapons. When she popped up, Laurence was surprised to see how young she was, little more than a girl. Despite her dirty face and the slightly crazed look in her eyes, she was really rather pretty. Shooting her a quick, encouraging smile, Laurence leaned over in an attempt to grab a stinger rifle that he'd spotted. Despite his best efforts, however, the weapon remained a good finger length away from his grasp. Frustrated, he straightened up, and it was just as well he did. The wild-looking girl threw a pulse rifle at his face without the slightest warning. If it hadn't been for his enhanced reactions, Laurence supposed that he'd have been relying on his fellows to carry his unconscious body to the dropships. The girl was shouting something inaudible at him. The expression on her face suggested they weren't gentle words of encouragement.

Awkwardly passing the pulse rifle over his head, Laurence became aware of a strange, roaring noise, and those around him, including the wild looking girl, turned their attentions heavenward.

His gut lurched as he looked up, already knowing full well what he'd see. One of those huge, bloody ships was coming right down on their heads. "Move! Everyone, get the hell out of here." Some were slow to react and continued to stare up in horror. Others were already trying to climb over the crates without much success.

His instinct taking over, Laurence reached across to the inside corner of the crate, ripped aside a safety catch, and pressed a button. Immediately, the crate gave way, collapsing as far as the remaining weapons inside would allow. Like water through a breached dam, Laurence and those around him burst through the gap. A man fell and would have been trampled underfoot if Laurence hadn't grabbed him and hauled him to his feet.

"Run. Run," Laurence bellowed and, taking his own advice, began scrambling over the rocks.

Just ahead, a torrent of rapid pulse fire from what must have been a massive gun was lighting up the increasing darkness with flashes of bright orange. But soon, even the noise of that weapon was drowned out as the roar overhead became almost deafening. Visions of being squashed flickered into Laurence's mind, but he ignored them and continued running as fast as his boosted muscles would allow. He was tempted to look up, but fearful of tripping, he forced himself not to. The ship was so close that the electric white light from the dry storm was all but blocked out. The roar above his head was merciless, threatening to burst his ear drums at any moment as an intense heat began to scorch the top of his head. Suspecting that the vessel would be crushing its way onto the rocks at any second, Laurence dove as far as his boosted, burning legs could manage.

Then, quite suddenly, every last flicker of light was completely snuffed out.

The two synthetic killers stalked like a pair of lionesses. Cal watched their progress intently on the distant screen. Fortunately, they were adopting a slow, deliberate approach, undoubtedly cautious of his five-click pulse rifle. Cal tried to ignore the increasing warm damp seeping from his injured side. He kept telling himself not to look down at the wound, but he couldn't resist a quick glance. He was a mess, that was for sure, and the pool of blood beneath him was a sickening sight.

The blood triggered a thought or, more accurately, a memory. He was standing over Laurence Decker's crumpled form, the faint buzz of cutting lasers the only sound to be heard. There was blood dripping from the man's nose and mouth, pooling on the floor where a single, white tooth settled. Despite the events happening only a handful of months ago, it felt to Cal like a different age. He had made a decision that day, a resolution to live a life free from responsibility. The thought of it almost made him smile. *The more you try to control life…* Now thousands of lives were hanging in the balance with nobody but him to tip the scales. *A whole world of responsibility.* Yes, fate really could be quite the bitch.

He took a deep breath, and the last of his lingering fear seemed to seep out of him and run dry.

An idea took shape in his mind.

As the synthetics crept nearer, Cal pulled Kaia's control wand from his sleeve and assessed his new plan. Ironically, it was the morbid thought of not being able to win this fight alone that had triggered it. It was an absurdly dangerous idea that would undoubtedly result in utter chaos followed closely by his death. But all of a sudden, he felt like going out with a bang. And just maybe, the ensuing chaos would give him those precious few moments to activate the dropships. There was really no alternative and therefore no choice.

Without further hesitation, Cal stood, feeling more than a little dizzy as he did so, and stretched both arms out in the direction of the synthetics. In his right hand, he held the five-click pulse rifle and in his left the little Godsend of a control wand. The two synthetics paused ever so briefly, assessing the threat now that he had so boldly revealed himself. The short length of their pause suggested he was barely considered a threat at all.

Cal aimed the wand directly between the lethal pair at a barrier inset within the far side wall then pressed a button. The heavy barrier immediately shot up to reveal a thick layer of smart-glass behind which was a brightly lit chamber and the crux of his plan. Once again, the two synthetics paused in their approach, one of them turning to observe the chamber. Within it, the Carcarrion drones reacted like a couple of bloodthirsty hounds as they fought against their bonds.

Much to Cal's dismay, the synthetic with the tattooed face kept her deathly stare locked on him while her partner calmly moved toward the two raging aliens. With the combined effect of the Xcel and his own adrenalin keeping him on his feet, Cal shuffled stiffly to his right and slowly and deliberately placed the pulse rifle down on a work surface. The tattooed synthetic watched his every move with cat-like precision, her focus concentrated on the control wand as he manipulated a couple more buttons and gave it a quick flick. Instantly, the far chamber's smart-glass divided and began to separate at a pace so lethargic it seemed to be giving Cal a chance to reconsider his reckless actions. Considerably less lethargic, the smart-straps binding the two Carcarrions snaked free, allowing the pair to burst forward in a furious symmetry to slam into the separating barrier. Satisfied, Cal locked eyes with the tattooed synthetic, placed the wand down, and moved back toward his console, both hands raised in a manner of truce.

She took the bait.

Finally removing her lifeless eyes from him, she turned and moved to join her twin in dealing with this new, far more dangerous threat. The Carcarrion drones were free now and moving slowly into the lab, sizing up their fearless opponents with a strange mix of caution and aggression. Cal didn't wait to observe the outcome. Instead, he turned his attentions to the console below him. He'd never been overly blessed with tech skills, and he'd need every available second to activate the dropships. Trying his best to ignore the sudden eruption of noise on the other side of the lab, he got to work.

Chapter Forty-Five
TIME TO FIGHT

The Insidion cube ship pounded into the ground with such force that it sent a huge wave of rock fragments and black dust billowing out from its edges. Just like countless others who'd been running alongside him, Jumper hit the ground only meters from one of those edges. Remaining face down, he used his arms to shield his head as fragments of rock pummelled his body. He could feel the reassuring shape of his bliss rifle pressed against his back. He couldn't remember having slung the weapon there before making his run, but after so many years of carrying it, the action had become automatic.

There were a few seconds when all that could be heard was howling wind. Then came the pop of a single, distant pulse rifle. Then a shout, or more accurately a scream. Then more gunfire, nearer this time, a repeat blaster. Then a third weapon. More shouting. More screaming.

Not wholly convinced that he wouldn't be blinded by rock dust, Jumper rolled over and cautiously opened his eyes, eager to check that a clawed fist wasn't about to make a grab for his spine. There was no immediate danger that he could see, but the air was still thick with grit. He dragged himself to his feet just as many others were doing around him. The sounds filling his ears were building in ferocity as those nearest him were also beginning to react. Peering upwards through the dust, he took in the strange, metallic wall of the cube ship stretching vertically before him. It towered further than his eyes could see, its surface seeming to swirl as if alive. With a sudden spasm of fear, it dawned on him that the giant cube had come down where the Star Splinter had been. He shook his head; no, Viktor must have taken off to avoid it.

He was about to call out to Toker and Eddy when a particularly strong gust of wind stole his words. Within seconds, the gust had whipped away the worst of the lingering rock dust to reveal a sight that was nothing short of terrifying. Well-accustomed to such sights, Jumper reacted quickly, dropping into a crouch that ensured his head remained firmly attached to his body. The huge, red claw swept over him with frightening speed. Instinctively, he dove to his left, his enhanced muscles carrying him three times the distance he'd normally achieve. In one fluid, practiced movement, he rolled up onto one knee, snatched his bliss rifle from his back, and fired a series of quick, hopeful rounds at his attacker. Then he grimaced as the bliss darts pinged harmlessly off the huge, armor-like carapace. The crab, or whatever the hell it was, stood twice the height of a man, its sprawling, spidery legs spanning a good twenty feet in width.

Jumper found all his senses suddenly overwhelmed as the people around him burst into adrenalin-fuelled action. Bright, fiery pulse rounds streaked through the air at erratic angles, many of which flew high, hitting the glimmering wall of the cube ship, which seemed to absorb them without damage. Massive red claws snapped and swished. Long, spiked legs rose and fell, thudding into the rocky terrain like thick, falling spears. Carcarrion drones began dropping down from their huge mounts, joining the fray with vicious enthusiasm.

Spinning his bliss rifle, Jumper allowed the weapon to slide through his hands until he was gripping its barrel. A Carcarrion was leaping his way, fangs bared and clawed hands stretched open. Jumper swung the weapon with all the force that his enhanced body could manage. His aim couldn't have been better, and the crunch of the rifle's butt connecting with the alien's head was sickeningly loud. There was no time to watch it crumple to the ground before another had taken its place. Falling back into the rocks, Jumper span the rifle again. The weapon's barrel was practically pressed against the attacking Carcarrion's muscled chest when the bliss dart fired.

Springing to his feet, Jumper swept his head around in a search for Eddy and Toker but was unable to see either of them. Everywhere he looked was utter mayhem with every single human now taking a stand. Despite less than half of them having a weapon, the broken prisoners had once again become highly trained soldiers. More than that, the Xcel had turned them into a blur of flesh and ragged clothing as they clashed with the alien drones. Where the humans showed incredible speed, the slower Carcarrions demonstrated raw power, swinging their clawed fists in thundering blows. The majority of the fights, however, were reaching sudden conclusions by pulse blasts or the razor sharp claws of the giant crabs. Jumper could see that the battle wouldn't last long and if it weren't for the pulse weapons would likely already be over. Even enhanced as they were, the soldiers were no match for the brute force and overwhelming numbers of the aliens.

Sweat poured from Jumper as he fired shot after shot, all the while attempting a careful retreat with those around him. Occasionally, the lumbering crabs would demonstrate their speed by lunging forward to snip off a limb or even a head. Jumper tried to shut his mind off to the brutality and concentrated on his aim. The longeye bliss rifle had always been his weapon of choice, but it was a sniper's weapon, certainly not designed for close quarter combat against an enemy that surged in such great numbers.

Seeing an opportunity, Jumper slung the rifle over his back and darted between a couple of stomping, armored legs. The crab's huge body loomed over him like a roof as he skidded across the scree to grab an idle pulse weapon. He had no idea of the name of the gun but, like all others, it had a trigger, and that was all he needed to know. There was also a single, black cylinder clamped to its side. This, he did recognize. Pulling the point grenade free, he looked up. The underside of the giant crab was full of openings where its multiple legs met its body. Without a second thought, he picked his target, activated the point grenade, and jumped up to shove the little explosive deep into one of the crevices. It stuck fast.

"*Fire in the hole,*" he bellowed as he barrelled his way out from under the beast. As he ran, a Carcarrion drone lunged at him. Swiftly bringing up his new weapon, Jumper emptied two rounds into the attacker. The drone's body was blown backwards only to meet an opposing explosive force as the point grenade detonated. To Jumper's dismay and utter amazement, the point grenade failed to blow the monstrous crab apart. A crack had appeared down the center of its huge shell, and two of its long, multi-jointed legs were now twitching on the ground, but still, the creature stood tall.

Seemingly angered by the attack, the partially mangled beast twisted slightly to fix its multitude of shiny, round eyes on Jumper. Then, its remaining legs pounded the rocks as it moved towards him like some sort of mechanical killing machine. Swiftly backing up, Jumper directed his weapon and held down the trigger. Blast after blast blackened the beast's hard frame, but it did disturbingly little damage. Even the creature's eyes seemed impenetrable. Continuing to back up, Jumper risked a few glances around, and a strange realization sank in; all the Carcarrion drones were avoiding him. It was as if the giant crab had labelled him as its opponent, and its fellows were respectfully acknowledging the claim.

In that moment, it occurred to Jumper that this was perhaps nothing more than a game to these invaders, a sort of sick entertainment. He'd already wondered why such a technologically advanced race were not making more use of weaponry. Maybe they relished the physical combat. The fact that they had created a technology to disable weaponry went a long way in supporting such a theory. These hijacked bodies were the only weapons they needed. And, if Kaia was correct in her theories, the invaders themselves would have no risk of injury or death. The bodies were simply avatars, much the same as Kaia's Infiltrator. Jumper grimaced at the realization. He wouldn't be surprised to find slug-like Insidions beneath each and every one of the massive crab carapaces. Probably an avatar of choice—the bastards were near indestructible.

With a long-practiced calm, Jumper began targeting different areas of the huge, armored body as it closed in on him, systematically searching for weakness. Before he found any, however, the gun ceased firing putting an instant dent in his calm. Glancing down, he saw a red, blinking light on its side. Throwing the useless weapon to the ground, he again snatched his bliss rifle from his back and considered the option of turning and running as fast as his Xcel-enhanced legs could manage. As appealing as the thought was, he couldn't bring himself to turn his back on the brute. Besides, someone had to take it down.

Then, someone was by his side.

Toker was holding a big, ten-click pulse rifle in his hands, the powerful blasts of which caused the massive crab not only to pause in its attack but even retreat a little. "Need some help?" he shouted, the pulse blasts illuminating his wide, determined eyes.

The sight of his young friend sent a wave of relief through Jumper. *That's one accounted for.* "Much obliged," he shouted back.

"Eddy about?"

"Yeah, but I lost her a couple of—"

Jumper's ears were suddenly assaulted by a familiar noise that completely drowned out the rest of Toker's words. The sound of the Gibson gun had the effect of demoting all the other weapons to mere toys. Looking back at the attacking crab, he saw that Eddy had somehow popped up behind the creature and leapt onto its carapace. With the Gibson gun firmly grasped in her small fists, she was directing its multiple, blazing muzzles at the crack down the center of the creature's broad back. The strength and skill the girl was demonstrating astonished Jumper, and he had to wonder whether the Xcel was having a more potent effect within her petite body. The crab reacted to the assault with a panicked, backward scuttle, which, to Jumper's horror, carried Eddy further into the enemy ranks.

"She's going to get cut off," Toker shouted between pulse blasts.

Jumper cursed. More and more Carcarrion drones were surging from the cube ship, many of them converging toward the girl atop mangled beast.

The crab shuddered to a halt. Somehow retaining her balance upon the tipping carapace, Eddy leaned all her weight against the Gibson gun as it thundered out its rounds. Then, with a loud crack, the thick shell began to separate. With its remaining legs jerking, the beast came apart like an old oak tree, splitting in two to reveal a wet, rotten interior. Her feet on either side of the crack, Eddy teetered for a moment, then she fell. Plummeting headfirst through the crab's mucus-like insides, she disappeared from view behind the swelling number of drones.

With a torrent of pulse blasts tearing through the air around them, Jumper and Toker desperately fought their way forward, all the while hoping to catch sight of Eddy. As they neared, it dawned on Jumper that the drones were now fighting among themselves, and it wasn't until he'd fired off another few bliss darts that he remembered that they weren't alone in this fight. Large numbers of Carcarrions with gray ash smeared over their muscled bodies had joined the fray with impressive ferocity. A great, roaring cheer erupted as the other soldiers joined Jumper in recognizing their allies.

Jumper turned to Toker, but his young friend had recklessly surged ahead, weapon blazing, seemingly fearless. Jumper swore and quickly picked off a few drones that were closing in on the bold young man.

Trying his best to move forward while laying down cover fire for Toker, Jumper caught sight of Eddy. The girl was covered in mucus and was darting around her fallen foe's entrails. The Gibson gun was laying idly on the ground while numerous Carcarrion drones circled menacingly. Dark yellow slime flew through the air in stringy arcs as Eddy fiercely swung her big survival knife in an effort to keep her attackers at bay and reclaim her weapon. Stopping dead in his tracks, Jumper concentrated his aim on the drones nearest her.

A cry of warning that Jumper was certain had come from Toker rang out above the din. Lowering his rifle, he immediately saw the reason for it: Distracted by her attackers, who were now backing away, Eddy had missed the huge, clawed beast that had crawled over the broken remains of its defeated kin to loom above her. Toker was already close, firing his weapon at the beast, but it was too little too late.

Jumper watched in helpless dread as Eddy suddenly became aware of the enormous foe and turned to face it, knife defiantly raised. But without her beloved Gibson gun, she didn't stand a chance. The giant crab snapped a razor sharp claw down with the speed of a viper and, in the blink of an eye, Eddy's knife-wielding arm was separated from her body and was dropping to the ground.

Jumper heard Toker scream, a sound filled with anguish and fury. Ignoring any lingering enemies, the young man was bolting toward the collapsing girl. Firing two last darts, Jumper slung his bliss rifle over his back and followed as fast as he could. By the time he'd caught up, Toker was standing over Eddy's unconscious form, wildly unloading his ten-click blasts into the eyes of the looming crab. He was roaring at the top of his lungs as if the sound might somehow increase the weapon's power.

Without missing a step, Jumper sprinted past him. Sliding beneath an attacking claw, he dove under the crab's body, hitting the ground in a roll. When he came up, the Gibson gun was in his hands. "Get her out of here," he bellowed at Toker as he directed the huge gun at the giant beast's underside and tugged on the twin triggers. The weapon's discharge rent the air and filled Jumper's vision like a blazing sun.

His whole body shuddering, Jumper turned his head to see Toker gather up Eddy's limp form and bound back towards the relative safety of the human ranks. The Gibson gun was slick with mucus and stank to the high heavens, but he gripped it tight and didn't ease his fingers off the triggers for a second. Jumper had never been one for big, noisy weapons, but as the gun's rounds hammered into the relatively soft underside of the giant beast, he had to admit, it was a hell of a way to unleash his anger.

It was dark. A complete and terrifying dark. Laurence could barely move, which, along with not being able to see, caused a sharp panic to stab at him. He forced himself to take slow breaths. They weren't deep due to a crushing pressure bearing down on his chest, but they went a little way toward diluting the panic. It was a searing heat that sent sweat trickling down his face and neck. Other than the sound of his own breathing and thumping heart, which seemed horribly amplified in the blackness, all he could hear was a distant, rapid popping. Also muffled words. Yes, he could definitely make out voices among the popping. The sounds were a huge comfort as they suggested that he wasn't dead, something he'd been questioning since coming to.

Finding that he could wriggle his left hand, he did just that. The hand met nothing but rock, but it was loose rock. He pushed with all the leverage and strength at his disposal. He felt weak, but something was cracking, giving way. Then, a long crevice opened up, and a spear of light struck him, causing his thumping heart to soar. It was a flickering light but bright as it penetrated a tiny, jagged gash in the rocks maybe three or four meters ahead. The gap brought with it louder, clearer sounds too. The muffled voices were now cries and yells, mixing with the rapid blasts of heavy gunfire. It sounded like chaos. But it also sounded like salvation.

It began to dawn on Laurence just how lucky he was to be alive. That bloody great cube had landed right on top of him. The fact he'd fallen into a suitably deep crevice was nothing short of a miracle. Most of the countless others fleeing alongside him certainly wouldn't have been so lucky. But of course, he was still buried. Those countless others might've had the luckier deal yet.

Wriggling his entire body, he managed to displace more rocks. He coughed and spluttered as they crumbled around him, causing little plumes of dust. Doing his best to blink away the grit, he kept his watery eyes on the flashing light that penetrated the gap like a guiding strobe. He could still barely move, but at least he *could* move, and every inch he shifted was a blessing. Soon, he managed to turn the shifting into a sort of forward shuffle, panic and determination battling it out in his head with every inch moved. Unfortunately, by the time he reached the light-filled gap, panic had well and truly won.

No, please no. The gap was too small, too small by a long shot. Laurence desperately peered through the gap. He saw figures. There were Carcarrions, hundreds of them like fast-moving shadows against the bright flashes of lightning and gun fire. He could see other moving shapes too, but those didn't make sense: huge, dark red things that must have been a trick of his grit-filled eyes.

All of a sudden, he wanted to cry. This was too much, too great a test for his newfound bravery. Surely, even his father would have given in to fear at this. *Buried alive... God no.* He sucked in a few shuddering breaths. Then, instead of crying, he found himself letting out a long, low growl. Anger was taking hold, bubbling up from the depths of his mind. If nothing else, it proved a blessed relief from the fear. There was no way he'd go out like this, not after all he'd been through, not after all he'd grown.

Urgently trying to steel himself, Laurence bent—practically contorted—his arms to feel above his head. There was a smooth, unyielding ceiling: the hull of the cube ship. He began slamming his palms against it, pounding at it with everything he had. Then he gave the rocks around the tiny gap the same treatment, letting his rage team up with a sudden burst of adrenalin to fuel his strength. Pushing, pounding, heaving as silent prayers repeated in his mind. He directed the prayers not just to God but to *all* the gods, to anyone, anything that had the power move a mountain.

The rocks didn't budge an inch.

The panic returned then like an invisible claw come to grip him around the chest and squeeze away any last drops of courage. Frantically, Laurence increased his efforts, slamming his elbows, knees, and mistakenly his head, against the walls of his tiny prison. The serum still in his system gave him strength, but his flesh and bones couldn't match it. Blood began running down his arms and legs, and only after he felt some knuckles and an elbow crack did he force himself to stop. He wanted to cry out for help or at least for someone who could ensure he didn't die alone, but as hard as he looked, he could see no humans among the outside chaos.

Eventually, with his breaths nothing but ragged gasps, Laurence dropped his head and rested it against a bloody forearm. He lay still for a while, the sounds of the outside chaos echoing around his little prison. So close but a world away. His body felt numb, a numbness that was blessedly creeping into his mind. Part of him still wanted to cry, but a larger part of him decided to simply close his eyes and quietly accept his fate.

Seconds later—or perhaps hours—Laurence's eyes snapped open.

An explosion was rending the air...no, maybe an earthquake. The ground was shaking, causing his rocky cocoon to crumble. Then, the ground began to shift, rocks began to churn, twisting him like an insect caught in a pepper grinder. Laurence broke his silence then. He screamed as loud as his raw throat could manage. Screamed for someone to help him, anyone, even if was an enemy wanting the pleasure of killing him, anything but being buried alive. He called out Tark's name, then random names, all those he'd helped in recent days, all those he'd been a leader to. Some leader he was now. Every muscle in his body burned in strain as he attempted to push, crawl, heave himself through the crumbling rock, through the gap to the outside world.

Even in his panic, Laurence could see that the gap had widened. Frantically, he thrust one arm out into the open air, his free hand finding a solid, jutting hand hold. Roaring with effort, he pulled with all his might. But the weight of the disintegrating rocks on his legs and body was too great. Then, the rocks were coming down on his neck then his head. He tried once more to cry out, but fragments of rock were pressing into his face and entering his mouth.

Then the light was gone.

Laurence remained conscious. The relatively cool, gusting air of the outside world teased the skin of his blood and sweat-soaked free arm. Possibly due to shock, the sensation felt oddly pleasant. Then, there was a similarly odd sense of disappointment as a new pressure began to bear down on the arm. It seemed fate wasn't going to allow death until every inch of him was buried.

His lungs were beginning to burn. It wouldn't be long now.

But there was a strange, tugging sensation.

Somewhere deep in his fading mind, Laurence dreamily became aware that the pressure on his free arm was different, very different. Not rocks but flesh gripped him. Multiple hands, no, claws. Then, the tugging became more violent. Loose rocks scraped across his flesh. His spine seemed to stretch and pop, and his legs felt they might leave their sockets.

Then, quite suddenly, he was free, the only pressure being that of the hard ground underneath him. Painfully, he rolled over and blinked his eyes open. With the amount of grit that had assaulted them, he was surprised that he could see anything at all. Nevertheless, there, standing tall over him, were four figures: three Carcarrions, their bodies smeared with gray, and one white-haired little man.

"The gods are most definitely looking out for you, young Laurence."

Trying to break free from his lingering shock, Laurence managed something akin to a smile. Then he attempted a verbal reply, but it quickly became a painful, bloody coughing fit.

With no time to catch his breath, Laurence again felt clawed hands gripping him then lifting him to his feet. It was at this point that he realized just what a sorry state his body was in. Fiery pain ignited in every joint, shot up every muscle, and burned its way down every ligament. He wobbled for the briefest of moments before being lifted again and thrown over broad, solid shoulders.

The bedlam all around him was overwhelming. Laurence was well and truly amid all the chaos now, and for that, he was pretty damned grateful.

Chapter Forty-Six
RELENTLESS

As he hit the last control for the activation of the dropships, Cal felt an enormous wave of relief wash over him. He just hoped to God his efforts weren't too little too late. He imagined it would be nothing short of chaos down on the planet surface by now—an easy thing to picture when a similar chaos was happening right before his very eyes. The far end of the laboratory looked as though it had fallen foul to a crate of pressure grenades. Amid the mass of smashed equipment and cracked workstations, he could see one of the synthetics in a fierce embrace with one of the Carcarrion drones. The din they were creating was bordering on absurd as they crashed around in a rapid, violent dance.

As he took in the rest of the carnage, Cal felt his heart begin to thud increasingly harder and faster. The second fight was over. The synthetic with the tattooed face was standing victorious over the other drone, its lifeless form slumped over a console. Even from this distance, he could see the slug-like Insidion crushed in her cybernetic hand, its long, torn tendrils hanging limp down her arm. Throwing it to the floor, she turned her deadly gaze toward him. Cal swore and clenched his jaw. If the activation of the dropships had taken even a few moments longer, he'd already be dead, and he wouldn't have seen it coming.

As if reacting to the sight of the tattooed bitch's gaze, the Xcel within Cal's body seemed to reignite, offering some blessed strength to his damaged body. The dropships were on their way. All that was left now was one last-ditch effort at survival, one last fight. Moving with all the speed available to him, he snatched up both pistols and pointed them towards the synthetic. He was breathing heavily, and the wound in his side was doing its best to oppose his will and fold him in half, but he was damned if he was going to give up now.

The synthetic began her approach, and Cal steadily tracked her movements with both pistols. He fired a couple of quick, controlled blasts. She was too far away to hit, but he wanted to get the measure of her speed. The swiftness of her reactions shouldn't have surprised him, particularly after spending so much time in Melinda's company, but still, they did. She was impossibly fast, leaping and spinning away from the blasts in a blur and only taking minimal cover before resuming her steady path towards him. It was as if she could see into his mind, fully aware of when and where he was going to fire the weapons.

Cal was careful not to become distracted by the almighty crashes at the far end of the lab. It seemed the other drone was putting up a far more effective fight than its companion. Strangely spurred on by the drone's unwillingness toward defeat, Cal let instinct take over. Taking a step back from the console, he leapt up onto it. The time for caution was over. He knew the synthetic would never be intimidated by aggressive actions but, just as Kaia had surprised Melinda on their first meeting, perhaps a bold attack might just throw off her programming for a vital second.

Launching himself forward, he unleashed a barrage of fire from both pistols, doing his best to track his opponent's movements as he did so. The rest of the lab became a blur. All he saw was that soulless, tattooed face, clearly framed amid the light of his blazing pistols. He leapt from one workstation to the next, his need to survive manifesting into a near animalistic fury.

Then one of his shots found its target, pounding into the synthetic's shoulder. Clothing and synth-flesh instantly disintegrated as the blast met her hard, cybernetic chassis. The blast did little damage, but the force tipped her off balance for the briefest of moments. Cal took full advantage. Continuing to bolt directly towards her, he made sure that every one of his shots found its mark, hammering directly into the synthetic's body, twisting her, never giving her a chance to regain form.

By the time he'd closed the gap, the force of the onslaught had turned the cybernetic woman almost one hundred and eighty degrees. Throwing down the pistol in his right hand, Cal launched himself through the air and slammed into her back. He felt as though he'd hit a boulder, but he wrapped his right arm around her neck and held on with all his might. Lab equipment flew and disintegrated as the two of them crashed about, slamming into anything and everything. Cal felt his body crunch under the impact, but still he clung on, Xcel and determined rage fuelling his arms.

Raising the pistol in his left hand, Cal pressed it hard against the back of the synthetic's neck and held down the trigger. Blinding, orange and white light dazzled his vision, and intense heat scorched his face as the pulse pistol objected to the point-blank range. But despite the heat, he retained his pressure on the weapon's trigger, holding it desperately like the lifeline it was. The weapon's discharge backfired and blistered into the air around him like snakes of pure energy, writhing furiously as they tried to bore directly into the near indestructible metal.

Once again, the synthetic slammed him back against a workstation, making him feel as though he'd been sandwiched between a tank and a wall. The pistol's grip became red hot in his hand, but it would be suicide to let it go. Calling upon every last spark of energy, Cal angled the weapon up toward the underside of the synthetic's skull, causing something to shudder violently beneath him. Every part of his being screamed at him to let go, but he roared back a wordless answer of defiance and somehow found it within himself to cling on to consciousness.

All sense of time and space seemed to slip away, and it was only with a vague, dreamlike awareness that Cal felt one of the synthetic's hands grasp his right arm. Over the sound of the pulse pistol's continuous discharge, it was impossible to hear his bones break, but even with his wildly distorted senses, he felt the crunch. One more drop of pain into a sea of hurt. He couldn't breathe. His muscles were refusing to respond. He tried his best to turn his face from the writhing, electric snakes, but he failed. It felt like staring into the core of a great sun, his eyes burning in their sockets. There was a terrible noise, a scream painfully filling his ears. Was it the burning weapon or the synthetic beneath him? Or perhaps it was issuing from his own throat. Then, quite suddenly, he was plunged into a dark ocean, no longer able to see, hear, or feel a thing.

Cal came to…but only just.

He could make out a distant commotion: fighting, crashing, thumping, screeching. Blurred visions were swimming dreamlike in front of his throbbing eyes. He was lying on his back, limbs sprawled awkwardly and unresponsive. His body was rhythmically searing with pain as if his heart was pumping liquid fire through his veins.

Slowly, his vision began to clear. He managed a weak shake of the head in an attempt to hurry it along. He felt confused. There was something coming at him, a horribly disfigured form. He shook his head again. It was a woman…a woman turned wild. She had a crazed expression made fierce by tattoos and thin, blackened scorch marks that wrapped around her face like the legs of some arachnid. The woman was stomping forward on one stiff leg. Her other seemed useless, twitching and dragging behind her. One of her arms appeared similarly useless—joints completely rigid, the fingers of the hand splayed and frozen. The other hand, however, appeared fully functional and was reaching determinedly. Reaching for him.

Cal's brain fought its way through the fog. He managed to disengage from the pain to capture some understanding of what he was seeing. He had damaged his opponent, *seriously* damaged her, but it still wasn't enough. Her reaching hand was close, seconds away. He attempted to get to his feet, but was far from successful. Instead he settled for a desperate, crawling retreat, keeping his back to the floor and his blurry eyes on the grasping hand. As he moved, he realized that, similar to his attacker, only one of his arms was any good to him; the other was shattered and barely had enough function to remain tucked at his side. He tried to ignore the trail of blood that he was leaving in his wake, astonished that his body still retained any. Unconsciousness continued to threaten, but he kept crawling back, relentless in his efforts, desperately shaking his head in an effort to keep the darkness at bay.

The demonic-looking synthetic loomed closer still, her spasmodic gait proving just that bit faster than his desperate crawl. Suddenly, her leg buckled, and she dropped down onto her knee. Cal felt a glimmer of hope that she was dying a cybernetic death. But the hope was quickly and brutally extinguished as he realized she was simply increasing her chances of getting a hold on him. Her hand was now practically touching his foot.

Cal searched frantically. He needed a weapon, anything to give him some sort of fighting chance. Then his bleary vision homed in on a pulse pistol—the very one that had already proved its worth tenfold. The weapon lay on the floor, thick, blue smoke oozing from its muzzle. It was a little further than an arm's reach away. He turned and stretched, his pain manifesting into an audible cry. His fingers scratched desperately at the smooth floor as he tried to pull his broken body closer. He touched the weapon, its metal grip still hot as his fingertips brushed against its surface. There was a voice in his head, encouraging him, urging him to stretch further, just a little further. Unfortunately, that voice could do nothing about the steely fingers that closed around his ankle. The pistol rocked slightly as his fingers pressed against its edge. Then, within one terrible blink of the eye, the pistol was further away. The hand around his ankle had given one violent jerk, and his reaching fingers met nothing but air.

Cal twisted onto his back, a grim sense of defeat pouring through him. He felt the steely hand grip his thigh. Another violent jerk, and he was again yanked through his own blood across the smooth floor. The synthetic leaned over him like a jackal over a carcass, and Cal couldn't help but focus on the hideous, scorched face. The hand was reaching for his throat now, soon to meet flesh and begin its squeeze.

Something exploded to Cal's right.

A workstation split apart, countless canisters splintering into a million shards that rained down on him along with bright blue liquid. Cal's fragile senses span in confusion as a large, jet black shape crashed down on top of him. He tried to make sense of the situation—a near impossible undertaking for his failing brain. Then he realized, with only a faint sense of relief, that the tattooed bitch had gone. He managed to stretch his neck to see the dark form of a Carcarrion lying across his legs. The drone looked to be in a similar state to himself: bloody, broken, and struggling with unresponsive limbs. There was another movement, a flickering that was almost lost in the haze of his peripheral vision. He turned just enough to see the dying throes of his tattooed foe.

Then there was foot fall, glass crunching under the weight of a heavy frame. The second synthetic appeared, fists balled at her sides like a prize fighter looming over a felled opponent. In contrast to those she stood over, her body still looked well within its physical limits. Other than torn clothing and long gashes to her already healing synth-flesh, the cybernetic woman appeared all but intact. Her gaze briefly dropped toward the tattooed synthetic. There was not the slightest hint of pity or grief as she assessed her broken sister nor did she show any sense of anger as she turned her doll-like eyes toward Cal and the fallen drone. Indeed, it was with an entirely impassive, machine-like efficiency that she dropped to one knee and began slamming her fist into the struggling drone—or more specifically, the Insidion that clung to its thick, muscled neck. With the drone pinning his legs, Cal felt every blow.

Once satisfied that her alien opponent was no longer a threat, the cybernetic woman looked at Cal. Strangely, he felt no fear. He didn't want to die, far from it, but in that moment, he felt too much pain, too much confusion. There was no longer any room for fear. At least death would put an end to the searing agony, and it would be quick; this cybernetic killer wasn't damaged or malfunctioning; she wouldn't falter or hesitate.

He gritted his teeth as she took one mechanical stride over the drone before again dropping to one knee. Her pale face filled Cal's vision as she leaned forward and drew back her right fist back for the killing blow.

But it didn't come.

A black arm had threaded around the synthetic's neck from behind, causing a hint of confusion to flicker over her face, briefly betraying the impassive countenance. Surprise hit Cal as hard as his delirium would allow. At first, he thought he was seeing the arm of a Carcarrion, but even through his damaged vision, he realized the arm was far too slim. Also, there was a hand, a *human* hand, feminine and pale with immaculate, snow white fingernails. Cal stared at it, time seeming to slow almost to a stop, a strange, disconnected curiosity fending away unconsciousness, denying it a hold. All he could see was that beautiful hand contrasted against the synthetic's deathly face. Then there was an abrupt, violent lurch that seemed to nudge time back into action. The synthetic killer had been wrenched away from him and forcefully pulled to her feet. Painfully, he craned his neck and watched as she was spun on the spot then launched through the air right over his head.

Then came a mesmerising sight. Seeming to tower above him, Melinda looked every bit the Amazon of myth: incredibly beautiful and entirely formidable.

Quite unlike the synthetic that she'd just launched through the air, Melinda's face was far from impassive. Cal could see anger there, which, as she looked down upon him, turned to undeniable concern.

Very nearly human.

As his vision began to fade, Cal recalled something his young friend Viktor had said when they'd first met, the words sounding in a loop in the back of his mind. *My Melinda could destroy those pathetic synthetics with one arm tied behind her back.* As he watched Melinda leap over him, he had no doubt the boy was about to be proven right. He had an overwhelming urge to laugh, but there was no chance of that now. As he slipped into unconsciousness, however, there was definitely something close to a smile lingering on his bruised and battered face.

Chapter Forty-Seven
TIME TO RUN

Laurence was finding it hard to breathe. The shoulders of the Carcarrion carrying him were repeatedly slamming into his gut and chest—not that he was complaining. As the alien leapt across the rocks, Laurence did his best to lift his lolling head. Everything was a blur. Multi-colored pulse blasts streaked through the air. Carcarrions leaping, diving, clawing, biting. Crabs, huge bloody crabs, stomping and snipping off limbs. A big metal spider, a rotating gun on its back creating a circle of destruction. More pulse blasts. White dreadlocks. Gray war paint. Bared fangs. Humans, lots of humans, fighting, shouting, cheering.

Feeling his brain could take no more, Laurence dropped his head, closed his eyes, and held on tight.

"Jumper, here! Over here, bro, run."

Toker's shout was distant, but somehow, Jumper managed to pluck it out of the mad din. He continued to bound over the rocks, his breath pumping through his lungs like some sort of steam-powered cyborg. Without slowing his pace, he tried to hone in on the sound and catch sight of his young friend. His vision was overwhelmed with blaster fire, battling aliens, and dropships coming down in dangerously rapid descents. On top of this was the fact that all his running was causing disgusting globs of yellow slime— remnants of the giant crab he'd killed—to drip from his hair into his face and eyes. Using a filthy sleeve, he did his best to wipe it away and was partially successful in clearing his vision. Just as well too because at that moment, a Carcarrion sprung from behind a rock not far ahead. Seeing no gray war paint, Jumper swung his bliss rifle back, ready to strike a club-like blow, the weapon's darts having long since run out. Locking its malevolent, pale eyes on the weapon, the Carcarrion raised its clawed fists and lunged forward to meet the attack. But it didn't come. Jumper had rolled beneath the lunge and was already continuing his speedy path across the rocks, safe in the knowledge that the alien could never match his speed.

Once again, he scanned the terrain for his young blond friend.

"Here, Jumper. Over here!"

The shouts were definitely closer, but still, Jumper couldn't spot him. What he did see, however, was Viktor's mechanical combat spider, or at least what was left of it. The metallic beast looked as though it had been half crushed, four of its long legs curled up tight, the remaining four flailing while the multi-barrelled swivel blaster attempted to spew out non-existent rounds. Jumper leaped over the defeated machine and continued on. Not far ahead, he saw swarms of people pouring into the dropships. As they boarded, the armed survivors were offering cover fire. Distressingly late, the escape was finally concluding as planned.

A blue bolt of light streaked through the sky high above Jumper's head. For a moment, he ignored its existence, then its likely source dawned on him: the Star Splinter. He slowed his pace, wiped again at the slime invading his eyes, and scanned the dark skies for the next blue streak… There, emanating dead ahead. Or perhaps slightly to his left. Because of the Star Splinter's ghosting net, the blue cannon blast had appeared to materialize out of thin air. Judging by its height, Jumper guessed the ship had already landed. *Good lad, Viktor.*

"Jumper, run, damn it."

This time, Jumper knew exactly which direction to look and spotted Toker almost instantly. Taking his young friend's advice, he summoned every last ounce of the Xcel left in his system and ran as if his life depended on it, which of course it did.

Numerous individual Carcarrions came at him as he closed the gap to the Star Splinter. He evaded every one of them, all without swinging a single blow. He'd always had a talent for ducking and diving, and with the Xcel in his system, he was a near impossible catch.

He was close now, close enough to see Toker running toward him, close enough to see the warning on his young friend's face. Dodging to his left, he twisted in mid-air, came down in a crouch, and skidded to a halt on the scree. Two giant crabs, each with at least three Carcarrion drones on their wide backs, were coming at him at an incredible pace. Barely having time to register their presence, a flash of blue sliced into their ranks. The crabs exploded in a shower of yellow ichor, and bits of Carcarrion drones flipped through the air in a high arch.

Thanks, kid.

Jumper didn't hang around to see the debris hit the rocks. Instead, he turned and ran toward Toker, ran towards the Star Splinter, ran towards his ticket off this damned hell hole.

Chapter Forty-Eight
SURVIVORS

The first thing Cal saw was a clear, coiled tube sticking out of his arm. His eyes followed the tube to a white box full of bright, blinking lights and low-pitched beeps. Other tubes coiled out of the machine. Sluggishly, Cal followed their paths; they all led to other arms, other people laying on white beds, just like him. His whole body felt numb, and he had the queer sensation that he was hovering in mid-air.

He could hear activity. With an effort, he lifted his head and saw the familiar sight of *The Orillian's* medical facility. The large, D-shaped room had been empty the last time he'd been in it. This time, it was anything but. The entire space was jam-packed with beds, people, and monitoring equipment. The vast majority of those people were in a similar position to himself, horizontal and immobile. Some, however, were apparently uninjured and on their feet, weaving their way around the beds, leaning over the patients, and tweaking monitoring equipment. Similar bustle was visible through the wide windows set high within the curved portion of the room.

The facility's occupants weren't limited to humans. There were a number of Carcarrions dotted about too, their dark forms stark against the gleaming whiteness. Cal's eyes drifted toward two of them, who were close by. Both were injured, their dried, purple blood bright where it mingled with ash war paint. Between the two hulking aliens stood a skinny, deeply tanned man sporting a mass of white, dreadlocked hair. Cal blinked. An odd trio.

A familiar, low whirring noise tugged at his attention. He looked to the far end of the room, where a pool hoist was lowering two people while two others were simultaneously being raised. Cal peered through the mass of beds until he caught sight of the shimmering, black surface of the healing pool. The sight of it was almost hypnotic. As he stared at it, he half expected Kaia's beautiful, pale face to break its surface. But there was no chance of that now.

The numbness he felt was beginning to fade, and in its place came an increasingly intense pain. The floating feeling was also fading, leaving him to the mercy of gravity, a broken body and an only partially forgiving bed. A machine near his feet began to beep, louder and higher-pitched than the others. The noise made his ears ring. He tried to ignore it and continued to take in his surroundings. A familiar face caught his eye; Eddy was laying three beds over, her eyes lightly closed. The girl's hair was no more than a layer of black stubble, and her face was a patchwork of small healing patches. Cal also saw a familiar tangle of blond hair on the far side of her bed. Toker was slouched on a chair, his face pressed into the mattress.

Eddy had lost her right arm. There was a healing cap on the stump that Cal knew would do little more than seal the wound and help minimize phantom pains.

"There'll be no fixing that wound, I'm afraid."

Cal turned to see a young man, maybe mid-twenties, who had approached the foot of his bed and was looking toward Eddy.

"That black liquid is pretty incredible stuff, but it doesn't regrow limbs." The young man turned to Cal and gave him a half smile before turning his attentions to the beeping machine.

Without saying a word, Cal looked back toward Eddy and Toker. It was hard to feel sadness about her lost limb; seeing them both alive filled him with a relief too great to leave room for anything else.

"Still, that magic black pool certainly did you a world of good," the young man continued. "According to that blonde synthetic, you were hanging onto life by a thread when you went in there." Finally, the machine stopped its infernal beeping. "Don't get me wrong, you're still in a hell of a state, but you're stable, and that's what counts. We'll get you back in there once the others have been stabilized." The man's voice was cheery, but it seemed a struggle.

"Ju...Jump...er." The word didn't leave Cal's mouth easily, like forcing treacle through a sieve.

"You'll have trouble speaking, I'm afraid. Your jaw is still partially broken, and you're on enough drugs to topple a horse. If it's your tall, black friend you're asking for, he's making his way over here now."

Cal tried to follow the young man's line of sight, but his neck wouldn't allow it. Instead, he studied the man. He was clean-shaven and wore an immaculate white coat, but his face was gaunt, hair roughly cut short, and despite his youth, his eyes had a haunted edge—the look of a man who'd spent months in a living hell.

Suddenly, Cal was confronted by a tall stranger...no...Jumper. The afro was gone. Just like Eddy, all that covered his old friend's head was a thin layer of stubble.

"Good to see you awake, Cal," Jumper said, giving him a smile that didn't quite reach his eyes.

"You'll not have long," the young man informed him. "The drugs will take effect very quickly."

Jumper nodded without taking his eyes off Cal. "How you

feeling?"

"A little...pissed...off."

Jumper didn't laugh at that, just nodded his understanding. "Viktor?"

"He's fine," Jumper replied quickly. "You'd have been proud of him. You'd have been proud of them all." He glanced across at Toker and Eddy. "They fought hard, saved a lot of lives. And they gave those invading bastards something to think about before the dropships arrived."

"I'm sorry...there were—"

"I know," Jumper interrupted him, saving him the effort of the words. "Viktor showed me everything on the lab's security feed."

"Took Kaia."

"There's no way you could have saved her. No one could have. It was a bloody miracle you managed to activate the dropships let alone survive those synthetics. Every soul on this ship and the starship following owes you their lives, Cal." Jumper gave a brief grin. "We're just damn lucky you're such a bloody relentless bastard."

Cal tried to shrug, but his body only half obeyed. "Thanks for...Melinda...dead without her."

Jumper nodded. "I just wish that mosquito ship had been faster." Then he shook his head. "Or I wish I'd sent her sooner. Hell, I wish a lot of things." He rubbed at his stubbly head, and his eyes strayed towards Eddy. "I tell you, Cal, I'm not overly keen on being put in charge of anyone but myself."

Cal managed a very small nod of understanding. "Must been...chaos."

"Yes." Jumper turned back to him. "I saw the recordings from your Infiltrator too. Saw the inside the Insidion base. Not what I expected."

"Ag… Agreed."

"It's as if this is all a game to them. A sport."

Cal could feel the drugs starting to reclaim him.

"And if Kaia's theories are right," Jumper continued, "we mightn't have even seen them yet. Not the real *them* at any rate—"

"How many?" Cal managed to interject. "How…many saved?"

"Of course, sorry." Jumper looked down and paused a moment before answering. "Half… Almost half. The others died fighting."

The two men went silent for a moment.

"A good deal of our Carcarrion allies made it too. I'm not sure how many they lost."

Cal could feel himself slowly slipping back into unconsciousness. It was a welcome feeling. Before he went under, however, he managed to mutter one last thing. "Kaia… She's…not dead."

Jumper nodded almost as though he'd been fully expecting the words. "I know, Cal. I know."

Eddy looked pale and incredibly fragile lying on the large bed. Her shaved hair had barely grown at all since Cal had seen her five days previously. She was breathing steadily, and her eyes were closed, eyelids hiding the wildness within. At that moment, all Cal could see was a young, innocent girl. He looked up at Toker, who was standing over the bed, staring at Eddy, anxiety clear on his face. He was rubbing at his neck, and he kept throwing Cal and Jumper worried glances.

"She'll be awake any moment now." The voice was that of a middle-aged woman, one of the few military refugees with enough medical experience to aid the injured. "Do you want me to stay and help explain about her arm?"

Instinctively, Cal glanced at Jumper then said, "No, that's okay.

Thanks though."

The woman gave them a warm smile then moved off toward another bed. Watching her walk away, Cal caught sight of someone being hoisted out of the inky depths of the healing pool.

"He looks a bit like you, don't you think?"

Cal turned to see that Jumper was also looking towards the pool.

"But he's a little skinnier."

With a raised eyebrow, Cal turned back as Laurence Decker stiffly transferred from the hoist to a bed. "He wasn't always so slight."

"I guess months spent on a prison planet changes a man."

Cal nodded. "More than you know."

"She's waking… I think she's waking up." Toker's voice was little more than a whisper, but it was loud enough to attract Cal's and Jumper's attention. Cal used his crutches to shuffle forward slightly. Toker was right; the rousing drugs were doing their job and stirring the girl from her long, induced sleep.

As Eddy's eyes flickered open, her look of confusion was almost instantaneous. Slowly, she turned her head and gazed briefly at each of them in turn. "Did we win?"

"We did…okay," Jumper answered. "All considering. How you feeling, kid?"

Eddy blinked a few times. "J man, where the hell's your hair got to?" she asked, ignoring his question.

Instinctively, Jumper reached up and rubbed his head. "I, um, well, I got a little too close to the slimy innards of the enemy. When it dries, the damn stuff sets hard as rock."

Screwing up her nose, Eddy turned to Cal. "Geeze, Cal, you're lookin' pretty banged up."

Cal tried his best to shoot her a lopsided grin. "Well, that's what happens when you piss off a synthetic."

Eddy screwed up her nose again, staring at him like she could see right through his forced smile. Then she continued to look at them each in turn. "What's goin' on? Why you all lookin' so flippin' sad? An' what's up with you, blondie? You look like your butt's been got at by a giant pincer ant."

Toker opened his mouth, but no sound came out. He coughed and tried again. "Well, er, we're...we were worried...you...there was..." He shook his head, swallowed hard, and looked imploringly over at Cal.

"I'm afraid you were injured, Eddy, during the fighting."

"Yeah?" Eddy said, continuing to look back and forth between Cal and Toker.

Eventually, she followed Toker's line of sight, and her eyes locked onto the healing cap covering the stump of her missing right arm. "My arm's gone," she said in a small, rather bewildered voice. "Where'd my arm go?" she asked, her gaze not shifting from the space where her missing limb should have been.

"It was one of those giant crabs," Jumper explained. "Like the one you managed to kill."

"Bastard snuck up on you," Toker added, his voice far from steady. "Don't worry though, Ed. Viktor's gonna...Viktor's gonna..." his words faltered as Eddy looked up at him, tears brimming in her big eyes.

Viktor took a step toward the bed. "Hey, Eddy. What Toker's doing a pretty crappy job of explaining is that I'm gonna build you a new arm. A cybernetic, nano assisted prosthetic limb actually."

Eddy turned her glistening eyes towards the boy, her expression suggesting she wasn't really understanding his words. Cal could sympathize. It was a huge thing to take in, particularly with a drug-addled brain.

"I've already started working on it," Viktor continued, suddenly eager as he turned to Melinda. The synthetic woman passed him a long, white box. "I took the dimensions of your left arm already, see. Then I started building the basic cybernetic skeleton. It still needs loads of work of course: tendon shifters, sensory pads, fiber optics, and of course sufficient tubing for the nano threads plus all the synth-flesh too, but the basic structure's there."

Eddy turned to Cal, confusion still evident on her tear-streaked face.

The sight made Cal feel like spilling some tears himself. "Viktor's making you a cybernetic arm, Eddy. Like a synthetic's arm."

Viktor nudged Toker out of the way and, setting the box down on Eddy's bed, opened it up like he was presenting the girl with a prize. Eddy awkwardly leaned over to stare at the cybernetic limb contained within.

"We won't be able to fit you with it on this ship though," Viktor explained. "But when we get to the research base on Alvor, they'll definitely have some decent surgeons and all the kit needed to meld the nano threads to your nerve endings. But that's good though, see. It'll give me time to make the arm top notch, way better than anything the military would ever dish out."

Eddy gazed into the box for a good long while before lying back on the bed.

"That'll be my new arm?" she asked, looking back up at Cal, her face unreadable.

Cal nodded. "Yes, Eddy, you'll be able to use it just like your old one."

The girl turned back to Viktor. "Will it be like one of Melinda's? Will it be as strong as hers?"

Viktor also nodded. "Yep. You'll be able to squish bones with this new grip."

Cal winced slightly and exchanged a quick glance with Jumper.

"As long as you don't go squishing my bones, little chick," Toker said with a nervous laugh.

Eddy didn't say a word. Instead, she turned her head to stare up at the high, bright ceiling.

Some time passed with the girl not saying a word. Cal was beginning to get worried, a sickening, helpless feeling taking hold. He looked around at the others and saw that his expression wasn't the only one turning grim. "Eddy, I… I mean, we…" he started to say, but he aborted the words as he caught the look on the girl's face. A smile had appeared. *Thank God.*

As had always been the case, Eddy's grin was infectious, and before long, a similar one was spread across each and every one of their faces.

Then there was laughter.

EPILOGUE

The distant blue and green planet was a beautiful sight. Even from this distance, staring at it through the smart-glass of *The Orillian's* viewing deck, Cal could see that Alvor was a planet bursting with diversity. Lush forests and jungles, immense mountains and deserts, lakes the diameter of large moons, and deep, blue oceans too vast to fathom. A giant-scale Earth of old, pristine and untouched by the industrial and technological age. Perhaps it would be the new hub of human existence. Cal hoped so. As long as they didn't push it to its limits like they had Earth, he had a feeling it could make an incredible home.

"Sorry I'm late, Callum."

Cal turned to see Laurence Decker entering the dim room, his progress slow due to his lingering injuries. The first-name basis was still catching Cal off guard. The man had obviously gone through a miraculous change over the past months, but the Captain Decker of old, with whom he was far more familiar, had never been a friend. Far from it. But Cal had never been one to hold a grudge, particularly against a man who'd recently played a big hand in saving thousands of lives. "No problem," he replied as he watched the man hobble toward him. "I was just admiring the view."

"So, that's Alvor, eh?" Laurence said as he came to stand next to him. "She's a beauty."

"That she is," Cal replied, turning back to gaze through the smart-glass. "With any luck, the perfect place for a fresh start."

Laurence nodded. "I'm sorry it's taken us so long to meet for a talk."

"Don't mention it. You've been in demand. And there's all the pool time we've both had. Not easy to chat in the inky depths."

Laurence grinned. "Yes, we both buggered ourselves up pretty good, eh?"

Cal returned the grin. Despite the miraculous nature of the pool, both of them still had a way to go before they were completely healed. "It was worth it though."

"Couldn't agree more. A shame it didn't go quite as planned."

Cal nodded. "Fucking pirates," he muttered. He still couldn't quite believe the timing of the bastards. "Still, everyone did well, despite the problems."

"Particularly you, Callum. I've never seen someone take out a synthetic before."

Cal stretched his right arm and did his best to flex his fingers. "You saw the footage?"

"Oh, just about everyone's seen the footage. Quite a thing, the way you dealt with those pirates. Even injured, you made fools of them."

Cal shook his head. "Wasn't enough."

"I understand one of them is still alive?"

"Barely," Cal replied as he thought of the female pirate he'd knocked out with the knife. "Not even the black pool seems to be bringing her out of her coma."

Laurence nodded. "I'm sorry...about the lady who was taken. Kaia. It seems we all owe her our lives." He placed a hand on Cal's shoulder. "I would tell you how there was nothing you could have done to save her, but you've probably heard that a thousand times already. I doubt hearing it again'll make you feel any better."

She's not dead, Cal thought, but he didn't voice it. Instead, the two men simply stood in silence for a while, gazing through the huge sheet of smart-glass at the distant planet.

It was Laurence who eventually broke the silence. "If you're able to forgive me, Callum, I'd be grateful if Alvor could also mark a fresh start between the two of us."

Cal turned to him, a little surprised by his words. "Why would you need forgiveness from *me*?"

Laurence shrugged. "Why wouldn't I? You know that I've made a lot of foolish decisions in my past, given bad orders, put people at risk." He looked at Cal with solemn eyes. "I feel guilt gnawing at me every minute of every day. I need to ask forgiveness, and in all honesty, I don't know who else to ask it from."

Cal stared back at the man, awkwardly rubbing at the back of his neck. He was unsure how to reply and after a moment said, "Surely, there's someone better than me."

Laurence shook his head. "Who better than the man who saw fit to knock out one of my teeth because of that same foolishness?"

Cal continued to stare at him. "I got a little carried away. I'm sorry about that."

"Don't be sorry. You did me a big favor that day, started a change in me, something that continued to change on that prison planet."

Feeling a little weird, Cal took a moment before he replied. "Okay… To be honest, I feel like a bit of an idiot saying it, but yes, I forgive you."

Laurence nodded his thanks, tense shoulders relaxing a little.

Cal studied him closely. The man must have been through hell down on that planet. But how could someone change so completely? Maybe sometimes, it took a true nightmare to wake a person up. "You know, I'm not just saying that because you've asked me to," he said. "By all accounts, you turned the tides down on that planet. Turned despair into hope. Whatever past mistakes you're guilty of, as far as I'm concerned, you've made a damn good job at turning things around."

Laurence looked about to object, then let out a breath and said, "Thanks. Hearing that from you means a great deal." He reached out an open palm.

Cal shook it as best he could with his screwed up hand. "Of course, you realize it's not over yet. Not by a long shot."

"No, I didn't think so."

"There's probably countless others to save…once we find them that is."

Laurence nodded. "You think we'll get away with pulling the same trick twice?"

Cal shrugged. "I imagine we'll have to get creative. And hope they don't strike back first."

Laurence turned his gaze back on the nearing planet. "You think they'll find us here?"

"Most likely. Eventually."

"We best be ready then, eh?"

Cal nodded. *How the hell do you prepare for something like that?* They fell into silence again.

After some time, Laurence tore his eyes from the view and looked down at the floor. "You, er, you mind if we sit down?"

"Christ, I thought you'd never ask," Cal replied. "My legs are killing me."

"Only your legs? Lucky bastard."

Both men chuckled as they stiffly lowered themselves to the dark, smooth floor.

"I tell you what, Callum, I feel about a hundred and two. I can't bloody wait to get in that pool again."

Cal sighed as he sat. "That makes two of us." He rubbed at his legs and after a few moments said, "You know, it's a shame your father couldn't see you now."

Laurence smiled. A sad smile.

For almost an hour, the two men sat in comfortable silence, staring quite literally into space, taking in the slowly expanding planet. By the end of that hour, Alvor was almost matching the height of the viewing panel, a mesmerising sight that Cal found pleasantly calming.

"I think that's got to be the biggest, lushest planet I've ever seen," Laurence said.

The words almost made Cal jump; they sounded ridiculously loud after the long silence. "I've been thinking the same thing," he replied.

"Probably holds a lot of secrets."

"A tonne, I'd imagine."

"Good place for exploring."

"Undoubtedly."

"Fancy exploring it together?"

"I do," Cal replied sincerely. "But I might have to take a rain check? There's something I have to do."

Laurence looked at him. "You're going after the scientist, aren't you? The woman. Kaia."

"I am."

Laurence nodded.

Rubbing at his face, Cal stiffly got to his feet, and after one last look at Alvor, he turned and reached down with an open palm. "A fresh start, my friend?"

Laurence grinned and took the hand. There was a good amount of clumsy stumbling and some chuckling as Cal pulled him to his feet.

"Aye," Laurence replied once he was fully upright. "A fresh start."

<<<<>>>

Author's Thanks

Firstly I'd like to thank you, the brave reader, for taking a chance on this debut novel! I hope you enjoyed reading Star Splinter as much as I enjoyed writing it. If you did (and you like the idea of putting a big grin on a first time author's face) I'd be incredibly grateful for a review, even a very brief one, on Amazon and/or Goodreads. I'll do my absolute best to return the favour by writing plenty more books in the Fractured Space series for you to enjoy. If you'd like to be notified of the release dates for these books please feel free to sign up to my news letter at www.jgcressey.com/news-letter/

Also a huge thanks to my wife, family and friends without whom this book may still have been adrift in deep space. For your unwavering support and occasional kicks up the arse, I'll be eternally grateful. A special thanks to my test readers (particularly those hardy souls who waded their way through the really early drafts!). Many thanks to Amanda Shore, my wonderful editor for your hard work and support. A big thanks to Alisha at www.damonza.com for her hard work on the cover. Also thanks to Oda and Keri for their work on the original cover. Also thanks to Polgarus Studio for the great formatting, I dread to think what my level of tech skills would have produced without your service!

Made in the USA
Monee, IL
13 December 2023

48553326R00268